LIFE IN HITLER'S CROSSHAIRS

BY
CONSTANCE KRAIL-SELF

ISBN: 1466450932
ISBN 13: 9781466450936

Library of Congress Control Number: 2011919063
CreateSpace, North Charleston, SC

DEDICATION

It's been estimated that approximately five million Catholic and other Christian Poles were murdered in the first four years of World War II. This story is in honor of those forgotten millions.

. . . And to my Polish mother and German father who proved through sixty-five years of marriage that the two nationalities can find mutual respect for each other. I miss you both every day.

ABOUT THE COVER

The inspiration for the cover art came from a Pro-Poland poster printed in 1940. An original is on display in the Polish Museum of America in Chicago, Illinois. The artwork was later made into a US stamp.

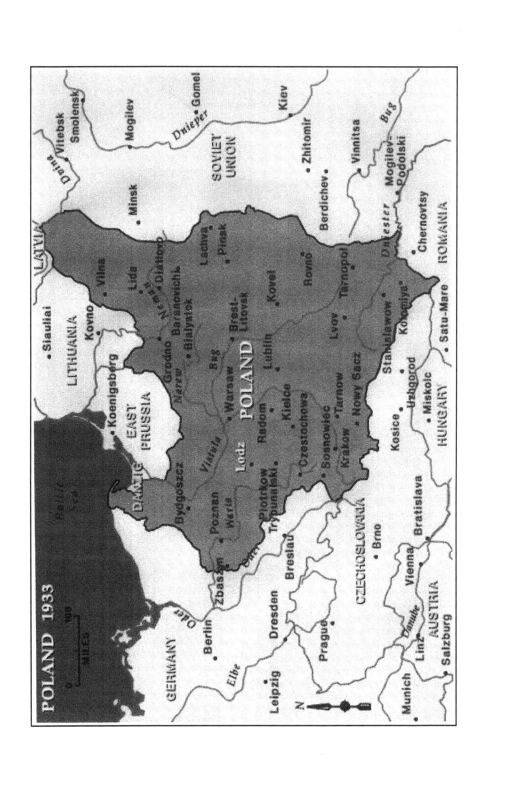

Part One

POLAND
1933 to August 1939

Germany has concluded a nonaggression pact with Poland...We shall adhere to it unconditionally...we recognize Poland as the home of a great and nationally conscious people.

Adolf Hitler, 21 May 1935 in his great "Peace Speech" at the Reichstag (Germany's parliament), Berlin

Chapter One

May 1933

CUCUMBERS

I have been told a scent can trigger a particular memory, good or bad. For me, it will always be the smell of cucumbers.

I clearly remember the circumstances when I first heard the name of the man who was to change my life and millions of others forever. We were seated at the breakfast table, Father reading the newspaper and Mother preparing a typical morning meal of soft scrambled eggs, fresh white bread, and sizzling *kaszanla,* or blood sausage. Mama's cooking skills were, in a word, abysmal, yet she continued her efforts in the kitchen much to the distress within our stomachs.

"He's in the papers again," my father remarked.

"Who, dear?" my mother questioned.

"That man Hitler—Adolf Hitler."

Sitting across from Father, nibbling on the fresh cucumbers mixed with sugar and sour cream Mother had set on the table, I heard the anger in Papa's voice.

"Oh, yes, I know," replied Mother. "Mrs. Schultz mentioned him to me. She seems very impressed with him. He is doing some remarkable things to bring prosperity back to Germany. Even established some sort of an organization for boys. And it seems so popular; something like two million members. Can you imagine? Very clever man," she said.

"When did you speak with Mrs. Schultz?"

"Oh, I saw her in our shop yesterday and we had a lovely talk. You know, Germany has had quite a difficult time since the Great War ended."

"Ach! We've all had difficulties," my father retorted, tossing the paper down. Poland had become an independent state after the Great War ended in 1918, struggling to find her footing for several years. After the depression in 1929, the worldwide economy sank to disastrous levels but life was now finally improving. "The whole of Europe had difficulties," he said, truly warming to his subject. "And that boy's group is no International Boy Scout Troop she's talking about, believe me. It is called *Hitlerjugend*, the Hitler Youth Group!" That organization was vaguely familiar to me. Cousin Antoni had expressed a desire to join but had been too old at the time.

"Today's article describes German university students burning thousands of books after a speech by Hitler's henchman, Joseph Goebbels. Book burning! This is sheer madness."

"Oh, that has to be an error, surely. Mrs. Schultz certainly would not be so keen on the man if he was involved in those kinds of things. Oh, dear. I think this sausage has burned. Well, I'll eat that one. What was I saying? Oh yes. I know you think the man has some unconventional ideas but who would want to burn books? No, I think the paper has gotten it wrong," said Mother.

"Perhaps," Papa said slowly, "but just the same, I want you to watch what you say to Mrs. Schultz in the future."

"Oh, Marek, why? I've known her for years."

"Bernice, this is important," my father said quietly. "Please do as I ask. Be careful to whom you speak about Hitler, understand?"

My mother and I just looked at him. I could not remember when I had heard him use her Christian name. Within the family she was called Birdie, a nickname so given because of her whistling skills and Papa addressed her with terms of endearment. The sudden flash of emotion on Papa's face frightened me, causing the hair on the back of my neck to prickle.

What he was referring to, of course, I later found out. The date was May 10, 1933. On that night, Joseph Goebbels spoke in Berlin to thousands of students stating, in part:

"...The breakthrough of the German revolution has again cleared the way on the German path...The future German man will not just be a man of books, but a man of character. It is to this end that we want to educate you..."

University students gathered in the capital city and throughout Germany, burning great piles of books, singing Nazi songs and anthems while dancing around the giant bonfires they created. It seemed almost paganish as students moved wildly around the flames with abandon. Literature by such greats as Sigmund Freud, Thomas Mann, Jack London, and H.G. Wells went up in flames, glowing ashes rising heavenward, as the demonstrators gave the Nazi salute in the midst of their frenzy. The words in these iconic books were deemed un-German, possibly rabble rousing in their ideas. Many years later, I found this quote by the poet Heinrich Heine written more than a hundred years prior to the book-burning event:

"Where books are burned, human beings are destined to be burned too."

I have never been able to eat or smell another cucumber without reliving that kitchen scene and feeling the tickle on my neck.

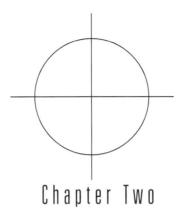

Chapter Two

THE BUTCHER SHOP

*E*ssentially, I was raised in the butcher shop my grandparents owned in Bochnia, Poland. Called Roman's Meats after my grandfather, Roman Koblinski, it was a wonderful place to grow up. The smell of freshly scattered sawdust on the floor would greet me whenever I entered. Once I was old enough to be of some help rather than a hindrance, I worked behind the counter after school each day.

We were located across the street and down the block from the requisite town fountain of which all Europeans seemed so fond. Certainly not as grand as the Trevi in Rome, it nevertheless boasted golden figures of Pan and Pegasus with clear water spouting from their mouths in such a wonderful rush we could hear it from our shop.

The flat above the shop was the home of my grandparents, furnished with good solid Polish furniture; Grandpapa would have no other. Somehow, my grandmother convinced him to purchase a delicate piece from Bavaria, a fragile dressing table. Painted in shades of red with narrow drawers in soft gold and green tulips, it was a childhood favorite of mine. I loved to sit upon the velvet stool and use the silver brush and comb set that had belonged to my great-grandmother.

Within a secret drawer of this table, my grandmother kept her most treasured possessions. When we opened it together, the process was almost ritualistic. She would close the bedroom door and grin while I opened the long skinny drawer filled with creams, lotions, and rouge. Removing all these, my hand sought out the delicate spring in the very back corner of the drawer. Snap! A long piece of wood would leap to one side, revealing a false bottom. Touching our fingers to our smiling lips, we kept this a secret between us.

Today, hearing the tinkle of our small silver bell placed strategically over the door, I looked up to see my cousin Filip Wozniak stride in. My familial relationships extended down many paths with step cousins, third cousins, half aunts, and other bonds I was never too sure of as a child. Filip, I knew, was my third cousin and my least favorite.

"Hello, Weegie," he said. I winced upon hearing this hated nickname, which is precisely why he used it. Because I resembled none of my family members (I was blue-eyed and blondish while they were brown-eyed and –haired), Filip had chosen a family gathering to intimate quite rudely that I had been left on my mother's doorstep. Mama had simply laughed, calling me her "little *Norwezka*," or Norwegian. Never one to be outdone, Filip began chanting "Weegie, Weegie" at the top of his lungs, forever nicknaming me thusly within the family. I really hated that Filip.

Approaching him today from behind the butcher shop's counter, I was pleased to see him noticeably back away. I knew why, of course. I had gotten my revenge upon him after the nickname incident by popping him severely in the nose, forcing him to run home bleeding to his mother. The entire incident had played out among the family for some time.

"Come in for your free handout, have you?" I asked. His parents owned two successful furriers, one a short walk down the street, the other in Krakow, forty-five minutes slightly southwest of us. Every day at noontime, Filip would come in to secure himself a free lunch. I was against it. He had money for the purchase, a fact he never let me forget, and the free meal was eating into our profits.

As luck for him would have it, my grandmother entered from the back room. Although I thought Buscha, my pet name for Grandmother, was not as fond of Filip as she was of her other grandchildren, he was still family. As such, we all tolerated him, some just more than others.

"Ah, Filip. Is it lunchtime already?" she asked. "What would you like today? I have just made sweet and sour cabbage and fresh *pierogi*." I knew those triangular dumplings filled with Buscha's seasoned ground meat were Filip's favorite; he could finish a plateful of those in a matter of minutes.

Jingling his coin-filled pocket to let me know in no uncertain terms that he could afford to pay for this meal, but would not, he grinned broadly at me and proceeded to order a towering plateful of food from our grandmother. Primarily, we were a butcher shop, but when my grandparents bought the two neighboring shops and enlarged their business, Buscha decided to expand upon the items sold. She prepared savory dishes of *spaetzel* and roast chicken, slow-baked beef ribs, even sandwiches to order, thereby enticing the lunch crowd to spend money. Schooling me in these recipes, I had developed into a competent cook and developed a light hand with pastry.

Noticing the look of frustration upon my face, Filip deliberately asked Buscha to add a few of her smoky ribs to the plate. Setting the rack of ribs upon the large butcher block, she proceeded to wield the meat cleaver with authority and force. Buscha reminded me of a photo I had once seen of the American Mrs. Claus: small, round, with a cloud of snow-white hair enveloping her pink circular face. It was incongruous to reconcile that vision of her with the one before me now, wielding her cleaver and chopping frantically at the meat.

When my cousin was satisfied not another tidbit of food could find purchase upon his plate, he proceeded to one of the small round tables we had positioned for our paying customers.

As Buscha walked to the freezer I automatically warned, "Latch, Buscha."

At that, Filip laughed hysterically. "Only Weegie could get locked into a freezer!" I ignored him; it was true, after all.

Our freezer had been purchased secondhand and was not very attractive but "did the job," Grandpapa said. The latch on the heavy insulated door tended to stick even though several repairmen had tinkered with it. When I was eight, the door had closed behind me and locked tight. Luckily, I was just tall enough for my head to be seen through the door's reinforced window but it was quite some time before anyone looked for me, hence our constant warning of the faulty latch.

"Marta, would you like to have your lunch with Filip?" she asked me. Thankfully, she and Grandpapa did not call me by that irritating nickname.

"No thank you, Buscha. I think I will take a walk." I would rather eat dirt than spend time in that cousin's company. I proceeded through the preparation room where Papa was chopping beef into roasts while my grandfather was practicing his newest set of jokes. I never knew which was funnier; listening to the punch lines or watching them laugh so hard the tears would roll down their cheeks.

With a smile and a wave to both, I walked into the room adjacent to the alley door to talk to Mama. She did the books for the business, had done so ever since I could remember. When she had applied for a job here as a student, Buscha, thinking she was as proficient in kitchen skills as all Polish women were, had given her the task of making a sweet soda bread called *babka*. Alas, the bread never rose, looking more like a brick than anything edible. Her pierogi and piecrusts suffered the same fate; dry, tasteless, or burnt. She tried her hand at many recipes and purchased countless cookbooks but with instructions to "beat butter, eggs, and sugar for one hour, and in one direction only" she very often gave up halfway through. Finally, in desperation, she had been given the position as bookkeeper at which she excelled. Luckily, Papa had the knack for cooking so we did not starve even though Mama continued to experiment on our stomachs.

Telling Mama I would be walking to the bakery shop, and receiving her order for cheesecake, I made my farewells and was out the back door.

Food is not mere sustenance to Poles, but a way of communicating hospitality and love. Great quantities of butter, eggs, cream, and buttermilk are used in Polish kitchens resulting in wonderful meals and light-as-air pastries. Food and drink are always offered to any caller, turning a simple visit into an event.

Most of these ingredients were easy to acquire for those of us in more rural areas. My family raised chickens and would often trade eggs for the milk of a neighbor's cow. Our climate favors the growth of nearly everything to make us a very self-sufficient area so vegetable gardens were a common sight. As a child, I would take great pride in the carrots I cultivated every season. For years, I thought it was due to my diligence that they flourished until I learned that a carrot could withstand almost any abuse and still grow large and sweet. The few staples we lacked—coffee, spices, citrus, and some southern fruits—we simply imported.

Wiping the excess sticky fruit off my face from the berry tart and exiting the bakery, I ran into Antoni Schreiber. Literally. With an ungraceful thud, I found myself sitting on the cobblestone road looking up into the deep, dark eyes of my wonderful older cousin.

"Weegie," he said as he helped me to my feet, "are you running from the devil or merely anxious to see me?" He bent down to retrieve the crushed ribbon-tied box containing my mother's cheesecake. Opening it, he proclaimed it slightly damaged. It looked as if I had sat upon it, I thought peering inside.

"It was for Mama," I said, knowing I would have to purchase another.

"Well, her tastes are much more discriminating than to eat this disaster. Perhaps Filip would enjoy it," he said with his wonderful lopsided grin. I laughed in return, knowing how Filip would eat even Mama's cooking.

"That boy will be as round as he is tall if he doesn't show some restraint." Where Filip could only be pleasant when he chose, Antoni lit up a room by simply walking into it. He reminded me of a Roman god: cheekbones that could cut ice, eyes that looked into your soul, a tall slender build, and wonderful wavy hair. To me, he was clever and sophisticated and I never tired of being in his presence. I absolutely adored him.

I think he was secretly flattered by my blind adoration. Occasionally, he would allow me to tag along with his friends, while at other times he refused. His rejection never really bothered me; if I elicited any attention from him, I was thrilled.

Antoni's father, my *wuj* (uncle) Teodor Schreiber, had been ethnic German but had passed away several years ago. Antoni's mother, *Ciotka* (Aunt) Cecylia, had married her deceased husband's brother, Edmund, which made him both Antoni's uncle and stepfather. (Did I not mention our complicated family tree?) Uncle Edmund was an apothecary and, as my father often said, a good man. He did his very best to be a friend and surrogate father to Antoni, whom he loved, permitting the boy to travel to Germany each summer to bond with those relations. He would come home with some wonderful stories to tell.

Because of his late father, stepfather, and his summer stays in Germany, Antoni spoke that language fluently and took great pride in his dual nationality. When he demonstrated his perfect *Deutsch* to our cousins, I annoyingly attempted to copy him. Imagine my delight when he offered to teach me the language, vowing I would speak "like a native." Because it meant that I would spend more time with him, I promised to study diligently.

Filip was secretly jealous of Antoni, I believed, competing with him in everything they did. Sports, schoolwork, running, fishing—everything. Filip dreamed of beating Antoni at something but never could and was furious at losing time and again in brains, brawn, wit, and looks to his older cousin. It was not the constant thrashing that angered him but rather Antoni's ridicule. Antoni only laughed at Filip; his cousin was simply out of his league. The situation never altered, though; the next family gathering, Filip was at it again. Poor wretched boy.

As he waved good-bye to me, I sighed, watching his straight frame stroll away before I finally turned to purchase more cheesecake.

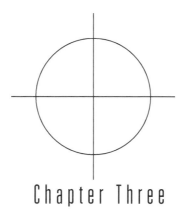

Chapter Three

THE BROOCH

*O*n weekends, European businesses closed their doors. The only establishments unlocked on Saturday and Sunday were churches, open to penitents and worshipers alike seven days a week. Government offices, restaurants, even public transportation systems were silent. Grandpapa said it was a dammed good thing the Great War had not begun on a weekend.

Saturday I spent with my friends, always making the most of it. One of our favorite pastimes was exploring the vast tunnels of our salt mines. Most of Bochnia's citizens and many members of my family were employed in the profitable salt mining operation. The finished product was exported throughout Europe, providing greater self-sufficiency to our town. Tunnels meandered through the mountains for hundreds of kilometers while in the center of the mine was Blessed King's Chapel where the pulpit, sculptures, and alter were carved entirely from salt. We were always at risk of getting lost but as far as I was concerned, the risk made the adventure more fun.

I was usually the instigator in these proceedings, as I seemed to be the adventurous one in my neighborhood group of friends. Olenka was the smart one and spent most of her time trying to discourage me from what I thought were splendid ideas for fun. Her mother was English and her father was Polish so she spoke both languages flawlessly. Through her and our English studies in class, I was also becoming quite adept at the language.

Arlene and her family lived down the road a bit, her house in view of ours. She was the pretty, sensitive one with lovesick boys frequently following her. I was in awe, perhaps slightly jealous, of Arlene's beauty. Blessed with the long legs of a dancer, she had perfect Hollywood-like features and glossy dark hair.

One boy, Maxim, (Max to his friends) was often in our company when we would scout for activities. Max was a very serious and quiet boy with an obvious crush on me. I was teased constantly about this fact but secretly I was pleased to have an admirer since I could not hold a candle to Arlene's beauty.

I would like to say I resembled a heroine from a romantic novel or movie, but that would be far from the truth. Those fortunate women are described in the same manner: "long, thick, golden hair that curled around her porcelain skin" or "limbs like a gazelle and a proud perky bust..." on and on ad nauseam. I often wondered how one could possess either a proud or a perky breast. My hair was long but extremely fine, maddeningly straight, and I continually forced stray hairs back into my carefully prepared braid. My nose, a bit too narrow; my hind end, *dupa* in Polish, slightly too large for my frame (this from my mother). Definitely not tall, destined to be at the most five foot in height, and as for the bust...well, I continually held out hope I might inherit that feature from my grandmother's gene pool. At any rate, I am just a regular girl among thousands of regular girls, blending in with the crowds.

Still, I reasoned, things could be worse. I wanted for nothing, had parents who doted on me, marvelous friends, and a wonderful extended family. With the exception of Filip. Nothing is perfect, after all.

Today, we walked into the center of town to engage in another favorite pastime—the cinema. All the world's problems and troubles would melt away as the lights would dim and the current story would unfold upon that bright, flickering screen.

We were not the only ones who enjoyed the rolling images; it was rumored that Adolf Hitler was an enthusiastic fan of Mickey Mouse and would have private showings of the cartoon in his home. For some unfathomable reason, I thought that very odd.

We all had our favorite American stars and movies, subtitled of course. I loved Norma Shearer and Myrna Loy; always so smart in the latest fashions and jewels. Arlene was fond of Fred Astaire and Ginger Rogers movies, those two gliding about in the most fabulous manner. Olenka could discuss Bette Davis and Joan Fontaine, the "mystery girls," for hours. (She just adored Bette's eyes). Swashbuckling and derring-dos were Max's interest with Errol Flynn capturing the title role.

Walking home, my three friends would often critique the recently viewed film. For me, who could only do what I considered a very good polka, I simply twirled my way behind them, pretending I was Ginger wearing a floating chiffon ball gown.

Sundays we reserved for God and family, gathering after Mass in my Grandparents' flat for Sunday dinners. The home was always crowded with family members, everyone bringing a dish of traditional food to share—even Mama, unfortunately.

More often than not, political discussions would begin, Grandpapa always speaking his mind, even when it would be wiser not to do so. I recall Buscha saving for a new hat she had fallen in love with at our local millinery. The black velvet piece was the new cloche style, sitting on one's head more like a puddle of cloth than anything else. After finally purchasing it, she made her grand entrance from the bedroom to show us. Grandpapa took one look at it and told her it looked as if an elephant had crapped on her head. She returned her purchase the next morning and did not speak to Grandpapa for three days.

Lately, Papa warned his parents to keep their voices down if others were within earshot. Papa said times were changing and it was better to be safe than sorry as one never knew who was listening. I was confused at this ambiguous remark but attributed it to another matter for adults only. Certainly nothing with which I need concern myself.

Having disposed of the Sunday meal remnants and hearing Grandpapa begin to snore lightly in his favorite chair, Buscha and I had our special time together. When I was very young, I would snuggle on Buscha's lap and listen to her stories of long ago. She was a large-busted woman who loved to wear very lacey dresses in somber colors. Pinned on her dress, as it was every Sunday, was her beautiful brooch, the most wonderful piece of jewelry I had ever seen and I could not wait to hear the story behind it.

"Buscha, tell me about you and Grandpapa and the brooch he gave you," I would request eagerly.

"Oh, Marta," she would say with a sigh, "you've heard that story so many times. Maybe something else?"

"No no, Buscha, I love that story best."

"Very well," she smiled. "Let me unpin it for you." And suddenly the marvelous brooch was in my hand, twinkling in the light. Set in the center of a hand-painted flower was a small diamond and encircling the pin were tiny, filigreed hearts of sterling silver.

"Do you remember the secret?" she whispered.

"Oh, yes," I whispered back. "You just touch it here and look," I said excitedly as it opened to reveal a recessed locket inside. "Tell me how Grandpapa gave it to you when you married and how you opened the box and saw a REAL diamond on it."

She laughed, "I think you just told the whole story."

"Nooooo, Buscha, you tell it and I'll help."

"Well, it was the night of my marriage to your grandpapa."

"And he was the handsomest man you ever saw, right, Buscha?" I interrupted.

"Yes, that's right. Anyway, on our wedding night, he gave me a beautiful gold box and said it was from his heart to mine. Then I opened the box. And inside was a most wonderful brooch made out of Polish Pottery."

"With a REAL DIAMOND!" I exclaimed.

"Yes, a real diamond in the center, right here, see? And I started to cry and your grandpapa said, 'Wait, there's more.' Then he touched this invisible latch on the side..."

"Just like I did, right, Buscha?"

"Yes, little one, just like you did. When he opened it, I saw a photo of the two of us on one side of the brooch and on the other side, an engraving with To My Beloved and then our wedding date; 1 *Maj* 1880."

"And you asked him why your names were not written, right?" It was normally the custom to engrave each name on such a gift, using the bride's new surname for the first time.

"Yes, I surely did. And do you remember what he said to me?"

"He said, 'Because as long as you and God know how much I love you, that's all that matters,'" I said proudly.

"That's right, and then I cried some more and he kissed my tears away."

Every time she told this story, Buscha promised me the brooch would belong to me someday. She hid it in her secret dressing table drawer, so I could always find it. This was another secret between the two of us and I was so excited to know I would be wearing this wonderful piece of family history one day. It would be Mine, Mine, MINE! I would proudly pin it on my dress just like Buscha! Of course, it never occurred to me that I would be wearing it only if Buscha was no longer in my life. As a child, I never made the connection between her death and my ownership of the brooch.

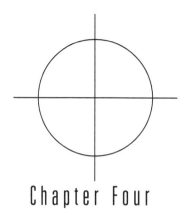

Chapter Four

KLEIN'S BOOKSHOP

*W*e may appear to be a country town but with our large railway station and a military airfield 31 km away in Czyzyny, just outside Krakow, we have great accessibility to the rest of the country. Still, we pride ourselves on a slower pace of life and our quaint establishments. None was more unique than Klein's Book Shop.

To improve my German language skills and thereby impress Antoni, I often embarked on outings to this favorite shop and its German owner, Mr. Klein. It was a wonderful old building and by looking at the exterior, a shopper knew the interior would be magical. It reminded me of a fairy tale from Hans Christian Andersen.

The roof had the requisite high pitch so the winter snow could release itself from the tiles. At the very top of the peak was a round stained glass window, inset with bright colors of blues, reds, and yellows. Next to the doorway, on the street level, Mr. Klein had recently replaced the multi-paned picture widow with a new single-pane unit that better displayed his current best sellers. It was much more useful to his sales but I thought the original window had more charm. A few of the large, flat rocks wrapping themselves around the building had crumbled with age while others held on doggedly for dear life and the wide, red door with heavy brass finishes was so glossy my reflection was nearly visible. Mr. Klein took great pride in that door even if it was a peculiar color for a shop entrance.

My friend was known for his window displays of delicate wooden puppets, the theme changing every few weeks or so. Today it looked like something from *A Midsummer Night's Dream*, a forest diorama featuring wooden sprites and nymphs, positioned in midair, ready to land on a stack of leather bound stories. One petite golden fairy hung in the air in the act of turning a page for a larger blue fairy. It was wonderful.

I entered to the tinkling of the overhead bell and saw that today my friend was assisting only one customer. The room was awash with the hues from the stained glass window above resembling the interior of a kaleidoscope. Books were not only situated by genre upon the many shelves, they were in stacks upon the floor, piled high on the front counter, and even wedged tightly into a large basket by the door. I could see the dust specs floating upward in the rays of the colored light like tiny souls making their way to heaven.

If his shop was busy when I visited I would help at the counter, accepting payment and making change for those lucky patrons who would be transported to other times and places through their purchases. If the shop was nearly empty, like today, I knew a book in German was waiting for me under the newspaper shelf.

Today's was a book of German fairy tales. How apropos, I thought. I greeted my elfin German friend and said hello to his customer as I made my way up the winding staircase to the equally stuffed office. The staircase had obviously been here for ages and I wondered when my friend would find the time to reinforce it. As I stepped on each worn board, I was greeted with croaking and cracking sounds like an old man's bones on a cold winter's morning. Each groan seemed to say to me, "I'm very old and delicate, you know. Please tread on me carefully."

Mr. Klein naturally began his lessons with very simple instruction booklets, mostly containing pictures of objects, and I worked my way up to complete stories entirely in German. The more confident I felt, the more difficult the books. After several years of this practice, he was so sure of my language abilities that he began issuing books in Yiddish.

Whenever my tutor was free, he would join me up here to brew the dark rich tea of which he was so fond. Here we would sit; I reading aloud while he patiently corrected my pronunciations, watching the seasons drift by the window, year after year.

Although ethnic German, Mr. Klein was very anti-Nazi. He was not overtly verbal in his opinions but if drawn out, he would tell you exactly how he felt about the new regime. He reminded me of my outspoken grandpapa in that respect. Often threatening to retire and live on the French Rivera, he was still a fixture on the street, more books than ever for sale.

Chapter Five

June 1933

RISE TO POWER

*I*n June 1933, Hitler once again captured headlines when he was installed as chancellor of Germany. The man was quickly rising into an ever-increasing position of power. Our ethnic Germans seemed to worship the man with German-owned restaurants and bars full of merrymakers, embracing the new chancellor. Papa said that it would be difficult for most men to remain humble with so much public adoration thrown at them. Grandpapa snorted and said that he did not think Hitler knew the meaning of the word humble. As Bochnia's demographics were a varied lot, so were people's opinions of the chancellor.

We were mostly Catholics, as was the whole of Poland; over 85 percent, in fact. Ethnic Germans, also primarily Catholics, called our town home as did approximately 20 percent Jews. Occasionally, we had the odd group of Gypsies arrive and make camp while they sold their handmade goods or, as my father would say, try their hand at whatever scheme they had perfected to part the town's people from their coin. After a few weeks, they would move on to another unsuspecting settlement.

Our town, indeed throughout all of Europe, lived in a general climate of anti-Semitism that could flare into violent outbursts and as such, the deliberate attempts made to divide Europeans against each other was widely successful. Newspapers and the wireless were inundated with propaganda from Germany, Russia, and even Great Britain separating us emotionally and psychologically. Each tapped into our religions and fears, playing one against the other. The German media appeared much more calculating in their efforts to foment unrest. Targeting the Poles, the blaring headlines professed Jews would be the downfall of our civilization. The Jews, on the other hand, were warned against the Poles. That nationality, they were told, would just as soon slit their throats as look at them. The ethnic Germans firmly believed both were inferior people.

The Soviets had their own methods of coercion, constantly bemoaning our poor status as a country while urging our government to let Mother Russia wrap us in warm, receiving arms. As for the Brits, their media was not above the stiff-upper-lip type of talk; all would be well in the world and evil was only in our imagination. When I asked Papa to explain such things, he simply summarized by exclaiming, "Adolf Hitler is a very difficult man." I was amazed that one man, located thousands of kilometers away, could be the cause of so much tongue wagging.

The constant barrage of information from the German media seemed to be hitting closer to home. Neighbors we had known for years became withdrawn and tense, our customers' attitudes were changing, and discussions were held in whispers. I often wondered, I said to Arlene with a laugh, if customers feared I would beat them about the head with a giant *pierogi* or stab them in the back with my pickle fork. Arlene giggled and said she caught herself looking sideways at her own parents one day. Papa said some Jewish families were selling their possessions and leaving for America or England. Since my family remained steadfast, it was no concern of mine. We were due for some good news, Papa said, and felt we received it in 1934.

Poland's current chief of state was anxious to avoid involvement in any quarrels with its neighboring countries. This was accomplished by signing nonaggression agreements with Germany and Russia in January, both pacts openly reflecting Warsaw's policy of maintaining friendly relationships with all parties concerned, a difficult balancing act to perform. A mutual trade agreement between Germany and my country soon followed that had many shopkeepers in both countries celebrating. With a bit more ease and acceptance, they could now enjoy a more profitable exchange with customers in both lands. Many of the Poles rejoiced and shared the notion that we had nothing to fear from Germany. Perhaps the Brits were right after all. Tension lifted and life would improve with the new treaty.

When I read that particular opinion from the newspaper to Grandpapa, he merely shook his head and said, "Fools. This allows more time for That Man to rearm his military. Mark my words, Marta, I'm right; he's up to something. You'll see." I sincerely hoped he was mistaken.

Chapter Six

August 1934

DER FUHRER

*T*oday, I decided I would visit Mr. Klein and see what new lesson he had in store for me. It was a beautiful summer's day and I wanted to enjoy it before fall officially arrived next month. Mama asked if I would deliver some food to Elias Fischer on my walk.

The rail-thin, longhaired man she spoke of had terrified me as a child, making me extremely uncomfortable by talking to himself. The town knew him simply as Elias but Grandpapa called him "an odd duck." When I mentioned my fear to Papa, he explained that Elias had fought bravely for our country in 1914 and had suffered head injuries from the enemy. He was very harmless, Papa said, but sometimes he talked to old friends who had passed on.

Never regularly employed, he worked at odd jobs that the people of Bochnia hired him to do for their homes or businesses. He resided in a back room of the church in exchange for general clean-up on the grounds. After my talk with Papa, I found the nerve to say hello to Elias when I saw him, the two of us eventually becoming very good friends. As promised, I stopped at the Basilica to give Elias the bread and sausage I had packaged for him. I found him sweeping the vestry, the priests' changing room, behind the altar. Often visiting, I enjoyed his reminiscences about the past, particularly the Great War. I wondered, however, how much was fact and how much was imagination, remembering what Papa had told me about his head injury in The War To End All Wars.

Today, he greeted me warmly and was extremely thankful with the food I brought to him. After he was satisfied I had done the baking and not Mother ("I'm sorry, Miss Marta," he would say, "your mama is a wonderful person but she does have some trouble in the kitchen."), I thought we would sit for a short talk.

"No time to talk today, Miss Marta," he said anxiously. "Father Benedykt is most particular about everything for the Sunday Masses. Sad goings-on, Miss Marta, sad indeed. He's preparing an important sermon and wants the church to look just so."

I asked Elias what sad thing he was referring to but could glean nothing more from him. Reminding myself that his conversations could be difficult to follow, I simply patted him on the hand with an assurance that everything would be fine and continued on my way to Klein's Bookshop.

Mr. Klein had always sold Polish newspapers in his shop but over the last several years had begun to sell German publications as well. More business that way, he had said. As I approached the shop on my bicycle, there were a great number of people entering and leaving the rather small shop, the gleaming red door swinging to and fro with all the activity. I imagined it must be crowded in there with not only the patrons but also the scattered books. It occurred to me that perhaps he was acting upon his threat to retire and was having a closing out sale. I thought how much I would miss my friend and teacher if that were so and I pedaled faster.

Propping my bicycle against the shop wall, I stood aside to allow people, German and Polish alike, to enter and leave, each holding a newspaper written in their own language. The headlines all seemed to announce the same news although the print was larger on the German paper. "Hitler Becomes *Fuhrer*" the lettering blared forth. According to the conversations I overheard, the Germans seemed ecstatic about the news; the Poles, not as much.

I finally made my way into the shop to find poor Mr. Klein struggling to receive payment and hand out change to his impatient patrons.

When he saw my wave from behind an irate lump of a man, he beckoned to me and said, "Marta. Please, come help me."

Pushing and shoving my way through the crowded shop all the while saying, "Excuse me, excuse me," I finally made it to the counter. "Mr. Klein, what is going on? What is happening here?"

"No need to worry, my dear. Help me finish these sales. The newspapers are almost gone and we'll have a sit-down about it all."

True to his word, after announcing to the customers that all the papers were sold and they must now annoy the shop two blocks down, he locked the door and we carefully crept our way up to his office. He put a pot of water on the hot plate for the eternal black tea and sat down, wiping his forehead with his blue-checkered handkerchief. "*Mein Gott*," he said reverting to his native vernacular, "that was exhausting." He set out two newspapers, one in German and one in Polish, and we began to read them together and sip our tea. I read aloud and he supplied the translation of many new political terms I had never seen before.

I knew the word *Fuhrer* in German meant leader or guide. The German paper was very enthusiastic in declaring Adolf Hitler as such, effusively proclaiming what a great man he has been for the people of Germany and the glorious future together that lay ahead, continuing to detail the country's prosperity. The Hitler's youth group was declared a magnificent organization, raising boys into men. Hitler was credited with the creation of jobs and the general high morale the people regained since the Great War. They made him sound so glorious I was surprised he had not been nominated for sainthood.

More cautious in the writing was the Polish newspaper. Although they admitted to "leader" in their translation, they also hinted at the word "tyrant" as well. Rather than sainthood, the paper implied that we Poles should proceed with prudence in any future associations we were to have with Germany.

I put the paper down and looked at Mr. Klein. "But what does it all mean?" I asked. "The German paper treats the man as a god and the Polish journalists are walking on eggs."

"I wish I knew," he sighed as he sipped his tea. "It is true; he has brought Germany up from the poor state it was in but I don't trust the man or the party. The Nazis in general seem to be a cruel, single-minded group who insist everyone think as they do. And Hitler...I'm not sure about him either. Several of my friends in Germany just adore the man and tell me they would give their life for him. My family, on the other hand, is not so enthusiastic, writing me of some terrible things happening. They are always being watched for any infraction. Very frightening and worrying. He promises much and I wonder how he can accomplish such guarantees peacefully.

On the way home, many of those I passed had an opinion on the latest news. Some were expressing it more loudly and more forcibly than others. I quickly dashed past two men skirmishing, fists flying and voices raised, until the local constabulary put an end to it. Two distinct sides had been taken, not necessarily split evenly between the Poles and the Germans. Some of each had slipped over to what I thought would be opposing sides. Perhaps they were just as confused as I was. For the most part though, the Germans were joyous while the Poles and Jews I passed spoke with more trepidation.

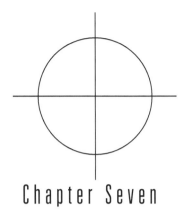

Chapter Seven

October 1934

TELKA THE CAT

*W*e were one of the lucky families in the area who owned a wireless and the family loved to listen to the radio shows and world news emanating from that wonderful box. Ours was a twelve-inch by eight-inch tabletop model made of Bakelite, a sturdy shiny substance, with glass tubes in the back that glowed eerily.

On this particular evening, several of my relations had come to visit and were now sitting wherever they could find room, listening to the world news. My cousins and I were still in the kitchen, munching on pastries Aunt Isabella brought, but still within sight and sound of the sitting room. My ears pricked up when I heard the name of Hitler coming from that tinny-sounding box followed by the words Treaty of Versailles.

I was far from politically minded but as I remembered it from the schoolroom, the Allies had signed the Treaty of Versailles after the Great War, around 1919. Ancient history to me, of course. It restricted the German government in many areas, stripped them of territories, limited their military personnel by abolishing the draft, eliminated the production of military equipment, and ultimately affected their economy by mandating reparation to the rest of the world for damages caused by Germany's initiation of the war.

A few years ago, a photograph appeared in our newspaper of two German schoolchildren flying a kite made of pasted-together Deutsch Marks. I could not understand how anyone would make such a thing out of money so I questioned my father. He told me the DM had continually dropped in value since the end of the Great War. In 1921, a reasonably strong German bank note stood at 75 Marks to the value of one American dollar. By January 1923, the DM was worth 18,000 to one dollar and by November of that same year, it would take 4 billion Deutsch Marks to equal one dollar. In December 1923 the rate of exchange was an unbelievable 4.2 trillion Marks to one dollar! Citizens were transporting wheelbarrows of cash to the store to purchase one loaf of bread. By then, the wealthy German citizen became practically penniless. In economics, as I learned much later, this is called hyperinflation; out of control inflation. At the time my father was trying to explain this to me, I could not grasp the concept. All I could see in my mind was that photograph. They were making a kite out of MONEY! Money was worth, well…**money**, was it not? It would always be money. I could not understand.

The treaty seemed harsh and punitive when I learned of it. Now, according to the voice on the radio, Hitler "may be" violating that treaty and "perhaps" raising great numbers for a new military, even conscripting citizens to forcibly increase that number. The report seemed rather vague and repeatedly hinted at the "possibilities" of such violations.

My grandfather, who was positive everyone wanted his opinion, tended to believe this uncertain news as fact. "That man is up to something, mark my words. What does he need an army for if not to fight?"

"Father," warned my own father, "please keep your voice down. The newscaster is only trying to create facts where there are none. It's just more propaganda."

"I won't! If he's not in violation of the treaty now, he soon will be. Someone must stop him! He is nothing but an egocentric maniac!"

I watched as Antoni slowly rose from his seat across from me, clutching something behind his back. He made his way into the sitting room and walked up to Grandpapa. In a flash, Antoni had a knife held against Grandpapa's neck and growled at him, "Never let me hear you say another word against Herr Hitler."

Conversation stopped and all eyes were upon Antoni, appalled at this development, frozen to the spot. I could not take my eyes from my handsome cousin as Uncle Edmund carefully approached the two main characters in this macabre scene. "Give me the knife, boy," he said. Antoni hadn't moved a muscle since he had sprung upon my grandfather but ever so slowly, my uncle slipped the knife from his stepson's hand into his own. Aunt Cecylia immediately began babbling apologies and excuses while Uncle gripped Antoni by the arm and strode out the house, the three of them leaving with a slam of the door.

{ I }

I was out the door early the next morning. With so much drama happening within my own family, I could not wait to share it with my friends. I found them at our usual meeting place, the back entrance to the mines. Arlene was sitting upon the old rickety fence nearby and I jumped up to join her.

"You'll never guess what happened at my house last night," I began. That was all it took for me to gain their attention. As they warmed to my story, I outlined the entire spectacle for them. I may have added a bit more color to the story—the wild red eyes of Antoni, and the length of the blade—but overall I stuck to the facts.

Having finished, I looked at them expectantly. I waited for their shocked questions and overall comments but I was disappointed in my expectations. Instead, the three of them were casting uncomfortable glances at each other. "Whatever is the matter?" I asked. "Did you not hear what I told you?"

"What happened next? I mean, after Antoni and his parents left?" asked Olenka.

"Well," I said thoughtfully, "everything went back to normal after a few minutes. No one spoke of it." I remembered, though, how the remaining relatives could not wait to leave.

"Were you frightened?" asked Max.

"Of course not! It was just Antoni acting funny." As soon as I said this, I realized how unbelievable the statement was. Antoni never acted silly to gain attention. That was Filip's trait.

The three of my friends were busy with furtive looks again, this time directed at me. "Marta," began Max slowly. "Perhaps Antoni has more of a temper than you might think."

As I was about to discredit this as so much nonsense, Olenka offered her opinion. "Yes," she said, "I think you should really examine his actions more carefully from now on. Remember what happened to Telka?" she finished.

"Oh, that was nothing. Antoni adored that cat. His mother said she just ran away," I said defensively.

"What was that? What did you say about a cat?" asked Arlene.

As I continued to make light of the whole affair from many years ago—I think I was only three at the time—Olenka pressed me to tell the entire story to the others. So, with regret, I did.

One day, I began, my parents and Antoni's were in their sitting room discussing life in general while Antoni and I were in his front garden playing with his cat, Telka. She was very sweet and I seemed to hold a place in her heart since she would continually seek me out whenever I visited. This day, Telka was sitting in my lap, content and purring in the sunshine.

"Why is my cat always on your lap, Weegie?" complained Antoni.

I just looked at him and shrugged my shoulders, smiling and petting her. My response seemed to upset him further and he narrowed his eyes while jutting out his chin. Then he began to call and cajole the cat from my lap to his. When she did not move, he grabbed her from me, surprising her so much that she scratched him.

Looking at the blood she had drawn on his hand, he said, "No one hurts me. You're my cat and you'll do as I say," he yelled. That said, he stood up and began to shake her.

I was up on my feet as well, screaming and crying at him, pummeling him with my ineffective fists when I finally heard the front door open.

"What is going on out here?" boomed my Uncle Edmond.

In between my screams, I saw my mother run over and pry the cat from Antoni's hands. "Enough," she said. "What has gotten into you? Come inside, both of you," and with that she handed the terrified creature to Uncle Edmond and led us inside.

Several weeks later, we were again at Antoni's home, enjoying cheesecake with coffee for the adults and milk for Antoni and me.

"This is wonderful cheesecake, Cecylia. I'd very much like the recipe," said my mother. Oh no, I inwardly groaned, another culinary experiment. I glanced at my father who looked as if he had just sucked on a lemon; he obviously had the same thought as I.

Trying to change the subject, I looked around and suddenly asked, "Aunt Cecylia. Where's Telka?"

"Oh, my dear, she must have left us—I haven't seen her in over a week. We looked everywhere for her. Antoni was simply devastated! I hope she is all right but cats do go off when they are dying. I prefer to think that perhaps she's found another family," she said.

"Oh, I hope so. She was such a sweet thing," my mother said.

Conversation went back to normal but I could not help looking at my father. He was staring at Antoni with a speculative look in his eye, as if Antoni was a newly discovered life-form. Antoni did not look the least bit devastated. He kept his eyes down, continuing to eat, and I noticed a slight grin on one side of his mouth. The event made a great impression on me and slightly uncomfortable at the time, although I could not say why.

Although I did not let my friends today know how I been bothered by this, I could see they were very upset as I ended the account

"But, that is terrible!" cried Arlene. "Do you mean to say that Antoni...that he...Oh, I cannot even say it!"

"Nonsense," I said unconvincingly. "Antoni did nothing wrong! I have already told you. The cat simply ran away." As far as I was concerned, this was the end of the conversation. I could not let my thoughts stray down the path my friends were leading them. Standing upon the top rung of the fence, I proceeded to walk across it like a balance beam, as far away from their talk as possible. I left my friends looking concerned and mumbling to each other, hoping that by the time I traveled down the entire dilapidated fence and back, they would have come to their senses.

The knife incident, as I referred to it, was the last I saw of Antoni for several years. Many weeks later, I overheard my parents whispering that my uncle and aunt had sent him to Germany to live with his father's family. Mother said that Aunt Cecylia had been weeping and begging her husband to allow her son to stay. For once, Uncle Edmund did not give in to my aunt's wishes and would not budge on his decision.

Chapter Eight

March 1936

THE RHINELAND

*F*ilip's family business, he bragged, was busier than ever. They could not keep enough furs in stock and were positively rolling in money, he said. He would often flip a roll of bills in my face to emphasize the point. I found out through Papa a very good reason existed for this sudden brisk business. The Jews fleeing from Europe were allowed to carry only the clothes on their back, nothing else. Hence, families sold their possessions and purchased the most expensive furs available. They crossed borders to the shop or ordered items sight unseen through the post. Upon arrival in their new country, the families sold the furs, obtaining funds to begin anew. I thought it was very clever.

I chose to remain disconnected from such boring subjects as Hitler, politics, and treaties. I was a typical teenage girl with far more immediate matters deserving my attention. School, friends, and boys to name a few. It was difficult, however, to remain completely under my rock and not notice changes in my hometown.

Frightened families from every walk in life were beginning to leave our town in droves. Houses sat empty and shopkeepers never knew how many helping hands would show up for the day's work. While thousands had left, millions of us stayed. This was our country. Besides, where would we go? Other countries were filled to capacity with immigrants and many refused to accept more. Many Poles had traveled to Russia. We had been under Russia's control for many years and some believed if the Germans gained control now, how could it be any worse than with the Russians? We had survived an atmosphere of mutual distrust between all three countries for generations. Why leave now? Apparently, according to Grandpapa, several reasons existed for such apprehension and change.

From the few conversations I overheard, I knew of Hitler's interest in regaining lands for Germany stripped from her years ago after the Great War. The Rhineland and the Sudetenland were, according to Grandpapa, two extremely fertile areas that had once been in Germany's purse. Austria as well, the birthplace of Hitler, was probably in his sights too, Papa said. Although Germany enjoyed political control over the Rhineland, she was not permitted to maintain troops there. Rather like owning a shiny ball and not allowed to bounce it, I thought.

At any rate, on March 17, 1936, Hitler took a large political and military gamble by assaulting the Rhineland and making it his own. Papa and Grandpapa were constantly listening to the news on the radio. Apparently, the whole world was waiting for Britain or France to stop him. France hinted that military action was a possible option. That country would be willing to fight if Britain agreed to assist. The British did not generally regard the German remilitarization as harmful. The future British ambassador to the United States, Lord Lothian, said Hitler's action amounted to no more than "the Germans walking into their own backyard." At any rate, Britain did not have the resources to enforce the treaty so they left it up to France to handle this problem. France turned to Belgium who opted for neutrality. At this juncture the Allies....did absolutely nothing.

Hitler was quoted afterward as saying: "The forty-eight hours after the march into the Rhineland were the most nerve-racking in my life. If the French had then marched into the Rhineland, we would have had to withdraw with our tails between our legs, for the military resources at our disposal would have been wholly inadequate for even a moderate resistance."

As far as I could see, the whole occurrence was not our problem. According to Grandpapa, it was brilliant, absolutely brilliant. Germany sat contentedly with its slice of the pie and zero bloodshed. The world, other than Grandpapa, seemed satisfied and thankful. The entire incident was accomplished in a most civilized manner.

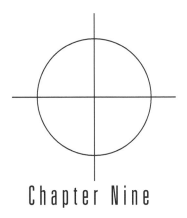

Chapter Nine

January 1938

THE WEDDING

*M*y second or third cousin on my mother's side (or perhaps it was my father's) was getting married and I was finally old enough to be a junior bridesmaid instead of the perpetual flower girl. My mother was in the process of sewing a wonderful creation for me in our country's traditionally bright colors. As my figure was maturing, my bust line was increasing (thank you, Buscha), and I filled out the blouse quite nicely. I could not wait for her to finish the frock.

Today, I was standing on a stool while she was on her knees, pinning the hem so it would hit my mid calf. "Stop fidgeting, Marta," she said. "This fabric is difficult to handle. I'll never get this hem straight if you keep this up."

"I can't help it," I said petulantly. "My back aches and I'm bored. We wanted to go see the new movie at the cinema today."

"Well, my back aches too. We have to get this done, Marta, the wedding is next weekend. Now stand still for just ten minutes longer. I only have this one side left."

Next weekend! I could hardly wait. There were rumors within the family that Antoni would be attending since the groom had been his best friend when they were younger. He would see me in the fabulous dress with what I believed were my new womanly curves. The closer the day came, the more difficult and excited I became.

"Marta, please! Whatever is your problem?" asked Mama.

"Ants in her pants," replied Papa, always my parents' explanation for any restless behavior. "I wonder, Marta, could you be hoping for someone special to attend the wedding? Someone you have not seen in some time?"

I turned crimson. I had no idea Papa had noticed my girlish devotion to Antoni. Looking back, though, I suppose it was obvious. Probably the whole family had known of my crush on my cousin, and I became more horrified than ever. Mama just looked at me with a very Mona Lisa-type smile on her lips. We knew Antoni had graduated from the Munich University some time ago although I had no current information about him and was anxious to find out.

"Never mind, daughter, I'm sure you'll have a wonderful time and even outshine the bride," he said with a chuckle.

Now that last statement I doubted. I had seen the bride's dress since Mama had been putting the finishing touches on it for the last month. It was white taffeta with a complete layer of heavy lace over it. The dress was high necked with a long flowing train and cathedral veil, and Mama had been hand applying tiny seed pearls until late at night. Her creativity with the needle and thread more than made up for her lack of culinary skills.

The day of the wedding finally arrived. All the women (except Mama) had been baking and cooking for days. (Mama had done her part by creating the wedding dress, she said, but we all knew the real reason why she was not asked to cook). Aunt Isabella had made the wedding cake.

The nuptials would be held in the large ornate St. Nicholas' Basilica. We made a most colorful group, making our way down the long aisle to the altar while the stringed musical group played. The ceremony was beautiful but I have to confess I paid little attention to the goings-on. My eyes were searching the congregation for only one face and I was exceedingly disappointed not to see it.

Leaving the church to the hymn of "Ava Maria," we all headed back to the parents' house for the reception. Most Polish receptions lasted a day or two, depending upon the family's finances. This family had an enormous house and the bride's father was rumored to be doing very well in his business, so I expected this party to carry on for some time.

I remember Mama telling me of a wedding reception lasting three days when she was small. She crawled upon a pool table, fell asleep for a few hours, and then rejoined the party. We Poles love any excuse to celebrate.

As we walked in to the large decorated home, the band began to play and I caught the first whiff of food. The long tables had been laid with every Polish food imaginable, fairly buckling under the strain. Oh yes, I thought, this is going to be fun!

After the bride had the first dance with her father, other guests joined in and the band played a lively round of polkas—of course! This was my chance to prove my talent and I grabbed a cousin next to me, dragging him out to the dance floor. Although I danced well, I had one problem when it came to the Polka—I liked to lead. Sometimes, this could be a concern but luckily this cousin was pliable so around and around the dance floor we went.

Guests were enjoying vodka and beer while queuing up for food. Still no sign of Antoni. Deciding I had enough dancing, I toddled over to fill my plate. Suddenly, the conversation around me stopped and people began whispering and pointing. The band played on as if nothing was amiss, but many of the dancers simply stood and looked toward the door. It was Antoni. I saw his head above others and felt my heart do flip-flops. Look, I thought, the other guests are actually clearing a path; they obviously respect him. Then I got a closer look. He was wearing a German uniform! No wonder guests had dispersed.

His mother had not yet seen him and I turned to look at her just as she spotted him. I watched as the color drained from her face giving her a chalky, ghostly complexion. I was rooted to the spot in which I stood, letting my plate droop in my hand, and watched as Aunt Cecylia rushed over to grab him, promptly bursting into tears. He held her tightly and was murmuring to her but his face was impassive.

Those guests who had been demonstrating their finest impressions of wax figures suddenly came to life. I heard many assessments of the situation as whispers floated around me.

"A German soldier? We can't have him here," I heard an unknown woman say, "We are not Nazis."

"Not just a soldier, my dear, it looks as if he is a lieutenant," answered a man, presumably the woman's husband.

"I can't believe he showed up. Why is he here?" said an obvious acquaintance.

"I should never have invited his parents." This probably from the mother of the bride.

"I didn't know the groom was German," said a limpid old man.

"Shhh, the family will hear you."

"But, what does he want?"

That, I think, was the question of the moment. What did this German lieutenant want? I did not really care—it was still Antoni. I made my way through the staring crowd and waited until he was through talking to his mother and shaking Uncle Edmond's hand.

"Hello, Antoni," I said.

"Well, well. If it isn't little Weegie," he replied. We exchanged the traditional three kisses on each other's cheeks. He laughed when he saw the sour look on my face. I silently cursed Filip again for that nickname.

"Please do not call me that. I'm much too grown-up for that silly name."

"I see. If you're so grown-up, then you shall be my dancing partner, for it looks as if I shall have no other tonight." He had obviously noticed the grimaces upon the guests' faces. With that, he whisked me on to the dance floor. I thought my grandmother would become apoplectic when she saw me in Antoni's arms. She immediately poked Grandpapa who leaned over to Papa and Mama. They all looked as if they had partaken of some extremely soured milk.

The band was playing a polonaise, a dance performed throughout Europe for centuries in one form or another but its roots were Polish. It was simple, really. Dancing side by side and clasping each other's hands with arms crossed, the couples walked along the floor in a circle. After a few steps, they did a short skip then repeated the first movement. The couples would twirl, turn, and eventually engage in more intricate steps while maintaining the circle. It was a lovely, traditional Polish dance and slow enough for a couple to carry on a conversation.

"See, isn't this fun?" commented Antoni. I was not sure if he meant the dancing or the reaction he was receiving from the family. "And I'm perfectly capable of leading, cousin. You needn't."

"Sorry," I mumbled.

"What! That is all I get—'sorry'? That is not the Marta I know." I looked up to find him smiling down at me.

"Now you're just making fun of me. And what are you doing in that uniform, anyway?"

"Now that's the little cousin I left behind. Do you not like it? It's a wonderful cut and color on me, do you not agree?"

I frowned, stung at the "little" reference. I had to admit, though, that the uniform looked wonderful on him. "So how long have you been in the army?"

"My dear cousin, you must learn to take notice of the different uniforms. I am in the Luftwaffe." By now, the music had changed to a polka and it was more difficult to talk while prancing and jumping along to this quick musical selection.

"Come," he said. "Let us sit this one out and I'll help you understand the differences between our military divisions."

I cringed at the term "our." He sounded so serious. Had he actually wiped from his mind and heart the fact that he was half-Polish? "Why would I want to know that? I'm not German."

He merely glanced at me enigmatically and ushered me out the door to the back garden, holding my elbow. Sitting on the iron bench next to me, he proceeded to tutor me with pride in the art of determining one German fighting force from another. I tried to present my best aloof countenance but secretly I was pleased we were now student and teacher once more.

Naturally, he began with the Luftwaffe, or air force. His uniform was dark blue with yellow collar tabs. "I'll tell you a secret," he continued, "all the officers' uniforms, indeed I believe in every division, have been custom tailored and designed. Do you see my belt? It is actually placed higher than normal, just a bit above waistline, to give the illusion that we are all taller than we actually are. Even Filip could look stately in one." I had to laugh at that. Filip was only a head taller than I and it truly irked him. He pointed out the silver and yellow embroidery on his ranking insignias. It really was beautiful work.

"The *Heer*, or army, has an entirely different color, that of gray-green, and the jacket is more of a double-breasted model. On the Heer soldiers' belt is inscribed '*Gott mit uns*,' God with us."

"You do not have to translate for me, Antoni. I have not forgotten my Deutsch," I said arrogantly.

Smiling his lazy grin at me, he continued my lesson. I had no idea how he managed to keep all this information in order. The *Kriegsmarine*, or navy, uniform was darker than the Luftwaffe. It was midnight blue and also double breasted but cut lower around the neckline than the Heer's so that any decoration at the shirt collar would show. The officer's cap was white with a dark bill. It sounded a bit like a jaunty seaman's uniform.

Different colored piping around the hats was used for further distinctions. As if that was not enough, even the shoulder straps and collar patches were color-coded: white for infantry, red for artillery, rose for *Panzer* or tank troops, and so on. The more he spoke, the more confusing it became. In addition, apparently all the officers had the option of purchasing variations on their division uniforms, opting for different shades, slightly different cuts, even different jackets. Then there were the caps. Peaked caps, field caps, helmets—the list went on and on.

These three combined armed forces of Germany were known as the *Wehrmacht*, the Defense Forces.

"Then there's another group that are not considered part of the Wehrmacht proper. You've heard of the *Gestapo*, *ja*? The *Geheime Staatspolizei*, or secret state police. Do you know how they got their nickname? No? It's taken from the first few letters of each word like this: GEheime STAatsPOlizei, ge..sta..po. *Verstehst du*? Clever, *ja*? They seek out those not fully committed to the Nazi way of life. They can be a bit of a nasty group; even I do not wish to cross them. The problem with the Gestapo is you can never tell who is a member, perhaps even your neighbor. They usually wear nondescript civilian clothing, although of a much better cloth than most civilians could afford. They have a gray uniform when they need to present themselves more as a military group. Occasionally I have seen members in leather trench coats with fedoras. For example," he went on to explain when I looked confused, *"Der Fuhrer* considers smoking to be very un-German so if your friend was discovered smoking a cigarette in public, your friend might get a visit from the Gestapo." I was horrified. I had never heard of such a thing.

"Then there is the *Schutzstaffel*, the Protective Squadron. They are more like an elite police force called simply the SS." This group, he continued, was a bit more complicated (at this point, I thought they were all complicated). This organization was split into three groups. The first section is *Waffen SS*, a military branch of supposedly true Nazis—elite soldiers who were trained in extreme ideology and motivation. They were fierce fighters, almost fanatical, who fought to the last bullet or the last man standing, and those uniforms were more or less the same colors as the Heer. They were ruthless and feared, killing on and off the battlefield and sent upon missions where the regular army could not succeed. Certain requirements were demanded of a man to belong. One must be physically fit and loyal to the Nazi cause, at least five ten in height, not wear spectacles, have no defective teeth, (I thought that was odd), and must be able to prove his Aryan race back to the year 1750. Antoni described them as the vanguard of the Nazi party and he obviously admired them. Alas, he would never be permitted within their ranks due to his half-Polish heritage, I thought to myself sardonically.

The second category of the SS is the Death's Head, who were given the task of organizing and operating the work camps. These were where, he explained, communists, socialists, and general troublemakers were confined. The most intimidating feature of the entire organization was the raised silver skull and crossbones in the middle of their black cap.

"The third group is the SD who deal with enemies of the state" (which to me sounded exactly like the Gestapo, but what did I know?). "They also act as Hitler's body guard detail." He went on to explain the uniforms of this SS branch were probably the most distinctive, all in black with a red, black, and white swastika armband. They seemed to take their work very seriously. Their other distinguishing mark was the runes "SS" on their collar tabs. At times, all the SS also wore dark gray uniforms.

I stopped him at this point. "Wait, wait, wait! My head is spinning, Antoni. All this custom uniform alteration; different color piping on caps; gray or black for each group that is split into three groups; even the different cap shapes. I pity you if you ever had to tell each other apart on short notice."

"It is our ranks, dear cousin. Those insignias never change and are placed in a prominent spot—just for such a reason, I suppose. After all, it would not do for a private to pass a captain and not offer a salute, would it? Our uniform rankings are always displayed on the collar tabs, shoulder tabs, and several other places, depending upon the branch of service."

"Well," I said, rising to my feet, "this is all very interesting but I really have no interest in this lesson. When would I ever need to know of German military units? I do not plan on visiting that country any time soon or joining their ranks. Perhaps we should be back on the dance floor in better view of my family."

"I'm afraid I have overstayed my welcome, little cousin. Possibly some other time. It seems my uniform is causing some disturbance among several of the wedding guests. I must say my good-byes to family, good luck to the happy couple, and return to my unit."

"But, I…ahh….we…we will see you again, won't we?" I felt sure he had heard the momentary betrayal of my tongue as I stumbled over the word "we" and came close to saying "I."

He looked down at me and smiled. "Perhaps."

And with that, he bent down and kissed the back of my hand. It was just like in the movies. When he looked up at me again it was with a look, I was sure, of admiration for my new maturity. Although, I thought later, a more reasonable explanation was his usual expression of mockery.

I watched his tall figure stride across the room, clasp the hand of the groom, kiss the cheeks of the bride. He then made his way to his parents, hugged them both, and strolled out the door.

{ I }

Of course, I was anxious to relay this romantic story to my friends. Arlene, Olenka, and Max were sitting with me under the great bartek tree that grew in the back of my house, nibbling on the pierogi my mother had attempted. Normally they were served warm but we liked to nibble on leftover cold ones and Mama always had several leftovers. "Still hasn't gotten the dough right, has she?" asked Arlene. I replied she was still trying but at least the filling was tasty.

Changing the subject from my mother's inadequacies in the kitchen, I began relating the entire wedding scene from two days ago when the party ended. I told them how handsome Antoni had looked in his uniform, our long conversation in the garden and the very best part, the kiss on the back of my hand. I neglected to mention he had also kissed the bride's hand in the same matter. I was met with a complete lack of enthusiasm on their part.

"And he wants to belong to the SS? I have heard they are a bit of a vicious group. And why did he explain the German uniforms? That's a peculiar conversation to have, don't you think?" I admitted my parents had said the same thing when I told them of the garden chat.

"My parents have a lot of strange conversations lately too," said Arlene. "And whispering. Are things different in your homes?" she asked. I still found myself envious of her beauty and today she seemed almost ethereal in the sunlight, as if she could shake pixie dust from her pockets. She was right though. Things seemed tense in the entire town.

"Several of my uncles and aunts are taking their families and moving east," said Olenka. "They say he is going to cause trouble."

For several years now, many of us had taken to substituting a pronoun for the name of Herr Hitler. It did not matter, though; we all knew who starred in the topic of the conversation. My father's favorite was "that man" and others would whisper and say, "He must be demented"; "Something must be done about him"; or "That filthy disgusting shrunken troll." This last was from Buscha, who was always very descriptive in her comments. When Father would warn her that the walls have ears, she simply replied that she was an old woman and she had earned the right to speak her mind.

"I'm going to be leaving too, I think," Olenka went on sadly.

"Leaving!" I said. "What, on holiday?" I asked hopefully.

"No, my parents have been talking of sending me to live with my mother's family in England. A district called Sussex. They thought I was sleeping but I heard them talking in the kitchen one night."

"England! But you can't," I cried.

"Well, I haven't left yet. Perhaps they were not entirely serious. That was over a week ago and I haven't heard them mention it since."

"Well, I'm not leaving" I said decidedly. "I'm not afraid!"

"You should be, Marta," Max said in his quiet precise way. "I believe things may get out of control. There is a man in Warsaw named Jan Piekalkiewicz. He is a Polish diplomat now, I believe, after serving in our army. He is outspoken but pro-peace, hoping we can all make a difference in the world. He is brilliant; educated in Poland and Russia—his family is Intelligentsia. I think I would like to be a part of it all, if it comes to that."

The three of us looked at him in astonishment. "Max," I said, "I think those are more words than I've heard you speak at one time since I've known you."

We all four chuckled and I felt the sun warm the tip of my nose, but it did not lift the chill in my bones.

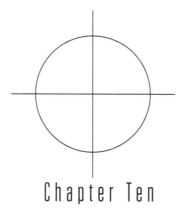

Chapter Ten

March 1938

AUSTRIA

*H*itler's idea of unifying all German-speaking people under one flag was neither new nor original; it had been bandied about since 1806 at the end of the Holy Roman Empire. Perhaps Hitler was simply more determined than other would-be conquerors.

Whatever the reason, on the morning of March 12, 1938, the Eighth Army of the German Wehrmacht crossed the German–Austrian border. There was no resistance by the Austrian army; on the contrary, the German troops were greeted by cheering Austrians with arms extended *Heil* Hitler style, Nazi flags, and flowers. Hitler was met with enthusiastic crowds chanting his name and presenting bouquets when he visited his house of birth and schools of his youth. He had complete control of his beloved Austria within three days, again spilling not a drop of blood or with an Ally in sight. The Austrian annexation, *Anschluss* as it was known, was a complete success. Austria was finally in Hitler's pocket.

Years later, I realized the Anschluss had not been that simple. Der Fuhrer's first course of action was to convince the Austrians they would be better off under the German flag and he began by working through the established Nazi Party in that country. When it became influential and strong enough to support him, it was time to invite the chancellor, Kurt Schuschnigg, to his home in Berchtesgarten. If the chancellor believed he would have a quiet, reasonable conversation with Adolf Hitler he was truly misinformed about Herr Hitler's temperament.

Not one to mince words, Hitler got straight to the point in the form of insults and threats. For hours, he preached his mission to create the Great German Empire, convincing the chancellor that Western Europe had abandoned Austria and would not come to their aid. "I have only to give an order and your ridiculous defenses will be blown to bits!" Hitler screamed at Schuschnigg. The words "quiet and reasonable" were not in Hitler's vocabulary. Finally, the chancellor caved in to Hitler's demands, signing a two-page document of agreement, as Hitler knew he would. He really had no other choice.

The world had an astonished reaction to these latest events. The wireless reported the news nonstop, offering predictions from learned men, and spewing propaganda either for or against Germany. Everyone had something to say and our family was no exception.

"What the hell is that man doing? And for God's sake, what the hell is wrong with those idiots in England and France? Why don't they just sign their own country over to that man while they're at it?"

"Now, Papa," said my own father, "please don't get yourself in a tizzy. It's just not good for your digestion."

"Pah! My digestion is just as good as anyone's. I told you that man was up to no good. Years ago; I told all of you. Now what do you have to say for yourselves?" No one said much. He was right, after all.

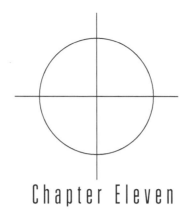

Chapter Eleven

September 1938

THE SUDETENLAND

*N*ow that I was older, I vowed to become informed of world affairs. It seemed, however, as if I had picked up a book with missing pages or vast portions of the plot missing. In the real world, years of pertinent facts and events had been occurring to bring us to this point, all of which I had been blissfully unaware.

In all fairness, Hitler was not the only topic discussed over Sunday dinners. For example, we were amazed at the photos of the world's tallest structure, the Empire State Building, which opened on May 1, 1931. (Only in America, stated Grandpapa.) We were thrilled with Amelia Earhart's around-the-world exploits in 1932 and mourned her when she disappeared in 1937. (Was she really a spy as the Germans claimed?) When the Olympics were held in Berlin, 1936, we sat in front of the radio, cheering on Poland. And none of us could forget the shock we felt when the Hindenburg airship burst into flames in 1937. I will admit, though, that Der Fuhrer never seemed to be far out of mind.

We had the chance for further discussion of the man in the latter part of 1938. Buoyed by his enormous success thus far, Hitler turned his attention to other territories to bring into the fold of German arms. So far, he had been unopposed in all corners. Publically, he spoke proudly to the world that the Fatherland had regained what had been lost, doing so without violence or bloodshed. Privately, with his General Staff, he was discussing his next move; the Sudetenland.

This land Hitler now set his greedy sights upon was a large area belonging to Czechoslovakia. The surrounding mountains in the territory created a natural barrier from any German aggression. It also contained most of their major manufacturing plants—coal, iron, and steel to name a few. Pried from Germany's hands by the despicable Treaty of Versailles, it was time for retrieval.

Hitler's shrewdness as a statesman was again evident as he developed a new tactic to regain this Promised Land. The method is tried and true now but in 1938 the undermining of a country from within using a political and social spy network was something very new indeed. Loyalists were placed within the territory to instigate dissention by fighting with the communists, social Democrats, and socialists.

So successful was the plan that on August 14, 1938, martial law was declared in the Sudeten districts. Quick to point out the mayhem within, Hitler insisted that Czechoslovakia had lost control of the region and Germany must have jurisdiction to promote order in the zone. At this point, some thought it was time for the Allies to step in. The wireless' tinny voice proceeded to educate us about Britain's possible assistance and the viewpoints of their current prime minister.

{ I }
Neville Chamberlain

A year prior to the Austrian Anschluss, Neville Chamberlain became prime minister of Britain. He was a man who truly did not understand the enormity of those circumstances in which he found himself. He was a staunch conservative whose world was spinning and changing faster than he could possibly control; he was lost in his ineffective pacifism. He acknowledged that the Treaty of Versailles had treated Germany badly and agreed a number of issues associated with that document should be corrected. He also acknowledged that England was no match for the new Wehrmacht, which was by now monumental. The prime minister felt if

Hitler's demands were met, another war would be prevented. This policy, adopted by Chamberlain's government, became known as the Policy of Appeasement and no more notable example of that policy existed than the Munich Agreement of 1938. Prime Minister Chamberlain; Italian Duce Benito Mussolini; and the French premier, Edouard Daladier, made their way to Hitler's home turf of the Bauhaus in Berchtesgarten on September 29, 1938. The Czechs were not represented at the meeting; they were not invited.

Once again, Hitler's demands were met. The Sudetenland would be returned to Germany with no further territorial claims made by The Fatherland. The Czechs were not only forced to accept this decision, they would be held responsible for any subsequent aggressions if they did not comply. The signatory parties were acting with the best of intentions; after all, the toll from the Great War was still fresh in everyone's mind.

The Munich Agreement was viewed as a triumph and an excellent example of securing peace through negotiation rather than war. The Sudetenland belonged to Germany and the Czechoslovakian government had resigned. Another victory, another bloodless campaign by Hitler. Chamberlain returned from Munich declaring the world had "Peace in our time." The photo was reproduced worldwide in newspapers and magazines, Chamberlain waving the signed document over his head, a large grin on his face. He had just accomplished an amazing feat for the Good of the World, he announced.

While the English and French were involved in discussions for the Greater Good, our way of life was being devoured the way a moth nibbles upon a favorite wool coat. Living and working with us as our neighbors was a secret organization called *Der Selbstschutz*, or Self-protection Squad. They actively cooperated with Germany by conducting espionage, political provocations, and propaganda. With direct ties to the Gestapo, they were gaining strength through numbers in our country. Unknown to us, many of these ethnic Germans with Polish citizenship had been trained in various methods of sabotage by the Third Reich. It was estimated close to 25 percent of the German minority were active members by the end of 1939. Fighting hostility from an enemy that is identifiable is difficult enough; fighting against an anonymous foe is impossible.

While the prime minister was touting his own good works that October, our Polish government had received word that Nazi Foreign

Minister Joachim von Ribbentrop would like to make a few alterations to our security-sealed pact of 1934. The proposals, he felt, were simple: renew the joint nonaggression pact in exchange for allowing the Free City of Danzig to be annexed peacefully by Germany. In addition, he went on, Deutschland will build an extraterritorial motorway and railway between East Prussia through the Polish Corridor and finally into Germany proper.

The Free City not only included Danzig but over two hundred other surrounding towns in northern Poland along the Baltic Sea. This entire region was known as the Polish Corridor. Sandwiched in between Germany and her province of East Prussia, it divided those two German territories. The area was an important port and trade center, one the Nazis wanted back.

To Hitler's way of thinking, the rest of the world had beaten Germany into submission; worse—into near poverty. Prior to the Great War, Danzig (renamed Gdansk by the Poles) had been the jewel around Germany's neck. Afterward, it became the Free City of Gdansk under the League of Nations' protection while Poland controlled its external affairs. To add to the confusion, the Port of Gdansk on the Baltic Sea had its own constitution, national anthem, parliament, and government. Due the city's largely German population, this split control was seen as a compromise between Poland and Germany.

Our cabinet members presented several arguments for both sides: give Hitler Danzig/Gdansk and avert possible war, or refuse and make war a certainty. It was well known that our leaders firmly distrusted Hitler. While Prime Minister Chamberlain thought all would be well with a "gentlemen's agreement," we Poles were confident that Adolf Hitler was no gentleman.

It was with a great sigh of relief, then, when Poland was given a guarantee by England and France; the Polish territorial's integrity would be supported with their combined defenses. With their assurances, we could continue as an independent country. Hitler would be foolish to advance on us now that we have publicized support and no one thought him a fool. Behind the scenes, however, Chamberlain was still hoping to come to a deal with Hitler over Danzig/Gdansk and the Polish Corridor. He continued to believe, or perhaps it was only hope now, that if Poland gave up this small area, Hitler would leave the rest of the world alone. Poor, misguided man.

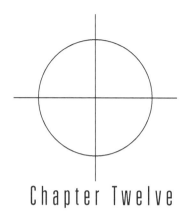

Chapter Twelve

December 1938

THE CONNIVING HITLER

$\mathcal{M}$uch to Hitler's surprise, country leaders were seeking out treaties and agreements with him to save their asses. Unbelievable! Had the European leaders gone mad or were they simply in awe of his power? The German generals were likewise amazed. Hitler had Europe eating from his hand.

His popularity rating in Germany was 98 percent, having personally facilitated the country's large expansions of industry and civil improvements plus the construction of dams, autobahns, railroads, and schools. In 1938, he was even on the cover of *Time* magazine as man of the year. Nazi policies reinforced the importance of family life and encouraged women to remain home, caring for the children while men assumed the role of breadwinner. As the women left the work force to free jobs for men, the unemployment rate miraculously dropped. Bit by bit, the German family circle was becoming more dependent upon Hitler to provide food, commerce, and a sense of self-worth. It was unfortunate that along with his military brilliance, oratory skills, and understanding of human behavior, there resided an equally dark and perverse side to the man.

His method of handling the Western nations was carefully orchestrated. Incredibly astute in his analysis of their emotional responses, Der Fuhrer played to those emotions as if in a fencing match. His earth- shattering announcements would occur on a Saturday, catching government offices closed and their executives off guard. When the dust would settle, he offered a conciliatory speech with reassurances and platitudes. Allowing a lapse of time to reinforce his promises, he would repeat the cycle with his next manipulation. He was extremely accomplished at the thrust, or attack move, in fencing, and equally good at the parry, or defense move. First, break the Treaty of Versailles by renewing military conscription; second, deliver a comforting speech promoting a thirteen-point peace program. Thrust forward, parry back. Obtain the Rhineland, then ensure the world he only wants what is rightfully German. Steady blade, in and out. Acquire Czechoslovakia, then sign another peace treaty with worldwide news coverage. Hitler handled the sword beautifully.

The astute politician in him had tapped into his peoples' resentment of that inequitable Treaty of Versailles and their desire for retribution. Each step had been completely strategized, slowly and carefully, from his first Munich speech in 1923. He would often mull things over for weeks or even months at a time but upon arriving at a course of action, he was unshakeable in his judgment. Many generals on his staff would try, but none would succeed. All of it leading to this place in time, worming his way insidiously into the Germans' lives. They needed him now, so devoted they would sacrifice themselves. Little did they know there was no turning back.

Chapter Thirteen

Christmas and the New Year

FANATICISM

*A*fter Germany's acquisition of Czechoslovakia, some were certain we would soon be wearing lederhosen. It came as a bit of a surprise, at least to me anyway, when Poland and Russia openly confirmed a prior 1932 nonaggression pact. With Christmas celebrations about to begin, this was considered very good news indeed. Hitler would surely direct his hungry eye upon some other country now, perhaps something small and insignificant like Liechtenstein. Perhaps too, this new affirmation will affect von Ribbentrop's request. We were in a more celebratory mood as a result of this recent development, and were looking forward to Christmas and the new year.

In our part of the country, some snowfall is always expected during the holiday festivities, adding to the fun. The center square of towns and cities all over the country would suddenly transform seemingly overnight to become one large Christmas market selling everything from hot-spiced wine to hand-blown tree ornaments. Days are spent in preparation for our traditional *Wigilia* or Christmas Eve dinner.

All day long, I could smell the delectable treats being prepared in the kitchen. (Buscha and Aunt Isabella were always persuaded to do the cooking and baking.) The Christmas Eve feast was a traditionally meatless meal but that did not stop us from creating our other Polish favorites; the more food on the table, the more promising the next year would be. The evening's celebration would end with passing out many gifts amid much oohing and ahhing, and then it was on to midnight Mass.

This year, 1938, my family greeted Christmas with more restraint. At the evening meal, our prayers centered on those we missed and the hope they would join us at this same table next year. We prayed for peace among nations and people. Filip, naturally, prayed in a very loud voice for someone to shoot Hitler. Obviously, this did not sit well with the adults, even if they agreed. As he grew older, I thought, Filip was becoming more difficult to ignore, although I continually tried to do just that.

{ I }

Because we are such an old land, we have many curious traditions and beliefs associated with holidays and the New Year is no exception. My personal favorite was one that ensured great wealth by holding a small bag of coins and running through the fields while shaking the bag as loudly as possible. It could be quite a peculiar sight, for lately folks had taken up the custom of running through the streets rather than the fields. Papa thought this was because the streets were much better lit; many folk had taken quite a tumble dashing through the snow-covered countryside in the dark. Funny but dangerous.

This year, I was determined to see the annual fireworks at Krakow with my friends. After all, I was no longer a child, quite old enough to be out celebrating this last night of 1938. I was especially looking forward to celebrating with Max. Since we have mandatory military service in Poland, as in many European countries, Max was of an age to join. Filip, also of age, had various excuses why he was unable to enlist; flat feet, bad eyes, ulcers, and so forth. Papa said that his parents pulled some strings, namely bribes, to keep him out of uniform. Coward.

Recently completing his preliminary training and aptitude tests, Max was lucky enough to attend flight school. He would be leaving soon and I wanted to spend time with him before he departed.

Mama, of course, was completely against Krakow but Papa suggested a compromise; we could have our night out in Bochnia. I am ashamed to say I became extremely pouty and childish over this development but neither of them would budge.

As it turned out, my other friends' parents were of a like mind about the adventure. Receiving an invitation to a schoolmate's party, we would settle for that. Besides, Olenka said, Bochnia was investing in an elaborate fireworks display in our own town square. It would have to do, I thought peevishly, but I exclaimed to all who would listen (especially my parents) that next year would be Different; Very Different, I promised.

Prior to the party, we took in a matinee. We linked arms and started off, comfortable in our friendship and hoping for a wonderful 1939. The air was crisp and cool, our breath forming wispy clouds in front of us. Christmas displays were still exhibited in store windows with lights strung around trees and outlining shop fronts. Other folks were also out, greeting each other with *"Dosiego Roku,"* Happy New Year, and singing Polish songs. One man had obviously begun imbibing, and he tumbled to the ground in the middle of a run with his bag of coins. We all laughed heartily; it was good to be young, healthy, and alive.

Prior to the feature film beginning, we sat through various news reports, a few cigarette advertisements and a cartoon or two. Tonight, the news of the world centered on Germany. Had I not known it was produced by the British Broadcasting Channel (BBC), I would have written it off as so much propaganda upon the screen. Nazi soldiers marched in huge block formations within a giant amphitheater, pointed toes strutting out the goosestep of which they seemed so fond. As each living block of men approached Hitler's dais, the soldiers snapped their heads in his direction and presented him with the Nazi salute, gloved hands all at the same angle. It was an awesome display of fidelity and power.

German planes soared across the screen in swastika formations, each one equally spaced from the aircraft next to it, the sound of their engines filling the theater. The viewing populace was waving and shouting their allegiance, some in such an emotional state they were in tears. With arms extended and fingers held tight, they were steady and unflinching. I thought back to the book-burning incident five years ago. The newspaper had described those participants as near maniacal. This display seemed so obsessive and extreme it was closer to sacrilege. How could one man elicit this much fanaticism? It was both an inspiring and horrifying demonstration.

I glanced at Arlene next to me and saw the same shock in her eyes. Then I thought of Max who had been issued our Polish uniform. I leaned across Arlene and saw his face had blanched. We held onto each other's hands and I wondered what that man with the strange mustache had in store for us. For some reason, my reaction to this was not so much fear as it was an overwhelming sense of despondency.

Chapter Fourteen

February 1939

MAX AND OLENKA

*A*lthough I knew Max would be stopping by our house to say good-bye, it was still a shock to see him wearing his crisp new Polish uniform and a recently shorn head of hair. He had gotten his orders to travel to Gdansk for further training.

After Mama pressed a meal upon him, he and I went out back to sit in our favorite spot under the bartek tree. We spoke of our waning youth and the mischief we used to get into as a group before taking on the more serious conversation we had been avoiding.

"You do know we may be involved in war, don't you?" he said.

"You mean with Germany? Some people think that since Hitler has what he wants, everything will settle down. Besides, he signed that last treaty, didn't he?"

He looked at me sideways, shook his head with that poor-misguided-girl look on his face, and said, "I think he'll do anything he can to get what he wants. Many of the soldiers I trained with think he will try to get Poland next. Or maybe France."

That tickle started on my neck again. "He already has everything Germany lost in the last war—why would he want us or France? He doesn't even speak Polish or French," I tried to joke.

Max just shook his head. He asked me about Antoni but I was forced to tell him that I had not seen Antoni since that wedding so I had no idea what he was doing. Aunt Cecylia only cried if his name was brought up.

Where had the time gone? Here was Max in his military uniform and I would be leaving for University soon. I was really very proud of him. I knew he still had a crush on me but he did not wear it on his sleeve any longer. I was not too sure how I felt about that.

We hugged each other tightly, my childhood friend and I, and I watched as he walked down the street feeling suddenly sad and frightened. Nonsense, I thought. He will be back on leave in a few months and everything will be as it always was. Still, I could not stop the tear that ran unbidden down my cheek.

Several weeks later, I was again forced to say good-bye to another lifelong friend. Olenka's parents had booked her passage to her maternal relatives in England. The bartek tree once more had the pleasure of our company as we promised togetherness again in Bochnia as soon as her parents came to their senses.

"What about your family?" she asked. "Will they be moving out of Poland?"

I shook my head. "Buscha and Grandpapa will not hear of it, Papa will not leave them since they've grown older and need more care, and Mama will not leave Papa. So that leaves me and I refuse to leave the rest of them. Some of my cousins have packed up though."

She tried to comfort me by telling me of the funny set of English relatives she would soon be residing with, their peculiar dialects, and their slang. "They are all barking mad, you know. Absolutely bonkers!" she giggled. "But veddy, veddy propah," she said in imitation, prancing around with her nose in the air. My laughter at her clever antics was forced; I could not seem to shake the empty feeling developing inside me. Once more, I stood on the front porch and watched a dear friend slowly walk away from me. Again, I told myself she would return soon, once everyone realized they were running from fear and not a real threat.

Chapter Fifteen

March 1939

ALLIED PACT

$\mathcal{B}$eing of a somewhat stubborn nature, our government officials felt the time had arrived to partially mobilize our military along the German-Polish border. Britain and France had requested we delay any such action as it may be seen as aggressive behavior. Eventually, they agreed that two-thirds of our potential manpower could be mustered. Since we were completely dependent upon their future support in a conflict, we did as they "requested." Grandpapa called it a form of blackmail.

Britain had begun air raid and blackout practices and opened factories to produce the equipment necessary to kill more efficiently. France, in the meantime, was not idle either. For years, they had been building a defensive wall along their German border called the Maginot Line. Less of a wall and more like interconnected concrete fortresses, it contained border guard posts, communications centers, infantry shelters, artillery emplacements, and barricades. The line boasted cinemas, a sunroom, air-conditioning, canteen, barracks, and rounded gun turrets protruding from the ground like giant molehills. Electric trains carried the almost half million French soldiers to and from their underground destinations.

The French had sunk three billion francs into the project over the previous ten years. Convinced this enormous fortress would be their best defense, the Line spanned eighty-seven miles along the joint border but stopped short of the English Channel by 250 miles. At the Maginot, the French felt "the gun would halt the Hun." Possibly true, providing the Hun came solely in this one direction.

The men in our town, too old for the service yet determined to defend their country, armed themselves with whatever they had. Grandpapa had a lightweight Iver Johnson .22 pistol seven-shot, not more than six inches long from barrel to grip, given to him by a distant relative in America. He kept this hidden in the butcher shop under the counter, reachable at a moment's notice. I thought of Max who would probably be forced to forego his pilot training for the more immediate needs of ground troops. Still, we held out hope that it would never come to what we feared. Perhaps our two countries could yet compromise with each other over the Danzig/Gdansk issue. Losses were still felt from the Great War. Surely, Hitler would not cause such devastation again.

Events continued to unfold swiftly with treaties signed and resigned, editing one to include a third country, revoking another and drafting a fourth. Our country finally presented a formal response to Germany's proposed treaty modifications: a resounding NO. Hitler cannot have Gdansk/Danzig, he cannot build a trade railway through the territory that belonged to Poland. Berlin was now disturbingly quite.

Newspapers sold out very early each morning, citizens anxiously grabbing at the headlines. Would today be the day Hitler declared war upon us? Or would he commit another transgression placing the world in an uproar? On April 28, 1939, it proved to be the latter. "Hitler Withdraws From League of Nations!" So there it was; the other proverbial shoe had dropped. He was no longer obligated to the League's explicit policy of armament reductions. I imagine those international phone calls between Poland and Great Britain became very costly.

We were told the world leaders would neither allow nor stand for another act of war. The world was more civilized now and our leaders much more educated in the art of negotiating. We placed our faith in God, treaties, and our allies. And so we stayed.

Chapter Sixteen

Late May, 1939

THE MEETING

*S*pring was arriving early to Bavaria in 1939. The weather was warmer and women tended to daffodils and tulips in window boxes. Light sweaters were de rigueur rather than the heavy fur coats of a few months ago.

Families in Munich were out walking, enjoying the Rathaus-Glockenspiel in Marienplatz strike it's tunes. Men were enjoying their beer at round tables outside of the Hofbrauhaus. Snow was melting in the Alps, yet some would ski until the last flake melted.

Several black touring cars displaying the Nazi red and black flags passed through this Bavarian town as they made their way toward Berchtesgarten. Many citizens stood on the sides of the road, waving and smiling at the obviously powerful occupants of the vehicles. Although the mountain was dotted with connecting homes and outbuildings for the elite of the German Generals, two of these luxurious residences belonged to Hitler.

The polished automobiles carried their passengers up the twelve-hundred-foot climb to the Berghof, Hitler's favorite residence. What had once been a small chalet was now maintained almost as a resort hotel with several housekeepers, gardeners, cooks, and other miscellaneous staff on twenty-four-hour call.

The home boasted coffered ceilings with hand carved wooden beams from the Black Forest, 18th century antiques and old engravings. A red marble fireplace, a gift from Mussolini, sat on a raised dais along one-half of the massive entry hall. Surrounded by several deep comfortable chairs and sofas, guests enjoyed movies here from a hidden projection booth.

In the rear of the home was Hitler's favorite space, his warm and inviting study. The view from here overlooked the snowcapped mountains of Hitler's native Austria. To provide a completely unobstructed view, a window fifteen feet high and ten feet long could be lowered electronically to slide within the wall of the floor below. On the wide terrace spotted with colorful umbrellas atop tables and chairs, Hitler relaxed in the casual attitude only his closest friends were permitted to see. Filmed and photographed at the Berghof as a carefree man, it become wonderful grist for his most efficient propaganda mill, ensuring his image as a gentle, caring man.

This is where Adolf Hitler spent most of his time and greeted such dignitaries as the Aga Khan, the Duke and Duchess of Windsor, Neville Chamberlain, and Benito Mussolini. Today he was about to meet with his most trusted men, the General Staff, to discuss the next item on his massive agenda.

{ I }
Himmler

Greeted first by the household staff was Heimlich Himmler. He was not much taller than Hitler, only by about an inch, and rather slight in build. His nondescript face was flattish with a slightly wrinkled double chin and an egg-shaped head. The rather squinty eyes behind round glasses gave him a myopic look. Coming across as shy and quiet, certainly not brutal, he was said to seem harmless, even dull, looking more like an elementary schoolteacher. A colorless man making little or no impression on anyone, he was inconspicuous; a most underestimated attribute.

He was proud of his stellar background; his godfather was Prince Heinrich of Bavaria and his father was principal of the prestigious Wittelsbacher Gymnasium Secondary School. Raised in a devoutly

Catholic family with his two brothers, he mastered the technique of an unassuming spy, as his father would often send him to scrutinize and punish other pupils at the school.

Although never completely comfortable with the opposite sex, he eventually married a woman seven years his senior who was a divorcee and a Protestant. They had one daughter together, whom he affectionately called Poppi. Himmler and his wife separated but never officially divorced one another. This small difficulty notwithstanding, he took his secretary as a mistress and fathered two children with her. Knowing that Hitler regarded himself as an upright Father Figure to Germany, Himmler did not advertise his immoral living arrangement. He often wondered, though, about the Fuhrer and Geli Raubal, Hitler's niece by his half sister. The two of them were inseparable with Hitler, often behaving in a very un-uncle like way toward her. However, with his mistress firmly ensconced in his life, Himmler had no room to judge.

Unnoticed over the years, he slowly wormed his way next to Adolf Hitler. Behind his placid face, he had a quick mind and was totally ruthless, brutal, and perfectionistic in his responsibilities to the Fuhrer, earning him the nickname of the Executioner. Perhaps because he was so insipid looking, it made his cruelty much more horrifying to witness. Surpassing Hitler, he was now the most feared man in Germany.

Himmler's frame of mind regarding his sense of duty and inner malice was summed up in a quote attributed to him:

The best political weapon is the weapon of terror. Cruelty commands respect.

Men may hate us. But, we do not ask for their love; only for their fear.

Having attained the title of SS Reichsführer, he was second in power only to Hitler. In 1936, the *Reichstag* (the German House of Representatives) passed the Gestapo Law, which included the following paragraph: "Neither the instructions nor the affairs of the Gestapo will be open to review by the administrative courts." The law essentially gave the Gestapo, and by definition Himmler, carte blanche to operate without judicial oversight. Now he had the additional control over internment camps and the prisoner labor force.

His position of power and worth was blatantly exhibited in his castle located in the Rhineland village of Wewelsburg. Himmler had been renovating the triangular-shaped stronghold into the Center of the New World, an educational training center for the SS, containing streets, parkways, opulent outbuildings, a dam with its own power plant, and an airport. The amount budgeted for this monumental estate was 150 million Reichsmarks, or RM, as the currency was now referred to. Prisoners from the nearby camps of Sachsenhausen and Niederhagen naturally supplied free labor. The death rate among the toiling prisoners was 63percent; a small price to pay for so lofty a goal.

{ II }
Göring

When Hermann Göring entered the room, he usually filled the space so completely, one needed to move from the area. The man enjoyed the label of *der Eiserne*, the Iron Man, but the once dashing, muscular fighter pilot had turned to flab and obesity. He did not particularly care how he was spoken about behind his back; it was taken by him as a sign of his great popularity "no matter how rude" the comment. He was without a doubt the most debonair and dapper dresser of Hitler's men.

He was Hitler's designated successor, and commander of the Luftwaffe. Without conscience and extraordinarily ruthless, he could be extremely charming and personable when needed and was almost as adept at manipulation as Hitler.

The standard color for a Luftwaffe uniform was a blue-gray. Göring, however, chose to have many of his uniforms custom made in a soft, pearl gray. He sported numerous styles and slightly different cuts to his uniforms with so many variations, he was able to change at whim several times a day. He also had a penchant for wearing double-breasted white uniforms. Unfortunately, when the German people saw him turned out in white, they would ridicule him. How, they wondered, could he keep such cloth spotless when they, who had their soap rationed, could barely keep their own attire clean?

His Reichsmarschall collar tabs of crossed batons surrounded by laurel leaves were of exceptional quality in silver and gold bullion. Each shoulder-board rank device was a golden eagle, wings outstretched atop a glistening swastika within an equally gold wreath. Two crossed batons were under these and the entire piece lay upon a golden roped braid. He was the only recipient of the Grand Cross of the Iron Cross (a prestigious award although redundantly named) and it hung around his neck along with the Knights Cross. The Pour le Marite cross, an award he earned while flying in the last war with Baron von Richthofen dangled in place along with the others. He cut a remarkable figure albeit a large one.

Göring also enjoyed an official flag befitting and announcing his rank handmade of gold bullion, aluminum, brocade, and embroidered yarn. The man was such an egocentric, when he gained his promotion to Reichsmarschall he also designed a personal flag. One side was emblazoned with a German eagle, swastika, and crossed Marshall's batons. The other side proudly displayed the Grand Cross of the Iron Cross between four Luftwaffe eagles, all in striped silk and gold bullion. Göring had this three-foot by three-foot ostentatious flag carried by a personal standard-bearer at all public occasions. Thankfully, today's scheduled meeting was not public.

Göring's questionable confiscation of others' property was probably known within Hitler's direct circle of confidants but was seemingly over-looked, as they all were opportunists of some sort. Often, he simply seized properties and acquired others for a nominal cost, or accepted bribes so a friend could assume the property. He received kickbacks from industrial-ists for consideration in Hitler's expansion plans and managed to acquire several other government titles with high salaries. Whatever his meth-ods, he had amassed a huge personal fortune.

His wealth was never more publically seen than in his personal vehi-cle that had been dubbed "The Blue Goose." The Mercedes 540K Special Cabriolet was aviation blue, his favorite color, reminding him of his piloting days among the skies. His family crest had been hand painted on both doors, the windows made bullet proof, and the sides were armor plated. Special modifications had been installed at the factory to accom-modate Göring's considerable girth behind the wheel should he choose to personally drive the automobile.

The pedigree he presented to his peers was impeccable. Göring was a descendant of Count Ferdinand von Zeppelin, the great German aviation pioneer, and related to the owners of the giant pharmaceutical company, Merck. He also had a few familial ties he preferred not to mention, skel-etons, according to Nazi standards. He could claim kinship to author

Baroness Gertrud von Le Fort, whose works were anti-Nazi; and Carl J. Burckhardt, a Swiss diplomat, historian, president of the International Red Cross, and who openly rejected German claims of superiority. His brother, Karl, had immigrated to the United States and Karl's son, Werner G. Göring, became a captain in the United States Army Air Forces. Even his parents were cause for worry since they were distinctly not anti-Semitic. Perhaps these last few scraggly branches on his family tree were the reasons he tirelessly proved his devotion to the Third Reich and to Hitler.

{ III }
Joseph Goebbels

Although Joseph Goebbels walked through the doors with a slight limp, he was still described as tall, athletic, and handsome. The man's deformed leg was attributed to polio as a child or a botched operation for a bone infection and he had perfected his stride to be as limp-less as possible. It was not something he chose to discuss. After all, infirmity and deformity were not tolerated in the Nazi philosophy. He was left with a shortened leg, which now necessitated a brace and special shoe to correct it. One of his greatest disappointments was his rejection for military service under the Kaiser's realm.

Owing to this rejection and his need for approval, he rose to power at an extraordinary rate and was appointed propaganda minister in 1933. Hitler was a genius and had "a sparkling mind," according to Goebbels who was intelligent in his own right, having earned a PhD from the Heidelberg University. He was now one of Hitler's closest associates and most devout followers, known for his almost zealot anti-Semitic views. Viewed as second only to Hitler in his oratory prowess, he often drove his listeners into frantic ecstasy through conscious psychological calculations. He once compared this ability to that of playing the German people like a piano, able to lead the masses wherever he wanted them to go.

The man was obsessed with film and movies, watching everything from Greta Garbo to Shirley Temple. Film, he thought, was the most efficient medium to influence the subconscious mind. As such, it was heavily employed during his reign as the propaganda minister, seducing the German people to accept the Fuhrer's ideals and objectives.

Dr. Goebbels first gained notoriety for the book-burning event in 1933 and was now directing his propaganda machine against Poland. He had been orchestrating a hate campaign against that country by fabricating articles and atrocities performed by the Poles toward the ethnic Germans. Additionally, he focused some of his attention toward accusing many minorities of attempting to destroy Germany from within, thereby reinforcing any self-defense actions against the Jews, Poles, and French.

As with his counterparts, Hitler had made Goebbels a wealthy man. Until the Nazi regime, he had been earning a mere seven hundred fifty Marks per month. Currently, he enjoyed three hundred thousand Reichsmarks a year in fees for writing his propaganda-based newspaper, *Der Angriff* (The Attack) as well as his ministry-appointed stipends and other dubious forms of income.

Herr Goebbels used his various talents in creating divisions of the Propaganda Ministry by forming chambers in control of the press, radio, film, theater, music, literature, and publishing—in short, all activities of the German people. Authors could not write, singers could not perform, painters could not exhibit unless they belonged to the correct chamber and their membership was conditional upon good behavior or the occasional bribe.

Goebbels was one of the most enthusiastic proponents of Germany regaining her territorial claims sooner rather than later. While Hitler was publically professing peace, Goebbels was deliberately leading Germany toward a confrontation for territorial claim. He considered it his mission to convince the German people of this cause and to welcome it—quite the daunting task but one he was well suited for. He used his propaganda techniques to prepare the German people psychologically for an aggressive war campaign and the complete annihilation of the lesser races by perfecting the "Big Lie" technique to control all aspects of the media and arts. A lie, he believed, if daring enough and repeated often enough, will be believed by the masses.

{ IV }
Wilhelm Keitel

General Wilhelm Keitel entered last, a tall imposing figure. Keitel was ramrod straight and dashing; a Kaiser-era trained, traditional Prussian soldier. He was more suited to be a curator to a museum than a general and had been described as "nice." Perhaps too nice; behind his back he was called *Lakaitel,* meaning lackey.

Completely spellbound in 1933 when first meeting Hitler, he would forever be at Hitler's beck and call, always loyal and faithful, as a dog was to his master. He was the ultimate yes-man and was never known to oppose any proposition that Hitler put forth. Unlike Hitler's other trusted men, Keitel had a very limited vision in regard to his own ambitions, and the rise to his current rank could be attributed to one woman: Erna Grun.

Fraulein Grun married Keitel's superior in 1938 with Hitler and Himmler acting as witnesses to the nuptials. Only afterward was it discovered the new bride had an immorality record using a pseudonym. Not only had she been arrested for prostitution, she had learned the oldest profession at the feet of her prostitute mother. As if that was not enough, she had also posed for pornographic pictures. Public humiliation seemed imminent for Der Fuhrer and Himmler, witnesses to the travesty.

Not surprisingly, Hitler was initially livid. However, always one to recognize and seize an opportunity, Hitler knew this was his chance to be well rid of Keitel's superior of whom he had grown increasingly weary Known as the Night of the Long Knives, he cleaned house completely, removing other outspoken generals and replacing them with men of a more pliable nature. Hitler took over the war ministry himself, renamed it the High Command of the Armed Forces, and appointed Keitel as his deputy and war minister.

Keitel was not without his abilities; after all, Hitler did not suffer fools in his midst. The new general worked tirelessly to increase the number of German troops against mandates in the Treaty of Versailles. Since heavy machinery was banned, the army trained using tank mockups constructed of wood and cardboard. Unlucky men pushed these mock tanks around open fields while unluckier recruits were practicing their maneuverability from inside.

Hitler's Nazi dictatorship scored a huge propaganda success as host of the 1936 Summer Olympics in Berlin. Using his organizational skills to develop the Olympic Village, Keitel was rewarded by accompanying

Der Fuhrer into the opening ceremonies—directly behind Hitler. It was a very apropos position.

The men who gathered here today with Hitler had offered him their *Kadavergehorsam*. Literally translated, it means Corpse Obedience. In the Nazi tongue, it meant "absolute duty and blind obedience till death." Several of these men were forever tied to Hitler because of their shared beliefs. Others professed the same lofty reasons for their loyalty but secretly knew they would not be in the political or monetary position they now reveled in were it not for Adolf Hitler. These, then, were Hitler's elite and his most trusted officers; mercenaries, opportunists, thieves, murderers, sadists, corrupt to the core, and ready to do his bidding.

{ V }
Operation Tannenberg

The niceties were attended to first with a hearty meal and a stroll along the terrace with his mistress, Eva Braun, and their pet dogs. This was the only area where smoking was allowed and as the men took out their tobacco of choice, Eva excused herself, allowing the men their privacy.

Although Adolf Hitler met here on several occasions with many different groups of men, this meeting was something more than receiving status reports. They eventually made their way to the gathering room with the enormous picture window. Antique hand-woven tapestries decorated the walls with various scenes of German country life and a sideboard stood along one side of the room where large portions of food and drink could be laid out for entertaining or all-night meetings.

Not only was this Hitler's favorite room, here the men would have complete privacy and could speak in a close group. The officers were instructed to make themselves comfortable while Herr Hitler remained standing, as was his habit, just for a moment; just long enough to impress his superiority over them. He strode back and forth, hands clasped behind his back, occasionally tapping the top of one hand into the palm of other, before taking his seat in the most comfortable chair. As he prepared to brief them of the next step on his agenda, none of his staff doubted that this was Hitler's schedule, Hitler's decisions that took place in this room.

He was the Man with the Vision; the others were the facilitators of that vision.

"Firstly, I would like to discuss Japan. Herr Himmler? Please brief us."

"*Ja wohl, Mein Fuhrer.* As you all know, we have recently received assurances of support from Japan. Together with Italy, we will have three in our Pact of Steel Alliance. They agree to provide financial and military aid if we should meet with aggression. I think it prudent on our part to keep an eye on the Japanese emperor; he seems to be hotheaded and he could be trouble. He instigated the conflict with China and Russia several years ago, although he considered it a draw." The others sniggered . Only Emperor Hirohito would call the thrashing a draw.

Himmler continued. "On another note, Poland is now in treaty with France as well as England. The French promise offensive support within fifteen days of any attack. Privately, we have learned another sequestered cabinet meeting resulted in..." he shuffled a few papers and concluded, "ah, here it is. 'The fate of Poland depends on the final outcome of the war, which will depend on our ability to defeat Germany rather than to aid Poland at the beginning.' Obviously, they are preparing to save their own skin."

Hitler chuckled. "The French have always been realists, yet cowards. Herr Himmler, what of Dachau? Is everything continuing as ordered?" Hitler asked.

"*Alles in ordnung*, Mein Fuhrer. Completely in order. Dachau now contains German Communists, Social Democrats, trade unionists, and any other political opponents of the Nazi regime. We have completed an extension of the camp using the prisoners as the work force. It is cheap labor and they have no choice but to do good work," he joked. "Last year, we began to utilize it as a training center for all SS camp guards. It will produce the model soldier for all future camps."

"*Sehr gut, sehr gut! Und so,*" Hitler continued, "it has come to my attention that Stalin has begun talks with the English. I have also been told these talks are waning. Soon Stalin will have no choice but to come to me for an agreement. Hah! Stalin, that shrunken gnome." Joseph Stalin was only five six, which pleased Hitler tremendously although he was just five nine. Nevertheless, he loved to lord those three inches over Stalin behind his back. "I shall indeed agree to a pact, allowing me to acquire half of Poland and Stalin shall have the other half—for the moment. I do not anticipate there will be much bloodshed on our part."

"Herr Fuhrer, what of the rest of the world? What of the English and the Americans? Surely they will oppose you," remarked Herr Göring. The General Staff had been apprised of their leader's intent to take Poland but they nevertheless had grave concerns.

"Ah, do you really think so? We were practically given Czechoslovakia on a platter by those ridiculous English and French. They are grateful to me for agreeing to their allowances and proceeding no further. Grateful! Do you really suppose they will object to both Germany and Russia combining their efforts to take the insignificant Poland? *Nein*! They will not oppose us! They will cower in fear and do all they can to avoid war. They will play the great pacifists and tell the world they have single-handedly averted a crisis! They will pat themselves on the backs as heroes! It is for the benefit of Germany and her people that we retake what is ours—the Free City of Danzig and the right to the Corridor." He had leapt out of his seat for this tirade, waving his arms about and slapping his hand into his palm, emphasizing each word, like that of a staccato scale played on a piano. "Poland will be ours!" Slap! Slap! Slap! Slap!

"Those ridiculous English and French. They have no idea I am serious about the advancement of our great country. For too long they have beaten us down, preventing us from greatness. They think my goals are too fantastic and unrealistic. And yet, they have given me everything I have demanded. And Chamberlain? He is shortsighted enough to think of me as any other politician.

"I am a visionary! We will have the perfect Aryan world without those sucking the life from our purpose. Not only will Danzig belong to the German people once again, but Poland will be a haven for the entire Aryan race. We will obliterate them and their culture. Their Intelligentsia must be eliminated first and we will strike fear into all others through terror tactics. Destroy their universities and high schools, libraries, museums, national monuments, scientific institutions, and laboratories. Churches and clergy will be a thing of the past. Whatever we find in the shape of an upper class in Poland will be liquidated! We will completely remove those Poles, bring them to Germany for slave labor, send others to Russia if we must, but the country will be free of all vermin to allow for the growth of the German people! We will have our *Lebensraum*!"

It was an extremely ambitious proposal, Hitler's "Living Space," one that a few of his generals were concerned about. The last thing Germany needed was another war. Nevertheless, it was obvious that Hitler did not intend to deviate from his plan. After all, had he not been correct when they occupied Czechoslovakia and Austria? The Allies had simply rolled over and allowed Germany to enter. They had to believe that Der Fuhrer could gain control of Poland just as easily.

"Mein Fuhrer," began Himmler, "perhaps the remaining Poles should be literate enough to only read traffic signs." There was some laughter at this agreeable joke. "Through the elimination of free thinkers, the Intelligentsia, there will be no oppressive regime to take hold. At this rate, we will have a completely Aryan country within three decades. We must make the parasites in that country disappear from the earth."

"My feelings exactly, Herr Himmler. Although Eichmann is not present today, I want him in charge of the trains and deportations. He has been doing an outstanding job with the Jews in Austria since we have her back. I feel sure he will utilize his organizational skills to remove these Poles just as efficiently. Heinrich, I will expect you to brief him on this and keep abreast of his progress."

{ VI }
Eichmann

The man to whom Hitler referred was Adolf Eichmann, known as the Jewish Authority within the Nazi regime. With his amazing organizational skills, unfailing loyalty, and detailed knowledge of the Jews, he had been the perfect choice to facilitate and manage the involved logistics of mass deportation. The previous year he formed the Central Office for Jewish Emigration. Although sounding magnanimous, its purpose was to forcibly deport and expel Jews from Austria.

It had been a daunting task and so far he was handling it admirably. Prior to the formation of this department, families stood in long lines from morning to dusk at the English and American consulates hoping for entrance to those countries. As far as Eichmann was concerned, the red tape was taking much too long; therefore, he began the process on his own. He was known for acquiring deportation papers in record time, although he was not above being compensated for the process. He would personally agree to an audience with Jews in his ostentatious Austrian office if he felt the Jews had something to offer. They usually did. More often than not, their entire worth found itself on Eichmann's money clip. He was once asked why he made it so easy for the Jews to vacate Austria. So far, he replied, he had rid the country of three thousand Jews, the only success he required. The fact that he was amassing a fortune from the adversity of others was an agreeable side effect. Now he would be given complete control over the transportation and deportation of the Poles as well.

Eichmann was extremely proud of sharing his first name with that of his hero. Additionally, there were other points the two men had in common. Eichmann was born in Germany but was raised in Austria, also attending the same schools as Der Fuhrer a few years later. Unfortunately, he was just as much of an underachiever.

It was understood that those with high academic qualifications held the top positions in the SS. Eichmann was the exception to the rule and it forever haunted him. Driven by his severe inferiority complex, he was desperate to show the world his capabilities and that he deserved the position given him. His loyalty was above reproach. He was asked, "If your father was a traitor, would you shoot him?" His reply was, "If it was proven, I would be bound by my oath of allegiance and shoot him."

Eichmann's sense of style was so well known he was often called the Conceited Dandy. As a social climber, he enjoyed all the trappings of power and sought the nation's notice. His dress was always meticulously elegant and a chauffeured Rothschild's limousine was his conveyance. When standing alongside others, he had a habit of swatting the riding crop he always carried against his polished black boot. Some would argue this was just another demonstration on his part to convey power and instill fear. Others would say it was a defense mechanism to combat his feelings of inadequacy. Whatever the reason, most of his peers agreed that it was an extremely annoying habit.

Herr Hitler once again sat, making himself comfortable, and continued. "Last year, our loyal Germans living in Poland received conscription lists to identify the Polish elites in their vicinity: all activists, scholars, actors, officers, and so on. Many of the lists overlapped and there was much duplication but having crosschecked them all, we compiled a list of over sixty-one thousand Poles who will be eliminated immediately upon occupation. The others will take a bit more time. This, gentlemen, is our *Unternehmen Tannenberg*, Operation Tannenberg.

"So…we are here today to fine-tune this process, to finesse the tactical maneuvers, choose the most opportune dates, and discuss how we will receive Stalin. I must have an agreement in hand with Russia by this summer. And we must determine the special unit to initiate the operation, find probable cause and place for invasion, and where to relocate these detestable people."

The men began discussing the success of Dachau and the possible creation of other work camps to fill with Poles. They were well aware of Hitler's views of Jews, Slavs, Gypsies, the infirm, homosexuals, and any race other than German. They were also well aware these work camps would become something more sinister, especially since Himmler had been given complete discretion over the camps' activities. The men knew all this but it was something they would never openly discuss; orders were simply to be carried out. In conversations with Hitler regarding mass exterminations, it would be referred to as Resettlement or Proposed Labor Forces, eventually the term Cleansing would be used. Hitler preferred not to specifically talk about the details, thereby claiming plausible deniability.

It proved a very long night, one that saw much food and drink laid out upon the sideboard.

Chapter Seventeen

August 1939

RECONNAISSANCE

Oberleutnant Lucas Weber was doing what he loved best: flying. The first lieutenant was in control of a Heinkel HE 45, a beautiful light bomber produced in his country since the early 1930s. The magnitude and strength of the Luftwaffe had been developed in secret since 1925 and today it had some of the most efficient aircrafts in the world. With an open cockpit, the Heinkel could maneuver or soar like a bird. The plane was designed to hold a gunner behind the pilot but today's passenger was anything but that.

The scrunched-up man seated behind Weber was bespectacled and wearing a battered long brown coat. As if that was not surprising enough to the pilot, the only items the man carried were various Leica cameras, lenses, and a case of film. The man seemed particularly clumsy and obviously not accustomed to moving about in a flying plane.

The serious passenger had been constantly instructing Weber to move to the left, lower the plane, travel east, and circle about. The lieutenant was determined to say some rather harsh words to the man if he did not stop issuing orders. After all, this was his plane and he was in charge of their safety. They had traveled over the complete country of Poland in this manner and the first lieutenant had finally had enough. When he turned slightly in his seat to release the barrage of words he had been holding onto, he noticed the man's wallet had fallen and lay open to his identification card: Gestapo. Oberleutnant Weber turned slowly back to his controls. Thank God he had kept his mouth shut.

His was not the only like mission that would ensue over the coming months. It was an inventive operation with historical ramifications that would become the norm in the years ahead; air reconnaissance. Not only was the dried up man a member of Gestapo, he happened to be an excellent photographer. With First Lieutenant Weber's assistance, he managed to capture on film the positions of railway lines, communication centers, military stations, aircraft depots, and the major city thoroughfares of Poland. It was another brilliant piece of espionage in preparation for the Nazis' anticipated campaign.

When they finally landed, his passenger was shuttled away in a black sedan for parts unknown to Lucas Weber. The plush vehicle eventually halted not in a German city but in the middle of the forest close to the Polish borders. Here sat a portable developing room, one of many scattered along the border containing everything needed to develop, print, and enlarge all photos taken. With these on-site field developing units, Germany could accurately pinpoint where to strike using up-to-date information. Poland would be cut off from the rest of the world before they were even aware of it.

Chapter Eighteen

August 23, 1939

STALIN

*T*rue to Hitler's insight, talks broke down between Josef Stalin and England. The man was now tentatively knocking at Germany's door. The German Chiefs of Staff were once again amazed at their leader's intuitiveness. Hitler was uncanny with his predictions and judgment in people. It was as if every detail had been preordained, each one coming to fruition as smoothly as Jägermeister sliding down the throat. Now he would begin the cat-and-mouse game with Stalin.

{ I }

As obsessive as Adolf Hitler was regarding the greater glory of Germany and Nazism, so too was Josef Stalin in his quest for his perfect Russia and Communistic society. Two men cut from the same bolt of cloth, both completely focused upon their respective fanatical goals. Both were extremely private in their personal lives yet where Hitler strove to project his altruistic commitment publically to the German people, Stalin did little to improve his image of a selfish dictator. When it was called for he could be charming and polite, mainly toward visiting statesmen, but was generally coarse, rude, and abusive

While photographs and portraits portrayed Stalin as physically massive, at five feet six inches he was anything but tall. For that reason he preferred, actually demanded, photos and portraits be taken when he was seated; he had been known to have artists shot if the image did not please him. Even the American politician, Harry, who was the same height as Hitler's five foot nine inches, would call Stalin "a little squirt."

In addition to the embarrassment over his short stature, he had several physical defects. At age seven, he contracted smallpox, leaving his face permanently scarred. In later life, he tried unsuccessfully to hide the marks behind a bushy mustache. After a carriage accident at age twelve, his left arm was damaged, leaving it shortened and stiff at the elbow while his right hand was thinner than normal. He was continually trying to hide these deformities under custom-made clothing. Simply put, the man had several reasons for overcompensation.

His first wife officially died of smallpox. His second wife reportedly shot herself after a public argument at a dinner party where Stalin cruelly flicked lit cigarettes across the table at her. Many believed it had not been suicide and Stalin had pulled the trigger. Even his son, Yakov, could not escape his father's abuse. When the younger man botched a suicide attempt resulting from his father's harshness, Stalin remarked, "He can't even shoot straight."

In his youth, Stalin was a published poet and enrolled in seminary school. He was reportedly expelled after missing exams although it was suggested he was unable to pay his tuition fees. After this failure, he became a full-time revolutionary and an outlaw, raising money for the Bolsheviks by organizing bank robberies, ransom kidnappings, and extortions. Repeated capture for his crimes led to exile in Siberia seven times.

The man worked his way through government ranks roughly within the same time frame as Hitler. He too was in the right place at the right time and, like Hitler, openly took steps to further solidify his power by forcibly and brutally ousting his rivals. Hitler's purge, the Night of the Long Knives, lasted three days while Stalin took more time and care with his Great Purge, beginning in 1936 and lasting until 1938. Mass exiles, transports to prisons, and executions were in store for those with any individuality of thought from whom Stalin felt threatened.

Additionally, if Stalin chose to have a person removed from his side by execution, the person would be summarily removed from historical records as well. During the 1930s, a photograph was taken along the banks of the Volga River of Stalin, his staff, and one young man positioned to Stalin's left. When the man was shot a few years later as an "enemy of the people," his likeness was simply edited out of the photo and negatives by Soviet censors.

Stalin may have been paranoid and a megalomaniac but he was no fool. He saw the Western Powers engage in what he perceived as collusion, handing over Czechoslovakia to Hitler like a blintz. So adamantly opposed to another war, would they perpetrate the same crime against his beloved Russia? Stalin's knocking upon Germany's door was finally answered and discussions began concerning a nonaggression pact between the two countries.

Stalin knew he required Hitler and Germany just as much as Hitler needed Mother Russia. As early as the end of May 1939, some three drafts of the joint pact had been reviewed and further edited, all while Stalin was still in discussions with Britain and France. Foreign Ministers from each country, Vyacheslav Molotov from Russia and Joachim von Ribbentrop from Germany, wrote and rewrote the pact until both parties were satisfied. The final document called for food and oil to be sold to Germany by the Soviets with an agreement for mutual nonaggression. Furthermore, each party pledged neutrality if the other was attacked by a third party. It was signed on August 23, 1939, and the world was shocked to see in the following day's newspapers a smiling Stalin and equally satisfied von Ribbentrop staring back at the reader, announcing the joint pact and its declarations. What the publications did not report, indeed did not know, was the secret clause ending the formal declaration, detailing plans for the partition of Poland and the further division of Eastern Europe between Hitler and Stalin. With a few simple signatures, Poland's demise was sealed.

{ II }

After all the appeasements and his belief in Hitler's promises, Chamberlain finally realized he had played the fool and Europe could be stumbling into another war. They had offered the sacrificial lambs of

Czechoslovakia and the Rhineland to no avail. Oscar Wilde once wrote, "It is always with the best intentions that the worst work is done." It had never been truer.

The street newsboys in Bochnia were shouting the headlines and waving their papers, urging passersby to purchase one for complete details. "Soviet-German Pact," they shouted, "Molotov and von Ribbentrop Architects of Treaty." Those who had already made their purchases were huddled in tight groups, some reading aloud, other groups reading quietly to themselves. A woman leaned on a man's shoulder, presumably her husband's, and cried softly. One man had been holding a lit cigarette while he read and jumped when the hot ash reached his fingers. Many were entering churches for solace, prayer, and understanding. Men were ranting and cursing while their wives attempted to shush them or simply wept. Some speculated that perhaps this would amount to just another worthless bit of paper, others were sure it meant war.

Two major military powers had promised to aid us in any aggressive action by Germany but our unease was far from suppressed. We had witnessed the honesty and longevity of such treaties. Unfortunately, we simply had no other choice and prayed to God that Hitler would change tactics. If not, we would be forced to trust in our allies and hope it would not be misplaced or betrayed. Now the world could only wait.

Chapter Nineteen

August 1939

THE SEPTEMBER CAMPAIGN

*H*itler was screaming at his generals, something that they had expected but still found unsettling.

"How dare you question my decision! All preparations have been met, the date has been set—we strike on the twenty-sixth of August!"

"*Ja wohl*, Mein Fuhrer, but you see, the Wehrmacht is not yet at full strength and our production rate should be higher. Plus, Mein Fuhrer, Britain and France have signed the treaty with Poland and if they should intervene…If we could just delay…"

"*Nein*! We settled all this in May! We have the world's finest armored corps, do we not? We outnumber them in every respect. Poland will fall effortlessly and quickly. Chamberlain and Daladier are weak, spineless men who even now are seeking further appeasement and peace from me at any cost. There will be no war from those corners. That treaty is a farce. As you know, Britain and France never promised territorial guarantees to Poland. Can you not see they left themselves an escape clause?

"Public opinion is with us as well. Europeans agree that the Treaty of Versailles was flawed and we deserve our lands back. Plus, fascism is a far greater threat to the democracies. They welcome our rearmament to serve as a bulwark against Stalin. *Nein*, this will be another victorious campaign. I have already ordered the *Schleswig-Holstein* to moor itself in the harbor of Danzig and Westerplatte with other ships to follow. The events will unfold as scheduled. If we are not prepared, then it is your blunder!"

As tactfully as possible, his generals continued to urge Hitler to give them time to set details in motion to ensure the least possible number of casualties to the Wehrmacht. Göring was predominantly concerned with the Americans and continually warned that above all else, America must not enter the conflict. In the end, the generals were given five more days.

{ I }
August 26, 1939

While the walls resounded with Hitler's thundering vilifications, the SMS *Schleswig-Holstein* was in the process of lowering its anchors into the mouth of the River Vistulia. She was proudly positioned in the channel of Danzig/Gdansk, a beautiful resort and health spa town.

The harbor channel separated a small, forested peninsula, called Westerplatte, from the Free City. On this spot, a Polish military outpost was situated with just over two hundred men. Behind the walls, the establishment was equipped with medium machine guns, one 75 mm field gun, two 37 mm antitank guns, and several mortars. The fortification was unimpressive with only a barbed-wire brick wall, five small concrete guardhouses, and a center barrack. Surrounded by trenches and barricades, the fortress should withstand an attack for twelve hours.

The SMS *Schleswig-Holstein* was one of six ships Germany had been allowed to retain after the signing of the Treaty of Versailles. She had fought valiantly in the first war, sustaining heavy damage. Having been refitted, she was the flagship of the Kriegsmarine, the German Navy, until 1935. Now she was used as a training vessel for German naval officers. She was still an impressive ship at 413 feet long, displacing over fourteen thousand tons full. With a nine-inch double-bottomed hull and better protective plating than ships before her, she was an efficient seagoing battleship. Her armament was impressive as well, with twin turret guns of 28 cm each. Positioned along the length of the ship were 17 cm and 8.6 cm guns with 45 cm torpedo tubes. She could run at a top speed of 17 knots and crew 743 men.

Today, she was here on a friendly courtesy visit, inviting many of the local inhabitants to come out, view her, and take pictures. She was quite a topic of conversation and folks were amazed to see such an old historical ship calmly docked in their harbor. The commanding officer had received orders to remain here unengaged with the Poles until further notice; a stay of execution. So, here she sat, quietly and patiently, for several days.

{ II }

August 29, 1939

On August 29, 1939, Prime Minister Chamberlain, true to his indecisive and appeasing policies, endeavored to persuade Germany in another round of negotiations. The ever-obliging Hitler made one last diplomatic offer indicating his desire to promote better understanding between Germany, Britain, and France as long as they did not get in the way of what he considered to be a just settlement in Poland. His offer came with various contingencies, one of which was the immediate arrival in Berlin of a Polish diplomat with the power to sign any agreement. The settlement was highly touted by the British to the Poles, stressing that the demands presented were not "that unreasonable" and Poland would probably "not get a better deal." He was told that unfortunately Poland was not seeking a deal, only to retain her independence.

The following evening, Joachim von Ribbentrop placed himself in the public eye once again by reading a sixteen-point proposal to the British ambassador in Berlin. The ambassador requested a copy to be transmitted to the Polish government. Ribbentrop, that solid representative of Hitler, refused. A Polish representative with signing power should have already arrived in Berlin, he said. Having been sent for as if he were a subordinate, Polish Ambassador Jozef Lipski scurried over to the negotiation table late that night. He indicated that, yes, Poland could be favorably disposed to the agreement but, alas, he did not have the authority to sign such an agreement. The German foreign minister promptly dismissed him.

Goebbels hastily cranked up his propaganda machine and informed the world that Poland had rejected Germany's proposal. They had tried, the media reported, Germany had attempted to sustain peace, but Poland had been stubborn and demanding. The world sat and waited.

{ III }
August 30, 1939

Buscha, Mama, and I were in the kitchen of the butcher shop putting up the end of the season's fruits and vegetables. Although nothing was said, I realized how important these provisions could become and we searched every last bush and plant for edibles to can. While we were busy at this task, I received an unexpected phone call from Max. It took operators on each end of the line a few minutes of wire exchange, finally connecting me to background noises that were loud and scratchy, like a dog's paw against a door.

"Marta, can you hear me? Hello, Marta?"

"Max! Is that you? Where are you? Are you OK?"

"I'm fine. Listen, Marta, listen to me. I am stationed in Gdansk. I am making this call at the post office here. Marta, a German battleship is parked in the harbor here. Marta, can you hear me?"

"Yes, Max, I can barely hear you. You said a battleship? What is happening? Is it war?"

"No, not yet. Nothing's been declared, but Marta, you should leave. You and your parents should leave Poland. The negotiations in Berlin are not going well and Poland is going to fall."

"How do you know all this? Max—tell me. Are you sure? How do you know?" I was frantic by now and the connections continued to hiss and scratch in my ear.

"Marta, is your father there? Please let me speak with him."

"My father? Why do you want my father?"

"I haven't got time to explain, Marta! Please, just let me speak to him."

As a child, I insisted upon an immediate answer to any question. I was older now but my need for on-the-spot information had not changed. I expected Max to give me a definitive answer to this boat problem while he continued to request my father. Before the connection completely faded away, I finally acquiesced to his appeal. It was odd, but when I told Papa who was on the phone, he fairly ran to it. Their conversation seemed all very hush-hush, lasting only for a minute or two.

After hanging up the phone, Papa said he would return in a few hours and under no circumstances were we to leave the shop. Mama merely shook her head when I asked for an explanation. Max sounded concerned but I reminded myself that the great ship was not causing harm. As far as my family leaving Poland, that had been settled long ago. Besides, I was to continue at University next month so leaving was not an option. In retrospect, I am amazed at my naïveté.

Part Two

WORLD WAR II
September 1939 to June 1940

It is of no concern what the weak Western European civilization is saying about me. I issued the command—and I will have everybody executed who will only utter a single word of criticism—that it is not the aim of the war to reach particular lines, but to physically annihilate the enemy. Therefore, I have mobilized my Skull Squads, for the time being only in the East, with the command to unpityingly and mercilessly send men, women, and children of Polish descent and language to death. This is the only way to gain the Lebensraum, which we need.

Adolf Hitler, 22 August 1939
The "Obersalzberg Speech" to his generals

Chapter One

September 1, 1939

0300 HOURS

*D*espite the emotional storms brewing, the weather in August had been splendid in Poland and September promised to be just as warm. Few folks were awake that September night in Gdansk, save for military men pulling their shift and late-night revelers who had not yet put head to pillow.

Max had drawn duty that night at the military post and he stood on the battlement waiting for the sunrise. His flight school training had been "postponed," as his commanding officer had phrased it. He and the other students were needed as ground troops until the German threat was concluded. I would have been a lieutenant had I been allowed to complete my schooling, Max thought.

With nerves on edge, he walked back and forth along the fortress' wall on Westerplatte. The idiom "ants in his pants" came to mind and he smiled at the thought of Marta and her family. This ammunitions depot was situated on the edge of the peninsula at the entry to Gdansk harbor, ready to protect the city should the need arise. He looked across the water at the Free City, too dark to see anything other than a few lights left burning. He could not see the battleship moored in the harbor either but he knew the *Schleswig-Holstein* was looming in the water. It was the source of much tension among his fellow soldiers. So far, the days had been uneventful but the men were as jumpy as, well…as if they had ants in their pants. Offense was taken at the simplest of comments and caution was practiced when approaching a fellow soldier. Fear of a bullet fired by a startled man was valid.

Behind his shoulder, he heard loud footsteps as another man saddled with the late-night watch approached him. Turning around, he saw the grinning face of Private Gorski. The man was forever cheerful and Max had never seen him without his smile. Even when he awoke in the morning, his mood was joyful. It was terribly annoying but it was difficult not to like the man.

"What ho, Max," the private said. "I was going to take a short smoke break. Join me?"

It sounded like a wonderful idea so Max drew out his own pack of cigarettes, and the two men leaned against the wall, gazing into the night.

"Should be light soon," said Max.

"Indeed," said Gorski. "Another day on this strip of land." The private had also been in the flight-training program and was itching to get back to their original goal. "So, what do you make of this ship? How long do you think she'll remain here?"

"She can't leave soon enough to suit me. Today would be fine. I just wish we knew why she was here in the first place. The civilians are acting as if she is a new puppy; everyone out looking at it and snapping photos. Makes me very nervous."

"Most of the visitors are German. Gdansk is mostly German, you know. No denying that she is a pretty ship, though. Still…do you think she's fully armed?"

Max just shrugged his shoulders and looked at his watch. It was 0430 and the sun was beginning to rise. It was a beautiful sight and some movement could be seen on the ship. The first day of another month. How many more days or weeks would we stand at the ready, he wondered. As it happened, it would not be much longer.

{ I }
Westerplatte
0447 Hours

In answer to Private Gorski's question, the ship was most definitely armed. At 0447 hours, the SMS *Schleswig-Holstein* opened fire upon Danzig/Gdansk and Westerplatte. The German commander had received his orders from Hitler: rescue the people of Danzig from Polish barbarism. Fifty-nine 150 mm light artillery shells blasted at the southwestern wall of the meagerly manned Polish station while the shells of eight 280 mm heavy artillery backed up the play. The weight of the large gun was 214 tons with a barrel length of over seventy feet. One shell was over 563 pounds with a range of 38.64 miles. A most impressive weapon for total destruction.

Located behind the massive weapons on board were machine gun operators. Their C30 machine guns shot off over six hundred rounds into the Polish fortification. Once a breach in the wall could be seen, rockets were sent into the air seeking further damage. The giant guns continued to pummel the town and fortress unmercifully.

Max and his friend held tight for a split second before they ran down the stone steps to man their weapon post. They watched as trees were split in half and portions of the bark went flying in all directions, some shards piercing through fleeing citizens as if they were pudding. It was incongruous; some people were still dressed in their evening finery while others wore nightclothes. Occasionally, a citizen or two ran from a building in both types of clothing as if they could not decide on either.

As the wall crumbled, dust from the falling concrete rose to mix with the smoke of the firing weaponry, making visibility almost impossible. The smell of cordite, salt from the exploding seawater, and the coppery odor of blood filled the air. Unable to see through the smoke and debris, men continued to fire in the direction where they had last seen the floating metal beast, hoping for a true shot. Screams could be heard as the civilians' attempts to flee the area were made all the more difficult by the onslaught of German infantry. The marching marauders found it easier to shoot the civilians out of their way rather than go around them. Messages were frantically sent out to Polish command centers informing them of the onslaught. The barrage was akin to tectonic plates sliding back and forth; one could only hang on and ride it out.

En route to man his machine gun post, Max heard a zing fly past his ear and saw in horror as the bullet struck the man next to him. He sidestepped a low-crouching man firing through a split between bricks. The fight continued throughout the day and into that night with the Poles successfully thwarting two assaults. One Pole died and seven others were wounded.

Max could barely see the streets below him and the ensuing chaos. Bodies and their parts were strewn everywhere. Flames shot out of homes and once-businesses with fury, further enveloping the town in a shroud of black smoke. He watched in horror as a woman and her child clinging to her dress ran blindly down the cobbled road straight into a German soldier. The German used his bayonet to run the woman through then stooped down to the frightened child's level, inflicting the same manner of death to her. He did not know if the two had been German citizens or Poles; they had been in the soldier's path and therefore an impediment.

Over the course of the following days, the Germans bombarded the peninsula continuously with men, aircraft, and heavy artillery including 210 mm howitzers. In a devastating double air-raid wave, the Polish mortars and the only 75 mm gun was quickly taken out. It had managed to discharge only twenty-eight shells before exploding before Max's eyes. One guardhouse was demolished with a 500 kg bomb. Once contact was made with the enemy, the Nazi policy dictated, it should never be lost. They were determined to keep pounding day and night. The German naval infantry, SS Police, and German Police simultaneously struck on land throughout the city. The thick black smoke and relentless fires erupting, completely enveloped the surrounding areas, carried along by the vacating wind.

With his vision obscured by the fragments of battle, Max nonetheless glimpsed some of his country's aircraft joining the battle. The planes could be seen intermittently as they passed from one concentration of airborne debris and smoke to another. Even so, it was plain that Germany's Luftwaffe not only overwhelmed the Poles in sheer numbers, but in quality as well.

The Nazi infantry was quickly approaching the fortress and would soon be crawling over the walls like ants on a sugar cube. Max looked over to the acting commander, Captain Dabrowski, who was attempting to issue orders over the noise by hollering into a soldier's ears. The official commander, Major Sucharski, had been shell-shocked by a 500 kg bomb and was presumably in the medical quarters with other wounded.

Running up to the captain, Max yelled into his ear to be heard. "Sir, the Nazis will penetrate our barriers soon. There are too many of them. Their second force is staying out of range and we are using up our ammunition."

The captain thought for a moment and said, "You are correct. The situation must be controlled if we are to be of rid of any Nazis today. Listen carefully."

After asking a question or two, Max darted off to relay the scheme of maneuver to the men. As the Nazi infantry entered the Polish fortification expecting an easy victory, they found themselves lured into an ambush. The Poles had positioned themselves in concealed spots around the inside perimeter as if they were holding up in a defensive area. With overlapping fields of fire, they established a choke point, picking the Germans off as they entered the complex. Bodies of both troops lay within the confines of the garrison walls. There was no time or space to bury the dead and the rotting smell of intestines and split tissue pervaded the area. The men were exhausted, barely able to stand on their feet, some falling asleep at their posts while the man next to them continued to fire.

By September 7, the Polish commander was forced to surrender. He had no choice. Water, food, and ammunition were almost depleted and without medical supplies, they were unable to continue care for their wounded. Before he officially capitulated, the captain instructed his troops to find any way possible to retreat to Gdansk and Polish borders to join the fight. Every man would be needed. The brave Poles proved their worth and determination, losing only fourteen men with another fifty-three wounded. The casualties of the Germans, however, were estimated between two hundred and five hundred. The two-hundred-fifty-manned garrison, expected to last just twelve hours, had kept over thirty-four thousand German troops at bay for seven days.

In the cloak of darkness, Max and other fit soldiers made their way into the Free City to see that it would remain so.

{ II }
The Free City
0447 Hours

The defenders of the City were hardly idle that dawn. While Polish soldiers were attempting to stop the enemy from taking the port, the townsfolk were busy with their own defense and evacuation.

The Danzig Polish Post Office was more than it appeared to be. It was comprised of several buildings and was designated exterritorial Polish property by the Treaty of Versailles. Since 1935, it had also become a crucial headquarters for the Polish Intelligence Organization and resistance. It was also secretly, and quite illegally, militarized, mostly with reserve noncommissioned officers and volunteers who had been trained in firearms. Trees surrounding the buildings had been trimmed, allowing for better aim, and the entrance had been fortified to withstand assault. In the day when international telephone calls were placed through scores of various operators, this Post Office was equipped with a direct phone line to Poland.

The employees maintained a cache of weapons, including light machine guns, various smaller firearms, and several chests of hand grenades. They would be expected to hold the buildings for six hours until reinforcements could arrive from the Pomerania district of Poland to the west. On that morning of September 1, there were fifty-seven people within two buildings, including the grounds keeper, his wife, and ten-year-old daughte.

At 0440 hours, their communication abilities were terminated when the phone line and the electricity to the building were cut. The German battle plan entailed storming the post office from two directions. The first, a diversionary attack, would occur at the front entrance while the main striking force would break through the outer wall. The frontal attack was repelled by the reservists although some Germans managed to break through the human barrier and briefly enter the building. This came at a cost of two dead Germans and seven others wounded.

After the second raid was also repelled, the Nazis brought in two 75mm artillery units. Even this did not break through the constant barrage of machine gun bullets and grenades from the post office. At 1500 hours, the Germans declared a two-hour cease-fire, using the time to receive reinforcements in the form of a 105 mm artillery piece and a unit of combat engineers called *Sappers*. This division dug under the walls of the post office's main building and planted a 600 kg explosive. When the bomb was detonated at 1700 hours, sections of the wall collapsed. With a tank as their cover, the soldiers crouched on the opposite side of the slow-moving giant, entered, and captured most of the buildings save the basement. The remaining half of the brave volunteers were preparing for a last-ditch defense against the Nazis in the room below ground.

Using automatic pumps and gasoline tanks, the soldiers flooded the basement with the flammable amber liquid. While artillery guns and a tank were blasting at the reinforced building, flamethrowers set the building ablaze. Polish capitulation came after three of them were burned alive. Sixteen prisoners were sent to a Gestapo hospital where six more died, including the child.

The remaining survivors of the post office and over three thousand Polish citizens were transferred to an empty girl's school, *Victoriaschule* (Victoria's School) being used as a processing and interview center by the Germans. Here they were met by other troublemaking Poles. Eleven railway workers had bravely foiled a German attempt to travel by armored train and were among these so-called subversives. All were tried and found guilty but not before being interrogated and tortured. Those loyal Poles met with a firing squad a month later.

{ III }
Polish Borders
September 1, 1939
0445 Hours

When the weather cooperated, the terrain of Poland was well suited for land warfare and today promised to be pleasant and clear. Poland consists of flat plains with shared German borders of over fifteen hundred miles. With the accumulation of Slovakia and its surrounding territories now under German rule, Poland's southern flank was left exposed. Over one million Polish troops had been called out for defense of her borders. Some areas were more strategically manned, allowing the British and French troops to defend their promised positions when they made formation.

The attack was brilliant in its simplistic terror and sheer manpower. At 0445 hours, a main assault poured over the western Polish border while a concurrent strike entered the country from the northern border of Prussia. Thickly armored tank units, known as Panzer Divisions, roared through the countryside and towns, blasting everything in their wake. The Panzer I was a lightweight tank weighing five tons, relying upon machine guns with which to do battle. As its name implies, the armor was only 7 to 13 mm thick, and its performance was limited, drawing strength from the massive numbers used.

The Medium tank weighed twenty-three tons with a turret ring large enough to hold a 50 mm cannon. With armor up to 30 mm thick, shooting at it was like throwing pebbles at a buggy. They had but one purpose: coordinate with other divisions of German military, push through the Polish lines, and isolate selected units. Troops and machinery would then surround them for the final destruction.

Following these mechanical beasts were various assault vehicles like the eleven-thousand-pound half-track. These impressive units carried eight troops, each man armed, and an antitank gun. This truck's main role was to tow a multitude of other equally dangerous weapons, such as antiaircraft weapons, that could be placed into position quickly.

Motorcycles too buzzed onto the scene. The manned sidecars used the NP18, a submachine gun that fired four hundred rounds per minute and only weighed nine pounds. The men were trained to be crack shots, even though they were turning and bouncing along at the mercy of the driver. Their task: clear the way for infantry aggression.

Finally, the infantry would break through wielding some of the finest handguns and lightweight submachine guns the world had ever seen. Among them: the karabiner 98k, a lightweight bolt-action rifle with a twenty-three-inch barrel; the Walther P38, a 9 mm pistol with sights set for eighty-two feet and a weight of less than two pounds; and the most popular of all, the Luger P08 pistol, elegant and dangerous with a semiautomatic rate of fire. This was the Third Reich's first opportunity to show world the exceptional new weaponry they had been developing during the last five years. And show them they did.

The ground shook from the thunderous tanks punching through the meager Polish forces. Buildings exploded with glass and bricks bursting into the air. The dust of fragmented cement hung over each town like a cloud and coated people with fine white powder. German infantry troops grabbed dead Poles on the battlefield and used them as human shields, forcing the Polish troops to shoot through one of their own in order to kill a German. Blood and brain matter sprayed over the land like champagne from a shaken bottle, adhering to the tunics of both armies.

Thousands of citizens were torn apart by soldiers with submachine guns as they hid in their homes, the four-hundred-round per minute weapons cutting them in half as they pleaded for mercy. Thousands of others fled for their lives, trying to grab the hand of a child or loved one, tripping over a burned torso or a detached leg, unable to see clearly between the smoke and fire, finally clogging the roads and rendering them impassable for other evacuees or their own rescuing troops. The panic was palatable.

Communications were essentially destroyed, making it impossible to send early warnings to other areas. Neighboring towns and cities had no concept of the terror heading their way. Once they did, it was too late and they could not call for help. People were loading up carts and cars with valuables, heading toward then free Romania. Others packed merely essentials. One man carried only a table lamp and a bemused look on his face. The evacuees did nothing but impede both troops. Upon seeing the oncoming Germans, many headed back to where they just left, many kept pressing forward, and many were simply shot.

The noise was so overpowering that the incessant screams of the frightened and wounded sounded no louder than cat mews. The ground shook and buildings rattled as the Panzers roared into each town, shelling indiscriminately at whatever caught their fancy. Infantry came through with the Germans' iconoclastic stick grenades, tossing them efficiently up to forty yards. When one was not enough, they would make a bundle of six, yanking the igniting wire on one but sending the blasting power of all six into a building. A seventy-nine-pound flamethrower was dragged through towns and landscapes by the half-tracks, purging its three gallons of gasoline compound into buildings, the conflagrations burning people alive in their homes. Shards of glass propelled from collapsing buildings and became weapons of their own, flying through the air with a power and force that drove them into the fleeing masses, severing arteries and slicing through small children's necks with the effectiveness of guillotines.

Units of the Polish Seventh Infantry were captured and held temporarily in a local school. The Wehrmacht soldiers eventually threw hand grenades into the building while they listened to the death cries of the men burning alive. It was painfully obvious the soldiers enjoyed their work far too much.

Brave citizens began blowing apart bridges and blasting holes into roads to impede the marching Nazis to no avail. The Germans had considered every scenario, even enlisting groups of engineers who instantly and effectively made any repairs needed, having a bridge serviceable before the next escape route could be sabotaged. They were like spiders repairing a web after a naughty child had destroyed it. Carried along were the materials needed: wooden beams, steel supports, gravel, and tar. When their supplies were exhausted, it was a simple task to commandeer more from the next Polish town. The edict of the Nazi ground troops: keep pounding the bastards.

The drone from what sounded like thousands of angry bumblebees burst upon the scene. Those would have been preferred to what was truly covering the skies; the Junkers Ju 87 airplane. These were German dive-bombers, so called because they dove to their targets at 60-90° angels. The gunner seated behind every pilot was well trained in firing machine guns at these sharp angles while traveling at decreasing altitudes. The plane was optimized to cause maximum damage.

Flying at fifteen thousand feet, the pilot located his target through a small bombsight window in the cockpit floor. He then rolled the aircraft 180°, nosing it into a dive to earth. When the pilot was close to his intended target, he released a 50 kg bomb and began his sharply angled assent back to the heavens. By releasing the bomb so near the target, they were assured of causing the greatest amount of damage and could almost look a victim in the eye. A bombing force of 366 aircraft was put into action that day. They were fascinatingly horrid to behold.

On and on they came, wave after wave of the flying arsenals, intent on inflicting more damage to the already burning and collapsing towns. Swooping down and then up, they resembled hawks diving for their prey. Up and down they flew, their buzz-saw noise drawing nearer, machine guns blasting at civilians and military units alike, littering the landscape with bodies as the aircraft neared the ground. Flying in formations of nine to twenty-six aircraft at a time, these air raids occurred more than fifteen times throughout this invasion. Using the detailed photographs of the reconnaissance missions, bombs of over a thousand pounds each were dropped destroying fortifications, railway stations, junctions, marching troops, civilians, and highway links. Oil containment areas burst into flames and fed off the fuel to become one giant mass of flames, burning continuously with black smoke shooting into the sky over 3 km high.

The Germans were magnificently efficient in their timetable management: a plane landing at its base was met by men with bombs at the ready. The plane was refilled, refueled, and back in the air. The edict of the Luftwaffe: isolate Polish forces as quickly as possible.

Aircraft dropped paratroopers inside city limits who were prepared to use their latest weapon, the MP36. With a firing rate of 550 rounds per minute and an effective range of 100 m, it was not only deadly but also simple to reload with a thirty-two-round detachable box magazine.

Expecting battles fought primarily in the trenches as in the Great War, Poland and the world were not prepared for this extraordinary display of complete power. This was the beginning of what the world feared but never believed and it had been orchestrated with precision. Hitler introduced a new term that day, one that would instill fear and gruesome memories in all who lived through the terror. It effectively described the happenings of September 1, 1939, as no other word could—*Blitzkrieg*, the Lightning War.

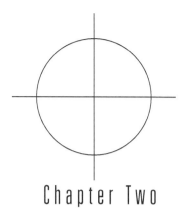

Chapter Two

September 3, 1939

WARSAW

*A*s the nation's capital, Warsaw was designated as a target to receive an unrestricted aerial barrage by the Germans. While the ground invaders were attacking from two fronts, the first in a continuous succession of bombings struck Warsaw beginning on September 1. At the peak of the raids, more than seventy German bombers and up to seventeen consecutive air assaults showered the city. By September 3, the Fourth Panzer Division broke through lines and made its way unhindered toward Warsaw, covering 140 miles in only eight days. From a range of thirty-one miles from Warsaw, the accurate German mortar and railway guns lobbed shells into the city, blasting day and night until nothing could be seen but smoke.

The entire city, as was the entire country, existed in chaos. Fires were destroying Warsaw as effectively as the German weaponry. The wooden interior of the buildings were gutted by the flames, burning heavenward through the roof. Nothing but the charred and crumbling outer shells of brick remained. Clouds of black smoke permeated the city, stinging the eyes and filling the lungs while four- and five-story buildings toppled over like houses of cards. It made for an impossible atmosphere in which to defend the city.

Fleeing civilians were cut down by machine guns on the aircraft's dive, bombs were dropped upon hospitals burning patients and staff alive. Schools, military facilities and water works were all targeted. Towns and villages in the area were deliberately destroyed to force evacuation, thereby effectively obstructing roads to any reinforcements. With drinking water all but gone and none left to extinguish the fires, the city continued to burn. So concentrated were the German land and air raids upon Warsaw, it became known as a "terror bombing campaign."

Using whatever skills and antiaircraft guns at their disposal, the Polish defense was initially successful with both sides suffering equal losses. Most of the city government withdrew along with large parts of the police force, fire fighters, and military garrisons, leaving the city even more vulnerable to destruction. Additionally, the garrison spokesman issued premature commands that the young and able-bodied should flee Warsaw, regroup and fight another day. Contrarily, the president of Poland insisted that Warsaw must be defended at all costs and must not fall. Complete and utter bedlam ensued. The city was left with four infantry battalions and one battery, amounting to less than five thousand men. Many of these were volunteer citizens, police and firefighters who had remained, and the newly formed Civil Guard.

By September 8, Nazi ground troops moved in, their furious assault continuing for three weeks. The Polish national anthem blasted day and night from speakers at full volume. We will not surrender, the music said, we will never capitulate, and we will fight to the death. The Poles fought bravely, hoping to hold out long enough for an Allied offensive strike in the west. They might have achieved their goal if it had not been for Hitler's ace in the hole: the Red Army.

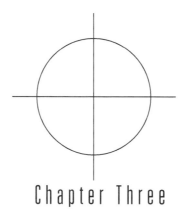

Chapter Three

September 3, 1939

THE GREAT BETRAYAL

*N*either country had made a formal declaration of war, yet thousands were being slaughtered. The British and French had estimated Poland was capable of defending itself for three months. The Polish government, on the other hand, had estimated six months, providing they received the promised treaty-ratified assistance. Yet no one had dreamed of such total annihilation. Poland begged for help from their allies, as they could not possibly withstand much more without them. Two weeks, they were told, just hang on for two more weeks. We are not fully mobilized yet, you understand, and we need additional time to do so, said the British. France, on the other hand, was continuing to strengthen that money-pit of a wall, the Maginot Line. However, they planned to send troops as soon as they were able, never fear. The president of the United States, Franklin D. Roosevelt, washed his hands of the entire affair. For several months, he had been reassuring the American people that he would not engage them in a "foreign war." This conflict fell into that category, he felt, and the US would remain neutral. There would be no aid from the Americans.

The Poles continued to fight bravely day and night, showing complete devotion and dedication to their country. Their forces were stretched thinly along the German-Polish borders and their army was still only partially mobilized. They lacked strategic defenses along troublesome terrain, leaving supply lines poorly protected. A full one-third of their mobilized men were stationed outside major cities but lacking the vehicles to travel quickly, their mode of transportation was primarily on foot. Two weeks would be an eternity.

Initially, on August 30, the Polish Navy had sent three of its destroyers to Britain's waters. It was hoped the Polish forces could hold out near the common border with Romania until relieved by the British and French offensive. The Polish Navy would then escort ships delivering munitions and arms to Romanian ports and act as a defense. Further supplies would be delivered from the west via ports and railways. Had Britain and France assisted in their defensive pact, it would have been a very good plan. Now, the three ships sat in the British harbor, their commanders hoping for a chance to prove their merit but unable to help in the annihilation of their country.

Even with their clear military advantage, the Germans had underestimated the capabilities of the Polish artillery. Their antitank gun was one of the best in the world and the light tank, the first in the world to contain a diesel engine, was superior to the Germans' tank in the same class. Unfortunately, the Poles were able to cause only minimal damage with these weapons since they lacked enough of the armaments for a concentrated effort. When towns were overtaken by the Germans, the defending tanks were absorbed into the German army like water into a sponge. Germans entered cities with such speed, the citizens had no time to secrete their weapons. They were systematically collected in town squares, adding to the Germans' already overwhelming cache.

In the end, it all came down to numbers. The Polish army had mustered almost one million troops but was hopelessly outmatched in every way. Almost two million German troops invaded Poland on three fronts with twenty-six hundred tanks against the Polish one hundred eighty, over two thousand aircraft compared to the Polish Air Force of four hundred twenty with the Germans holding two thousand more in reserve. Nazis ran rampant through Poland with fifty-six divisions of men, four complete brigades, and over nine thousand guns. Like giant swarms of locusts devouring crops, they decimated everything in their path. How could Poland possibly defend the land with half of those defenses And where were the Allies?

{ I }
September 3, 1939
Berlin

The British ambassador made his way by foot through the streets of Berlin the morning of September 3, 1939. It was a beautiful morning and he hoped the walk would do him some good, clear his mind, and bring forth the words he sought for this difficult task. This should not be his job, he decided. He was only an ambassador, more of a token position for having assisted the prime minister in his last election. Germany was a beautiful country but the members of the government, meaning the Nazis, could be especially difficult, and he did not enjoy dealing with them. They all seemed to be one giant mouthpiece, for Hitler, none of them able to think on their own. Or perhaps they were afraid to. He had seen the atrocities the SS and Gestapo had executed upon their own people, "executed" being the operative word. He had no desire to be subjected to any retaliation should he be met with threats. Again, he reminded himself that this was not his job. Surely, they would not kill the messenger. A faint voice inside his head said, "Oh, yes, they would."

Looking up, he realized he had arrived at his destination. With a deep sigh, he mounted the steps to the ostentatious building, swastika flags flying above him. Having made an appointment, he knew the office was expecting him yet he still had not found the words to ensure his safety while delivering the forceful message with which he had been entrusted. Clearing his throat, he began.

"Mein Herr, I have come as an envoy and the voice of the prime minister of Great Britain. He has sent this final letter stating that unless the German government responds by 11:00 a.m. today with the full intention of withdrawing all troops from Poland, a state of war will exist between our two countries." He waited a moment after handing the attaché the hand addressed letter. The officer never flinched, never opened the letter, never said a word; just quietly dismissed the ambassador by turning on his heel and proceeding through a connecting door.

The ambassador left quickly the way he had entered. He realized he was sweating and it was not until he had reached the street that he began breathing normally again. Well, he thought, now it is up to them.

Chapter Four

September 10, 1939

SITZKRIEG

*H*itler's lungs were in fine form that morning. Himmler was sure the screaming could be heard down length of the mountain until it reached the village below.

"War? WAR! Who do those buffoons think they are, declaring war on ME?" France had indeed followed suit with England and declared war upon Germany on September 3, as did Australia and New Zealand. "And what the devil are you doing out there in Poland? Those wretched people are still fighting us. And, I might add, causing us great injury! WHAT ARE YOU GENERALS DOING?" He was standing behind his desk, both palms flat upon the surface of that serviceable piece of furniture. He leaned in even further toward his generals at those last words.

The generals looked at each other before Himmler decided to speak. It was amazing; their Fuhrer was truly surprised that war had been declared though they had been warning him of this possibility for months. "Mein Fuhrer, we had no idea they would be able to fight this long without the promised support. They do not have much, but the equipment they have is very good."

"But not as good as Germany's! Our Fourth Panzer Division has lost eighty tanks. They began with two hundred twenty and now they have lost eighty! Do you realize how much money this will cost? My divisions have retreated! Germany DOES NOT RETREAT FOR ANYONE! Do you know how these tanks met their demise? I will tell you! Those Poles took turpentine from a nearby factory, poured it on the street to a town's entrance, and simply waited for our tanks to arrive. Those Poles, with no weapons of any kind, destroyed OUR tanks by simply lighting the street on fire! They never fired a shot! Not one single SHOT! This is your doing!" Once again, the generals looked at each other. Hitler had conveniently forgotten that all battle plans, all mobilization, every move made, had either been orchestrated solely by him or had received his utmost approval before any engagement was undertaken.

Taking a different tack, Himmler asked, "What of Stalin? Was he not to be entering into this arena by today?"

"Pah! That worthless Stalin. His army should have been in that miserable country on the third. Now he tells me he will not authorize his army into Poland until he is certain the country has collapsed and the Allies have not intervened! We do all the work, he receives the spoils! Cowardly insignificant gnome! I should have known better than to trust a country of cannibals."

Hitler referred to events in Russia that few people in the world knew. Thankfully, the Nazi network of spies in Russia was very thorough. Because of natural factors and bad economic policies in the 1930s, famine was rampant in Russia for several years beginning in the Ukraine and ultimately engulfing much of that country. Also rampant was the practice of cannibalism. Government posters were affixed to city walls declaring, "To eat your own children is a barbarian act" since children in particular seemed to be the sustenance of choice. Thousands perished in such a manner. To Hitler, this heinous act proved the subpar human nature of the Soviets.

As for the Poles, never had Hitler or his staff expected them to hang on so tenaciously. This was supposed to be quick; fly in, fly out, with minimum damage to their Wehrmacht. It was not proceeding accordingly. Hitler and his staff had underestimated their capabilities, their ingenuity, and the dedicated pride in their country. The burning tank story proved they would use whatever was at hand to attempt salvation from the blitz.

Himmler was slightly surprised at the very formal declaration from Britain and France. It was an insignificant gesture at best but tiresome. Neither country was prepared to fight; that had been verified some time ago. Still...there was always the possibility that America might join in if Britain convinced them. Himmler preferred not to think of that possibility. Göring was constantly insisting that the Americans be prevented from entering the war. Himmler did not see how they could control that. He was sure Germany had not the manpower or arms to win against the three major countries. Thank God, Russia had sided with them. With the Red Army's additional resources, anything was possible.

"Herr Hitler, if I may ask...so far we have had no interference from any country since their statements of war. Have you any news from our people within their government as to their intention?"

"France will put up some resistance; however, it will amount to nothing against our troops. And the British, those ridiculous people—have you not heard of the pamphlets? *Nein?* Hah! Chamberlain has organized the printing of propaganda leaflets to convince our citizens to denounce me. They have been dropping these by aircraft over Germany! Have you ever heard of such nonsense? They prefer to use a Sitzkreig method to win a war." He laughed at his play on words. "They would never stand up to our military achievements. I promise you; soon we will have control of that island."

The generals were slightly apprehensive at this remark. They had often heard of this intent but it would be difficult to capture England. Hitler was brilliant, although he tended to be slightly obsessed with his Lebensraum. Perhaps they should wait to see what transpires in Poland before stepping across the pond.

Chapter Five

September 17, 1939

THE BATTLE FOR WARSAW

*T*he German infection had half of Poland in its clutches and still Warsaw fought on. The Polish initial air strength of four hundred had been whittled down to a mere fifty-four. Air opposition had ceased although ground troops and volunteers were continuing to defend the city with their antiaircraft guns and anything else they could devise. Their border defenses, however, proved to be a dismal failure and the Germans had not been slowed. Day and night, the bombing resounded within Warsaw while the people were pushed farther and farther back. Only a strip of land toward the Kampinos Forest, 650 km of central Poland to the west of Warsaw, and the Modlin Fortress, one of the largest nineteenth-century fortresses in Poland just north of Warsaw, remained securely in Polish possession or was not under siege.

Finally, the German Twenty-third Infantry Regiment attempted to enter Praga, a historical borough of Warsaw. This was to be the single largest battle in the September Campaign. Using every source at their disposal, even riding into battle on horseback, the Poles completely annihilated the enemy with defenders of the Twenty-first Children of Warsaw, a prestigious infantry regiment. Over eight thousand Nazi soldiers lay dead and four thousand had been captured. Additionally, the Poles had seized fifty tanks, one hundred cars, and twenty artillery pieces.

After countrywide orders for retreat from the borders, troops and equipment made their way to Warsaw. Max and his compatriots had been prepared to assist Gdansk but it had been useless to try once they had made their way to the city from the crumbled fortress. The Free City was no longer free, much less standing. A dozen or more men from the garrison were making their way slowly and carefully toward the capital city. They had found others with the same intent and they now comprised almost a company. On foot, they had traveled primarily through the forests and across towns that were now ruins, attempting to remain out of sight from the passing Germans. They caught the few railcars still active or hitched rides from citizens in anything that moved. The few houses still standing were quick to offer accommodations and food, but in the wooded areas the men scrounged for whatever they could find. Hunting was not an option; they could not chance the smoke from a campfire.

By the time the Battle for Warsaw commenced, the Poles had strengthened their number to one hundred twenty soldiers. Max and his companions had been traveling nonstop and were practically starving. Yet their adrenalin was pumping in anticipation of the battle they knew was coming. They were one of the first of the newly arrived to grab whatever ammunition they could find, join in, and assume firing posts.

Thankfully, Private Gorski had been one of the men who had come along with Max to face this new battle. For once, his cheery attitude was encouraging rather than irritating and Max was happy to have him. "So, what do you think our chances are?" he said now to Max.

"I wish I knew. I think we may be more evenly matched than they know. At least I hope so."

"What I wouldn't give for a nice hot pierogi or a huge slice of babka," said the private as his stomach noticeably growled in reiteration of its emptiness.

Max could not help but think of Marta and the various culinary experiments he had tried at her mother's hands. "I have a friend at home in Bochnia," he told the private. "Her grandmother makes the best babka you could ever taste."

"Is she married?" asked Gorski.

"The grandmother? I should hope so or it would be difficult for her to have a granddaughter."

"God, no. I mean your friend."

"No, she is only two years younger than I."

"And pretty?" pressed the private.

"Very pretty."

"Well, then. You shall have to introduce me to her when we leave here. Women are absolutely mad about me, you know," he grinned.

Max laughed and was just about to answer him when the sergeant on duty called for attention to arms and to look sharp.

Looking around him, Max saw the worst lot of defenders ever assembled. Manning the perimeter of Warsaw were soldiers, old men, young boys, even women prepared to fight to the death for their city. Some carried pitchforks, others had hatchets; even kitchen knives were wielded. No one backed down, no one left his or her position. Runners would scramble day and night to bring what food and water they could find to the defenders. They were as prepared as they could be to fight the Nazis, thought Max. He hoped it would be enough. He could never have imagined the reality.

The Germans, preparing for an all-out assault, had gathered one hundred seventy-five thousand soldiers. Close to evenly matched, the Poles might have held out longer if it had not been for the over eight hundred thousand Soviet Red Army troops that came pouring into their country from the east like a tidal wave. On September 17, 1939, Stalin had finally produced his promised forces. Their numbers were staggering; over thirty-three divisions, eleven brigades, almost five thousand guns, forty-eight hundred tanks, and thirty-three hundred aircraft were joining Germany's still vast amount of men and arms. Whatever remained of Polish-owned territory stood a slim chance of continued possession.

The final battle commenced on September 25 for Warsaw. Five German divisions attacked the western part of the city while four other divisions harassed the east. Seventy batteries of field artillery, eighty batteries of heavy artillery, and two complete fleets of aircraft joined them. At first glance, one would think the capital of Poland would be in ashes within hours.

Again, the Germans had underestimated the Polish aptitude and their determination for freedom. The Germans were fighting for one man's obsession, the Poles were fighting for their lives. The citizens actually repelled the first attack, forcing the Germans to retreat. That night, the Polish freedom fighters managed a counterattack, destroying several Nazi outposts. Warsaw had managed to gather enough men and confiscated armaments to hold on just a bit longer, even if it was by their fingernails.

And still, on they came. The enemy seemed to be everywhere—the air, the ground, in tanks, wherever one's eyes roamed, there was sure to be a Nazi or a Soviet. It was unimaginable. Never had Max seen so many people in a single location. No matter how many fell, others appeared from behind. He reloaded his weapon too many times to count and still they kept emerging through the smoke like apparitions.

From the corner of his eye, he saw an extremely large, sturdy woman standing atop debris just slightly above the shoulders of the marauders. She was wielding an enormous mallet with ease and accuracy as if she held the Hammer of Thor, screaming obscenities at the onslaught of soldiers. Again and again it fell and he could hear the crunch of bones each time she brought it down. She crushed arms, shoulders, and jaws as the soldiers stepped over the barricades. As if possessed, she never tired or quit until a bullet finally caught her in the throat as she poised midstrike. She collapsed like a rag doll.

He turned to Private Gorski to ask for another round of ammunition from the box next to him. There would be no answer from that quarter. The private was crumpled on his back, his face and that winning grin having been blown to an unrecognizable state.

The situation within the city was dire; no running water, communications cut, scant electricity, and not enough sustenance to feed the remaining civilians or troops. The wounded and dying were too numerous to count and first aid materials were being depleted at an alarming rate. Families were caught inside bombed buildings and men assisted in rescue attempts until they were needed on the front lines again. Hospitals were nothing but rubble and makeshift aid stations were set up wherever it thought safe. These units were constantly moving about the city, struggling to care for those in need while scouting for safer places to stay. Parents lay dying on blankets under temporary canopies while their children sat alongside, holding their hands and crying. Blood was needed for transfusions but there was none to be had, save for that running down the streets. People were screaming in pain with an arm or a leg missing but they used pain medication sparingly; there was not enough to go around. Neither men nor ground could be spared to bury the dead who lay in every street. The city simply rotted.

At long last, the deputy commander of Warsaw began discussions with the German commander on September 25, 1939. The following day at noon, a cease-fire agreement was signed and fighting stopped. The incessant reverberation of battle noises that made it impossible to hear was now replaced by a ringing in one's ears. There was never a formal surrender or armistice from Poland to the German forces; there had never been a formal declaration of war either. The Poles intended to fight another day and cause disruption wherever they could to these foreign totalitarians. With this in mind, soldiers and civilians began hiding any weapons they could get their hands on. Whatever was too large to hide, they destroyed; better smashed than in German hands. Many made their way out of the city, hoping to reconnect with others who would not give up the struggle. Max escaped with them, vowing to fight in whatever capacity he could.

By the end of September, the remaining Polish forces were evacuated from Warsaw to German prisoner of war camps. The Polish army had lost over six thousand men with sixteen thousand wounded in the battle for the capital city. Approximately five thousand officers and ninety-seven thousand soldiers were transported to the camps. Warsaw's dead civilians amounted to twenty-five thousand, eight hundred with over fifty thousand wounded. Just over 85 percent of the buildings were reduced to ruins or rubble. The German casualties were minimal; fifteen hundred killed and five thousand wounded.

This Polish September Campaign—sixty-six thousand Polish dead, one hundred thirty-three, seven hundred wounded, and nine hundred sixty seven thousand Poles taken prisoners by Hitler and Stalin—marked the beginning of World War II. It would be a war that would forever change the world like no other that had come before it.

Chapter Six

September 1939

BOCHNIA

*T*he German infestation arrived at Bochnia's doorsteps on September 3, 1939. We had suffered great casualties by air upon our railway station and the fallout from the bombing at the military airbase in Czyzyny. As the second-largest Polish air base in the country, it was hit especially hard in the Blitzkrieg. Now they endeavored to complete the task on foot.

They barged through our inadequate fortifications and into our town square with thundering tanks, trucks, and troops making their position as captors undeniable. With communications cut off, we could not rely on outside assistance. Anyone with firearm training or owning a gun attempted to forestall the approach without success. Even Grandpapa, with his tiny pistol, hid behind buildings and got off a shot or two. He was extremely proud of himself when he managed to blow out a knee of one soldier and a tire of a half-track until Papa brought him inside to safety.

Little was left of our cathedrals from the bombing and we watched in tears as the Nazis took pleasure in pulling down the great basilica's bell. The metal clapper rang against the brass as it sang its last song and came crashing to the ground. Some of the Nazis stayed in Bochnia while the heavy equipment kept traveling, undoubtedly to ensure the capture of some other town, intent on destroying us one village at a time.

Although radio stations had been destroyed, we could occasionally receive the BBC if we angled the antenna just right. Knowing radio signals could be traced by the enemy, we utilized it fleetingly. Our plight was the only item mentioned and the broadcasters were dissecting our position in every way imaginable. These disembodied voices plainly had no idea what we were facing. How can you halt a tank with a shotgun? How does a woman with a kitchen knife fight off soldiers with machine guns?

Polish households were stormed by groups of soldiers who searched and seized any weapon or radio they found. They tossed anything confiscated into a pile beneath the fountain in our town square and the heap grew each hour. Luckily, Grandpapa hid his treasured pistol within the secret drawer of Buscha's dressing table. Unless the table was physically carried from the house, the Germans would never find it. At least that was our hope. Buscha took to wearing The brooch beneath her clothing, pinned to her undergarments. She was old, she said, and she felt no threat of a German ever venturing to her bodice. She would not let it go without a fight, she said.

Hope entered our lives when the radio reported Britain and France had declared war against Germany. Now, we thought, now we will show them. Now the Germans will turn tail and run. And so we waited. The French had promised a fifteen-day mobilization in our joint treaty, the British even less. France touted themselves as one of the finest Armies in the world and the Royal Air Force (RAF) was considered equal to the challenge presented. With these two countries rushing to our aid, Germany's troops would not stand a chance. And still we waited.

Sadly, our Allies had neglected to reveal the true number of defenses they could muster on our behalf. At the snap of his finger, Goebbels could put into the air over forty-seven hundred aircraft, including their very sturdy and reliable Junkers, and nine squadrons of the Ju 87 Stukas. The Royal Air Force could barely manage thirty-six hundred, most in dire need of repair, many downright obsolete. The French, those farsighted men with the Maginot Line, had virtually no modern bombers or aircraft. We lost most of our eight hundred aircraft in the first month of fighting, relying upon our Allies' reassurances and aligning our manpower under their strategic orders to coincide with their oncoming troops. Put simply, we had been duped.

Great Britain finally took a stand on September 4. We were told the RAF soared into action and bombing raids ensued upon Germany's battleships. Finally, I thought, our freedom should be restored within the year. I could not have been more wrong. Britain lost seven bombers during their brief assault, and directly ceased fire. Dreadfully sorry, but they could not afford to lose any more men or planes. What if Germany should attack their island country? Oh, no. No, no; that just would not do. Instead, someone had the brilliant idea to drop anti-Nazi propaganda over Germany during the dead of night. Surely, when the German citizens read of Hitler's scheming and trickery they would rise up and defeat him from within. There was one condition employed upon these paper-flights: the British soldiers must unbundle the ties around each packaging before the drop. The English did not wish to harm any citizen with a heavy bundle of paper leaflets landing upon a head, so afraid were they of German retaliation.

And the French? What of their aid? They were almost as unsupportive as the British. It is true that they offered some offensive moves along the Rhine River Valley area. Eleven units from their army, one hundred two division-strong, were mobilized on our behalf on September 12, just under their fifteen-day promise. By the sixteenth, they set out to do battle and were successful in seizing the Wandt Forest, a three-square-mile heavily mined area of Germany. Here they were met with German resistance and retreated to hide behind their Maginot Line, tails between their legs. They simply could not risk having their troops blown to bits from the mines. Many apologies, but we did try. The French press asked the question, was it worth French lives to fight for Danzig? Obviously not.

Our Allies rationalized their actions, or rather non-actions, by reminding our Polish government of the specifics in our joint treaty; it obligated them to assist us only against Germany. Nothing was mentioned about Russia and they chose not to declare war upon Stalin; Russia was too powerful to irk. Additionally, the treaty guaranteed Poland's independence and not our "territorial integrity." It seemed a matter of semantics as far as I could see. If Britain and France thought we were still an independent nation, they were more naïve than I was. For six months after our country fell, our allies engaged in what was unflatteringly nicknamed the Phony War. There were a few skirmishes here and there but nothing to send the Germans packing; more like a bop in their collective noses.

We referred to their broken treaty as The Great Betrayal. Not only was it dishonest in most of our minds, but it was sheer military stupidity. Together with the French army's manpower and whatever troops England could have mustered, Hitler would have been stopped in Poland before the Soviets had entered our territory. While Hitler was fighting a western battle with us, England and France could have directed their firepower upon the country of Germany. Deutschland's Wehrmacht would withdraw troops from Poland to defend the Fatherland. If Poland had not fallen, Stalin would never have entered the conflict. The world would have been a different place.

We were now known as Occupied Poland, a very nonviolent term used by unoccupied countries. This generic phrase was easier for people to use rather than the more accurate descriptions of war-torn, bombed-beyond-recognition, body-strewn streets, motherless children, or burned alive. "Occupied" was innocuous, salving the guilt and uneasy conscience of our so-called Allies over their treachery. The word implied humane and civilized treatment of the indigenous people.

Those of us who owned a wireless spread the word to others when we learned of the Soviet power struggle for whatever was left of our country in the east. We kept our radio well hidden since the Germans had forbidden ownership of those informative electronic boxes. Buscha said Stalin and Hitler were carving us up as if we were a Christmas goose; the breast for Germany, a leg for Russia. We wondered where we would eventually fit onto either of their plates.

Germany's propaganda minister was working overtime. We had been forgotten by our allies, said the German newspapers and pamphlets circulated throughout our country. Britain and France had promised you assistance and where were they now? Even America has turned its back on you. German publications proved just how insignificant we were to the British by describing that country's latest form of entertainment.

It seemed the Brits were enjoying a new dance routine. Partygoers positioned themselves in a star pattern, raised their hand in the Hitler salute, and tightly goose-stepped around the dance floor. Photos and newsreels of the dancers' smiling faces were publicized throughout our country. We had been torn to shreds and the English were dancing! To them, the decimation of our country had been a joke! Disgusting! I secretly wished the Germans would invade them tomorrow.

In addition to the half-truths of the German newspapers, the only kind now allowed in Poland, we often received some accurate news. It seemed as if Hitler and Stalin, amid a large smiling photo of them shaking hands as if they had just completed a well-played soccer game, had agreed upon the division of our country. The quote by Hitler within the article was, "Poland never will rise again in the form of the Versailles Treaty. That is guaranteed not only by Germany, but also Russia." Not exactly the words of encouragement we longed to hear.

The eastern half of Poland was collected by the Soviet Union. It amounted to 52.1 percent of our country with over thirteen million people. The Germans annexed ninety-four thousand square kilometers of western Poland where ten million people lived. The remaining block of land in the middle of Poland was placed under German administration called the General Government. The actual title of this area was *Generalgouvernement fur die besetzen Polnischen Gebiete* meaning General Government for the Occupied Polish Territories. Someone in the Reich seemed to have a penchant for long, difficult expressions and for every lengthy term devised, someone else would devise a sobriquet. This phrase was simply shortened to *Restpolen*, the Remainder of Poland.

Within this General Government area were four separate districts, each one named for the main city within it. The Lodz District contained the city of Lodz, the Warsaw district held Warsaw, and so on. We, that is, our town of Bochnia, were in the Krakow district. Each district had a separate German administrator but Hitler appointed his good friend, Hans Frank, the supreme chief administrator for all the occupied territories. The newspapers explained this Restpolen was under Nazi military occupation but was not directly annexed to the Third Reich. We were still subjected to all the rules, regulations, lack of rights, and abuse as the annexed part of Poland so, again, it was a matter of semantics. Grandpapa complained that government officials never could speak plainly and sought the most difficult explanation possible. Perhaps, I thought, this was purposeful so words could be twisted and construed to suit a later objective much like our allies had.

{ I }

Still attempting to maintain some normalcy in my life, I made my way into town as unobtrusively as possible. Along my walk, I noticed groups of people reading official-looking documents posted on walls or upon information pillars scattered around the town. It was difficult to miss the thick black Swastika preceding every notice. People were complaining among themselves or simply shaking their heads. Wiggling my way closer, I saw our sentencing as captives. Written in a flourishing hand, the notice was both in German and Polish. As I read, I realized these rules of our enslavement had not been drafted overnight. Much thought had been put into these itemized restrictions with probably thousands posted throughout Poland. This entire campaign had been premeditated for quite some time, meticulously planned, and methodically carried out.

I reread the notice, hoping I had misread it the first time:

As of today, all young, able-bodied Polish men will be drafted into the German Army

The Polish language is forbidden, either in the spoken or written word

All secondary schools and colleges are to be closed for an undetermined length of time

All shops, stores, or businesses will remain open until noon only

Polish newspapers and publications are banned; only those in German are allowed

Streets and towns shall be renamed to reflect the occupation of Germany

Cinemas are no longer allowed to run anything not sanctioned by the German Government Official in charge

German soldiers or other members of the German Establishment are allowed to search any person, business, or household under suspicion of subversive acts

All things American are banned

Curfew is set at 2000 hours unless signed authorization can be presented

Rationing coupons will be issued at a time to be determined for all citizens of Poland

Identification papers will be issued at a time to be determined for all citizens of Poland

The list went dizzyingly on. Now I realized why those around me had been grumbling. But how, I wondered, can they obliterate the Polish language? Most Poles spoke not a whit of German. It was outlandish. How could we communicate with one another if not in our native tongue? Then I thought, perhaps that was their intention.

I was particularly concerned about my friend, Mr. Klein, and his bookshop. I had visited a month ago and was shocked to see a red, white, and blue display in his storefront window. In the middle of this, was a book entitled *Learn English Before the British Arrive*. I rushed into the shop and told him he should remove the entire display. I was afraid for his safety, I said.

"Ach!" he said. "What can they do to me? I am an ethnic German citizen. I am one of Them, after all. Not a Nazi, but definitely a German. Do not worry, my dear, I will be fine."

Today I ran to his shop to see his fate. From outside, all looked normal at Klein's Books. Then I saw his display window. Surrounded by Swastika banners and tiny flags sat a new book. *Learn German Before our Friends Depart*, the words proudly announced. Oh my God, I thought, how could they have accomplished this so quickly? The only word holding hope was "depart." Would they, I wondered.

I hurried inside to find my friend. The shop had been completely transformed. Not a book, newspaper, magazine, or even a guidebook written in Polish was for sale. Instead, German propaganda in the form of newspapers, poetry, German history, and dozens of the same book displayed in the window were prominently stacked around the room.

I found Mr. Klein in his upstairs office, where we had spent many a peaceful and informative afternoon. The place had been ransacked with poor Mr. Klein sitting in the middle of it all. His face was badly battered and puffy, one eye swollen shut, and his arm in a sling. Dashing over, I knelt down next to his chair.

"Oh no! Mr. Klein, what happened?" I asked inanely. Anyone could plainly see what had happened.

"At least they did not kill me. Not good press for them to murder a fellow German, I suppose."

"But why? How can they do all this?"

"They do it because they can, my dear. Who is there to stop them? The English? The French? We have already seen how concerned they are about us. When people have no consequences for their actions, they do what they like. They are in too deep—the German citizens, I mean. My family tried to tell me months ago. Those who protest are taken away and never seen again or shot in front of their family as a lesson to others. Few Germans feel comfortable with the turn the world has taken but the SS and Gestapo are everywhere. You can no longer trust your own neighbor and individual opinion is no longer tolerated; only a regurgitation of Hitler's is allowed."

I brought a cool cloth to him for his eye and there we sat, each lost in our own thoughts, wondering what would become of us.

{ II }
September 28, 1939

My grandparents had been huddled with us trying to receive even the tiniest bit of hopeful news from the radio when a knock was heard at the door. Quickly hiding the illegal box, Papa proceeded to the door. It was Max! He had survived the Battle for Danzig (as it was now officially called) and made his way home. We had so many questions for him but Buscha would not tolerate conversation without first feeding "this poor starving boy." It was all we could do to sit there quietly and watch him eat.

Finally we tore into him with one question after another. It was overwhelming, the amount of facts he had to give us: General This, Commander That, The Something Battalion, The Whatnot Aircraft. So much information to be garnered about the whys and wherefores of what really happened but after he went on and on it was just one big blur. As far as I was concerned, we were in a terrible mess and no other country cared about us.

After we had temporarily exhausted ourselves of questions, he asked to speak to my father in private. Private, I wondered. Now what was all that about? They were locked in my father's study for an eternity before they emerged, looking serious and troubled.

Mama offered us a slice of her apple cake for us to nibble upon ("No thank you, Mrs. Koblinski—perhaps just a glass of tea," said Max, looking over at me. I was gently shaking my head side to side. Mama had concocted this on her own.) and we took our usual spot under the bartek tree.

"Max," I began, "I can't tell you how wonderful it is to see you safe. What are you going to do now? Do you have orders? Must you leave Bochnia again?"

"There is no longer a Polish army to issue any orders, Marta. We are done fighting as Polish soldiers. Many of our pilots have left for France and even Britain, hoping to fight on if the Allies should ever get their courage up," he said angrily. "They have all betrayed us and any hope we had for freedom. At least as far as fighting in Polish uniform." He looked at me somewhat strangely after saying this and I waited for him to continue. "I have heard our country will be treated differently, more harshly, than Czechoslovakia or Austria. Living here will become much more difficult. Once the battles are over and we have been shared between Russia and Germany...well, I think it will be very bad. You know how both countries have hated us for generations."

"But, Max, how do you know this? I don't understand."

He moved closer to me and took my hand very earnestly. "Listen, Marta, I have something to tell you but you must swear by all that's holy, for my sake and that of your family, you will never breathe a word of this. Do you swear?" I nodded out of curiosity but inwardly a wee voice told me I really did not want to know anything he was about to tell me. "Good. For the past four years, I have been involved in a movement with thousands of like-minded people. Do you remember when I told you about the man named Jan Piekalkiewicz?" I nodded again. I was beginning to feel like a pigeon, bobbing my head up and down. It seemed to be the only part I played in this tête-à-tête. "He uses the name Jan Karski now. He escaped from a Prisoner of War or POW transport train and made his way to Warsaw.

"He and another man, Stefan Rowecki, have been playing an important part in getting us established. By us, I mean the resistance, the underground. Are you familiar at all with this group?" Again my pigeon-like head bobbed. "Some of us have been working in secret for years; others are displaced military men who are now seeking us out. We plan to get as much information to our people and to the world as we can. We're not intended to be a militant group, but we will do whatever is necessary to free ourselves."

"Max, no! You could be killed just for talking about this. You cannot blow up Germans and Soviets. My God, what are you thinking?" I was shocked then had another thought. "Is that why you and Papa went into his study? Were you trying to have him join you in this crazy thing?"

"I can't tell you that, Marta."

"Max, he isn't as young as you. He can't, he just can't! Besides, why are you telling me all this?" I felt that tingle down my spine again and wished I could be anywhere but here.

"Marta, calm down." He held on tighter to my hand. "Please, listen to me. We need you. You speak German fluently and English beautifully, even some Yiddish. My French is passable but to what use? We fight Germany, not France. We need a person with your skills. I want you to join our organization and help fight these monsters that have overrun our country."

I grabbed my hand away from him and stood up. "Max, are you mad? What are you thinking? You cannot do this, you simply cannot. And neither can I." I had wrapped both of my arms around my body, holding myself intact as if I might fall apart.

"Marta, listen to me, please. Come, sit back down or it will look suspicious. Look, I'm not asking you to blow up bridges or German outposts." My eyes widened even more at that remark. "Honest. But I think you could be of great assistance in translating things that are bound to surface or possibly pretend you are German. With your fair looks, it would be easy for you and perhaps you could get some needed information. I do not know how, exactly, but I do know we can use you."

"It is not up to us to change things, Max. Let our government untangle all this. It is not our business and I will not sacrifice my life to try and change things. Look at me, Max. How do you expect someone this small to stop the Germans?"

He became more agitated as he spoke to me. "This is our country, Marta, our way of life and our families! You cannot put your head in the sand any longer. You have to grow up and face what is going on around us! One person can make a difference. Some of us already have."

My eyes were watering when I looked up at him. Max had never spoken so harshly to me but I needed him to understand.

"Max," I began, "I just can't. And it is not safe for you to be involved either. Please, let our officials and president handle this. Please, it is not for us to make waves here. Too many people have already died for doing nothing wrong. Can you imagine what they would do to us if they find out? Whatever you hope to accomplish is impossible." I was speaking quickly now, as if I had to get it all out before I changed my mind. "I know I was always the foolhardy one when we were younger but what you ask is not the same as climbing the tallest tree. What you are asking is completely crazy and I may be stubborn and outspoken, oh and many other not so endearing traits—but I am not crazy! There has to be some type of an agreement our countries can come to." I actually said this with a straight face, knowing full well how the many agreements and treaties had worked in our favor so far. "I'm sorry, Max, I just cannot do as you ask," I finished lamely.

Max just looked at me. Taking both my hands in his he said, "No, I'm the one who's sorry. I should not have asked this of you. Please forgive me. You may be ready later, but not now. Look," he said and he began scribbling something on a scrap of paper, "if you ever change your mind or need me for anything, send a telegram to this post office in Warsaw. Or you can send a letter there marked General Delivery. We still manage to have communication lines there most of the time; the Germans use it frequently. Remember your old horse, Irina?" Once again, my head bobbing began. "All right, just relay the message 'Irina sends her love' and I'll come here no matter what. Now, repeat it for me." I felt foolish but did so. "It may take some time between receiving the message and arriving here, but I will come, OK? And make sure you send it in English. Polish is forbidden now. My English is not as good as yours but this I will understand, all right?" Again, I bobbed. "And do not look so sad. Truly, it is fine. I am not upset or disappointed. You see, I know that when you are ready, you'll be the best. You always are."

He gave me a huge hug before he left. "Max, where will you go? Are you staying at home?"

"No, too dangerous for my family. Don't worry, though; there are plenty of safe houses throughout the country. I cannot tell you where because I am not even sure yet. But Marta, I was serious about the terrible time ahead. I think those posted rules are just the beginning. Make sure you have plenty of food put up in your larder—fruit, vegetables, even some smoked meats if you can." He smiled and went on, "Maybe you and your grandmother should do the canning, though."

Chapter Seven

October 1939

DEATH SQUADS

*N*ear closing time, I was keeping Papa company in the prep room when Mama came in, red-faced and flustered. "Birdie, What happened?" said Papa rushing to her side.

"Oh, Marek. Mrs. Schultz was just in and she told me something I just…It cannot be true."

Telling her to calm herself, she related the story. Mrs. Schultz had a confession to make. Several years ago, being ethnic Germans, she and her husband were formally requested to provide the names of anyone who might be conspirators against the Third Reich. In particular, the identity of Intelligentsia, business owners, teachers, doctors—the request, she said, went on for pages.

"Marek, she said they provided names of those who had already moved out of the country, or at least out of the area. They have never been pro-Nazi, you know. But there were thousands of these requests sent throughout all of Poland. She thought we may be in danger of having been written on someone else's list. She said they are leaving Poland and we should do the same. Marek, what does it mean?"

Papa just shook his head and said the time for us to leave had passed. Ethnic Germans were allowed complete freedom to come and go as they pleased. All we could do now was keep our heads down and stay out of trouble.

As unbelievable as Mrs. Schultz's story sounded, it was correct. Almost two hundred Polish civilians were killed during the raid upon our country in September. Many were killed from the bombings, others shot as they attempted to flee, begging for their lives. Some were even forcibly drowned. At least five hundred thirteen towns were burned to the ground and seven hundred fourteen mass executions occurred throughout the country in one month.

These men, the Nazi Death Squads, were the best of the worst. Those who had been well trained in the art of hatred, those who were the best educated and most fanatical in Nazis ideals, and those who loved to kill for killing's sake alone made up this intense group of men. With conscription lists at hand, they drove into towns after the Wehrmacht had disarmed its citizens and engaged in whatever atrocities they devised, all in the name of cleansing. Some were in SS uniforms, others in civilian clothes. They were all dangerous.

They began with our Intelligentsia, our elite: doctors, scientists, military veterans, nobility, judges, and teachers. Catholicism was hit exceptionally hard since the Roman Catholic Church has historically been a strong advocate for Polish independence. It was more than the Church's support for our freedom, however. Since 1932, the religion had been the fiercest anti-Nazi group, therefore the most troublesome. In Hitler's eyes, all religions must be put down. Without sanctioned religions and their interference, Nazism would rule supreme. Catholicism in Poland was not successfully squelched, however, and Sunday Mass celebrations were held in secret within private homes or basements of bombed churches.

Even our clergy were not spared. Throughout the German-annexed regions convents, monasteries, seminaries, Catholic schools, and any other religious institutions were brutally closed. Our own priest, Father Benedykt, was shot in front of his church after Mass one Sunday. Other priests and even bishops were equally executed, taken away, or shipped to the General Government, Bochnia's territory. Nuns suffered the same fate as the priests, with some special treatment administered first.

I will never be able to erase the picture in my mind of Sister Mary Lina's suffering. A month into our occupation, I made a trip to the church. Elias was still living there, now in hiding under the wreckage, and I was bringing him what food we could spare. As I walked carefully alongside the side of the church behind a border of trees, I could hear a woman's screams and the laughter of men. It was rather like a car wreck; I did not really want to see the disaster but I was compelled to look anyway. I crept up to a shattered stained glass window and peaked in through the bottom where the glass was a clear rosy color.

Through this pink haze I could see Sister Lina lying in front of the smashed altar. She was spread-eagled, arms and legs held by two SS men, with her habit around her waist. A third man in civilian clothing, his buttocks exposed, was on top of her, bouncing away as if he was riding a bucking horse. Blood was everywhere, underneath her and flowing from her face where they had apparently beaten her into submission. She was still screaming and the bouncing man seemed to find this most amusing. One kicked her in the ribs, ordering her to shut up. This was my first exposure to such an intimate act between the sexes and it was terrifying. I knew I could do nothing without being subjected to such treatment as well but I felt so guilty, slinking away and running home, my original errand forgotten. The following day I heard that Sister Lina, that sweet and innocent nun, had hanged herself.

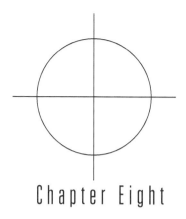

Chapter Eight

October 1939

THE EINSATZGRUPPEN

*W*olfgang Becker was looking forward to his new assignment. The October weather in Poland was close to the same temperature of Stuttgart, his city of origin. He was a member of the SS, a captain in fact, but one would never have known it by looking at him now. He wore none of his *Hauptmann* ranking or uniform on this mission and felt initially awkward without the security of his officer trappings. Captain Becker had a face that would blend in with others, no particular feature that stood out, and his clothing was not exactly shabby, but certainly not ostentations either. Just run-of-the-mill cuts and fabric anyone might purchase in any average clothing store.

He had been selected with many other zealous True Germans of the Third Reich to form the *Einsatzgruppen*, a special task force unit sometimes known as the EGR. Although ambiguous in term, it was anything but that in directive. Formed from SS ranks, German police forces, and volunteers, they traveled in the wake of the Wehrmacht. The men in this special force all had similar beliefs and characteristics in common: their dedicated trust in Hitler and the dark streak of cruelty running through their veins.

They were originally formed in the summer of 1938 prior to the invasion of Czechoslovakia and when the Nazis descended upon Poland, this group was reformed on the orders of the Deputy to Heinrich Himmler. Prior to their departure into Poland, the group had been honored with a rousing speech by Der Fuhrer. The Great Man had been mesmerizing, enthralling them with his goal for Lebensraum, the highlight of their careers. Even now, Hauptmann Becker could feel his Fuhrer's passion when he had said, "Whatever we find in the shape of an upper class in Poland will be liquidated!" They were to remove anyone considered hostile to the Third Reich, beginning with the Polish Intelligentsia. His men received orders to continue down the ladder, eliminating life unworthy of life such as the mentally ill, and small children who were of no use to the Reich. Mercy killings, really. Intriguingly, the EGR had been given carte blanche in their decision-making process and method of disposal.

Additionally, among the German minority in Poland as well in other European countries, the Self-Protection Groups were at the ready. They would be available to assist the EGR with whatever was needed. By November, the anticipated members were estimated to be eighty-two thousand strong throughout Poland.

To make their assignment easier, divisions were provided with the conscription lists of names forwarded to Germany prior to the war. The joy of the hunt was somewhat removed from the task with so many names at the ready. However the captain considered himself a man of style and had been entertaining some interesting ideas as to the obliteration of this Polish vermin. Der Fuhrer had chosen well with Captain Becker. Yes, indeed, he planned to enjoy himself for the next few months.

Following the destruction of a Polish region by the Wehrmacht, handfuls of men belonging to this special force would swoop in to further pick apart the remaining populace. Becker was particularly good at the selection process, concentrating upon the Intelligentsia foremost but always allowing enough time for the more choice pieces of Polish flesh. Young women were his passion while some of the men preferred children. Well, he did not really mind their proclivities—as long as the job was done before the fun.

They rounded up several victims and transported them outside city limits, usually to secluded woods or forests, where his men had prepared a large open pit; the prisoners' final resting place. Forcing them all to strip naked and binding them together, he allowed his men time to grope and fondle them before selecting a woman for himself. After satisfying themselves until their energy was spent, the captives were of no further use. The frightened group would be lined up against the edge of the hole and shot or stabbed. Some men preferred the more personal approach of strangulation, staring face-to-face until the life and fear dwindled from the eyes. Afterward, the men would gather their own belongings and those of the fallen victims to follow the Wehrmacht into the next community.

As with most German departments and official establishments, the Einsatzgruppen were painstakingly accurate record keepers. In ten regional Polish actions during the first month of German occupation until spring of 1940, over eighty thousand Polish nobles, teachers, entrepreneurs, social workers, priests, nuns, judges, government employees, and other would-be "political activists" were murdered. Next, they turned to Jews, Gypsies, and other rebellious individuals. According to their meticulous reports, the Einsatzgruppen and Selbstschutz were personally responsible for over one million murders, primarily civilians. They slipped into settlements unrecognizable as the monsters they were and conducted their massacres with great effectiveness. The Selbstschutz, those patriotic ethnic Germans with the conscription lists at the ready, were more ghost than human. They would emerge from the safety of their home and protected race, assist the Einsatzgruppen in their ghoulish duty, and quietly slip back into the mantel of a law-abiding citizen while their neighbors were unaware of the late night entertainment.

Wolfgang Becker and his men were professionals, after all.

Chapter Nine

End of October 1939

ARLENE

*T*hroughout the centuries, warmongering men had wielded their power over their conquests in cruel and sadistic ways. From the Trojan War to the Holy Crusades, women played a major role in their methods of debasing the citizens in conquered countries.

I never mentioned to anyone what I had seen in the church that day. How could I? It would be much too embarrassing to talk of such a personal act. I blushed as I remembered the man's dupa bouncing up and down. I could never discuss this with Mama and, with Papa...well, that was impossible. He was a man, after all, and some things women should never discuss with a man. Yet women talked among themselves.

It was mentioned quietly and usually in whispers. Mothers would glance at their daughters and a look of fear would flit across their faces. Older women would warn the younger ones and the word hung in the air like a curse. Men could never understand the terror women felt whenever we heard the term: rape.

Muffled screams of women being assaulted could be heard from behind the closed doors of their homes. Some brave citizen might attempt to assist only to be swiftly cut down. I remembered what Max had said about one person changing all this and shook my head sadly. I had seen too many individuals murdered as they came to the aid of someone else. I had been right to refuse him.

Other screams were louder, with girls being raped alongside a transport truck preparing to take the battered woman to suffer even greater indignities. Some were caught fleeing their homes or in hiding. All would receive mistreatment from their captor, stripped and beaten in the street, or raped in front of their loved ones. Some Nazis took pleasure in the insertion of whatever was at hand, prodding over and over till enough blood had been spilt to satisfy their sadistic nature or their physical inadequacy.

Months later, we would see an influx of War Babies from these brutal inceptions. The mother would never know the father of her baby, only if he had been German or Russian. If the child's looks were Aryan, the youth would be snatched up and sent to Germany to enhance the glory of the German empire. They would never know of their conception or their birth mother. Others would starve to death from the lack of food the mother could provide. Many would lay clasped in the arms of their mother in the street, a loyal Nazi having put a bullet through them. They were considered unnecessary baggage for the German Good.

So far, my only association with this most heinous crime had been my guilty voyeurism with Sister Lina. Unfortunately, it would be brought closer to home sooner than I had thought.

We heard the soldiers' boisterous voices and racing engines heralding their arrival on our street one terrible evening. It was apparent they had consumed too much alcohol and were looking for adventure and trouble. Since we were located in a very rural area, adventure would be difficult to find. I was afraid trouble would be easier.

We were hoping our house would not be noticed, hidden behind the large full trees along the road, but Papa insisted the three of us conceal ourselves in the long cellar under the floorboards of our pantry. Always cool, the space accommodated fruits, vegetables, and canned goods. Having lowered our shades and doused the lights, we lifted the almost invisible trapdoor and climbed down the ladder-like stairs to hide among the shelves. Here we waited, hoping our home would blend in with the gloom of the night.

The vehicles seemed to roar past us without even pausing. We could hear the raucous laughter and the breaking of glass from some other home not as fortunate as ours. The sound of screaming broke through the silence and shots were being fired, some seemed to echo in the air, others sounded as if they had hit something soft. I heard heavy banging as houses were looted and destroyed. We were lucky, I thought, our house was set back from the street and the trees were terribly overgrown. Then I thought of Arlene who would surely attract the eye of any soldier. Her home was built close to the road in plain sight. I rose and began to climb out of our self-imposed tomb.

"Marta, where are you going?" Mama cried. "Marek, stop her!"

I scurried out of their grasps faster than a ground squirrel and threw open the trapdoor. As quietly as I could, I crept into the front parlor and peeked out from under the drawn shade. I could see nothing through the pitch of night. I had to try to help Arlene, I thought. Grabbing a dark overcoat, I was just about to open the front door and exit when my father gathered me in his arms.

"Marta, what are you doing? Get back inside. It is not safe yet."

"Papa," I said, "I have to see what is happening to Arlene. Please, Papa, just let me go to her. I promise I will not let anyone see me. I will walk in the shadows and behind the other homes. Please, Papa, I have to go."

He could see that I meant to leave whether he allowed it or not. "All right, but I will come too."

With that, we crept out the door and, walking in a crouched position, hid behind the trees as we scooted along. We were only one house away from Arlene's when we knew it was too late. Her house was ablaze and her parents lay on the front walkway. From our vantage point, I had no idea if they were alive or dead. I heard my friend's screams and watched as she was dragged out of the entry door, her dress barely on her body, half of it torn away. What was left of her white slip seemed to glow against the dark grass as her captor continued to drag her by one arm. It too was ripped away from her body exposing her pale flesh underneath. She was trying to regain some modesty by clenching together what was left of her clothing.

Papa had turned away. I could tell he was embarrassed by her nudity. "Daughter," he said, "do not watch this." He grasped my hand to prevent me from trying to rescue her. I knew he was afraid I would suffer the same fate and I realized he had a right to be concerned. All the same, something should be done, although I had no idea what. I watched in horror as she was released in the middle of the dirt road where another soldier pounced upon her and I saw a reenactment of Sister Mary Lina's abuse. I could not allow my same lack of help to reoccur with Arlene. Behind him, other men were waiting their turn, drinking and shouting encouragement to their friend. Think, Marta, I told myself, THINK! There must be something you can do. I suddenly remembered Arlene's father and the odds and ends he collected. Arlene's mother fondly called him a pack rat.

"Papa, let me go. I have to stop this. I promise I'll be right back." Not waiting for his comment, I quickly drew my hand from his and ran to their back door. The men were so occupied in front, no one noticed me creeping in the rear and darting down to the basement. The light from the burning parlor slid halfway down the basement stairs, preventing me from falling headfirst to the packed dirt floor. Stifling a desire to cough against the smoke, I began to madly search for the item I sought. Aha—there it is. An old hand-crank siren. I only hoped it still worked. As quickly and as quietly as I could, I made my way back to Papa. As soon as he saw what I carried, he smiled, giving hope to my idea. He cranked the handle as hard as he could and the sound cut through the night with authority.

The soldiers snapped their heads up like children caught at some misdeed, their stationary figures casting long shadows in the road from the now completely engulfed flaming house. Even though the Germans were now in control, perhaps this was not the position in which an officer should find them. Gathering up their clothes and booty from the houses they had looted, they bundled themselves into their vehicles. I tensed my muscles, ready to leap up and grab my friend as soon as they left when one man stopped and looked down at Arlene, lying in the fetal position in the dirt.

"*Du, kommst mit mir!*" Bodily picking her up, he tossed her into the nearest car and hopped in after her, all of them taking off with haste.

"Oh, no! Papa, they took her with them. What do we do? We only made it worse! Where are they taking her?"

"No, daughter, you tried. I am so sorry. Perhaps we can make some inquiries to find her. Come. For now, let us go back home to your mother."

First, we saw to her slaughtered parents, burying both in their back garden. Slowly, we made our way home. Would I ever see my friend again, I wondered. I looked back at the collapsing house and wondered what Max would have said if he knew about my single attempt at bravery. It reinforced the refusal I had given him.

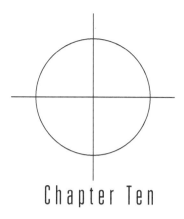

Chapter Ten

October 1939

THE PIT

*T*hroughout my country, libraries and bookshops were burned, art centers and museums were destroyed, colleges and secondary schools were trashed and boarded up. Hundreds of our leaders—mayors, local officials, teachers, lawyers, judges, senators, and even doctors—were shot or beaten to death in public as warnings to the rest of us not to resist. It was cultural genocide at its worst. To the Nazis' way of thinking, it was merely the harassment of a disliked minority, hardly murder. Hitler was determined that Polish knowledge and world contributions be erased from sight.

While the buildings were taken down to their very foundations, their treasures were not destroyed. Instead, glorious artwork by Jan Matejko, cherished original copies of Chopin's writings, authentic equations by Copernicus, and tributes to Madame Curie were shipped to Germany. We watched helplessly as our paintings, sculptures, ancient artifacts, and holy relics were carted away, probably to decorate Himmler's chalet or Keitel's parlor. It was sickening and we were helpless to stop them.

By September 9, the Gestapo passed a regulation giving them the right to arrest any "misbehaving" Polish citizen and send them to Dachau,

Germany. An odd place to send us, I thought. What was in Dachau? Two months later, another decree legitimatized the same fate to any Pole who left a German-controlled workplace without permission. Soldiers would rain upon the truant workman's home, seizing the hapless man and possibly his family, never to be heard from again.

At the end of September, our government officials had found circuitous routes through Romania into France where they optimistically set up temporary shop. From this location, the Polish government called the shots when it came to our struggle for freedom. Many of our pilots were also in France, joining forces with that nation's military, intent on fighting. From the rumors I heard, and they ran rampant, our underground had received governmental approval to harass the enemy by whatever means at hand.

Most journalists had been killed outright, printing presses smashed, telephone and radio companies destroyed, leading the Nazis to believe we were completely cut off from the outside world. Quickly our resistance developed tactics to outsmart the Germans. Within days, broken printers had been repaired and outdated ones had been revived to crank out the news. Eventually we could boast 110 different newspapers operating throughout the country. Volunteers listened to one-way radios, acquiring information from Great Britain. Inside of a few hours the news would be published and sent out for us to read with women and children risking their lives to deliver these forbidden publications. This they did on a daily basis and were seldom apprehended. Once a family read the news, they would hand it off to another family to read. We were all at risk; the publication, circulation, or possession of these illegal papers was punishable by death. The black Gestapo uniforms seemed to extricate themselves from the very foundations of our buildings, searching us out with perverse delight.

It mattered not what we did or did not do; being Polish was excuse enough for punishment, although formally we were classified as "political prisoners" no matter what the offense. If we did not show the proper respect to a passing soldier, we were taken away. If we looked them in the eye, we were beaten. If we looked down at our feet, if we moved from their path too slowly, if we scuttled away too swiftly, we were shot. If we complied with their requests we were spineless, if we did not comply we were possible subversives. If we smiled, if we frowned, if we ran, if we stood stock-still, it made no difference. It was a delicate dance we performed to avoid capture and we practiced the steps in our sleep. Around and around we would go, plying the Germans with effusive compliments, bowing and scraping, or simply retreating at their footfalls.

And where, I wondered, were my countrymen taken, those who were dragged down our cobblestone streets in spite of their fancy footwork? After they were beaten and tied, loaded into flatbed trucks, what then? Curiosity nipped at my heels like a dangerous dog. I had to know, one of my most troublesome traits.

Clouds had been forming throughout the day and it proved to be a Godsend in the evening; the stars and moon were shrouded by the low-hanging, cottony-white mist. No rain as yet, but the October night air was cold. A truck packed to bursting with human cargo passed through the outskirts of Bochnia; it would be completely dark before long so I assumed their destination was nearby. Traveling on foot, I maneuvered around buildings, carts, and trees like the drunk we had seen last New Year's Eve. Was it only eight months ago we had been celebrating the New Year? It seemed as if I had lived two lives since then.

With a sense of self-satisfaction, I had only to follow the vehicle out of town to the edge of the woods. Not too far at all, I thought. Making no attempt to hide their actions, I could have paraded up to them and no one would have stopped me. Of course, I did not; I may have been nosey but I was not foolhardy.

With the Germans' ever-present efficiency, the people were unloaded and forced to strip, placing folded clothes in one pile, valuables in another. Women were crying by now, some were comforting others while being pushed, shoved, and occasionally groped by the soldiers. I could just make out a long and presumably deep hole in the ground, its maw opening wide. Women and men, children too, were marched to the edge of the pit, some covering their nakedness, others holding hands tightly with a loved one while tears streamed down their cheeks, most muttering in prayer.

It took only one quick, precise shot to the back of each head for them to fall like broken china dolls into the grave. In silence, soldiers retrieved shovels from the ground and began tossing dirt on the hapless victims. Others gathered up the clothing, shoes, and trinkets and placed them into the back of the truck. Moments ago, the vehicle had been full of caring, loving people. Now, only three boxes of their belongings remained. No one bothered to verify if those shot were indeed dead. It mattered not; if anyone had been living, the person would soon smother within the grave.

The execution squad was long gone and still I sat under the tree unmindful of the moisture seeping into my dress from the damp ground. Someone needed to shake me awake, for this had to be a nightmare. How could anyone point a gun at someone, watch the person's head explode, and calmly walk away? If this is how bloodthirsty and ruthless the German Wehrmacht had become, then God help us. I slowly rose from the ground and began a long walk back home, filled with an overwhelming sense of sorrow and hopelessness.

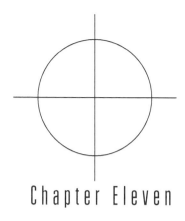

Chapter Eleven

November 11, 1939

OWINSKA, POLAND

*T*he mind-set of the German Reich never ceased to amaze me. They were like machines, always so efficient and capable in every movement, always blaming orders to release them from personal responsibility. Whenever an elegantly dressed officer looked my way, the image of a cruel boy about to pull the wings off a fly came to mind. So far I had been uncommonly lucky; my wings were still intact. The massacre in the woods must be the most heinous cruelty devised, I thought; nothing could top that. Once again, I was proved wrong.

Sister Mary Klara walked slowly up the stairs of the Owinska Hospital from the convent nearby. It was time to face facts; she was getting old. Seventy next month, in fact. She had been a nursing nun for almost fifty years and could still carry out her responsibilities with ease but these steps would be the death of her. She could swear, although she would not dream of doing so, that Sister Petronela, who loved inflicting practical jokes on the other nuns, had miraculously added several more steps during the night only to torment her. She quickly made the Sign of the Cross and said a quick prayer of forgiveness for such an uncharitable thought. She should have taken the rickety old elevator but Doctor said stair climbing would be good exercise for her. As if she did not get enough dashing about the hospital floor. Ah, well. Perhaps Doctor was right. At any rate, she was doing as he suggested.

She loved this hospital. Owinska was the oldest mental home in Poland, a beautiful, stately place with a tall clock tower and steeple. The staff usually cared for a thousand patients at a time, all with incurable and severe mental or physical maladies. Sadly, this number even included many children. It was the children Sister Klara thought of as she finally reached the entrance to her assigned floor. Such sweet dears…well except for a few who screamed at the top of their lungs at the least provocation. They could not help it, poor things, their minds were gone and they had no one who cared anymore except the nuns and doctors; no one wrote, no one visited. Very sad. She knew it must be heartbreaking to see loved ones bang their heads against the walls or sit in one spot all day long, drooling, and soiling themselves, but still…

Then came the invasion. Now the German Council Association, or *Gau-Selbstverwaltung* as it was officially known, was here and a Nazi commissioner placed in charge of Owinska. She had to admit the care and treatment of the patients had been permitted to continue as before. So far, most things went on as usual. But that questionnaire they received still bothered her.

An organization calling itself the Charitable Foundation for Institutional Care, *Gemeinnutzige Stiftung fur Anstaltspflege* in German (Dear Lord, why is every German word so long and sounds as if I am clearing my throat, the kindly nun wondered), had submitted an odd request to the hospital. The patients would be moved to another location, stated an attached letter, combining their numbers with those of another hospital. The patients, they assured the staff, would continue to receive the utmost care by German doctors and nurses.

With that result in mind, the letter went on, department heads of the hospital—"men, of course," snorted Sister Klara aloud as her thoughts went off on a tangent. "If women ruled this world, we would not be having this war. No woman, certainly no mother, would send her country's sons off to fight," she continued to mumble under her breath. Now where was I, she thought. Oh yes, the department heads were to provide the name, age, sex, and illness of the patient to the Reich Group of Sanatoria and Nursing Homes, which was completely unpronounceable in German. Patients must be reported if they suffered from schizophrenia, epilepsy, senile disorders, therapy-resistant paralysis, syphilitic diseases, retardation, encephalitis, Huntington's disease, or neurological conditions. The oddest request, according to Sister Klara, was to designate those patients who were institutionalized for at least five years, criminally insane, were not German citizens, or not of related German blood. This last category was subcategorized to include Jews, Negroes, and Gypsies. They were even to report all known homosexuals. Well! Quite an undertaking and very invasive! Homosexuals indeed. As if the nuns would ever discuss any such subject matter with their patients. There was, of course, a date by which the list must be received at *Tiergarten Strasse* 4, Berlin, Germany.

Since that date, all male patients had been loaded into military trucks, the black-uniformed SS men standing close by. The trucks held about twenty-five patients, some even less when the more difficult patients were situated. Two days ago, the female patients were taken. The nuns asked where the final destination was located but were told, and most rudely too, to stand back from the truck. The question was never answered.

Today they would be coming for the children. Oh, how she would miss them...well, most of them. Alfons could be most disgusting at times. Perhaps if he would just quit spitting, it would be a start in the right direction. It suddenly occurred to her that she would no longer be needed here. No patients meant no nurses. Well, she had the convent work to keep her busy until reassignment. That might take some time since communications were virtually nil throughout the country. It had been several months since they had received any communication from the diocese.

As she cleaned up after the children, gave some their required medication, read them stories, and changed diapers, she was surprised how the day had flown by. It was almost noon. Just then, Sister Joanna rushed in. "They are here. The doctor wants us to gather in the foyer for an announcement. Can you leave just now?"

"Oh yes," answered the diminutive nun. "I have just finished with Alfons."

"Was he any better today?" asked Sister Joanna as they proceeded down the stairs to the first floor.

"A little. He only spat once," replied Sister Klara as she thought how much easier it was to travel down these stairs than up.

"That boy," said her companion shaking her head, knowing full well how badly Alfons could behave.

By now, they had reached the foyer and joined the rest of the staff for the announcement.

"*Meine Damen und Herren*," began the SS officer reading from a piece of paper. Looking up to see his audience wearing habits and vestments, he glanced at his translator and made the adjustment to "*auch Vater und Schwestern*" (also Father and Sisters). "I know how much your patients mean to you so our wonderful organization has decided you shall all be permitted to join them at their new home. We will need your insight into their conditions and I am sure they should miss you." There were some gasps among the staff, handclapping, and many smiles. Well, thought Sister Klara, God certainly does answer one's prayers. How wonderful. We will all be allowed to stay together.

They were told to quickly pack what they could carry. The rest of their belongings would be sent for, as well as all medical supplies. The children had been packed for several days so this transfer should go smoothly. Making her way down the long hallway to her small overnight room, Sister Klara happened to glance out the window into the courtyard.

"Sister," she said grabbing at the sleeve at another passing nun. "Look out there. What do you make of that? Does it not seem strange to travel to another hospital in vans marked *Kaiser's Kaffee Geschaft*? Where are all the military vehicles?"

"Kaiser's Coffee Company? Are you sure?" With that, she peered out the window, knowing older eyes can have poorer vision. "Well, perhaps they ran out of military vehicles. I suppose this is occurring everywhere, yes? As long as we all arrive safely, I suppose." Then she was off, flying up the stairs to her lodgings. Sister Klara watched her in envy. Perhaps the next hospital would not have quite so many stairs, she sighed.

The other nun was probably correct. There were only so many cars and trucks to go around and several needed for other duties. Still, she could not rid herself of the niggling feeling in the back of her brain. Trying to shrug it off, she proceeded on her way to pack her belongings.

Reassembling in the courtyard, several nursing nuns traveled in each vehicle with the children. It was hoped the sisters would be able to keep them calm along the trip. Sister Klara was seated next to Alfons. With a huge sigh and a quick prayer for patience, she placed her arm around him. He disliked change of any kind and this would be a major adjustment in his life.

The walls of each vehicle were lined in metal and the floor was made of wood. A half hour into the journey, Sister Klara noticed a fog-like air coming from holes along the bottom of the van. The nun closest to the driver's cab began pounding on the wall. "We have a leak in here. Do you hear me? A leak," she said in her best halting German. Sister Klara was surprised the vehicle did not stop or at least slow down. There was no reply from the driver as they both banged on the truck panel. As their eyes met, the two nuns suddenly understood what happened to the rest of their patients. The children began to scream and stand on the seats as the fog floated higher in the van. Holding as many children in their arms as they could and praying over their cries, Sister Klara felt the tears run down her cheeks. How could they do this to children? How can they continue to drive and listen to these pitiful screams? Watching their charges slump to the wooden floor, the two nuns continued to bang and pray until their coughing and choking prevented their cries. Then they too collapsed upon the floorboards.

Following the complete "fumigation" of Owinska Hospital, the building was quickly converted into comfortable barracks for SS personnel. All indications of prior occupants were removed, as if patients, caring nurses, and hardworking doctors never existed on the premises.

Officers from the Central Office for Transfer of Sick Persons prepared stock death certificates on blank forms by merely completing the sentence "Death was caused by..." Fabricated reasons such as apoplexy, heart attacks, accidental, and other innocently worded excuses were sent to the victims' families to allay suspicions. The excuses were easily accepted; transportation of mail was extremely haphazard if not altogether absent in most of the country or the victim's next of kin was missing. The disintegration of the Poles' way of life was so complete and so chaotic, if a family member received the certificate they were more intent upon self-perseveration than a feebleminded relative who was institutionalized for life.

Other mental homes were equally eradicated. This portion of the population was the least able to defend itself so the killings were easy. Records were burned and family members who became too inquisitive were eliminated. Over thirty thousand nameless mental patients were murdered in Occupied Poland. The domiciles of hospital staff were converted into residences to accommodate ethnic Germans arriving from the Baltic countries.

{ I }

Euthanasia was not a new term to the world. The expression was first used in a medical context by Sir Francis Bacon in the seventeenth century. Literally, the word meant "good death" but the Nazi regime had a different attitude regarding its meaning and implications. Hitler used his twisted vision of the concept when he first attained power in 1933. It started with an extensive propaganda campaign, that extremely helpful tactic Hitler could always rely upon, convincing the people to give him what he wanted. In newspapers and magazines, film and radio, the suggestion was carefully and divergently made; life could be better for everyone if the sick, deformed, or unproductive could simply be removed. Think of those poor parents who watch their child suffer from crippling diseases and mental retardation. Think of your loved ones who are forced to face each day in pain from an incurable disease. And what of those poor souls who will never be able to talk, think, or walk because of their vegetated minds? Would it not be better to rid them of their burden and pain? Slowly, cautiously, and repeatedly the idea was planted into the fertile minds of the Germans. State-sanctioned murder would be a path gradually and diversely traveled.

In less than six months after his election as chancellor, Hitler introduced a regulation denoted "The Law for the Prevention of Genetically Diseased Offspring." Compulsory sterilization was announced for those people who suffered from any one of a wide variety of disabilities. An estimated two hundred thousand to three hundred fifty thousand people were sterilized in Germany by the year 1939. It did not matter if they were True Germans—they were declared unfit to propagate and could thereby weaken the Master Race.

In the same year, the Nazis enacted the Law Against Dangerous Habitual Criminals. This act skillfully blurred the distinction between criminal behavior and that of the mentally ill. Often acting in socially inappropriate ways, the mentally ill were continually hospitalized or arrested, conveniently falling into the "habitual criminal" category. Utilizing the same reasonable tactics practiced in his methodical acquisition of territories, Hitler was gaining approval to strengthen the German race by eliminating the weak.

Swiftly, seemingly small regulations were dispensed out to the public. Individually, the laws were regarded as somewhat rational but as a whole, the pattern became more sinister. The newly enacted Marriage Health Law prohibited a union if either party suffered from mental abnormality, a hereditary disease as defined by a previous law, or suffered from a serious contagion, particularly tuberculosis or venereal disease. Since so many excuses were available, if an official wanted to stop a marriage many opportunities were available to do so.

Unbelievably, by the end of 1938, Hitler's regime received requests for "mercy killings" from parents of infants born with severe brain damage or physical deformities. In Germany and Austria public health authorities, doctors, and other medical personnel urged families of affected children to admit them to a pediatric clinic specifically created to provide the medical care they could not supply at home. The relatives were not informed that these clinics were in reality killing facilities. Medical staff, recruited for their stoic nature and belief in only strong bloodlines, murdered these helpless youngsters by lethal injection or starvation. This covert venture took the code name T4, so named for the address of the program's coordinating office in Berlin; *Tiergarten Strasse* 4 (Zoo Street in English, a name that brings to mind a joyful afternoon viewing animals, not the cold-blooded murder of children).

So successful was the undertaking, the Reich expanded their venture to include youths up to age seventeen. Since that program too was sanctioned by the masses (or at least never openly challenged) the next logical step would be to include equally disabled adults.

When war seemed inevitable, the fate of mental hospitals was discussed behind closed doors. The first plan was to severely reduce the amount of food issued to the patients. After all, it was more important to keep the troops fed than deranged individuals. The doctors of such

German institutions were appalled. Slowly starve to death these poor helpless adults? Unthinkable!

Well then, the Reich would follow the current course of action. After all, Hitler reasoned, if people did not protest the killing of their own relatives and children, they would surely not object when Poles, Jews, Gypsies, and other undesirables were slaughtered. Therefore, in October of 1939, Adolf Hitler signed his name to a short sentence on his personal stationary protecting physicians, medical staff, and administrators from any prosecution while complying with the T4 initiative. It was back-dated to September 1, 1939, to coincide with the beginning of World War II, making it plain this effort was solely related to wartime procedures. Initiative T4 became a dress rehearsal for actions eventually leading to the death of millions.

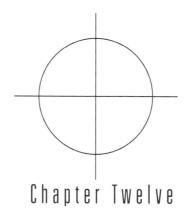

Chapter Twelve

November 1939

REGULATIONS

*F*ulfilling the promise of that first posted bulletin, we were issued identification papers. Conducted in a very orderly and capable method, we were told to queue up in the town center and find our position by last name. The Nazis decided that vehicles equipped with loud speakers were an easy and efficient method to pass information to us. *"Raus, raus, raus,"* they called out to us. Our instructions were blasted in both Polish and German but I had a feeling Polish would be eliminated eventually. For now, however, the identity papers were important enough that our native language was allowed.

We found our designated area, stood with others with similar surnames, until we finally reached the desk of a German official.

The soldier asked me, in understandable but not good Polish, if I required the use of the translator standing nearby. Should I let this Nazi know I spoke German? As I was deliberating his question, he turned to his aide, saying I must be an idiot; otherwise, why had I not answered a simple question. I straightened my back and heard Mama whisper "No, Marta, no," but paid no heed. "I certainly am not an idiot. Perhaps it was your extremely poor Polish that gave me pause," I said in perfect German. I heard my father sigh and saw the astonished look on the German's face. Oh, boy, I thought, here we go.

Astonishingly, the man let my critique of his language skills pass. "Ja, Fraulein, very good German," was all he said. The questions he asked me were extremely detailed. Our name was written in a massive ledger always at hand. They weighed us, measured our height, wrote a verbal description of our looks, and then finally snapped a photo. As I was turning to leave the station, I was told to return here in three days to receive my documents. Three days! How could they possibly produce complete papers for us all in only three days?

As ordered, we once again wiggled our way into the throng of waiting people three days later. Finally reaching the assigned desk, mine was handed to me unceremoniously with instructions to "carry it with you at all times." Slipping away from the people, I stood to one side and looked at my booklet. Of course, it was completely in German. Then I glanced at Mama's; hers was written in German and Polish. I looked over my shoulder at the soldier I spoke with on my first visit. He was staring back at me, one corner of his mouth turned up in a sarcastic grin. Teaching me a lesson, I thought. Hoping I would slip up without translation on my papers. Mama saw the look pass between us and whispered into my ear, "You could have been shot instead, Marta."

Ignoring him, I became familiar with this document indicating I was now a possession of the Third Reich. Made of oilcloth, it was four inches wide by six inches long, gray with a black border, and an embossed black eagle perched atop a swastika on the cover. Above this ostentatious symbol were the words *Bezirk Krakau*, District Krakow, while under the swastika was printed *Personalausweis*—my very own Personal Identity Document.

On the inside front cover was printed everything, and more, that anyone would want to know about me. While the categories were pre-printed, the facts had been handwritten. My first name and my family name, where and when I was born, place of employment, nationality, street name where I had lived on September 1, 1939, and other imperative information filled the top half of the page. Under all this was my physical description: eye color, hair color, height, weight, even particular characteristics.

On the opposite page was a reprint of the photo taken of me three days ago. Under that, official-looking stamps and the scrawl of some German who had deemed the booklet to be in order. Probably some large, fat scoundrel of a man, sitting behind a confiscated desk, drinking our vodka, smoking one of our cigars, stamping and signing hundreds of these identification papers, one by one. He and I would never meet and he cared not who I was or what dreams I had prior to this takeover. I was an now official piece of German property. Other pages had blank lines and columns, a table of sorts, to be filled in when I had permission to travel. Time out, time in; date out, date in. All very concise and detailed. The Nazis did not wish to lose track of us.

Chapter Thirteen

November 1939

EDUCATION IN POLAND

On November 6, 1939, *Obersturmbannfuhrer* SS (Lieutenant Colonel of the SS) Bruno Müller sent a message to the University of Jagiellonian's rector, Professor Tadeusz Lehr-Spalawinski. He was requested (in other words, commanded) to invite all resident professors to attend a lecture regarding plans for continued Polish education. The rector, of course, complied and sent the requisite invitations to all 144 professors.

The college had a long and impressive history since 1364 and was the second-largest university in Poland. The building in which the professors were to meet was the *Collegium Novum*, the Administrative Center containing lecture rooms and offices. It was a beautiful neo-Gothic building built in 1873 of red brick and adorned with intricate carvings in white marble. The windows were leaded and beveled glass while the arched entrances were trimmed in more carvings. It was a testament to a culture rich in architecture and academics.

The professors arrived at noon in room 66 of the picturesque building, hoping for the best. As Senior Storm Unit Leader Müller strode to the podium onstage, the professors heard the clicking of the door bolts sliding into place. There was to be no lecture. Instead, the 144 men along with an additional 39 individuals attending lectures in other parts of the building were arrested. The charge? The university was operating without German consent, therefore the men were considered traitors to the Third Reich. They were immediately taken to the Sachsenhausen concentration camp located 35 km outside Berlin.

This newest German operation had yet another code name— *Sonderaktion Krakau* or Special Action Krakow. The message was clear; education was forbidden.

The university's equipment, along with trade schools' and laboratories', were shipped to Germany to aid in educating that country's youth. The dignified buildings that had educated the minds of Copernicus and Chopin were now reused as German offices and military barracks.

{ I }

Contrary to the constant teachings of the Nazis, we were not a country of uneducated barbarians, dragging our knuckles on the ground as we walked. Education was highly valued and prized in Poland. As early as in the mid fifteenth century, our Krakow University became Europe's leading academic center for mathematics, astronomy, astrology, geography, and legal studies. The strong racist theories in practice by German propaganda assumed educating the Poles was unnecessary. Education was not required or desired for slaves.

The official decree came down from Heinrich Himmler to the German officials in each district. The directive was:

"The sole goal of this schooling is to teach them simple arithmetic, nothing above the number 500; writing one's name; and the doctrine that it is divine law to obey the Germans. I do not think that reading is desirable..."

To further enforce the Divine Law, by the end of October the penalty for any disobedience was death.

Being of a somewhat stubborn nature, we Poles were not about to let a world war interfere in educating our next generation. Our resistance movement went about the arduous task of establishing underground schools, which spread rapidly throughout the country. Teachers organized secret elementary, high schools, trade schools, and even special course studies in forbidden subjects like the Polish language. In private apartments and homes, professors taught flying universities, so called since the classrooms constantly moved location. We had underground law and social science faculties as well as the humanities, medical schools, mathematics, biology, and even surgical facilities.

Major cities set up secret military colleges. Some were designated as noncommissioned officer or NCO schools, others offered officer curricula. We even accommodated our young boys with an underground Polish Scouting Association. Religious education was also welcomed with Talmudic schools and the Roman Catholic Church operating seminaries for future priests.

Thousands of students received master's degrees at these secret universities and hundreds received their doctorates while over one million, two hundred thousand children in the underground elementary schools would be educated. Printing houses sprang up providing handbooks and exam papers for students. It was a wonderful, successful endeavor, one in which student and teacher risked their lives each time they met.

We were banned from a cinematic show unless the Nazis had permeated the screen with their propaganda. We were no longer allowed to attend plays, concerts, or go to museums. The penalty for a Pole engaging in any of these activities was, of course, to be shot. Therefore, we began forming acting troops to perform in private homes. Movie shorts were also made by those in hiding and book readings were popular. We were determined to promote Polish education and cultural longevity by any means necessary.

I was fortunate to have met a very gifted young man as he entered an underground seminary. He spoke twelve languages besides his native Polish, was an avid soccer player, and had been a student at the Jagiellonian University prior to its forced closing. By the age of twenty, he had lost his immediate family at the hands of Germans. At this still young age, he was credited with saving the life of a Jewish woman, who, having escaped from a labor camp, happened to come upon him while she stumbled down the street. The young man carried her on his back to the train station, purchased food and a traveling ticket for her, and placed her on the train to safety. I knew him as Karol Józef Wojtyła. To the rest of the world, he would become known as Pope John Paul II.

Chapter Fourteen

November 1939

DESTRUCTION

*N*ew and more inhumane restrictions were placed upon us with another Order to the Poles tacked up on our town walls. We were informed in October that the members of the SS and all German police were exempt from any public jurisdiction. Jews over ten years of age were ordered to wear yellow stars sewn on their garments at all times rather than the armbands previously required in our area. Restrictions were placed upon marriages; no German could marry a Pole, no Pole or German could marry a Jew. Sanitary conditions were lowered and the amount of water provided to us was limited. Much of the food we produced and refined was transported to Germany, leaving marginal amounts for us. Our salt mines remained operational with Poles as slave labor and the salt shipped to Germany.

On October 26, we were notified that male Poles aged sixteen to twenty would be forced to relocate by enrolling in Reich *Arbeitsdienst,* the Reich's Labor Service. These young people would be "unselfishly occupied" by repairing roads, building and repairing airstrips, con-structing fortifications along our borders and coasts, and engaging in various agricultural works for the Powerful German Nation. While it was mandatory for Poles, it was strictly a volunteer service for Germans. As Grandpapa so succinctly put it, we were now forced to repair everything those bastards had destroyed a month ago.

Thousands of young Poles were transferred from their homes and, presumably, taken to these labor camps. After what I witnessed in our forest, I hoped such a camp was the intended destination. Perhaps they would be given an increase in food for their labors. After all, the Germans needed laborers so starving us was not an option.

The Death Squads were no longer as secretive of their mass executions, now conducted in broad daylight and almost as sport, flaunting their power even further. Children were used as target practice as they ran down the streets while the soldiers awarded themselves points for hitting certain body parts. Their constant persecution led to a complete reign of terror. Arrests were carried out on a massive scale and we suffered through constant street roundups and shipments to Germany. At the onset of the war, over two hundred executions were held daily throughout my country. The unspoken threat was always there; if we attempted to inform others or interfere, that person or family would be next. Who could we tell? We remained on our isolated island in the middle of Europe, cut off from the world.

Even though enormous pits had been dug for burial of those exterminated or who had died from a growing typhus epidemic, many of the bodies were not collected in a timely manner. The dead and dying were littered everywhere throughout my country.

In the outskirts of almost all towns, one would see the large earthly bulges recently covered with fresh dirt. We all knew they were "mass graves," a new wartime phrase becoming too common a term. When internal gasses built up in the buried bodies, they erupted with a brownish-red liquid that oozed continuously from the mound of dirt. It flowed day and night, slowly trickling down the mounds and into the surrounding dirt. I wondered if we could ever cultivate anything other than misery in our soil.

By November, the smell of putrefaction slid through my country like a serpent, slipping under our doors and crawling into our beds in the dead of night. It seeped into our pores and embedded itself into our nasal passages so every breath brought the acrid, rotting odor of death. There was no refuge as it seeped firmly into our floorboards and walls. It took particular pleasure in glomming onto our hair. No matter how frequently we shampooed, the odor was still present in our locks.

As if the pervading odor was not enough, we found ourselves contending with those living creatures who subsist on such decay. Insects and rats had moved into our once pristine town and living quarters. We stuffed rags along our doorjambs and local merchants were unable to keep enough traps in stock. Many of us took to creating our own killing devices for the vermin using old clock springs, bits of wire, and anything we could find for a base. If windows were opened, we spent the day swatting and spraying flying pests. Thinking the last of the flies had succumbed to our outrage, we would begin our murderous rampage again when sticky maggots would creep out from their nest. No matter how much death and destruction I had seen, I was still squeamish about maggots. Just their sight brought an immediate reaction of revulsion. I often reproached myself for being weak and useless in respect to these creatures, but I did not have the stomach for those rice-like pulsating bits of pulp.

Chapter Fifteen

November 1939

THE SOVIETS

*S*talin had his own methods when it came to the obliteration of the Poles. The Nazis performed the initial invasion while he sat back and observed their progress. With a minimal amount of effort, Russia was now in control of two hundred thousand square kilometers of Eastern Poland, securely clenched in Stalin's stubby fingers. Now began the cleansing portion of his campaign. Soviets were no more fond of Poles than Germans and they were in complete accord with their elimination. A pestilence-free Poland should be easy to achieve.

Although the Soviets were not known for such obsessive efficiency like their German counterparts, they were still just as thorough. They too began with the Polish Intelligentsia removing five hundred thousand educated and professional Poles from their homeland. To further complete their obliteration, all official institutions were closed and reopened under approved Soviet supervisors and all political parties were converted to the Communist Party.

Polish literature and language were decreed illegal and replaced by the Russian language and reading material. The Poles found themselves in the unheard of situation where half their country was ordered to speak German while the other half, only Russian. While many Poles spoke neither language, communication became exceedingly difficult and essentially dangerous if the Polish language was overheard.

All Eastern Polish media was now controlled by Moscow, with that city spewing lies and propaganda as the only news source. Religions were targeted and persecuted, believing that without spiritual guidance the chance for uprisings would be less and, as a further demoralization, the ringing of church bells was banned. Quickly and indiscriminately, all privately and state-owned property was confiscated and redistributed while national treasures found their way into Russian homes. The Polish currency of the Zloty was suddenly withdrawn without an exchange offered to the Ruble resulting in life savings lost overnight. All Polish banks were closed and savings accounts were blocked. Taxes were raised on property as well as goods sold, although businesses were mandated to sell products at prewar prices. According to the new Soviet law, all citizens of the annexed area were now eligible for Soviet citizenship. They were strongly urged to do so. Those who did not were transported to the German side of the country where their fate was promoted by the Soviets to be "extremely harsh."

The Polish expulsion by Stalin began in February 1940 with other deportation waves following in April and June of that year. The trains were packed to overflowing, no room for sitting, inadequate room for standing. Anyone who had provided service to the prewar Polish state was considered to have committed a "crime against revolution." Others were exiled because they had simply been born Polish. Over one-third of those who died in transport were children who stood a slim chance on their own in Siberia; starvation and cold claimed many. In all, over 1,200,000 Poles found themselves shipped from their homes like cargo during these four mass cleansings. They would make excellent slave labor under Stalin.

The free state of Poland had ceased to be recognized upon the invasion. Since neither Russia nor Poland had declared war upon one another, the Soviets considered all military prisoners not as POWs but rather as rebels and dissidents against the new government. As such, they were treated like common criminals. Those who were not immediately shipped to Gulags were executed by firing squads beginning with more than 250,000 military personnel.

An intrinsic part of the Soviet administration was to rule by terror. This originated with the NKVD, the Soviet Secret Police. Through their own long-tested propaganda techniques, past ethnic tensions were exploited to their maximum by inciting and encouraging aggression against the long-hated Poles. The ethnic Russians living in the territory were persuaded to "rectify the wrongs they had suffered during the twenty-year Polish rule." Since prewar Poland was painted as a capitalistic government who exploited the ethnic Russians, Soviet city officials openly incited mobs to murder, rob, and otherwise eliminate and harass their perceived persecutors. Many victims of these Soviet inspired mob killings were unidentified and their numbers never known.

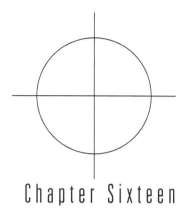

Chapter Sixteen

December 18, 1939

BOCHNIA'S PRIVILEGE

*B*ochnia's small resistance group was called *Orzel Bialy*, the White Eagle. I am sure like-minded groups were also formed throughout the country since our town's temperament was no different than any other Polish community. While many touted our small organization's first attempt a success to retrieving our freedom, I thought it a dismal failure.

The Germans quickly overtook our military bases, post offices, railways, and police stations, embedding their own people in control. It was in the latter department where members of the "Eagle" attacked and killed two German police officers including the commander of the station.

The following morning, the eighteenth of December, two of Bochnia's Polish citizens were hanged by their necks on a street lamppost in a very public demonstration. To compound our terror, fifty-four more were rounded up at random and executed on the edge of our woods. The German soldier in charge of this mass murder announced to us with pride of our town's dubious honor. Bochnia would be remembered in history where the first Nazi reprisal killings occurred on Polish soil, he said.

Immediately thereafter, truckloads of Poles were gathered and deported to labor camps. Even so, the resistance movement in Bochnia continued their efforts and remained active in the outskirts of our town. It was rumored they hid deep within the salt mines. As I said, some considered this a successful deed. Two Germans dead, fifty-six murdered Poles, and hundreds of us whisked away. If this was success, what was the definition of failure?

Chapter Seventeen

January 1940

THE VOICE

*W*e were unsure if and when our business would be confiscated but for now, we had to earn an income even if it was only half of each day. We were fortunate to have a business at all. Most of the Polish- and all of the Jewish-owned business had been supplanted with transferred Germans. Much of our business came from German soldiers and the tension in the air was thick when they were in the shop. The place would empty immediately of other customers once they walked in. After neutralizing each town, the bulk of Nazi soldiers would move on, leaving only enough staff to ensure we abided by their rules.

One day, Buscha was at the counter and I was in the back kitchen, preparing some of the side dishes for display. I heard the front doorbell tinkle, indicating a customer had entered. All was quiet until I heard Buscha suddenly raise her voice in Polish and the would-be customer was answering in equally angry German. I crept just inside the adjoining doorway where I could better hear their conversation, ready to step in and quell any situation.

"Give me my money!" Buscha was saying. The two of them were playing tug-of-war with a wrapped sausage. "I will release the sausage but I demand my money!"

"You Poles need to learn who's in charge now," replied the soldier. "You people are here to do our bidding. Slaves do not receive payment!"

I was just about to step in when I heard the tinkle from the front door again. "What is the trouble here, Private?" asked what I took to be an officer, speaking in German. The voice was smooth and seductive, reminiscent of a mahogany-paneled room and the scent of warm brandy lingering in the air. I had never heard such a sensual voice before, one filled with such an intoxicating timbre.

"This Pole," said the soldier in disdain, "will not release the *wurst* that I have purchased."

At that point, I felt it necessary to intrude in order to illuminate the officer. He is SS, I thought in horror as I saw the black uniform. Still I plodded on.

"*Mein Herr*," I started in German. "That is not the truth. This soldier refuses to pay my grandmother for the sausage he is trying to pull from her hand. He said he needn't pay slaves yet you are only paying half its worth already," I voiced more defiantly than I probably should have. I looked up into the face of a German major with the brightest blue eyes I had ever seen, tall and elegant in his tailor-made black uniform. He had a slight ruddy complexion as if he had been outdoors recently and his nose looked as though it had been broken at one time. Still, for a German he was extremely handsome.

"Is this true, Private?"

The private lifted his head belligerently and answered, "*Ja wohl, Herr* Major, but we are the master race here. Why must I pay her for what should be ours? She is only a Pole after all," he finished. I thought that this private either brave or stupid; he was only army and should know better than to speak to an SS officer in such a manner. I settled upon stupid.

"You are quite right. She is only a Pole. However, if this establishment does not have the funds to purchase more meat and make more sausage, there is the likelihood you will not have your precious *wurst*. Now pay the woman what you owe and leave," which the private promptly did but not before uttering to Buscha, "This is not over yet, old crone."

I looked at the major in some surprise. I had never expected him to come to our defense, although I supposed he did it for the logical reasons he gave.

"Your German is excellent," he said to me. "I apologize for that man, Fraulein. I doubt he will bother you again. Do not look so surprised—we are not all brutes," he said with a smile and for the first time I noticed his extraordinarily deep dimples; I had been so mesmerized with his voice. With a slight bow to my grandmother, and an *"Aufwiedersehen"* to me, he left our shop.

Perhaps you are not all brutes, I thought, but you are still all Germans. And the SS is only one notch above Gestapo in my book. In the future, I must remember not to let my anger or defiance show. Perhaps the next major would indeed be a brute. But that voice—I could wrap myself in it forever.

Chapter Eighteen

February 1940

THE PILLAGE OF POLAND

*B*y the end of 1939, thousands of Poles had been forced from their homes, which were now occupied by Germans who yearned for Lebensraum. When providing space in towns for the displaced Polish Jews, thousands more non-Jews were sent to outlying areas of Poland. Sequestered living quarters were designated for the Jews, with many families crammed into a home that had previously housed one Polish family. It was not unlike shuffling a deck of cards; we never knew where we would end up. In the Soviet-owned portion of Poland, it was easier to ship both Poles and Jews to Siberia and forget about them.

Christmas and the New Year came and went without much notice on anyone's part. Since the Nazis frowned upon too many of us gathering in one place, most families had a small meal from tins within the confines of their own homes, those that still had homes.

By February 1940, all ethnic Germans were being relocated to the General Government section of Poland. The Poles were evicted to the work camps springing up seemingly overnight, or to remote areas of the country. It was abundantly clear that we were to become a second

Germany with Poles reduced to serfs in our own land. Eventually realizing this continued relocation was cumbersome, Poles were shipped directly to Germany as slave labor.

Unknown to us at the time, Himmler had conducted a meeting with the *Kommandants* of the labor camps, clearly stating the Reich's hatred and designs for us. "All skilled workers of Polish background are to be used in our war industry," he began. "Afterward, Poles will disappear from the world...Every German's time is coming. That is why it is necessary for the great German people to see their main task in the destruction of all Poles."

An alarming protocol was installed for children under twelve years old resembling the Master Race. Mothers were forced to walk as far as 2 km with their chosen offspring where the child would be torn from the screaming mother's arms and placed in a railway carriage. They would be reconditioned by German families who would raise them as their own. Re-Germanization they called it. The children would never see their birth parents again. Believing the world must be made aware of this benevolent act of the Nazis toward otherwise useless Polish children, Prussian script announcing "Polish children taken to be fed in the Reich" was posted above each rail car. Over two hundred thousand children were adopted by loyal German families over the next few years to further the cause for the Fatherland.

My mother hovered over me continually after hearing of this development even though I was much older than twelve. My coloring was a great concern to her and she was convinced I would be snatched from the street. To keep her happy, I wore a kerchief over my hair and kept my blue eyes downcast; it was the best I could do.

Naturally, Filip had been in our home when Mama voiced her concern of my inevitable kidnapping.

"Ha Ha Ha! Weegie's going to Germany, Weegie's going to Germany!" he said laughingly. "You'll have to learn how to do this," and he began goose-stepping around the sitting room, "Heil Hitler-ing" in circles.

"Stop it at once!" cried my mother. She was close to tears by now.

I stood up and walked over to Filip. "You may be slightly taller than I am now, Filip," I said in what I hoped was a menacing tone, "but my fist can still find your nose." I balled up my hand and shook it in front of his face. He backed away but I could tell he was furious I had brought up that long ago loss of his dignity.

My possible Re-Germanization was the least of our problems. By now, rationing of goods and the economic pillage of our country was in full force. Public and private property had been confiscated, personal belongings had been absconded, and any luxuries like furs and jewelry were probably adorning the necks and shoulders of fat *Fraus* in German towns. Now they meant to remove our staples of life.

Each registered person was issued rationing cards for general foods such as meats, fats like butter or oil, bread, and sugar. The cards were printed on durable paper and contained small tabs or in German, *Marken*. Everything was divided into subdivisions and their values by weight. Butter, for example, ranged in 5g to 100g Marken. Every purchase of a rationed good required the appropriate tab and money to be exchanged for the food. Restaurant menus indicated the number of coupons needed and a waiter would cut out the required tabs to equal the meal. This many tabs are needed for soup, another for meat and so on. Vegetables and locally grown fruit were not rationed since they would spoil if not eaten quickly. Many people took to establishing a vegetable garden in any soil they had.

As shopkeepers, our difficulty was twofold. In the evenings, we would spend time affixing the daily collected tabs onto large sheets of a prepared document. These were submitted to the proper authorities at designated times to be carefully double-checked. In order for us to replenish anything we sold it was mandatory to verify we were selling only to customers within the rationing system.

Coupon books were issued every two months. However, owning such a booklet did not guarantee the acquisition of any indicated item. If a desired item was not available, it could not be purchased. Additionally, unscrupulous merchants were known to alter the item sold. It was not unheard of to hand over a coupon for flour only to discover it had been mixed with sawdust.

Many Poles began raising rabbits for food, not having the money to purchase meat and butchers unable to order enough to go around. Rare foods were often more difficult to come by, with items like coffee becoming nonexistent. We developed some creative ideas to concoct substitutes for our coffee. The most common was a mixture of roasted and ground barley seeds or acorns. Yeast could be found, although it was difficult to obtain enough to make daily bread. Tobacco would become another limited luxury once the Royal Navy blockade was launched. Rubber for anything other than military use was a thing of the past, forcing us to replace things like bicycle tires with those made of cork.

Potatoes were still easy to come by; most people had no difficulty growing those oblong tubers, which developed as well as my childhood carrots. Women became very creative with them, disguising them in different evening meals. One such recipe for fried sausages was popular:

Mock Fried Sausages

White cabbage
1 pound of boiled potatoes
1 cup breadcrumbs

Salt, pepper, caraway seeds
Soft boil the cabbage and put through a mincer together with the potatoes.
Add spices, mix well, and roll into small sausage shapes. Fry in a bit of fat and serve.

Initially, few food restrictions were placed upon the German people. The popularity of the Nazi party was partly due to the prosperity the Germans enjoyed. Hitler could not afford to lose public respect or faith in his quest, although he was eventually forced to ration certain products to ensure the strength of the military.

Germany was secure in producing nearly 80 percent of her food with few imports. This meant an enormous amount of labor used for food production, and once the war began, much of this labor force was shifted to military service. Overcoming the lack of able-bodied men increased the importation of slave workers. Over two million non-Jewish Poles were carried by train to the Fatherland for grueling workdays. That is, if they survived the journey.

Germans who were involved in heavy industry for the war effort were given extra rations and a sufficient income. The pay for the transported Poles and other forced laborers was half what their German counterparts received and only if the Poles worked hard enough. Their hours were longer and holidays or time off was unheard of. Also, 15 percent of their gross wages were deducted for taxes, social insurance, dues, and contributions to the *Deutsches Arbeitsfront*, the Nazi employment union, though they were prohibited from receiving benefits. If the production of a forced laborer fell 60 percent below the normal German production, ration cards were withdrawn. If the output was 68 percent above the Germans,' they received 113 percent of the normal labor camp ration. If the worker produced 80 percent above the average German output, he received half the German ration. When one man died, another followed on the next train.

Naturally, a distinction was drawn as to how many coupons each nationality would receive. The amounts were further classified as to sex and age with special ration cards issued for children under the age of one. Ethnic Germans in Poland were allowed rations totaling twenty-six hundred calories per day; Poles received six hundred and Jews three hundred calories. The planned hierarchy began with the Germans, then Belgium, Czechoslovakia, France, Luxembourg, the Netherlands, Norway, the incorporated area of Poland, down to the General Government of Poland, and the Jewish population of Poland.

Food rationing was severe beyond belief. In many cities, the amount allotted represented only 20 percent to 30 percent of our daily needs. When one considered the tampered food we received, the percentage was probably less. Mothers would neglect themselves, giving their rations to their children. Malnourishment was something we continually fought against and bodies of those who starved littered every street in every town. Animals too, until someone dragged them off for that night's evening meal. Housewives would stand in line for hours waiting to use their coupon on one loaf of bread, only to be told the last loaf had just been sold. People scrounging trash bins and streets for anything edible was such a common sight, we were almost immune to it. Many of us began to trade anything of value for food.

When winter reached our country, we faced the additional challenge of surviving the cold. Food was difficult enough to afford, firewood added another burden to our wallets. Freezing to death was a real possibility so families began dismantling furniture in their homes. Everything from simple chairs to valuable family antiques went up in flames. Buscha was adamant about safeguarding her dressing table but everything else was slowly reduced to ashes. We had taken to living, sleeping and eating in the single room we heated, conserving wood. As the war dragged on, few things of any value were left with which to trade, contributing to our country's starvation.

This was one reason the black market business was so successful in our country. The other reason was a familiar and sinister one—greed. The cost of necessities through this illegal business was outrageously high and few had the money to purchase goods, but we desperately needed the nutrients, clothing, coal, or medicine they sold. Bartering often took place with a family treasure traded for a sack of grain or flour.

Sometimes it was a simple one-man operation with a farmer smuggling in freshly grown fruit or vegetables for sale. Other times, the undertaking was on a much larger scale and represented big business, generating enough profit to pay local Nazis to look the other way. If caught, the penalty could range from simply handing the goods to the arresting soldier to being shot on the spot; occasionally it was both.

If the goods for sale had been stolen, the prices might be less than those smuggled in. After all, the seller had no monetary investment in their acquisition and made a profit at whatever the final selling price was. One was never sure of the product's quality, making it risky to purchase medicines or food.

Despite the threat of punishment, the soldiers were known to utilize the black market services quite frequently to obtain luxuries like tobacco and real coffee. For a high enough price, almost anything could be had.

Purchasing meat for the butcher shop was becoming more difficult. We affixed the miniscule tabs on the tally sheets for everything we sold each day. It was difficult to refuse a neighbor or friend without a coupon and Papa would often turn a blind eye and hand the poor soul enough to feed the children that night. He could have been shot for such an action but that never stopped him. "We have to help each other, no matter what the cost," he would say. "We cannot let the Nazis have our country through starvation." Politically induced famine was the least expensive method the Nazis had found to eliminate us. No bullets or military action was needed, simply withhold food and water.

The supply of meat was becoming scarce, often not enough to order for the shop. If we could not acquire a beef shank, we began to think creatively, ordering enough meat trimmings to crank out our special wursts only. By increasing our garden size at home, we sold vegetable stews and made unleavened bread when we could not purchase yeast. Buscha made dishes like the mock fried sausages and even created a mock goose made with potatoes, apples, cheese, and spices. It was tasty but I asked her why she called it "goose." Marketing, she said. If it sounds more appetizing, it will sell better.

Military rations at this time had nothing in common with our struggle for food. Divisions of the Nazi army usually carried at least a ten-day ration for each man. Well, why should they not? After all, the soldiers were confiscating the food we produced and sending it to Germany by the tons in rail cars.

The allotted amounts for the field or fighting army soldier were increased by several ounces compared to civilians. Their ideal daily intake was 1.5 pounds of bread, a half ounce salt, 5 ounces meat, 2 ounces each of fats, fruits and vegetables, and 1.5 ounces of sugar or milk. Additionally, each man should receive 11 ounces of potatoes, and either 7 cigarettes or a half ounce of coffee per day. Every member of the regular and replacement army was given special treats for Christmas; 125 grams peppermints or some other similar candy, 125 grams sweet biscuits/cookies, 100 grams chocolate, 3 apples and ¾ liter of wine.

All this was transported by the rolling kitchen division; carts and wagons containing portable ovens and stoves. If game was caught during the day, hearty stews could be made for the evening meal. The army rations often contained vast amounts of cheese, onions, canned fruit, and several types of sausages. It was more food than we would see in six months. Additionally, each man carried emergency rations consumed only at the order of the company commander. Hitler believed his army marched on its stomach.

Chapter Nineteen

March 5, 1940

KATYN, RUSSIA

*L*ieutenant Rudolf Kozenski was tired. He was cold and hungry as well. His uniform had been new issue nine months ago but the shoes had never really been broken in and his feet hurt tremendously. Overall, he was in a miserable state. Under normal circumstances, he would openly and loudly complain about his unfortunate situation. He may have been a malcontent, but he did not consider himself a stupid man. Unlucky, perhaps, but not stupid. For this reason, he kept his grumbling to himself. It was safer.

The lieutenant, along with thousands of other captured Polish soldiers and civilians, had been "interviewed" at great lengths in one of those unpronounceable POW camps in Russia. The enlisted men had been sent home while the officers were forced to remain. Rudolf was a cartographer, certainly not a professional officer, and the commission bestowed upon him was more of an honor. He cursed the combined honor and bad luck, convincing himself if he had been a private he would be home by now. Adding insult to injury, tomorrow, April 19, was his birthday.

It had been an odd group of men sharing the Gulag with the lieutenant. He had expected officers, of course, and there were certainly enough of those. High-ranking officers at that. Colonels would share coffee with majors, captains with privates. Pilots enjoyed card games with naval captains. He had even seen a general or two, and rumor had it that an actual admiral was mingled in with the lot of them.

Yes, the officers he could understand but the civilians? Chaplains, of course, were part of the military but they were priests, for God's sake. Why hadn't they been sent home with the enlisted men? Since his capture in November, he had shared meals with university professors, physicians, and lawyers. He had exchanged Merry Christmas greetings with city officials and writers, and Happy New Year 1940 with journalists and refugees. His commanding officer had told him that an honest-to-God prince was among them. If any captive had more painful feet than himself, thought the lieutenant, it would be one of the confined wealthy landowners. The snow and slush had made a mockery of their expensive leather shoes. At least his own feet were dry, thought Rudolf ruefully.

The men had been told this journey was a deportation to another camp. Food, bath, and bed would be at the ready for them and they could wait out the war in some solace, seeing their respective families soon. They had been traveling for hours in cell-like compartments aboard the cold train, the clickety-clack, clickety-clack and the jostling back and forth about to drive him mad. Occasionally, the scent of pine trees wafted in through the floor boards intermingled with the belching smoke from the engine.

Many of his compatriots had been keeping their spirits up by pulling out dog-eared photos of loved ones to share with others. One man had six children, a good Catholic he said, and his friend remarked, "Thank God they look like their mother!" Several were passing around cigarettes, leaning their heads back, and thinking about their next home cooked meal while the clickety-clack kept time with their thoughts.

One man wondered if they were still in Russia. "This is sure one Goddamn big country. I thought we'd be in America by now!" The laughter was polite, at best.

The two "real" officers in the corner had been deep in conversation and Kozenski wondered again what the hell he was doing here. He drew maps, for Christ's sake! Stretching out his foot, the blister on his heel chose that moment to burst open and Rudolf's attention turned to the additional pain in his foot.

Upon arrival at their final destination, each carriage was quickly unloaded and divided into two smaller groups. After so many hours confined in only slight illumination, the morning sunlight caused the men to squint. They had but a moment to regain their breath and bearings, catching a glimpse of road signs that positioned them somewhere in the vicinity of Smolensk and the Katyn forest. Well-armed Red Army soldiers were on display. The lieutenant's name was ticked off an official-looking file and he found himself with a handful of other Poles inside what was commonly called a Black Maria, like a police transport or an American paddy wagon. They could no longer ignore what they had long suspected; the Soviet's promises had been empty ones.

The fragrance of pine and nettles was more noticeable now, and they bounced over tree roots, listening to the sounds of distant machinery. They traveled caravan-style, dozens of the conveyances heading into the nearby forest. One man motioned out the window, a crack really; duplicate Black Marias traveling the reverse route maneuvered by on the adjacent trail. No one shared photos, cigarettes, or conversations any longer. Rudolf joined in with the Lord's Prayer someone had begun.

They had stopped now, the grinding of heavy machinery all around, smoke thick and black. The sound of faint pops reinforced their suspected plight. Odors of gasoline and heavy oil obliterated the forest scents. Even the birds were silent in the midst of so much human activity. Someone jerked open the rear door and roughly pulled out one of the Poles. Ropes dangled in the Russians' hands, and blood adhered to their tunics, while other Soviets stood by with weapons and dogs. Each time the door opened, the stench of decay progressively assailed Kozenski's nostrils.

The first man taken resisted and tried to scramble back into the car before he was up-righted and the door slammed shut. Other car doors opened and slammed closed as they were presumably unloaded one by one. The major was next. With a few kind words to his fellow captives and outwardly unafraid, he walked out on his own accord, a credit to his rank. His praying voice grew fainter before the anticipated shot echoed among the trees.

Lieutenant Kozenski's time had come. The Soviets' timing was precise and swift and yet the lieutenant felt as if he were moving in slow motion.

Even his senses seemed heightened. The Russians' breath smelled stale and oniony as Rudolf was dragged from the car. He could feel the soft leather of their gloves as they held him and began their bindings. The rough hemp-made rope still smelled green as he was trussed up with a series of loops like a roast chicken. His hands were brought up to shoulder blade level where they were tightly bound, the knot duplicated with the additional length of cord around his neck. The soldiers were well practiced; the constraints completed in a matter of seconds would cause strangulation to the bound man with the least amount of movement.

He watched other officers and resisting civilians being frog-marched toward a long deep pit. Some men were hooded, while others had rags in their mouths. With legs feeling like jelly, he was forced to join his fellow victims standing alongside the open ground. Below him, hundreds of bodies were laid out in rows, one upon the other, ten to twelve corpses high and five across. Red Army soldiers were casually strolling among the dead in the open jaw of Mother Earth occasionally stabbing one with his bayonet, ensuring his demise. Red-brown liquid was congealing on the bodies at the base of their heads and the smell of decay hanging over the grave was so overpowering that Rudolf thought to vomit.

He was determined to uphold the principles his uniform stood for and began to pray loudly when the back of his hair was grabbed and sawdust was thrust into his mouth. Standing as tall and as proudly as he could, Lieutenant Rudolf Kozenski's last thought was against his character and wholly altruistic; "God bless Poland."

He heard the click of the gun pointed at the base of his skull and heard the shot, but felt nothing as he fell to lay with his friends and fellow officers. He had been one of the lucky ones that day; the bullet allotted for his head had killed him instantly. The man next to him had not died when he fell and the Russians were forced to finish him off with a bayonet, stabbing again and again until death overtook the man. Throughout the day, others joined their fallen countrymen and friends, line by line, row by row, into the hole as if the Russians were planting bulbs for the spring.

These brave men would never know of the short document prepared just a month earlier that had brought about their murders. The official order was dated March 5, 1940, and had instructed Russian POW camp commanders to "...decide the cases without summoning the prisoners and without presenting charges. The sentence: to be shot." With a few signatures, thousands were sentenced to death.

Throughout three other Russian POW camps, Poles were shot in a felt-padded room on a daily basis for three months, one prearranged shot to the back of the head. A brief respite occurred to celebrate May Day before executions were renewed on May 2. With assembly-like precision, the Poles were murdered, delivered to transport trucks, and trekked over the Russian countryside to that fateful clearing in the forest. Day after day, month after month, the trucks rolled through towns and villages, carrying their bloody cargo. Over one-half of all Polish officers on staff and over six thousand influential civilians had been senselessly massacred. In all, over twenty-two thousand Poles had been slaughtered and buried in the Katyn area, their families never notified.

The graves were filled in by bulldozers, patted down, and left to the elements. The Russian soldiers returned to their various posts and the war went on. A carpet of forest flowers eventually covered the ground and its silent residents, the only tribute or headstone they received for their sacrifice.

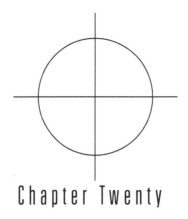

Chapter Twenty

May 1, 1940

MAY DAY IN BOCHNIA

*T*he annual May Day carnival held special memories for me with games, food, and most of the townsfolk in attendance. Polka music would play in the large tents while we danced and chatted with friends, enjoying our meals and sweets. The entire day culminated in the traditional May Pole Dance in the center of the celebration. Ribbons of various bright colors had been attached to the top of an incredibly tall pole, each ribbon hanging down to touch the ground. Dancers in traditional Polish clothing would each grab a ribbon and begin to skip around the pole, over and under each other, until the pole was plaited with the brightly colored streamers. It was a day filled with simple activities but it was one of my favorite holidays.

This May Day of 1940 resembled nothing of my childhood memories.

The day began nicely enough with lovely weather and an air of excitement in the town. We were pleased when an official decision from the German powers-that-be permitted the celebration providing there were no transgressions committed. Rudeness, real or imagined, toward any member of the Wehrmacht would not be tolerated. The soldiers were already roaming the streets disbursing small groups of gathering Poles. Our red and white national flag was torn down and replaced with one bearing a swastika.

Rather than spend the money on constructing an outdoor booth, Papa and Grandpapa would be selling food directly from our store. Signs proudly announced we were open for business and were placed strategically around the party area while a sandwich board describing our delectables was situated outside our shop.

Mama and I stayed in the shop most of the day, serving the hungry and sometimes tipsy revelers. We had an occasional German soldier as a customer but for the most part they did not bother us. When we finally had a lull in business, I was able to venture out to the other open shops and booths, greeting friends and family. The general mood of the celebrants was tense this year. The reason was clear; the soldiers were noisy, generally unruly and extremely visible. I kept my head down and tried to ignore them.

Music began signaling the Pole Dance and I strolled over to the makeshift stage to watch the nimble feet do their magic. Colorful skirts and lacy petticoats were swirling around legs while feet were flying as dancers began skipping and prancing around the giant pole. With each step they took, another set of bright colors began winding themselves into the familiar patterns high upon the pilaster. I could sense the people around me begin to relax, feeling the beat of a Polish Polka in their souls. Some were clapping or tapping their feet while others were dancing within the crowd. All was as it should be and I smiled.

Unexpectedly disrupting this happy scene was the sound of screams from behind us. Turning, I saw a young girl flee from a group of men. At first, I thought the men had been harassing her but then I noticed their intent on something within the middle of their mob. A flash of blue-gray fabric caught my eye through the spaces of the angry men. Legs began swinging and kicking, arms were raised and lowered with strength and force. The blue-gray cloth seemed to slip from someone's hands and fall upon the ground. As the mob dispersed and fled, I saw the material clothed a Nazi soldier, now in a twisted and bloody heap. He's dead, I thought, the German soldier is dead and Poles killed him. A quick sideways glance snapped me into movement as I saw oncoming soldiers and screaming people flee.

I ran for all I was worth until I finally made it to the back alley of the butcher shop. Bursting through the rear door I realized how I must look to my family—panting, sweating, wild eyes, barely able to speak. With their eyes upon me I finally gasped, "He's dead! A German soldier...is dead. Poles...they killed him!"

Papa jumped into action. "Quickly, Marta, hide in the back room. Put on an apron. Start chopping something. Birdie, Father—behind the counter. Look natural and just go about your business. The rest of you come and get your food, calmly. Remember, we have nothing to fear, we have been here this whole time." I had not even noticed the shop's customers, some of whom followed Papa's advice while others simply ran out the door.

I seemed to hear that girl screaming again and thought it just my imagination until I looked at Mama; she heard it too. A loud baritone voice followed, yelling something unintelligible in German. Our storefront window provided the only view to the events taking place. We watched with a perverse curiosity to the unfolding scene through our pane of glass.

A man suddenly entered the macabre diorama at a mad dash and kept moving out of sight, the fading sound of slapping shoes upon the cobbled road following him. Soon, other rushing citizens joined the first, sliding in and out of our view. One unlucky person was not quick enough; a disembodied black-garbed arm reached into this panorama, grabbing the man by his hair, dragging him backward.

The spectacle became our reality when an SS officer strode past the glass and over our threshold. He blocked the light from outdoors with his enormous height and bulk as he continued to stand in the narrow doorway observing us. I felt like the mouse to his cat as he decided which of us looked tasty enough for his meal.

Making his decision, he pointed to my father and grandfather and said, *"Du. Und du. Kompt!"* telling them to come with him.

Against my father's attempt to hold me back, I approached the officer and said politely in Deutsch, *"Was ist los, mein Herr?* What is wrong? We have done nothing, only provided food for anyone hungry. Perhaps you would like to sample our freshly made wurst?" I proffered a plateful of samples toward him.

"I will tell you what is wrong, Fraulein. There has been a deliberate murder of one of my men by you Polish pigs. You people must be taught a lesson and some respect."

I reiterated that we had been in the store all day, only cooking and serving. There was a momentary thawing of ice in his eyes; he was going to leave the store with only a warning, I thought. It was unfortunate that another soldier walked into the shop at this point. My eyes widened as I recognized the private who had the altercation with Buscha over the sausage. I could tell by the gleam in his eyes that I had lost the battle.

"Mein Herr, I know this family. They are nothing but trouble who blatantly disregard the German uniform. It would be best to be rid of them."

"*Ja, sehr gut*! Very good. Bring them!"

I started to beg now, Mama gripping my arm. Papa smiled at me and said, "Do not worry, daughter. We will be right back. It is just a misunderstanding. It will be fine, do not worry,"

Mama and I followed at a safe distance, hoping, praying that Papa was right. Our two men were thrust into a waiting group of other Polish men. The large officer spoke in German and a private next to him translated his speech into Polish. Understanding both languages, I heard their fates twice.

"We have allowed you to hold your May Day festivities here today," he began, waiting for the translation of each phrase before continuing, "and this is how you thank us! You have murdered a soldier of the Third Rich, of the Holy German Empire, in cold blood. There will be a reprisal for such an act. There will always be reprisals. For every single German soldier killed, I am authorized to kill up to one hundred of you Poles." I gasped at this and Mama looked questionably at me before she heard the translation. I felt her begin to shake next to me. "This will not happen again," the cruel German rhetoric went on, "for if it does, I will come back to shoot one hundred more and next time it will be your children."

Throughout this oration, I had noticed the gathering soldiers were pushing and shoving the selected Poles into a straight line against a brick wall. My father looked at us and smiled, mouthing to us again and again "I love you, I love you."

I began to make a move toward him when my mother wrapped her arms around me from behind, preventing me from leaving no matter how hard I struggled. The soldiers lined up too, facing the doomed. A few of the Germans faced the crowd of mourners prepared to discourage us with their weapons should any of us try something foolish. All we could safely do was pray harder for their safety.

The officer raised his hand and I heard the multiple click-click-click of safeties being released. *"Feuer!"* As his arm dropped giving the signal to fire, the guns made popping sounds and emitted short puffs of smoke, the smell of gunpowder filling the air. My father was holding on to the arm of his own parent as the two of them fell together to the street. The crimson liquid seeped onto their clean white aprons from some unseen source, becoming darker and darker until the bibs were completely red.

I heard the girl screaming again, shrieking and wailing, so earsplitting in its intensity it seemed to echo within my head, on and on, until my mother grabbed me and turned my face into her chest, muffling that agonizing sound. Thank God, I thought, the girl has finally stopped her screams. As I smelled the fabric of my mother's dress, I realized the cries had been mine.

Mama and I fell onto the cobbled stones of the road, clasping onto one another when we were abruptly pulled to our feet and were told we must remove our dead; toss them onto the waiting death cart to be taken away. Take them away where? To one of those horrible mass graves I had seen? How could I allow my loved ones to be laid in such a nameless hole?

Feeling a slight touch upon my shoulder, I looked up into the kind eyes of Elias Fischer. "Come with me, Miss Marta, Miss Birdie. Come with me. I'll take care of your papa and grandfather." We allowed ourselves to be led into our butcher shop where we plopped down into chairs. Elias brought us cups of water, knelt down between our chairs and took our hands. "Don't worry about them, Misses, I'll find a nice place where they can both be together. I promise. They were always good to me and they cannot be dumped like garbage. I promise."

We saw him walk out and past our window to where our two men still lay. I was about to get up to lend assistance when Mama touched my hand and said Elias could handle it. If he promised something, he always did it; he would be insulted if I helped.

Instead, I closed my eyes and inhaled the fresh scent of sawdust. The aromas of our special sausage and red cabbage floated about the room. No longer would I see Papa greet me with his smile and wave as I entered, no longer would I hear the two of them engage in comical banter over cuts of meat. I would never enjoy one of their long jokes or hear Grandpapa argue with the newsmen on the wireless. Even now, I expected one of them to come out from the storeroom in their bright apron and smile at us. I opened my eyes, stinging with tears that would not fall. Thoughts tumbled in my mind like marbles in a jar. How could I ever walk in here and not see them behind the counter? How could we possibly keep running the butcher shop? Mama, Buscha, and I could never fill their shoes.

Then I remembered; oh my God—we have to tell Buscha. I turned to look at Mama and it was clear from the horror I saw on her face she had just thought of the same task before us. She took my hand and brought me out of my seat when we heard light footsteps echoing down the stairway from my grandparents' flat. It was Buscha and clearly she had been crying. I had forgotten about her large bay window; she had watched our entire loss unfold.

We stood in the middle of the floor, we three women, holding each other, unable to speak, asking ourselves why God would allow such a thing to happen to those good men. Very softly, Buscha started to pray. We joined in with her, reciting the words to the Hail Mary we had each learned as girls. I thought of the Blessed Mary losing her Son before His time too and I prayed for some of her strength. No matter what happened, we were still alive and we had to stay strong.

That evening, Elias came into the shop and asked me to come with him. I have no idea how he did it, and I never asked, but he had kept his promise. In one corner of the church cemetery was a mound of dirt, recently patted down with a crude white wooden cross at its head. On it was printed my father's name and my grandfather's with the words "They were much loved."

"I thought they would like to be buried together. I hope that's all right, Miss Marta," he said, worrying his cap in his hands.

In response, I hugged him and said softly, "Thank you, Elias. Thank you so much." With that, I knelt in the soft earth to pray, my friend joining me.

I decided then that I had a job to do. I would see to it the Resistance would learn the details of all that transpired here. Somehow, we would make the Germans pay for this. I vowed to send a telegram tomorrow. Irina would send her love.

Chapter Twenty-One

June 1940

THE HOME ARMY

*I*t took several days after sending the telegram before Max arrived. I was in the kitchen when I saw him approach the back door.

"Perfect timing, Max," I said, hugging him. "We can talk in here."

I made us a cup of weak tea and we sat at the table like two normal people having a conversation about everyday things. I am not sure what I expected; perhaps for him to have been in disguise and the two of us to quietly slip down to the canning room where our only light would be one candle. Very cloak-and-dagger stuff. I told him this and he laughed.

"You always have the craziest ideas, Marta. I am afraid it is nothing so exciting. So, now. Tell me why Irina sent her love."

I proceeded to walk him through everything that had happened to us on May Day, including the day I had first seen that horrible private. He let me talk at my own pace, interjecting a few questions here and there, holding lightly onto my hand. By the time I finished, I was emotionally exhausted. We sat there quietly for a minute, holding hands, letting it all sink in.

"Let me warm up your tea, Marta," he said as he took my cup to the stove. "I am so sorry. Your father and grandfather were wonderful men. They will be missed." He sat back down and handed me my fresh cup. "Here, drink this. The sugar will do you some good." I dutifully took a sip. Warm, sweet, and soothing. Max looked intently into my eyes. "You know this is happening all over the country, yes?" I nodded. "The question remains, why did you contact me? Is there something I can do for you and your mother?"

I set my cup down and looked hard at him. "I want them to pay. I want to do anything I can to make them all pay. Tell me what I can do and I will do it. Whatever it is. I would just as soon go out there right now and shoot any German I see rather than have someone else's father be shot down like mine was. I can shoot, you know; Papa taught me. I bet I can still outshoot you."

He grinned slightly at that last comment of mine. "Well, I do not think you are quite ready to arm yourself or blow up trains just yet," he said. "But before you decide, we must have a serious discussion about all this, Marta."

He began by explaining details of the resistance movement to me. The country had many independent organizations, he said, ranging from youth groups to older civilians. The largest number of members belonged to the *Armia Krajowa* Underground. Meaning Home Army in English, it was simply knows as the acronym AK. He went on to tell me of Jan Karski's exploits. In January 1940, the man organized courier missions from the underground to the Polish government in Paris. Personally making several secret and dangerous trips between France, Britain, and Poland, he was arrested by the Gestapo during one mission. They tortured him severely, finally transporting him to a hospital when he was of no further use. There he was smuggled out by underground members. After rehabilitation, he returned to duty in the Information and Propaganda Bureau of the Home Army headquarters.

"This is not playacting or something you can join and then leave; once you are in, you are in for the long haul. This is considered high treason by the Germans and if you are caught, you will be killed. But not before they take measures to persuade you to tell them what you know about the organization. In a woman's case, they would probably rape her first. Then they will proceed to more painful measures."

"Max, are you telling me this to frighten me?"

"No, I am telling you this so you will know exactly what you could face should you agree to help. Even some of the resistance members may be traitors. Someone who thinks about his own skin first. You can only trust me or someone I directly connect you with, no one else. I want you to know all the dangers and be prepared if you agree."

I sat and thought about this for a moment while he waited patiently. At last I said, "OK. Tell me what you want me to do. If I can't blow things up it does not sound like I shall have any fun at all," I said with a grin.

He smiled back at me and brought out a small packet from inside his coat. "We have people installed in various post offices. Now, all mail sent by a Pole is opened and read, any incriminating information is copied down by the German employees, then the letter is destroyed. The writer of the letter is often tracked down, taken away, or shot—sometimes the whole family is shot. This is one reason why we cannot get any information to the outside world. Even telegraph offices are censored for outgoing and incoming telegrams.

"On the other hand, mail postmarked to Germany with a soldier's return address usually goes straight through. I suppose the Germans feel their own people will not betray them. I imagine that will change someday too, but for now, those are opened if the address is unclear or for some other minor reason, but not very often. Anyway, our people open those letters and quickly photograph them with miniature cameras. Then the letter is resealed and sent on its way. The film is developed and those pictures are what I have here." He spread them all out on the table for me to look at. "What we need from you is their translation into Polish and English. We'll set up a timetable between the two of us, then meet to exchange the information."

"How could you accomplish this in such a short amount of time? And who are the other people?"

"I cannot tell you that, Marta," he said. I promptly pouted at his refusal to include me, brat that I was. He chuckled and flicked my out-turned bottom lip with his index finger and said, "It's not that I will not tell you, Marta, but I do not know who they are. It is much safer that way for everyone. The more we know about each other, the more danger involved. Everyone has their own connection or two, but none of us knows who all the connections are. We do not even use our real names."

Well, when he explained it like that, it made perfect sense. "Can you at least tell me why I would be doing all this?" and I waved my hands above the table encompassing all the photos. (The implication of his coming prepared with these letters hoping for my assistance was not lost upon me.)

"Yes, that I can tell you. Remember Stefan Rowecki? Either he or Jan Karski will travel to England and America to talk some sense into them and let their officials know of our terror. For that, they need information on all events with concrete proof. They are hoping these letters might offer some or at least a start."

We sat and worked out the details of my resistance effort. I thought it would probably take a couple of weeks to get the request accomplished; some of the handwriting was terribly difficult to read. We would meet at a different place each time and if I needed anything in between visits, I should send another telegram and mention Irina in some context. Finding a safe place to keep the bundle was a bit difficult but we settled upon a loose brick surrounding the cistern.

With a quick hug, he was out the back door and out of sight before I knew it. Now I faced the task of telling Mama what I had agreed to.

She arrived at nearly sunset, peddling steadily on her bicycle. She knew as soon as she saw me that something was up.

"What is it, Marta? You have that look about you."

"Mama, I think you should sit down. I have something important to tell you."

I had expected her to burst into tears or stand up and loudly refuse to let me do such a crazy thing but instead she just sat there with her hands in her lap.

After heaving a long sigh, she said to me, "I had been expecting this from you. Your father was insistent too." I was stunned. Did she intimate that Papa had been with the Polish underground? I looked at her questioningly and she answered my unspoken query with a sad smile. "Yes, your father had been a part of it for some time. I understand why you are doing this but I do not have to like it," she finished with a smile and a kiss.

I realized how much sense it all made. That phone call from Max while he was at Danzig, those evenings when Papa would leave for hours at a time. What a little fool I was. I had seen my father only as Papa and not as the patriot he was. I was following in some wonderful footsteps.

Chapter Twenty-Two

June 1940

ERADICATION OF ALL THINGS POLISH

*S*ince the Germans had us firmly in their grip, it was decided that all things Polish would be renamed to reflect the new ownership. All towns and cities, streets within each town and city, office buildings, railroad stations: in short, anything that could be renamed was. It seemed petty and particularly spiteful to obliterate our centuries' old landmarks.

All revisions were written in extensive ledgers and memos made available to all members of the Wehrmacht. Unfortunately, we did not have that luxury. It was strictly through trial and error we were able to understand our new bearings. We were essentially lost within our own country, which, I felt sure, was intentional. It was a common sight to see men climbing ladders and attaching new street names to signposts. I constantly marveled at how efficient these people were and wondered just how long this had been planned.

My town of Bochnia was now engraved upon some Nazi officer's map as *Salzberg*, meaning Salt Mountain. Because of our salt mines, it made obvious sense. Happily, some of the names had not been drastically changed. Darz was now known as the town of Daarz and our wonderful city of Krakow was now Krakau. Other towns were not so lucky. The Polish town of Bagienice, mostly a farming community, was now Althofen, meaning Old Yard or Farm. Several newly tagged locations had the misfortune of sounding like a tongue teaser when the names were strung together: Brosen, Briesen, Bresin, and Bresen.

Outside of Krakau, one rather substantial town was fortunate its name had not been completely butchered with the German version. The population of ten thousand people lived in the thriving five-hundred-year-old Polish and Jewish culture. Many ethnic Germans had called it home as well. It was a very quaint town where most wage earners were artisans or merchants. We Poles had always called it Oswiecim. The Germans renamed it Auschwitz.

Part Three

THE CAMP
June 1940 to December 1941

We shall solve this problem, and afterward Warsaw as the capital and the pool of Intelligentsia of that nation will be destroyed.
Heinrich Himmler August 1944

Chapter One

June 22, 1940

MARTA'S JOURNEY

*I*t was impossible to ignore the blaring headlines and the noise from the Germans' speaker trucks. The reports were everywhere and one would have to be more of an ostrich than I not to have heard the news. "France Falls," shouted the voices from inside the vehicles, "Hitler enters Paris," screamed the giant caption in the German press. Details of the glorious Reich's victory were not spared. Hitler had generously given Finland to Stalin with Denmark, Norway, Belgium, Holland, and France all under the Nazi flag, giving further glory to the Third Reich. Josef Goebbels took joy in reporting how many were killed and injured from the other side but I noticed German casualties were not mentioned. It would not be prudent to advertise any Nazi fallibility. They must continue the pretext at all times; Hitler and Germany were indestructible.

Many of us still hoped and prayed for the Americans to enter this annihilation of European countries but they remained exasperatingly unmoved. Did they really believe America could remain untouched by this evil indefinitely? England was probably all that remained between democracy and Americans learning to speak Deutsch.

Max informed me that our exiled government officials were now in London where they positioned themselves to direct the Polish resistance movements. Also, and Max was especially proud of this, after the fall of Poland, thousands of our military men had made their way to France and Norway where they had their chance to fight the Nazis once again. Our fighter pilots numbered over one hundred thirty-three, won fifty-five victories, and lost only fifteen pilots. Over one hundred thousand Poles had fought for European freedom in this latest campaign.

I also learned from my friend that the British had deserted the French after the fall of Dunkirk. (Apparently, this was a pivotal battle for the occupation of France). The president of France claimed the British had "let them down." Irony at its height. I had no sympathy for the French. Now they understood exactly how it felt when betrayed by an Ally.

From France, Polish military personnel also found passage to England where they formed armored divisions, a rifle brigade, a parachute brigade, and trained pilots all at the ready. I could tell when he spoke of this, Max still yearned to be one of those pilots, ready to get into it with the Germans. I patted his hand and for once did not ask how he came to learn of all this detailed information, only told him he was doing more good here than if he had taken his chances in the sky.

Terrified citizens were attempting to flee by the thousands but by now, Germany controlled the surrounding countries of would-be emigrants. England would no longer accept Europe's doomed and it was too risky to attempt travel to America. It was pandemonium.

While the truck speakers continued to blare, Mother and I partook in what was now our customary bits of bread and one shared egg. After washing our few remaining plates, my mother announced she would be going into town.

"There's not much to do in the shop this morning, Mother."

"I'm not going to the shop," she replied. "I'm going to see Mrs. Feldman and her daughter. She's been very ill with cancer and Uncle Edmund mixed up a draught to give her for the pain."

I looked at her astonished. "Mother!" I cried. "You cannot be serious. Let Uncle Edmond take it to her. Do you realize what will happen if they see you there?"

I was correct to be concerned. In all of occupied Europe, ours was the only country where the penalty for assisting Jews was instant death for the Good Samaritan and possibly everyone in their household. It was not unheard of that an entire neighborhood had been slaughtered due to one person's good deed toward a Jew. Knowing this, I felt sure they would feel no compunction in making my mother suffer for her medical assistance. The Germans were determined to eradicate all of us for any reason.

"Mother, please. They will be sure to kill you or worse. She's a Jew, you mustn't help her. She has cancer, for God's sake—she is already dying. What can you do to keep her alive?"

"You are right. I am not a doctor and I cannot extend her life beyond what God wants, but I can ease her suffering. She has been a longtime friend—you played with her children—and I cannot let my fear get in the way of my humanity. Your papa was not afraid," she said pointedly.

No amount of pleading or threatening would persuade her from the dangerous notion. I could only pray that she would return safely.

Hours later, she still had not arrived home. It was dark now and I was sitting by candlelight trying to mend a torn dress that had already seen several such ministrations when I saw my young cousin, Emilia, running in the shadow of the trees toward our house. I let out the enormous sigh I had been holding in.

"Cousin Marta," she panted. "It's Aunt Birdie! They have taken her. Mama sent me to fetch you as soon as we heard."

"Slow down, Emilia. Now, tell me all that you know."

The Germans had stormed the streets once again, searching for Jews. An acquaintance of my aunt's had successfully evaded the soldiers and rushed to her home to relay the horrible event. He lived in the same building as Mrs. Feldman and knew that she, her daughter, and her small grandchildren had prepared a skinny cupboard behind the closet wall in which to hide. If they remained quiet while inside, they felt sure they would be undetected. He was hiding far below his floorboards and did not know what tipped the Germans off but loud voices in both German and Polish could be heard from their flat. He thinks my mother was trying to tell them she was not a Jew but rather a Pole. Perhaps, he said, the soldiers were accusing Mama of helping the Jews but he was not sure. Someone was sobbing then he heard men laughing, a gunshot, and then another shot rang out. The sound of women crying and something heavy being dragged down the stairs echoed in the hallway. When he finally crawled out of his hiding spot and entered the Feldman's apartment, the old woman was dead along with her two grandbabies. The only helpful clue he overheard was the word "Chrzanow." It was a town about an hour and a half west from Bochnia past Krakau where a labor camp had been opened in January.

Jews had been sent to that town since the Germans first marched into our country and Herr Himmler was intent to see it overflow with traitors. He was becoming more indiscriminate with whom that was accomplished if he sent my mother there; she was not a youthful laborer. It did not take much provocation for a soldier to rape or kill for sport, I thought. If Mama could overcome her fear of the soldiers for the sake of a friend, I could certainly do so for her.

"Emilia, can you make it home without me?" She nodded at me. "Are you sure? I have to try to save Mama. Keep in the shadows. Tell your mother where I've gone in case...well, just in case."

Nodding again, she took off and I watched to make sure she followed my instructions. She had obviously done this before; within a few seconds, she was invisible. I grabbed my kerchief and hurried out the door too, running in the opposite direction toward Leonarda Street where the Jewish settlement was.

I first tried this containment area in Bochnia, hoping they had taken her here instead; many people had been. I knew the area extended down many blocks but I was astonished as to the size of this formidable place up close. I had heard that sanitary facilities were virtually nonexistent and the electrical supply disconnected. Up close, I could believe those rumors as I saw only flickering candles. Smelling the stench of urine and excrement from behind the walls, my fear for my mother increased.

Barricades surrounded the area and there were tales of these walls becoming much more permanent. I approached what I thought was the main entrance, where two soldiers stood smoking. One was jowly with moist eyes and the other one kept licking his lips. We had all learned at the beginning of the occupation to recognize the various ranking patches on the uniforms and recognize which branch of the Wermacht they were from. I was loath to admit it, but that long-ago conversation held in the garden with Antoni had come in handy. Our well-being now depended upon us not stepping on the toes of an SS officer versus a Heer, or army, private. Even then, a sergeant in the blue-gray Luftwaffe uniform we could usually pass unscathed whereas a sergeant in the black SS uniform we carefully avoid.

"Well, well, Hans. It looks as if we missed one. Where have you been hiding, *Juden?*" said Jowly.

"She is very *schon*; a lovely morsel," the other one said. He was circling me and licking his lips as if I would soon become his snack. He touched the pleat of my cuff and ran his hand up my arm. "It's a pity she's a Jew," he said, licking his lips once again.

I suddenly remembered my kerchief. Whipping it off in what I thought to be very Greta Garbo-esque, I said dramatically in German *"Ich bin nicht Juden!* Do I look Jewish to you? Do you see a yellow star on my clothing?"

Taken aback, his hands quickly fell away from me noticing for the first time my coloring. *"Entschuldigen Sie, Fraulien.* Please, pardon me. I was not aware…"

"I'm looking for the officer in charge," I replied with more courage than I felt.

"Ja wohl. Please come this way." He was suddenly all business as I was led around the corner of a wall to stand before a tall, portly lieutenant who, I hoped, would have the resolution I sought.

He stared at me, unblinking. Turning to the Licker, asked him, "What do you mean interrupting me? Who is this?" and he motioned at me as if swatting a fly.

"Herr Leutnant, she insisted on seeing you. I thought since she's a German citizen…"

The seconds ticked off as the officer gave a withering look to the man before he turned his gaze to me. "I will deal with you later," the lieutenant said to the Licker. Secretly I thought, good; let them fight among themselves.

"Und so, Fraulein, what is so important that my good soldier would forget his orders, hmm?" He asked this but I could tell he did not really care what I replied.

I launched into the only excuse I had devised. "I'm afraid, *Herr Leutnant*, that there's been a slight misunderstanding. You see, one of the prisoners taken today is not Jewish but a Polish civilian. If she is here, I would respectfully request that she be released."

"Jewish, Polish—what does it matter? They all have to go." He squinted his left eye at me. This man was no fool and I must tread carefully. "What is so special about this one woman that you would come out here in the dead of night?"

"I'm afraid, *Herr Leutnant*, that we, the few German citizens here, have been utilizing her talents as a healer to assist us with the many illnesses running through our people." Now his right eye squinted at me. I pressed on. "She is especially good with the youth and babies, the next generation of the glorious Third Reich. The medical facilities have been so overcrowded, you see. We would all like to request from you that she be returned to us, at least until the last of us have found other more appropriate homes with our kind." Dear God, please let this work, I thought.

He visibly relaxed. Maybe he was more of a fool than I thought. *"Ja, Ich verste.* I understand. She sounds useful, and that's the only time they should be kept alive, *nein?"* He guffawed. I felt obligated to laugh along so I gave what I hoped was a proper lady's giggle.

"However, I cannot help you. Alas, they have not seen fit to award me such authority. Besides, she may have been taken to one of the labor camps. You will have to discuss this with someone else." And with that I was summarily dismissed.

I thought furiously at this. "I'm sure that can only be a temporary oversight on their part, *Herr Leutnant*. It seems impossible the Reich does not realize your worth. Tell me, *bitte*, do you know of someone else I should speak to? I realize the authority is, temporarily, in some others' hands but we have several sick children that need tending to and we are not privy to her herbs." Dear God, please do not let me sweat so profusely; he will surely see my fear.

He looked at me, softening some, I thought, so I smiled. He smiled back. "Well, there's an officer in a type of adjutant's department controlling the proper handling of the Jews in this area. You might see him. From what I hear he's rather a stickler for rules and regulations but he favors pretty blondes." Another guffaw exited this horrid man's mouth. "His name is Schreiber, *Hauptmann* Schreiber. Their offices are in Krakau."

Oh God, no, I thought, it cannot be. "Excuse me, but would that be *Hauptmann* Antoni Schreiber?"

"Ja, ja, that's him. I don't know if he will assist you, but you could do worse."

"Danke, Herr Leutnant. Vielen dank. Many thanks." I took my leave of this dreadful place, listening to the obvious pleasure in his joke.

Cousin Antoni! I knew he had returned, but as a captain? So fast? Filip had once said Antoni's family in Germany had connections in some very high places. Apparently, he told the truth for once.

Daylight was fast approaching and I had no time to lose. Somehow, I had to make my way to Krakau; no easy feat. Traveling outside of one's area was strictly forbidden without a pass. As a Pole, I was not allowed to purchase petrol, so the shop's vehicle was not an option. I thought of public transportation but it was never very reliable. Plus, I reminded myself, I had no excuse to obtain a pass. Whatever my means of transportation, there was the further problem of being granted access to my cousin.

I went home to prepare for the long walk, my only option. My old blue frock hung in my closet, practically the only serviceable one left. It no longer fit particularly well; snug in the hips and with the torn lace around the neckline, the bodice was now lower. It would have to do. If I did get in to see my cousin, I was not about to show him what terrible straits we were in. I rolled the dress up, placed it into a rucksack along with bits of food and what money I could find. This would not be an easy journey.

{ I }

I was beginning to panic at my slow progress. I had no idea how desperate my mother's position might be and I was anxious to see to her released as soon as possible. Without a travel pass, even on foot I could easily be arrested if some wayward Nazi stopped me. Naturally, I had my papers but even that was a worry to me. My name and address were clearly noted and my family could pay for my misdeed. Never did I imagine that we would have to think in such a twisted fashion to move about in our own country but there it was. I read somewhere the average person can travel about 6 km by foot in one hour. If that were true, I would have a seven-and-a-half-hour trip ahead of me.

I had worn mundane clothing, hoping I would blend in traveling by daylight. At the onset, I left Bochnia at night so I walked as long as I had the cover of darkness. The night not only hid me from view of others but the road obstructions were just as invisible to me. The entire countryside had been blasted away, with large remnants of buildings and farms everywhere. I used these to walk and crouch behind but more often than not, I stumbled and tripped, ending up on the ground. I finally had enough; I needed some sleep.

When dawn approached, I crawled into the scraggly hole of a broken building to catch a few hours rest. It was almost 5:00 a.m.; I had been walking and fumbling through the countryside for hours. I peeked at the food in my rucksack and settled for a gulp of water. Every noise startled me, making me think that either Germans, human scavengers, or animals had found my hiding place. My fitful rest finally came but not for long. It would take me hours to reach the city and then locate my cousin's offices. I looked down at myself and added to that list another half hour to make myself presentable. Muck covered my arms and clothing and I could only imagine what my face must look like.

In daylight, the many dead were clearly visible, causing my stomach to reach my throat. Animals too were rotting in the fields, bits and pieces of them scattered to where predators had carried them. I shuddered to think of how many I had fallen over during the night.

{ II }

Antoni's building had been easier to find than I thought—I had only to locate the most ostentatious one left standing with the largest flags flying. Seeing the former center of government in the historical town, I inwardly wept at the current destruction that greeted me. Prisoners were attempting to clear away broken bits of life from streets while guards watched their every move.

Cleaning off the debris from my trip had been more difficult. Clean water was next to impossible to come by but I had passed a stream, not more that a trickle, and had scrubbed my skin clean. I ran my fingers through my hair, and changed into the blue dress, hoping I was presentable enough.

Slowly and calmly walking up the long marble steps to the entrance, I listened for someone ordering me to stop. It never came, thankfully. Perhaps I looked more respectable than I thought. Finding "Hauptman Schreiber" proudly printed on a lobby directory, I took the lift to the fourth floor, Suite F. My destination approached quicker than I had hoped.

The doors slid open to reveal an oversized walnut desk in a spacious foyer and various pieces of art on the walls. Behind the desk was a Luftwaffe *Gefreiter*, or air force private first class, according to his insignia patches. He reminded me of a chipmunk; chubby cheeks with protruding front teeth and dark beady eyes. Sitting on the corner of the desk was another soldier smoking a cigarette. Resembling a basset hound with a long hangdog face, it was obvious he had gotten the meals I had been spared since his stomach strained against his jacket. I could not see his military insignia from this angle but I resolved to be "Nice" even though I felt far from doing so. The two of them were telling stories and Chipmunk Face was laughing at Basset Hound's joke too enthusiastically, too deferentially since the joke was not all that funny. Ah, I thought, Herr Basset Hound is the ranking officer in this scene. I should address my flattery and request to him.

They had not noticed me until I was within a few yards of the imposing desk. Herr Chipmunk jumped to attention very impressively insisting that I "*Halt.*"

"*Wie heist du?* And what is your business here?" I was a bit miffed—he had just asked my name using the German "familiar" pronouns, something strangers never did upon meeting. He was, I guessed, putting me in my place to further impress the soldier that outranked him. I was determined to use only formal German in my conversations with him hoping it would imply my subservience.

Herr Bassett Hound had by now turned in my direction and I could make out his rank. *Obergefreiter*—only a corporal, I thought. Not much better than a private. I did not have to overly worry about offending him, however I replied congenially to them.

"Good morning, *Herr Officieren*," I said "I am here to see *Herr Hauptmann* Schreiber."

They turned to each other and laughed. "And what might your reason be, *Fraulein*? What does such a pretty flower like you want with a captain?" Well, I thought, I suppose I should be flattered; I had moved up from morsel to flower.

"*Ja ja,*" said Corporal Bassett Hound, eyeing my bosom. "You needn't see the captain about anything. We are perfectly capable in servicing all your needs. Correct, Private Reiner?" With that, he leaned over and actually leered at me. As he was about to place his hand around my waist, I slapped it away. He was immediately all business.

"I think you need to be taught some respect for this uniform I am wearing," he said, grabbing my elbow, attempting to lead me God-knew-where.

"Take your hands off me!" I shouted, jerking away from him. "I demand to see Hauptmann Antoni Schreiber immediately. If you don't, I swear you will rue the day that you ever manhandled his cousin...his favorite cousin." I had learned an important fact these many months; if you are acquainted with someone of higher rank than the person you are speaking to, you hold the upper hand. To be related to a higher-ranking officer was even better.

My threat seemed to have the desired effect; perhaps my cousin had a reputation for punishing his subordinates. At any rate, I was escorted down the hall to Suite F where the door was opened ceremoniously for me. *"Herr Hauptman*, this woman claims to be your cousin," Chipmunk said doubtfully.

The look of surprise on Antoni's face was more than I could have hoped for. He was seated behind a wonderfully carved marble-topped desk, artwork adorning the walls, cut crystal glasses and a bottle of schnapps on a round antique table in the corner. The room was spacious and bright with a fireplace on the opposite wall to provide added heat in the winter ahead. It was opulent and masculine and I could not help but notice my cousin had grown even more handsome.

"So," he said, "you are the reason for the commotion in my building. It seems you still have a habit of causing disturbances wherever you travel."

Then he turned his gaze upon Private Chipmunk nearly trembling in the doorway. Antoni simply narrowed his eyes, slightly jutting out his chin at the man. I remembered this affectation from my childhood indicating Antoni's displeasure and smiled to myself. The unfortunate man, I thought. My cousin never said a word yet the soldier felt compelled to offer an explanation.

"She said she was your favorite cousin and if we did not allow her to see you we would forever regret not doing so for the rest of our lives." Not exactly literal but he understood my meaning.

"Favorite cousin?" he said with one raised eyebrow toward me. To the man he said, "Leave me. *Raus*! I will discuss this with you later."

He rose from his chair, walked around his desk and loomed over me. I had forgotten how tall he was. Or perhaps I had grown shorter. He stood there for a minute looking down at me then sat on the edge of the marble desk so we were now eye-level. I was not too sure how to play out this scene—would he assume the role of my cousin or my conqueror?

"So little Weegie, you have grown. In tongue-lashing abilities and in form, I see," and he gazed at my cleavage so prominently on display. "Would you like some schnapps? No? You will forgive me if I have some. I have a feeling I shall need it." He rose again and made his way to the crystal decanters, polished jackboots glistening in the light, every crease on his uniform razor sharp.

"It has been a long time, Cousin Antoni. My congratulations on your military advancement. And so quickly. Your father would be proud."

"Enough, Weegie," he said with boredom. "You did not come all this way to compliment me upon my career path. And how you got here is another question I should be most interested in hearing the answer to. Breaking curfew, traveling outside of your limits, verbally abusing soldiers of the Third Reich—all very serious transgressions, you know."

I decided to get to the issue at hand. "Antoni, please, I need your help. It is Mama. I believe she has been sent to the camp in Chrzanow. Please, you must help her."

"Must I? I seriously doubt that, little cousin. If she has been quarantined within those walls, there is surely a good reason for that, *ja*? Why don't you tell me what that is."

I could not tell him she was there because she had been helping a Jew. That would be certain death for her and possibly for me. So I told him my mother was in a Jewish home collecting money owed from the sale of meat. Things had not been going well for us, I said, and we needed what was due. As I was telling this, I could have kicked myself for wearing this dress. I should have let him see our troubles and worn my usual old garments. My pride again.

Antoni just continued to calmly look at me and did not say a word but I was used to his stares and had been quite adept at deflecting his attempted intimidation as a child. Perhaps I still had some talent in that respect.

Heaving a sigh he said, "Really? Is that the best tale you could think of during your long travel here? *Nein*, I do not think I believe you, not for an instant."

"Oh, please, Antoni, what difference does that make? She is my mother, your aunt. I am begging you to help release her. Please, I'll do whatever you want! She has been in there for days now and I fear for her health and life. Remember the happy times when we were children. She loved you." I was frantic by now and rambling.

A strange glint came into his eyes and he stood so close to me I could smell the pomade in his hair. "Tell me, *Liebschen*, have you any suitors?"

"What...what does that have to do with...?"

"Answer me, Marta. Any suitors or beaus? Or perhaps one of my soldiers has already taken you and no Polish boy will have you now, hmm?"

I was appalled at what I thought he was referring to. "No, Antoni, nothing like that. And no beaus either. We have been too busy with survival!" I hoped that last bit would throw some guilt his way.

He chuckled. "I thought I warned you about your tongue, Weegie. No matter. Perhaps we can come to some arrangement." With that, he reached his hand out to my neckline and drew one finger down along my exposed flesh. I went stock-still. If I struck his hand away as I had his subordinate in the foyer, all would be lost for my mother.

"I have certain means at my disposal to release your *Muter*, but I warn you, it may take some time. It may not be high on the priority list of things to do during these times. I may need some...incentive"

Realizing what he had in mind, my eyes grew wide. "Antoni, please. You cannot be serious. We are cousins, after all."

He leaned in further to lightly brush his lips upon my neck raising goose bumps on my skin. "Only third or fourth cousins, Weegie. Meaningless! Besides, I know how you felt about me when we were younger. Do not tell me all those feelings have disappeared." I could feel his excitement grow upon my leg and knew he was determined to see this through. Dear God, help me, I thought, I do not know what to do. If I refused, I would anger him. If I agreed to this insanity, I was completely inexperienced and would certainly disappoint him. All I knew of the sexual act was the violence with Sister Lina and Arlene.

His hand cupped the back of my neck and he kissed me, lips working against mine, his tongue finding its way inside my mouth. He pressed himself firmly against me, kissing me so hard I felt he would bruise my lips. Sliding his free hand down my side, it found the fullness of my breast and he cupped it lightly, allowing his thumb to slide across it. In spite of myself, I felt my tummy flutter and I cursed the dormant feelings that he was arousing within me.

As if heard through a long tunnel, we both became aware of a knocking at the door and someone calling for Hauptmann Schreiber. I quickly backed away from Antoni, noticing the slight smile upon his lips, and felt my face grow hot. I could still feel his kisses and was afraid my lips were crimson.

Antoni was quickly at attention when the door opened and a colonel entered the room.

"Hauptman, I need you to…" and he stopped when he noticed that Antoni was not alone in his office.

"*Herr Oberst* Müller, I would like to introduce you to my cousin, Marta Koblinski," he said grudgingly.

"It's very nice to meet you, Fraulein," said Colonel Müller and he leaned over my hand to plant a polite kiss on the back of it.

"She is Polish, *Herr Oberst*," said Antoni with a smirk.

"Being Polish does not make her any less lovely, eh Hauptman? But we have met before, have we not?" he asked me.

I could never have forgotten That Voice. "*Ja wohl*, Herr Colonel. You were of great assistance in our family butcher shop in Bochnia some time ago."

"Of course! I remember. It seems one of my more irritable privates was causing some trouble. You were the girl who spoke such perfect German, *ja?*"

"*Ja*. You were a major at the time, were you not?"

He actually looked slightly embarrassed at this. "*Ja ja*. But it so easy to rise in rank during wartimes."

I did not think he meant this as a personal affront to Antoni's promotions, but I hoped it deflated my cousin a bit.

"My cousin Antoni is whom you should thank for my perfect German—he is the one who taught it to me as a child." I hoped this attention to his past in front of his superior would sting him a bit.

"*Ist das richtig?* He did an outstanding job if that is so. But what brings you here, so far from that small town? Surely not a family visit so late?" and he looked to me for an explanation. In reply, I looked to Antoni to give it.

"Herr Colonel, she has been telling me of her mother's...difficulties with a detention center."

"I see. I am assuming this is an error, *ja*? Are you able to assist in this matter?"

"*Ja wohl*, Herr Colonel."

"Gut. Then do what you can. Family is important, now more than ever. I would see you in my office, Hauptman. Fraulein, have a safe trip home," and he turned to leave. Turning back to me he inquired, "Tell me, Fraulein, do you speak any languages other than Polish and German?" I replied that my English was also excellent but my Yiddish was only passable. He laughed at that and said, "Well, she certainly is honest in her self assessment, *ja*, Hauptman? I ask because our offices here always need translators and perhaps we could use your talents. My English is less than fair but my French is better." When I looked doubtful, he clarified. "I would be willing to pay you, although it would not be much, but it may help you and your mother along *ein bischen*, but only a little."

"Mein Herr, you could use me as slave labor as you do so many others I see. Why would you pay when you could use me for free?"

He laughed again and asked Antoni, "Does she always speak what is on her mind?"

"Unfortunately, it has been a problem since childhood, Herr Colonel."

"That is most unusual, Fraulein, and even dangerous in these times. A trait you must keep in check now, I'm afraid. Truly, think about my offer, *ja*? As I say, my English is only tolerable so perhaps I could learn more from you. Pidgin English, I believe it's called." And with that comment, he cleared his throat and attempted a sentence in that language. "Hello, I want a pie piece and with a milk cup would like." He stood there, beaming at us as if he had just swum the English Channel. I could not help but smile.

"Ah, you smile. Is that not correct? No, no, please, I insist. Tell me the truth."

"Well, Mein Herr Colonel, you see...well, I think even the English pigeons would have a difficult time understanding that." I clapped my hand over my mouth, trying to replace the words back into that treacherous orifice with which I have so much trouble.

The surprised look on his face gave me well-deserved cause for panic. Suddenly, he threw his head back and laughed out loud. "Touché, Fraulein. I see you have wit as well as intelligence. *Sehr Gut*! Very, very good."

Continuing to chuckle, he attempted to become more businesslike again, although he was still smiling, those prominent dimples on display. "*Ja*, well, as I say, I could do with more practice. So, see to your mother first and then you may always contact me here if you would be interested. Do you have access to a telephone?" I nodded. "*Gut*. Here is the phone number to my office and Antoni's, if I am unavailable." He handed me a business card after adding Antoni's information upon it. "I am not sure how long we will have these particular contact numbers. It is possible our offices will be moving. However, I feel safe in telling you that these will remain active for the next several months. I urge you to think about this offer. *Aufwiedersehen*, Fraulein. Hauptman, in my office in *funf minuten*." And with a slight salute, he once again turned. "Oh, and Hauptman," he said walking into the hall, "see that she has a public transportation pass for her return journey." The door closed behind him.

I looked at Antoni, amazed at The Colonel's proposal, relieved at his suggestion of a transport pass, and wondered where things now stood with my cousin. Surely, he would not presume to continue where he had left off. The Colonel had given him only *funf minuten*, five minutes, to spare, after all. How much could he accomplish in that short time? I hoped I would not find the answer.

"Please, Antoni, will you help me?" he was leaning against the large bookcase, legs crossed at his ankles, arms folded across his broad chest, never taking his eyes off me. It was quite disconcerting and I wondered if my dress was still mussed.

I could tell he was considering my request. "*Ja*, all right. I will. But do not come here to ask for her release again. I was correct when I said it would take some time. You will have to be patient for her return. And, Marta—you only get this one favor from me. Never ask for another one."

"Oh, Antoni, thank you, thank you so much. I promise." I turned to leave.

"Remember, little cousin, we are not done yet. We will be meeting again." I took his tone to be more of a threat than a promise.

{ III }

I had been waiting impatiently since my return from Krakau. Days became weeks, which added up to nearly a month now. I kept my promise: I had not been back to beg Antoni again. The question was, would he keep his promise? A better question might be, could he keep his promise? Perhaps his connections were not as strong as he led me to believe. Also on my mind was his parting remark. I knew he was serious in his intentions.

Today, I was once again alternating work in the butcher shop with glances out the window, praying for her safe return. Then I saw her. She was crossing the street toward me, looking older than Buscha, with a sort of shuffle-walk. I ran out to grab her, holding her close, trying to warm her.

She could barely walk into the shop, and she had lost weight. I gave her some warm broth and thin slices of bread, making her finish them before attempting to tell me her story.

She had arrived without incident at Mrs. Feldman's flat, she began, and gave her the medication for the pain. She and Mrs. Feldman's daughter were only chatting for a moment and she was leaving when they heard the noise in the street. "*Raus, raus, raus*. All Jews—out!"

The daughter took her children and placed them in a cupboard behind the boards in the closet. They both helped Mrs. Feldman inside and my mother was about to flee when the daughter told her if she did not want to die on the spot, she must hide as well. They were all confined in this dark space, barely large enough for two adults and two children, now even more cramped with the additional person. Standing there for hours, they could see the light leave the room as the sun set, all the while hearing whistles blow and Germans shout. Heavy boots resonated off the stairwell walls and doors were kicked open. Occasionally they would hear a scream or a gunshot.

The children had been so quiet but they got hungry and thirsty so began to fidget and cry. In desperation, their mother urinated in her hand and gave them each a sip to drink so they would be quiet. The baby just continued to whimper. In a last hope, the mother held the baby to her chest but it was no use. Within twenty minutes, they were found. After they piled out of the cupboard, the Germans began laughing and pointing at the baby. The mother had been holding it so close she smothered it. "Since she doesn't care about her children, why should we," one of the soldiers said and he shot the other child.

A second soldier grabbed Mama and demanded papers. Mrs. Feldman, half-unconscious from the combined heat and the pain medication, tried to tell them that she was *"Polska, nicht Juden, nicht Juden.* Polish, not Jew!"

"Polish or Jew—you're all the same to me. This one is almost dead anyway," the soldier said and another shot rang out, killing Mrs. Feldman.

After that, the two survivors were dragged down the stairs, shoved into a transport vehicle, and brought to the labor camp.

"Oh, Marta. It was worse than you can imagine. People called this place a ghetto. I never heard that before, have you?" I shook my head. New terms and phrases were the norm now. Some German must lie awake at night dreaming up such things. "The Nazi officers called it an isolation area but whatever they want to call it, the place is worse than anything I could ever have imagined. There were over eight thousand people, Marta. Eight thousand! There was no water or electricity. The toilets were all full and people took to urinating and defecating in the streets. I saw political prisoners, Jews, and so many others. We tried to remain strong, tried to help each other but it was no use; so many were dying from starvation and disease. Typhus is running rampant in there. Some of the Poles outside would smuggle in food or toss it over the walls at night but it was never enough."

She told me about two fat guards, merely boys, who liked to torment the inhabitants. They would stand on the sidewalks and toss empty bottles across the street at any passersby. If they hit one, the unlucky person was propped against the nearby wall and shot. Occasionally they changed up their gruesome game. If the bottle did not break, the person would be allowed on his way. If it shattered, the prisoner was shot, the boys laughing gleefully. They seemed to enjoy the people scrambling down the street in fear as much as the killing.

In a moment of guilt, I asked after Mrs. Feldman's daughter. Mama simply shook her head and I did not press the matter. Whatever her story, I was glad it had not been Mama's even though it was selfish of me. She sat in one of the short chairs that had not seen a customer's use in quite some time. I kept filling her cup with weak tea or broth while the few people who could afford to buy meat came and went. She never said a word the rest of the day or on the slow walk home.

Two weeks later, July 10, we again awoke to the sounds of those enthusiastic speaker trucks. Now what, I thought. They were traveling at a snail's pace so every neighborhood (what was left of them) would hear the entire bilge they were spouting. After reiterating the glorious achievement of Germany over the Frogs, (my term for the French, not the Germans') those shouting vehicles went on to proudly explain that Britain would be the next country to join the Third Reich, as the Luftwaffe was now harassing that island country. According to those disembodied voices, the blitz upon England would end in defeat for England. We, meaning the Poles, would do well to cease all aggressive activity against the Third Reich. There was no one left to assist us. That much would be true, I thought, if England was occupied. The Americans would be all that was left of democracy and they were adamantly remaining out of the picture.

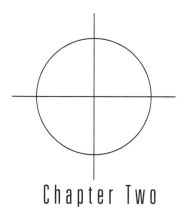

Chapter Two

August 1940

THE PARTNERSHIP

*T*he reasons for affording Jews safety were many and varied. Some had family links, strong friendships, or even professional bonds. Much of the aid given was simple human empathy or the Christian belief in helping one's neighbors. Many offered concealment in return for payment, not out of avarice but of necessity. Those in hiding did not have official ration cards; consequently, food was purchased on the black market at exorbitant prices. Altruistic Poles were saving thousands of Jews, knowing the Germans were murdering complete Polish families and entire communities for this act of treachery. Whatever the reasoning, it was always done at great personal risk.

Alternately, the motives for relinquishing those Poles who helped the Jews were also varied. Many let the Germans know of these perpetrators for self-survival or that of their family. Some ethnic Germans felt it was their duty, while others believed the propaganda spewed from the German radio and newspapers. Others did it purely through greed.

Filip Wozniak was one of the latter. He had been sneaky and malicious as a child and was shifty and cruel as an adult, forever on the watch for any possible moneymaker. Listening to private conversations or reading someone else's mail were not beneath him if it proved profitable. He cared not if such a venture would harm another person, even another Pole. At a time when family solidarity should be at its strongest, he had not changed his priorities; Filip was interested only in himself. He was always flush with money but it was spent entirely for his own pleasure or the pursuit of another money scheme. Some of his more successful ideas had involved burglary, muggings, even committing a beating for a price. Other times he stole food from one household and sold it to another. So far, no matter how many get-rich schemes he came up with, he had not realized the enormous purse or the power he desired.

It was not surprising, therefore, when he thought of chatting up a German private in one of the few coffee shops doing business. He was always open to possibilities. Perhaps he would be able to secure a few coins from the soldier with a card trick or two. Perhaps something more lucrative would come of it. Picking up his coffee cup, he walked over to the other table and plopped down in the adjoining seat. His German was halting and thick with a Polish accent but it was understandable and he smiled into the soft-boiled eyes of his new friend. The Heer soldier was the requisite blond blue-eyed Aryan and his overfull, spongy lips gave him an almost feminine appearance.

The private seemed surprised by this intrusion but Filip was using his most complimentary and conciliatory approach so before long the two were engaged in conversation. They both wanted something out of this war; Filip wanted money and status, Private Johann Schafer wanted promotions in rank.

"It would seem, my friend," said Filip, "that between two such intelligent men as ourselves, we should be able to come up with an endeavor that would get us both what we want."

"I agree wholeheartedly," said the German." My promotions can only occur with some outstanding act and I certainly will not get that opportunity stationed in this decrepit town. One can only kill so many Poles and Jews, after all, and there would be more opportunity for that if I were in the SS."

Filip tried not to wince at the remark about murdering Poles. He was aware how tenuous his situation was in his own country. "Would a promotion be forthcoming if you were to inform your superiors of illegal activities?"

"That would certainly impress them but where would I get any such information? I'm only a private and have nothing they would be interested in."

Filip thought the man dim witted. This suited him well and he was beginning to form an idea of sorts to aid them both. "What if I supplied you with something valuable to take to your superior? Would you be willing to pay for such information?"

"As I have said, I am only a private with limited income. I could only pay a few RM, I'm afraid."

"I have an idea, though, and if it works, not only will your income increase, but so will your worth among your commanding officers. Meet me back here in two days. If you like the information I bring you, I shall accept your Marks. I will continue to bring you useful bits from time to time and if your pockets increase in wealth, so will my payment. Agreed?"

"I have nothing to lose. But you will buy the coffee at our next meeting, *ja?*" And he laughed at his joke.

"Ja!" said Filip and they shook hands on their new venture together.

Two days later, Filip walked into the coffee shop and saw that the private was already seated. "Where have you been? I have been waiting for ten minutes. As a soldier of the Third Reich, I should not have to wait for you."

"I am so very sorry, Mein Herr, but traveling about town is not as easy as it once was." He ordered two coffees for them and paid with money from his pocket. This seemed to put the private in a better mood and he leaned back, taking a sip of the brew.

"Ach! This is not nearly so good as coffee in Deutschland. So, my friend, what have you for me today? Anything exciting?"

"Well, I hope this will impress your superiors. What would you say if I told you I knew of a family that was harboring Jews? How much would that be worth to you?"

Filip watched the man's soft-boiled eyes grow bigger and he could see the wheels turning in his head. "Where? Tell me where they are!"

"Ah, not so fast. How much?"

"I have only three Marks, all that is left of my weekly pay. Is that enough?"

With that last sentence, Filip knew he had found the perfect partner. Anyone who does not know the value of something can always be expected to pay more. Filip drew out a scrap of paper and wrote an address on it.

"The entire family will be home by five tonight along with the Jews." The soldier grabbed at it eagerly.

"Mein Herr, might I make a suggestion that would not only put some coin in your own pocket but will ensure that someone else does not take the credit for this?" It was clear Private Schafer had not thought of either of these possibilities. He nodded his head dumbly. "What is your superior officer's name?"

"Major Schmidt," he replied.

"Good. Now first, write a note to be sent to Major Schmidt's commanding officer. Do you know how to reach him? Good. Tell him only that you know of a family of harbored Jews and you hope to capture them as well as those who aid them with the assistance of your Major Schmidt. Then, when you present this plan to Major Schmidt, do not reveal the location until he has given you permission to head up the raid for tonight. Do not tell him the time either. He will naturally threaten you but do not give in. Tell him that you have already informed his superior officer of your plan and if it is not completed, perhaps Herr Major could explain to his commander why it was not. He will not be happy, but eventually he will agree to your terms. Everyone is afraid of his commanding officer, *nein*? Can you do that?"

"I cannot! How can I threaten my commanding officer like that? I will be shot!"

"You must, Johann! Do you know of anyone who has suddenly risen in rank? Yes? And how do you think this comes about? From remaining a good soldier, complacent, agreeable? *Nein*. By being ruthless and looking out for yourself. Soldiers around you are doing this all the time. Hell, the entire Wehrmacht does this—whatever helps get a person ahead in this war. *Verstehen*? Understand? So, if the raid goes well, and I see no reason why it will not," said Filip quickly when he saw the momentary look of panic on the private's face, "tell him the next time you would also like to be recompensed for the information as well. Then, eventually, you shall ask for promotions in rank. Believe me, he will agree. He knows these raids will not go unnoticed and he will be rewarded as well. All of us gain, *ja*? And I promise you, I will have more information and you will be shown to be invaluable to their efforts. Do we agree?"

Poor Private Schafer—he was so excited he looked about to pee in his pants. And so began their business association together. Traitorous activities were becoming a very profitable enterprise.

Chapter Three

October 1940

NEW POSITION

*A*s promised, I had been diligent in my efforts to translate the German letters into English and Polish although I firmly believed they could have put me to better use. Hadn't I just walked 40 km to Krakow, gotten past several guards, and made it back home in one piece? I should remind Max. Maybe then, he would use me for something more dangerous against these horrible Germans; Russians too, for I could not forget what my countrymen on the other side of Poland might be suffering at the Soviets' hands.

When I first began reading these snippets of the soldiers' view on life, I found it difficult to continue. I was amazed and disgusted by the descriptive details of the many atrocities conducted by these men. These carefully penned messages were posted to family and friends and I often wondered how a mother could read these confessions of persecution from a son she loved. Granted, most of the pages reported normal everyday activities; friends they were serving with, and complaints of military food. But many of the soldiers wrote openly about their belief in the Master Race and their personal hand in the exterminations.

I would be meeting with Max shortly to give him my finished notes. I glanced at my translations of selected parts of these letters. One was posted to a soldier's sweetheart. He proudly wrote, "I am one of those who are decreasing the number of partisans. I put them against the wall and everyone gets one bullet to the head...very interesting job." I was reminded of a cat who brings his master a dead mouse, waiting for approval.

One comment seemed to be directed solely at the Poles. "...This nation deserves only the hangman's noose. Only by that can they become educated...I have become convinced that we are the masters and all others are beneath us."

While in the middle of another note, I had a moment of excitement; it was beginning to sound as if this soldier was not happy with the murders and tortures of our people: "No newspaper can possibly describe what I have seen here. It verges on the unbelievable, and even the Middle Ages do not compare with what has transpired here..." And then I read the final sentence of this passage: "Photos give only a limited impression of what we have seen here and of the crimes committed here by the Jews." I felt deflated. The propaganda served up was not limited to the Occupied but spoon-fed to the military units as well. Blaming the Jews for the evil now living in our country fomented more hatred lending further conviction to the Nazi cause.

Photographs were often included in these letters home to loved ones. Many seemed innocent to the recipient, merely photos of their soldier-son smiling into the camera. To me, however, I had seen those smiling faces just prior to firing a pistol at a child's head or dragging a woman behind a deserted building. That smile could be more frightening than a scowl. Others were not so innocent to gaze upon, photos of mangled men hanging in trees or another one of a young girl with the familiar braid down her back whose detached legs were being held proudly by another soldier. I thought of a picture of my papa after a fishing trip. He had posed in that same stance with his catch, as if he hooked the largest fish in the pond.

One photo I could never forget. It was marked simply on the reverse "The Warsaw Ghetto," the largest ghetto in our country. Although I did not know it at the time, it would eventually house four hundred thousand people in an area that should hold one-fourth that number. The main character in this sepia-toned photo was a small girl, probably no more than three. She was lying in the fetal position on a cobbled road, limbs resembling sticks, eyes closed, mouth slightly agape, and obviously dying in the middle of the street. Just slightly to the left of her were three passing youths, each carrying a bundle in their arms, looking down at her. The picture of that scene troubled me greatly. I found myself hollering at the three older children in the photo as if they could hear me. "Don't you see her there? Help her! Why do you continue to walk past? Save her, save her!"

There was no reference to this photo in the letter accompanying it and perhaps that is what bothered me most. What message was the writer trying to convey to his family? Was he demonstrating the power of the Nazis over us? Or perhaps the photo begged the question, why should Nazis care about these people if they allow their children to die in the street? Either way, it was a sad commentary upon life in what had once been a great city.

As always, I was glad to see Max alive and well, although he seemed thinner each time I saw him. My mother insisted he eat something and produced a plateful of canned and dried food in front of him with a fried egg and vegetables from our garden. He raised his eyebrows at me, asking the safety of this prepared meal. I nodded back to him; yes, it was safe. Mama did not prepare it. We smiled at each other, each of us still remembering our unspoken shorthand when it came to Mama's kitchen skills.

Clearing away the plate at the table, she left us to our own devices, knowing we had business to attend to. Max began to pore over my notes. "This is excellent, Marta. You are getting faster at this each time. So many good items here."

"Good?" I questioned.

"You know what I mean. Jan or Stefan will certainly be able to use this information. Perhaps if we can get it to England, someone will finally know what is happening here."

Jan Karski and Stefan Rowecki were still determined to get to England and the United States to beg for help. Max had told me they were hoping this was the proof needed in order to get the Allies' collective asses (Max's words, not mine) out of their chairs and doing something. "It is utterly amazing how these Nazis can take snapshots of all this terror and send it home as if they were photos of family outings. These people are fixated on record keeping and photographing everything in sight. Perhaps it will prove to be their undoing some day, hmm?" he said as he continued to flip through my many pages of translations. He seemed to be in a very good mood today, although I had no idea how that was possible after reading those letters. Sometimes the letters were so distressing, I needed time away from them. Perhaps now was my opportunity to propose a transfer to another more rewarding task.

"Max," I began, "all this...this...tripe that these men write—it is truly beginning to bother me. That photo of the girl in the street, for instance. I had nightmares about her for days after I saw that. Maybe it is time for me to do something with more...well, action involved." He finally looked up from his reading. I decided to plow ahead since he had not automatically said "No" as he usually did. "I could take a job at an inn or café that the Germans frequent and listen to their conversations." My cinematic imagination was getting the best of me. Uh oh, he was beginning to frown. "Or maybe be a courier to another underground unit. Oh, Max—I have to do something other than this!"

He sat there a moment, just looking at me, before he said, "Marta, really, you do not know how important this work is. Some of these men... it just proves everything we already know. They hate us and want us gone. It's as simple as that. The rest of the world needs to know."

Now I was getting testy, as Buscha would say. "Max, really! This is ridiculous. If these letters are so important, just send them to England. Let the Brits find a translator. Maybe I should have taken that job with that colonel! At least it would not be so depressing!"

His head snapped up at that comment from me. Good, I thought, maybe now he will realize someone else recognizes my talents. "What did you say? What colonel, what are you talking about?"

His eyes had a peculiar gleam in them and I was forced to relate the entire story when, the then- major, first entered our shop, the help provided, and my subsequent meeting with him in Krakau. He urged me to describe in great detail about the job offer from the now-colonel. Max seemed particularly interested in that offhand comment of a location change. He asked a few questions here and there throughout my narrative and I reversed myself a time or two but when I finally finished, I sat back and watched him. I could not see why this provoked such thought; it was no problem as far as I could see. I only mentioned it so he would offer me something more exciting to do.

"Marta! But this is fantastic! Do you know what this means?" Obviously, I did not but I felt sure he would tell me. "I think this colonel of yours and Antoni are going to be moving to Auschwitz. I have heard that the Germans are enlarging the staff at a camp there, especially their administrative staff to act as liaison to Himmler. You could be right there, in the middle of it all. Just think of what you could accomplish there; all the information you could accumulate."

I was shocked. Did he actually mean I should take a job at a work camp, surrounded by nothing but Germans all day long? And where would I live? "Wait, Max, for one thing he is not 'My Colonel,' and I certainly do not want to be around Nazis all day long, alone. How would I get home every night to be with Mother? Oh my God, what if I should be caught? They could torture me!" This was getting out of hand. But wait—a thought just occurred to me. "Oh, I see! Teasing me because I asked again for a transfer. You made your point. I will contentedly continue these translations and I promise I will never ask again." I held up my hand in a solemn vow, smiling at him.

Max was not smiling back. I felt that old tingle on my neck. "You are deadly serious, aren't you?" I exclaimed, sorry I had chosen that particular phrase. He took both of my hands in his and began to talk to me, quietly and slowly, making a plan as he went along, enlarging upon the idea little by little until I had enough. I reiterated my decisive "NO."

Max just sighed and said, "All right, I will not mention it again. All I ask is that you do one thing for me."

I made the mistake of asking, "What?"

"Come with me and talk to someone I know. Actually, just sit and listen; he will do the talking. Will you do that for me?"

"Impossible," I said shaking my head. "I cannot leave the area; I have no travel papers." I said this hoping it would put an end to all this nonsense realizing it was a ridiculous thing to have said. Max has no travel papers and look at him; he travels all over the country.

"I can arrange the travel papers for you. I think we could leave in three days. Will you come with me?"

I finally nodded yes, wishing very much I had not.

{ I }

As promised, three days later Max handed me an official-looking, forged document. I vowed to keep it well hidden until it was absolutely necessary to show anyone.

Surprisingly, we were allowed to step into the rail car without any trouble. The Nazi standing at the end of the doorway carefully looked over my papers while I tried not to look guilty, a rather tricky undertaking for me. As we were making ourselves comfortable in the car, I asked Max where we were going. "It will not be far, only about forty minutes or so," he said obliquely. Since he would not give me a direct answer to my question, I decided I would find it by reading the train stops. Now that every hamlet in my country had been renamed, the newly painted signs did nothing to enlighten me. With an irritated sigh, I flopped back in the seat.

We ended up setting foot in a village known as Wojnicz. (I asked the conductor when Max was not listening). At fifteen square miles large and out in the middle of nowhere, it was so isolated the Germans had not yet bothered to rename it. The train depot sign had been removed but nothing had replaced it. I wondered if anything ever would.

Max and I traveled through the town-with-no-name to the far end of its borders. The crumbling homes and other buildings were sparser out here. Max directed me to a ruin among other ruins and made our way inside the roofless hovel through half a window. Max rolled over a few rocks for us to sit upon and we waited. He had been keeping very quiet and for once I followed suit but just as I was about to ask how much longer we would have to sit here, we heard a crackle of twigs outside the building. Max held his hand up to forestall any noise I would make.

Around a jagged wall peered a man, tall with close-cropped hair, lending him a military appearance. As he came fully into the space, Max stood and shook his hand, bringing him closer to me. "Marta, I would like you to meet Major Jan Slodarkiewicz, formerly of the Forty-first Polish Infantry." I rose and the man took my hand, placing a slight kiss upon its back.

"Miss Marta, I have received some very nice reports about you from Max," he said in a quiet voice. "You are quite accomplished in translating the letters from the Germans." He motioned for us all to sit once again on the uncomfortable rocks. "I haven't much time but Max thought perhaps I could offer some information about our work and how important it is to our freedom."

So, I thought, called in the top brass to convince me to accept the job offer. I was determined to remain stubborn but was still curious what this man was prepared to tell me.

He began by providing me background of the underground. He and his wartime companion/deputy, Witold Pilecki, had formed the Secret Polish Army within a week after our occupation. With the man that Max had held in such regard, Jan Karski, they had convinced thousands of men and women to join their cause; more were joining every day. A few radical groups had also sprung up but attempts were underway to incorporate them within the Home Army. Another underground cluster had young girls and boys ages fifteen and up as their members who had been giving the Nazis some considerable trouble, he said proudly.

The Home Army was destined to become the largest resistance organization answering to the government in exile. So far, they had managed to destroy a battalion of German infantry in a village to the east then another had been taken in an ambush near the village of Szalzsy. "We inflicted heavy casualties there," he said proudly. Most of their members were armed with machine guns and several anti-tank rifles. Although the number of members never amounted to more than three hundred at a time, the Germans had recently sent eight thousand men to secure a town. Imagine, he said, eight thousand Nazis had been taken away from other duties to control a handful of his men.

He asked me if I had heard of the Blue Police. When I shook my head no, he explained that they were members of the Polish police, who, wanting to keep their jobs and uniforms, had agreed to work for the Germans. One evening, members of his resistance unit had surrounded the office of a Blue Police group by boarding up the windows and rear door, and simply stole everything they could carry; food, weapons and ammunition, uniforms, everything except the underwear the traitors were wearing. The Germans were called in to locate his unit but they had left the area far behind. Members also derailed trains carrying goods back to Germany, confiscating as much as they could from the fallen rail cars. Sometimes, the cache would be weaponry, sometimes clothing or food. Whatever goods they found were carried away.

"Did you know they have arrested and imprisoned almost five hundred thousand of us and executed sixty thousand Poles since the war began? No? It continues every day.

"Have you ever heard of an Enigma machine?" I shook my head. "It is a German typewriter-like machine that translates messages into code. In 1932, our Polish Cipher Bureau broke their code. Five weeks before war broke out, we were able to transmit the entire code book of this machine to Britain. So far, they have deciphered many messages among the Germany military."

This is what the resistance is all about, he said. All over the country, people have sworn to fight the interlopers and carry out sabotage. They have vowed to destroy the supply lines to the armies and to disrupt their ordinary business as much as possible. Poland has offered nearly two hundred troops to the countries of France, Britain, and the Netherlands to name a few. Through the courier services developing, he was convinced the Allies could receive information.

"And now," he said, "I come to one of the most important missions we are currently undertaking. Witold has allowed himself to be captured and brought to Auschwitz. Other talented people within our organization gave him false identity papers. He volunteered for this, you understand, and we let him go, mingling in with the crowds at Warsaw during a rounding-up of dissidents. He was collected with over two thousand other civilians and tortured for hours before being sentenced to the camp. He is there now, organizing a resistance movement within the camp. We are sure, you see, that this establishment is much more than just a work camp. Witold is convinced information can be smuggled out of the camp and all the way to America or Britain. People are dying in these camps and he is determined to get the truth out. Jan Karski, who has a photographic memory, has agreed to travel to the Allies and talk to anyone he can get a sitting with. Someone must believe what is happening within our country if we have the proof. Now, Max has told me of the most fortunate opportunity for us to have someone working within the offices, able to travel in and out of the camp. In short; you, Miss Marta."

Of course, I had dozens of questions. "How do you know I will be privy to any information there? I may only be a simple filing clerk or typist. And as for venturing into the camp, you do not know that I will have permission to do any such thing. What makes you think they will trust me with secret information? They know I am Polish; you have not forgotten that, have you? They could just as easily make me a resident of the camp instead of an employee there."

The major looked at Max and said, "You were right, she does have quite a lot to say on the subject." To me he said, "We can only hope you will come across something of interest. This will have to be your choice, of course, but I cannot tell you how important having you placed there might be. If this camp becomes what we suspect, information from there could be the most vital we could send to the British. I will not lie to you and tell you it will not be dangerous because it will be."

"You are worried about your friend too, yes? Have you had word from him yet?"

"Some, but the conditions there are not good; in fact, more than cruel. It is important for him to live, not only for the mission but because he is my friend."

"But how will I know him and pass information back and forth to each other? And how will I get the information, if there is any, back to you?" I had so many detailed questions but the answers were not very consoling.

"I am afraid I cannot go into any more detail with you until you have agreed to take up this challenge. I have already given you much more information than I should have, than I usually do in fact." He said this with a sad smile. "If you agree, Max has been briefed and will answer everything when the time is right.

"And now, I must go." Clasping Max good-bye and kissing the back of my hand again, he looked me in the eyes and said, "My dear, I hope you make a good decision, one that you will be able to live with for the rest of your long life." And then he was gone.

On the way back to the train, I asked Max about the vague farewell statement of his. "You have to make the decision that is right for you, Marta, that's all. Whatever it is, we will all stand by it."

{ II }

Max stayed at our house that night. I'm sure he slept like a stone; he did not have to think about a decision he would have to "live with." I tossed and turned all night and dreamt of Germans chasing me through town and all around the butcher shop. When I awoke, I was physically exhausted.

Max was sitting at our table finishing his meager breakfast when I stumbled down the stairs. Mama told me to sit down and eat something. I tried but I wanted answers instead of food.

"All right, Max, I will do as you ask. Please tell me I am not crazy and I will be safe."

He reached across the table to hold my hands. "We have taken all the precautions we can think of, Marta, and the details have been carefully thought through. I think you will be safer than most of us." If meant to comfort me, he did not.

Later today, I would go to the post office and place a trunk call to the colonel accepting the job offer. (Unfortunately for me, I had retained the business card the colonel had given me). And, Max instructed, I should do so politely and respectively. (He knew me too well). The position should not be too difficult. Carry out whatever tasks the colonel gave me while paying attention to all that transpired around me. Take mental notes of the camp, talk to some of the prisoners if possible, get their names and any other details I felt I could remember.

He told me that Witold had many contact names but the one forged onto his new documentation was Tomasz Serafinski and this is the only name I should use. He was also known as prisoner number 4859, another means of identification for me. He had me repeat this information to him several times. I was to memorize it and never write his name down for any reason.

"Marta," he said seriously, "every person in that camp has a different identity number. It is the same in all the camps. You will see this when you get there. Now, listen carefully. This will all be a shock to you; you have to be prepared to witness terrible things done to these people. It may be worse than what you have seen in our hometown and you have to learn not to react to what you see. At least not in front of the Germans. Your first instinct will be to help these prisoners but you have to stop yourself and remember that the information you can smuggle out will do more good to us all. You will have to be stronger than you have ever been, Marta, in order to help them and stay alive."

I was frightened now. I wondered if I was prepared to be constantly exposed to worse conditions than I had already witnessed. I knew he was waiting for me to let him know I could perform this important task without hesitation. I nodded my head firmly, telling him that I would not let him down.

Then he showed me a key. It was an ordinary key with a long ornate handle, thick and sturdy. This key, Max said, was a duplicate to our butcher shop lock with one tiny difference. He proceeded to unscrew the locking portion from its long neck and told me to look within. "It's hollow," I said.

"Exactly. This is how you will receive information from the camp. Tomasz has an exact copy and the two of you, or perhaps even others within the camp, will pass them back and forth. Once you retrieve a key with the information inside, you leave an empty one in the same spot. After you arrive at the camp and contact Tomasz, you two can decide upon a hiding place for it."

I looked suspiciously at the key in my palm. "How can any information fit into this tiny thing? Even if it is hollow, it will not hold much."

"It will be filled with microfilm, Marta, either stolen from the camp or duplicated. And you would be surprised how small a piece of paper can be rolled. Also, learn as much about the prisoners as you can but memorize it only, do not write anything down, understand? Do not worry if you cannot remember everything, whatever you know will be useful."

When I was able to come home for visits, Max continued, he and I would meet to exchange information. I was not to open the key until he and I were together. As far as I was concerned, it was just a key to my family's shop. Also he would try to call me from time to time just to make sure everything was progressing smoothly or pass on some urgent information if need be. And most importantly, he stressed, we would only converse in English over the phone. Since Polish was not allowed in our country, this would seem reasonable. Our conversations would be in such vague terms that only he and I would understand but if anyone overheard my end of the conversation, well…he felt sure I could come up with an on-the-spot explanation. I hoped he was correct.

It all sounded very well and good, this crazy idea of his, but I admitted to him that I was still frightened. "Do not worry, Marta. Although you cannot tell him of your reason for being there, I am sure Antoni would protect you in a pinch." Oh, my. Now that made me feel much better!

The next morning, Max and I went to the post office and waited for the connection to be completed through the tangle of operators involved in seemingly every call. Finally, my name was announced by the clerk. "Booth number 2, please, Fraulein."

My legs felt like limp cabbage as I walked to the designated telephone booth. Max came in with me and closed the glass door to the booth behind us. I hoped he would help me along with my rehearsed speech, as I was drawing a blank.

The operator on the other end of the line told me to "go ahead" and then I heard The Voice say *"Ja, hallo. Colonel Müller hier."*

The words would simply not come out. I stood there with my mouth open until Max nudged me in the ribs—painfully, I might add. *"Hallo, Herr Colonel Müller?* I am not sure if you remember me. This is Marta Koblinski, Antoni's cousin."

"But assuredly, I remember you, Fraulein. How very nice to hear your lovely voice." (My lovely voice, I thought. I was about to swoon just listening to his.) "Is there something I may do for you?"

I realized he had just asked me a question and I tried to answer it, all the while Max was mouthing my reply. "Oh, yes, Herr Colonel. I… ah…have…ah…had a chance to think over your kind job proposal and I should very much like to accept it, the job I mean, if you still have it available for me to take, I mean." God, could I possibly babble any more than this? I glanced at Max. I had no idea his brow could furrow so deeply when he frowned.

"Well, I am so glad you have reconsidered, Fraulein. I promise you, the job should not be too taxing. Some paperwork, filing, perhaps some personal translations…mostly office work. And your mother? I seem to remember some concerns regarding her when last we spoke. I am assuming she is in good health and she agrees with this decision?"

Oh God. I had not even mentioned this to Mama. Max was pushing on my arm and nodding over and over again as if that would encourage me to continue this insane conversation. "Oh, yes, I am sure it will be all right. She still has the butcher shop, you see, to tend to and since we have to close it by noon now, the extra money will come in handy for both of us. By the way, could you please tell me exactly how much money we are discussing?"

Apparently, I should not have asked about money or mentioned the German law of early shop closing; Max's eyes were popping out and he was shaking his head so hard I thought it would fall on the floor. The colonel, however, merely laughed that deep-throated chuckle of his. "My dear Fraulein. I am content to know you have lost none of your outspoken charm. Shall we say ten Reich Marks per week to begin? If your talents prove useful, then we can discuss an increase. Is that agreeable?"

I replied formally, to calm Max, that it was most agreeable. We talked a few more minutes regarding my travel documentation, the train station where I would be met, and how he felt Antoni would be looking forward to seeing me. Oh, God, not Antoni again. That would have to be a bridge crossed very carefully, I thought. The colonel also promised to reserve a room for me in a respectable boarding house near the office building. Thanking him for all his effort to ensure my comfort, I hung up the phone and shook like a leaf.

"Marta, you carried that off well. I was worried there in the middle but it turned out fine. So, we will go over all the details again," (I thought this a splendid idea based on that telephone conversation), "and then I shall place you on the train myself. Wait until Jan and Stefan hear about this. They will be thrilled!" Thrilled was not the emotion rattling around in my stomach at the moment. Fear was more like it. Now I must tell Mama what I would be doing. Hopefully, Max would stay with me while I tried to explain all this to her. Oh God, oh God, why do I keep opening my mouth before thinking things through?

I had been correct to be concerned about Mama's reaction to my latest bright idea. Truly, though, unlike our childhood adventures I was totally blameless this time. I looked to Max to explain those details he safely could. By the time he had finished, my job sounded harmless and merely the means to earn a few RM for the family. The one saving grace they both believed in was Antoni. How nice it would be to have him nearby and protective of me, they both said. For an instant, I thought of divulging the truth about my cousin. That would surely forestall this idiocy and I could remain home. I did not, for once, open my mouth, knowing how it would upset my mother. Perhaps I was finally growing up.

Chapter Four

October 27, 1940

ARRIVAL

*T*wo days later, a Nazi soldier came to my door and very formally, along with the requisite Heil Hitler salute, presented my work authorization documents to me for non-Germans. Max saw me to the train station as promised with our traditional three-cheek kisses and a hug, entreating me to be careful. He told me he would attempt a phone call the following week to see how I was fairing. To see if I had been caught yet, more than likely. A one-way ticket was waiting for me along with travel papers to ensure my non-harassment along the way. Surprisingly, the station and the train cars were busy and crowded, although mostly with Germans. The handful of civilians like myself were making a great effort to stay out of the way of the Nazi soldiers until the very last minute. With mixed feelings, I was allowed on and made myself comfortable in the coach. The railway train was bound for the small town of Libiaz with one scheduled stop at Krakau.

The colonel said he would send a car to bring me from Libiaz to the office building where I would begin my new duties to both him and the underground. It was only a fifteen-minute car ride from the station to

Auschwitz, he had said. Unless the Germans had completely changed the path of the railway track, the train could have deposited me at a station in the heart of Auschwitz. If that was so, I wondered why he was so insistent my journey end in Libiaz.

True to the colonel's word, I saw a tall soldier with a thick mustache resolutely approaching me. Apparently, he had gotten a very detailed description of me since he wavered not from his path toward where I stood. I had barely set my traveling case down when he picked it up with one hand and presented me the Nazi salute with the other. "Fraulein Marta." It was a statement, not a question, but it was said politely. I nodded in response and he introduced himself as Corporal Konig, asking me to follow him to the waiting automobile.

It was a beautiful machine; a new Mercedes Benz staff car, buffed so shiny that the black and chrome gleamed in the sun. The corporal opened the car door for me and I leaned back into soft-as-butter dark brown leather that smelled wonderful. Before he closed my door, I was informed that the tray in front of me contained some refreshments sent by the colonel for my enjoyment. It was a pity I would be under my enemies' roof conducting a traitorous act and probably would not live long enough to enjoy another ride in such a vehicle. With that dismal thought, I chose to enjoy myself and munched on the tempting candied fruit. It was less than fifteen minutes when we reached the office building. What a shame. I would have liked more of the fruit. Reckless thoughts for one about to enter the lion's den.

The building in question was two stories tall, made of red and white brick. It was long and wide and probably held far too many German officers for my own good. Situated a short distance outside the wire of the camp, it was behind another even longer, wider building located within the wire enclosure.

The corporal said he would bring my bags up for me while I proceeded to the third floor, Suite G. Thanking him for his kindness, which I sincerely meant, I did as I was instructed. The foyer was paneled in rich, dark woods adorned with gorgeous works of art. I wondered from what museum they had been stolen. The elevator was silent and fast, not unlike a German bullet, I thought.

Following the signs to Suites G through J, I turned right until I stood in front of the frosted glass door with the words "Colonel Müller" hand painted in gold upon it. Trembling, I took a moment to take a deep breath before I knocked lightly upon the door.

My tapping was immediately answered by a *"Ja. Kommen Sie"* in a booming voice.

I did as ordered and opened the door. The Colonel was upon his feet with his hand outstretched to take mine in welcome. I made a timid, wobbly curtsey as if meeting royalty. He smiled broader at that, offered to take my coat, and bade me sit in one of the very comfortable-looking leather club chairs in front of his desk at the end of the room. As he hung up my coat in a wardrobe cabinet and I sat in the oh-so-soft chair, I had a minute to look around his office. It was a long wide room with marble floors, and a fireplace against one wall surrounded by deep and colorful divans. Across from this wall stood a beautiful sideboard topped with crystal glasses and decanters. The large windows in each corner of the room looked out over a grassy area adjacent to the Sola River. I sat in front of a sturdy hand carved desk and the large slab of marble on top gleamed like glass. Under one of the corner windows sat a wonderful old Victor Victrola with flowers painted on the inside of the huge horn. The room was beautiful and masculine, even larger than Antoni's prior office.

The most obvious item that caught my eye, and I imagined everyone else's who entered this room, was the ceiling-tall bookshelf behind his desk. It was beautifully carved with the full relief of several country folk positioned in the middle of the unit. They were all poised with their arms above their heads, giving the illusion of supporting the many shelves above them. What gave me cause for a second look were the items contained on the shelves. Toys! Twenty to thirty perfectly maintained toys. Some were colorful, hand-pulled wagons; others were hand carved puppets. Many were American toys, others looked French. They had to be very old, perhaps family heirlooms, yet they were all in excellent condition, their colors bright and dust free. It lent an air of a happy carefree atmosphere, incongruous considering where I sat.

"Ah, you have noticed my vice," said The Colonel as he stood next to me. "The one thing I can never pass up is an original old toy in pristine condition. Silly, I know, but..." and he shrugged his shoulders as if to say, "what can I do?"

"Well, I think they are absolutely wonderful. You must have been a collector for many years. Some look quite old."

He smiled at my enthusiasm. "Some were my father's, some my grandfather's. I even have one or two of my own, those that I did not break or chew apart as a child." I grinned to think of him as a small child and I wondered if his voice was this beautiful when he still wore short pants. "Perhaps someday I shall be able to show you the rest of the collection, *ja?*"

"Oh, yes. I would like that very much," I responded honestly.

"*Und so*, I have refreshments here for us while we discuss your duties and answer the many questions I am sure you have, *ja?*" With that, he brought a tray from the sideboard containing drinks and sweets. "Would you like a small glass of vodka or iced lemonade?"

I thought about that for a moment. As our national drink—it was invented in Poland (although the Russians would argue that fact)—vodka was usually consumed by my fellow citizens from an early age. However, I found the spirit loosened my tongue and since I continually had trouble with that particular muscle without alcohol, I opted for lemonade. Oh, and a slice of Kasekuchen; cheesecake. A moment of guilt passed through me; here I was eating and drinking like a queen and so many others were starving. I tucked in anyway and with great bites, I am ashamed to say.

As he took his own seat behind the desk, The Colonel became all business. The Kommandant of the camp is Rudolf Höss, he told me, a very calming man and easy to get along with. His office was in the building I had seen within the perimeter of the camp. That, he went on, was the Administrative Building where prisoners were first brought, rather like an induction center. Our office acts as a liaison between the camp, Heinrich Himmler, and Adolf Eichmann. "Have you heard of these men?" he asked me. I nodded. Everyone had heard of these men. "So, you know how important they are to the Third Reich. Occasionally, we may expect a visit from either one of them. Nothing has been arranged, you understand, but one never knows.

"This camp operates as a Prisoner Of War camp—POW camp for brevity's sake. At this moment, the camp contains mostly criminals and agitators. The camp is also a work camp and the prisoners are used for labor in the surrounding farms, camp maintenance, and so on. These offices are newly constructed but the buildings within the camp are not.

"Your duties will be primarily confined to messenger service within this building, requisitions for various goods, and accounting ledgers. Herr Himmler likes to be kept up to date of expenses and it is this office's duty to ensure that there are no unexplained expenses. When you wish to travel home or elsewhere by train, Corporal Konig will gladly take you anywhere you wish. He has been with me for many years. You have met him, I believe, at the railway station as your driver."

"Oh, yes. Thank you for sending him. Although I could not help noticing the train tracks that would have allowed me to arrive directly at the camp. I could have traveled here without using the corporal's services."

He shook his head decisively. "Those tracks are for prisoners only, not for public transportation," he said. "So, now, where was I? Oh yes, I hope to eventually use your language abilities to communicate with the prisoners or even the *kapos*." I raised my eyebrows at that. Kapos? "They are German political prisoners that have been given some measure of authority over the other detainees so our soldiers are not kept from other duties." Like killing Poles, I thought. "Also, the fences surrounding the camp are electrified so you mustn't touch them under any circumstances. At times, you can hear them humming but you will become used to that. Do you have any questions so far?"

I shook my head and set down my cheesecake. It tasted wonderful but I seemed to have lost my appetite. "*Gut*. Oh, yes—we have a *Kanteen*, a cafeteria of sorts, on the lower level for staff and soldiers. The food is very good and it would be included with your pay, of course."

"I have one suggestion for you, though Fraulein. Please do not think me presumptuous but it has to do with your hair." I involuntarily reached back to touch my braid. "You are aware how very German your coloring is, *ja*? I think it would be to your advantage to promote that likeness. Many may be suspicious of you and possibly not as friendly if they know of your heritage. I would like to suggest that you wear your hair unbraided. Perhaps you could just loosen the braid or tie it back? I am not suggesting that you should cut it, by any means, just something a little more...German in style."

"Do you mean a ponytail?" I asked.

He seemed relieved that I understood. It was obvious he was uncomfortable attempting to describe anything feminine in detail. "*Ja, ja*—that is what I should have said. Ponytail. Or simply loose. I would hate to have you spoken to in a rude fashion. I do not have the time for reprimands over such a trivial situation."

And I had thought he was worried for my safety. I had to admit, though, it was a very good idea. It would probably be much safer if everyone believed I was German, considering how disliked the Poles were. I readily agreed with his suggestion.

He seemed to pause before he continued. "*Ja*, well, now about your accommodations. I promised to reserve a room for you in a boarding house, but none was available where I felt you would be...comfortable. Few are privately owned any longer and many of the rooms are let out to soldiers who prefer to live in town or reserved for their...personal use." He was not about to tell her these rooms were used for the entertainment of prostitutes or mistresses. "If you would please follow me, I think I have a solution if you are agreeable."

With that, he rose from his chair and I followed suit. Crossing over to a little side door with a frosted glass window, he flung it open and allowed me to enter first. The room I walked into was about a quarter in size to that of The Colonel's office. To the right against the wall were several tall filing cabinets. Next to those was a solid wood door leading, presumably, to the hallway of the building. Across from the cabinets was a small table with one long middle drawer, a typewriter, and a multi-line telephone situated proudly on top. Directly in front of the table/desk stood two straight-backed wooden chairs, something akin to kitchen chairs. The other chair in the room was a swiveling office-type situated behind the table. It was padded in all the right places, and looked exceedingly comfortable when compared to the other available seating. Directly across from the adjoining door to The Colonel's office stood another duplicate door. I looked up at him questioningly.

"This will be your office. The connecting door will make it easy for us to work together. That door," he said pointing to the duplicate on the opposite wall, "leads to Antoni's office. Your phone has three lines attached to it; one is my phone number, one is yours, and one is your cousin's. I told him you would be happy to answer his line when it rings. That is agreeable with you, *ja*? I did not think you would mind." I was surprised at that bit of news, but I nodded my answer to him.

"This is what I particularly wanted you to see." He strode over to yet another door behind the table/desk and opened it with a flourish. I peeked over his shoulder to see a small room furnished with a bed topped by a colorful quilt and an equally colorful pillowed seat under the large bay window. In one corner stood a serviceable washbasin and mirror above it, and on the opposite wall sat a narrow cabinet closet and heating unit. The walls were painted a very bright yellow instead of the military gray on the office walls. It was crowded but cozy. "Originally, this area was one large room and used for surplus furniture storage until all the offices had been completed. The room was empty so I took the liberty to have a wall built to create both your office and sleeping quarters. Across the hall is the ladies WC and next door to that is a bathing room. There are several other females working in this building so you will not be without companionship. My housekeeper provided the bedding and furniture for you. You two will meet, I am sure, or at least speak on the telephone. The most difficult item to acquire was a paint color other than the usual dull gray. I hope this yellow is not too bright for you." A sunrise had never been so bright. "A locking mechanism is situated in the handle and a sliding bolt to use from the inside. Both of these two connecting doors and the one leading into the hallway also lock so you would be perfectly safe here." With that, he held out a key for me to take. I took it from his hand and walked into the little room. "It is lovely, thank you. I appreciate the feminine touches. Tell me, though; do many staff members work very late that I need be concerned for my safety?"

"Not very often; it depends upon the current situation within the Reich and the camp. Eventually, information from any other camps may travel through this office as well. We may become very busy at some later date. So, will this be satisfactory? We can always search for other accommodations in town if you would like."

I replied that this would be fine and thanked him once again for his efforts. It had been only days since I accepted this position and in that time span, all this reconstruction had been completed. Efficient to the core, these Germans. Still, I hoped this would only be temporary. If those dammed Americans would only become involved maybe this war would be over soon.

Chapter Five

February 1941

BOREDOM SETS IN

I spent the first few months in my new position primarily in the office building during the day and my private sleeping cubicle at night. I had thought Antoni would be surprised to see me sitting at my desk, looking every bit the Polish collaborator. He had obviously been told of my arrival and simply presented me with a slight smile and a gleam in his eyes when we first met. So far, he had kept his hands to himself but I could not deny the heat I felt whenever he leaned in closer than was required to impart information or when he perched himself upon my desk, allowing his leg to touch my knee. It was all conducted innocently enough with outward propriety; only two cousins quietly conversing. Had it not been for his wolf-like smile when he believed no one else was in view, I might have believed his nonchalant attitude. Remembering his kiss and hands on my body, I knew better than to underestimate Antoni.

I had developed a sort of friendship with a slightly older German girl who worked downstairs in the communication office. Taller than I (who was not?), and quite a bit bustier (again, who was not?), Berta was loud and bawdy, funny enough to make me forget she was German, and she took me under her ample wing. We made a habit of taking meals together in the Kanteen. The more we saw of each other, the more I actually liked her. She was impressed to learn who I worked for ("Oh, he is dreamy.") and told me if men ever bothered me I should use my colonel's name to extricate myself. She, on the other hand, never seemed to extricate herself from any man's attention and I had the feeling she had "been around the block" a few times, to quote Buscha. I kept her suggestion in mind but for the most part, it was not men I had difficulty with but rather one particular irritating mechanism in my office.

My duties were simple enough and, luckily, Colonel Müller knew of my shortcomings with the written German language. He wrote any personal letters needing to be hand delivered within the offices or posted which, he said, were usually confidential anyway. His copies were locked in a desk drawer and I need not concern myself with them. That is where the trouble with the typewriter came into play.

I knew the Germans were a detail-oriented lot; I had only to read the many facts on my identification papers to bear this out. However, until now I had not realized just how notorious they were at gleaning information and passing it along. Everything I typed was at least in triplicate, usually more. My fingers were continually smeared with traces of carbon leavings in my attempts to control the shifting of so many copies between the paper guide and the platen. Occasionally, the hungry machine would shred the form I had worked so diligently upon as if it were gorging itself. I was sure it took great pleasure in torturing me because it was German made. Even Nazi machines hated Poles, I thought.

As organized as the various war departments seemed to be, I wondered why the documents could not have been easier to use. When pushing the return lever, none of the lines fell within the area of the typewriter's type guide. The entire process would take far longer than it should have. Several times, in complete frustration, I gave this device of torture several hearty thumps with anything at hand resulting in many of the lettered type-bars to become jammed together.

Most of my required typing was the transference of information from spidery handwritten ledgers to forms for Berlin. I was becoming, in a word, bored. Even the avoidance of my cousin was becoming tiresome.

I had been able to keep out of Antoni's clutches these several months, however difficult it was. When I traveled to other parts of the building,

I used the stairs and always peeked around corners first. Occasionally, I would be forced to duck into an office on some excuse when I would see or hear him approaching. The whole thing was becoming ridiculous, I thought. This was still the same person I had known my whole life and now I was running from him.

One day, I was outside carrying a large stack of books and requisition files, making my way across the grassed rear of the office building toward an exterior entrance in this maze of offices. As I rounded the corner, I saw my cousin with his back toward me, smoking a cigarette. As quickly as I could, burdened as I was, I turned around and scrabbled back the way I had just come, rather like a hobbled crab, my bundle slipping precariously in my arms. When he did not burst in after me, I counted my blessings and made my way to another exit to continue my journey, ever on my guard.

Several weeks later, I stood in front of The Colonel's desk having been ordered to report to him prior to a weekend trip home. I stood there until he had decided to address me.

He briefly looked up at me before turning his attention again to the papers on his desk. "So, Fraulein, I have received a report on your efforts from Kommandant Höss. He compliments your very precise and clear ledger transcriptions. For the first time, he said, he can actually read his carbon copies quite nicely.

"*Danke, Mein Herr.*"

"And you have not had any concerns with soldiers of the camp or in these offices?" When I did not answer immediately, he stopped writing and lifted his gaze to me.

I did not want him to know I had taken Berta's suggestion and used his name to disentangle myself from a few of the more amorous advances. I was not sure how he would respond to that. "*Nein, Mein Herr.* Nothing to speak of," I offered. I realized he was waiting for me to continue. "Only a few looks here and there but I have been able to outrun any problems," I finally responded, keeping my eyes down.

At that, he sat back in his chair, folded his hands, and brought his two index fingers to his chin saying, "Really? I seriously doubt that. You do not run very well, you know. I have seen you."

I was horrified to realize he had seen my awkward crab routine from his window as I fled from Antoni. I turned scarlet.

When I looked up, I saw that he was smiling and I could not help but offer a slight smile in return.

"Ah, a smile! You wear it much better than a frown, Fraulein. Enough for today. See to your mother."

"*Danke, Herr* Colonel. *Auf wiedersehen.*" He had resumed his writing before I had even offered my good-byes and I realized he was no longer paying attention to me.

Chapter Six

February 1941

THE CAMP

$\mathcal{M}$ax was disappointed I had no information other than food consumption amounts to report. When I told him I had not been allowed to enter the camp, he sighed and said we would just have to give it time.

Today I made a monumental decision and decided to broach Colonel Müller with it. He stopped writing and looked up at me with a smile. I noticed he always seemed genuinely glad to see me when I entered his office. "Ah, Fraulein, how nice you look today. *Was kann ich for Sie tun? What can I do for you?* Please, sit, sit," he said as he rose from his chair and gestured toward one of the usual club chairs. Looking idly at his toys, I noticed he had a few new ones displayed.

"Herr Colonel," I began, deciding to plow directly ahead, "I would very much appreciate it if I could have another task that might take me out of the office building for a while. It is no reflection upon you, you understand, but those requisition forms are becoming monotonous." He had stopped smiling. I began to speak faster. "I realize their importance but perhaps I could help in some other way as well? Even walking to the camp and retrieving the ledgers on my own would be a break in routine.

Perhaps it would release the messenger to perform some other duty." His stoic expression had not changed and I realized I was beginning my customary babble. What did I know of a messenger's timetable? The wheels of the German Reich seemed to spin faultlessly enough without my suggestions.

He leaned back in his chair and clasped his hands while bringing his two index fingers to his chin in the thoughtful manner I knew was habitual. After several minutes of having him stare at me, he said, "Perhaps you are right. The fresh air and walk may be good for your health. I will have an entrance pass prepared for you so perhaps you can visit the camp by the end of the week, *ja?*" I nodded. *"Gut.* You shall formally meet Kommandant Höss; in fact, I shall take you myself then you can proceed with your errand. New ledgers would involve different documents to complete but perhaps these will not involve beating the defenseless writing machine." He said this last bit with a dimpled smile and I smiled back. How could I not? The conversation had ended friendly enough so I wondered why my request had given him momentary unease.

Three days later, The Colonel rang my telephone line at 9:00 a.m., asking me to come into his office. He looked very serious as I sat in my usual chair, my hands clasped in my lap, waiting for him to speak. I had taken special care with my toilette this morning, curling my loose hair and giving me what I believed to be the look Veronica Lake had sported in movie magazines. Any look was preferable to my danger -ridden Polish one. "Fraulein, before we make our way to the camp, there are a few…details I wish to discuss with you. First, I have your pass," he said as he handed it to me across his desk. As my fingers found his, I tried to ignore the tingle I felt from his touch. Stop it, I told myself; you have a job to do here.

My photo was at the top, a duplicate to my identification papers. At the bottom was his complete signature, Colonel Wilhelm Müller. Wilhelm? Funny, I never knew his first name. In fact, I never thought of him as having a first name, although I suppose all Nazis do. He was simply The Colonel to me.

As I read the information under the photo, I was shocked to see my name listed as Marta Wolf, distinctly not a Polish surname. I looked up at him. *"Ja,* as you can see I have…adjusted your name slightly. I thought it safer." He looked at me as if I should completely understand but I was frowning; I preferred my good, solid, Polish name. He sighed and went on, "The guards in the camp are not as...tolerant of others as I am. In fact, many have an intense dislike for Poles. I did not wish you to be harassed by any of them if they should see your pass. Also, the prisoners might think of you as a traitor. I understand they have their own form of punishment for traitors." Prisoners harming other prisoners? I understood but I did not like it. I nodded my head in compliance anyway.

"Now, as to the camp. Auschwitz is conducted under the most confidential means; nothing you see or hear will ever be discussed outside these walls, *verstehen?*" I nodded my head quickly in comprehension. "These are prisoners, you understand, and as such are treated accordingly. We do not mollycoddle prisoners; they wear prison clothing and their heads are shaved to keep the lice population under control. We spray for the infestation regularly, but..." I was not sure if he meant the lice or the prisoners. "Many will have lost weight, prison food not being on the same caliber as in our Kanteen." He stopped at this point and I thought he was trying to tell me something left unspoken. I could only look back in puzzlement since I was far from clairvoyant. Placing both hands upon his desk, he stood, saying, "No matter. You will soon see. Remember, you wanted a walk," he finished enigmatically. I have to admit I was slightly alarmed at that but he was right; I had asked for this, not only out of boredom but because I felt I owed it to Max.

The Colonel and I left directly, walking around the office complex toward the front of the camp. I knew the rear gate was closer to our office and I wondered why we did not use it. We passed several soldier's *Kasernen* or barracks along with officer quarters. Kommandant Höss, I knew, had a very nice two-story home he shared with his wife and children a little farther from the camp.

The train tracks were along one side of the camp necessitating the walk from a railcar to a hard surfaced clearing at the front entrance for any newcomers. As I stopped to stare at it, The Colonel said shortly, "Crushed brick and granite. Solid but allows for drainage. We call this space Kanada. The prisoners' belongings are sorted here. Kanada is considered a country of wealth and riches, hence the term. Ironic, *ja?*" Ironic and sick, I thought.

I had seen the intimidating curved iron archway announcing *"Arbeit Macht Frei"* but had never passed beneath it. I wondered if it was truth or pacification; would work really set the prisoners free? The statement was constantly tested as I knew the prisoners were loaned out to commercial establishments and worked around the camp for long hours of unpaid labor. I saw several of them through the wire who were so enveloped by the black-and-white striped garment it looked as if the uniforms were wearing the men.

The closer we walked toward the arched entrance, the more I could hear the constant hum of the electrified fences. Looking up I could see the guards moving in the cramped watchtowers, machine guns at the ready, trying to stay alert during an obviously boring assignment.

The entrance guard sharply saluted The Colonel as I showed him my pass and I caught my first view of the camp. Straight ahead was a wide road rather like a main boulevard. Jutting off this were many others lined with long brick buildings. Sidewalks ran the length of the streets with wide grassy areas adjoining the cement. In these patches of green grew tall flourishing trees. This did not look like a work camp but rather the site of a university or large commercial facility. The buildings were all two stories with a third smaller floor under a steeped roof.

Turning right, we passed a long, white wooden building with a dozen chimneys protruding through the roof. "Kitchen," he said. We turned slightly right again toward the long brick Administration Building lined with windows and dormers.

The Colonel entered without knocking and I was close behind. The secretary who was masterfully typing away at the same machine I seemed to have so much difficulty with, smiled coyly to The Colonel as she announced his presence via an intercom system. Striding through the connecting door was a man shorter than Colonel Müller but stockier in build with close-cropped hair against a rather square head. He smiled and presented another of those snappy salutes with The Colonel responding in kind.

Since my assignment here, I had learned from Berta that the salute became an ordinary and mandatory way of life since Hitler and the Nazi party came into power. Postmen used the greeting when they knocked on people's doors, department store clerks were instructed to greet customers with "Heil Hitler, how may I help you?" and dinner guests often brought glasses with "Heil Hitler" etched upon them as house gifts. To alleviate punishment, small metal signs reminding citizens to use said salute were displayed in public squares, on telephone poles, and street-lights throughout Germany.

Children were indoctrinated early in life using simple innocent methods. Kindergarten children were taught to raise their hand to the proper height by hanging their lunch containers across the raised arm of their waiting teacher. First-grade primer books contained a lesson on the greeting, class and teacher would salute each other at the beginning and ending of the school day, between classes, and whenever an adult entered the room.

It was a deplorable practice, one I wished to take no part in. To avoid my participation, I pretended to trip instead.

"Herr Kommandant, I would like to present to you Miss Marta," said The Colonel after gripping my elbow to steady me. His touch brought a quick bolt of electricity down my arm but he seemed unaffected by it. "We are very glad she consented to be our secretary and generally keeps our office running smoothly." The Colonel made it sound as if I had done them a great favor and I was pleased at the introduction. It would serve me well to make friends with everyone connected with the camp. As an afterthought he said, "She is also fluent in Polish and English. Perhaps you could use her translation talents from time to time."

Herr Höss took my hand and planted a wet kiss. "But, *Herr Oberst*, you did not tell me she was so pretty. You will have to spend much more time within the camp, Fraulein." I smiled my most flattering smile and thanked him very much for such nice words.

During our small talk, another officer entered. "Ah, Fraulein, allow me to introduce to you my *Schutzhaftlagerfuhrer* Karl Fritzsch. Karl, this is Fraulein Marta. We will be seeing much of her in the future," said Herr Höss.

Again, the hand kiss and my forced smile to the Deputy Commander I must not cross. "A pleasure, Fraulein," he remarked. I thanked him and kept the smile on my face. He was a tall, thin man with a long face. His blond hair was receding and he had what could be called a patrician nose: long, narrow, and rather Romanesque.

Waiting for me to speak, I decided to begin my underground assignment immediately and try to learn about the camp. I must also find my contact, the prisoner known as Tomasz Serafinski, and I had no idea how to accomplish that. "This camp is much larger than I had expected it to be," I began. "So many buildings and fences. I suppose having the railway tracks so near was helpful with the building materials."

Höss and his deputy looked at each other and then presented me toothy grins. "Building materials?" laughed the Kommandant. "Not so many of those, Fraulein. Twenty-two buildings were already here, you see, although filthy and infested with rodents and vermin. It had been an abandoned Polish army camp. The cleaning alone took months. I drove 90 km just to scrounge teakettles and pilfered the barbed wire wherever I could. A monumental task, I assure you. Now, of course, the electrical fence is doubled and we receive goods regularly. Did you know that fourteen of the buildings were only one story high when I arrived? Since then, they have all been expanded to two stories, many with an attic space on top. We have done our best to match the style and even the bricks to those of the existing structures." Naturally, I thought. Conformity above all else. "You see, Fraulein," he further explained, "I was expected to have this camp ready in a short time to house ten thousand prisoners.

Ten thousand, I thought. Dear God. "But, Herr Kommandant, I did not see that many prisoners on the way to your office. In fact, very few. How many are here?"

"Oh, that is not surprising. Most are out on work details or maintaining the buildings in the rear of the camp. The others are in the medical ward. But we have 10,900 prisoners now, correct Herr Fritzsch?"

"*Ja, Mein Herr*. All Polish political prisoners. We are overcrowded at present but they do not last long," he said with a laugh.

"You see, true opponents of the state must be securely locked up. Only the SS are capable of protecting the National Socialist State from such threats. All others lack the necessary...fortitude," said Höss.

I did my best to retain an unemotional expression on my face. All Poles, I thought, probably all Intelligentsia or those who proved any threat, real or imagined. I noticed Kommandant Höss was watching me intently, waiting for a reaction. Did he know I was Polish? "I see. Well, it seems you have accomplished much considering how remote the area is."

"Ah, but it was not always so. The Polish population was...removed and we enlisted three hundred Jews to improve the camp. We have a 40 km clearing surrounding the camp giving the impression of isolation. Perhaps the Fraulein would like a tour of the camp. Deputy Fritzsch, would you be so kind?"

"Oh, I do not wish to be a bother, Herr Kommandant. I should get the ledgers and go back to the office. Really, you must have more important things to do."

"I assure you, Fraulein, it is no bother. I would be most happy to show you the workings of the camp," said the deputy.

I glanced at The Colonel, hoping he would say that we had overstayed. Instead, he said, "The ledgers can wait. The Kommandant and I have business to attend to. It should take *dreizig Minuten.*" He turned back to Herr Höss and I was dismissed.

"Fraulein, after you," and I was led out the door for my thirty-minute tour.

Walking out of the Administrative Building, my guide informed me that this building was also the induction center for new prisoners. Here they would be registered, deloused, head shaved, and given uniforms. I could well believe it; the building was enormous with various wings stretching out in several directions. Slightly behind this was a most elegant structure, also of brick, with a beautifully constructed turret extending from the second story. This, said the deputy, was the original theater building. It had been left exactly as they found it. Now it was used to store prisoners' personal effects.

As we passed the length of the kitchen, I noticed a dilapidated guardhouse the size of an elevator or lift with a square steeple on top. "It is an old sentry box original to the camp and simply left in place. Now, it stands on the *Appelplatz*, our Roll Call Place, where the prisoners gather every morning and every evening to be counted. It is quaint, ja?" I agreed, then asked about the music I heard each evening. "Ah, the camp orchestra. They are actually quite good. They play each morning at 0430 hours for first roll call and when the prisoners return at 1630 hours. Also when new prisoners arrive, for special occasions, even for entertainment."

"Do you mean the prisoners begin each morning at 4:30 a.m.?" I asked.

"They have time to wash and have breakfast afterward. Then they go to their work detail."

The weather was getting cooler and as we walked, I gathered my sweater tighter about my shoulders. I wondered how the prisoners stood in the cold each morning as all 10,900 names were called. It must take hours. "Ah, but you are cold," noticed the deputy. "Here, we will begin in the kitchen. It is warmer in there. This is the prisoners' kitchen," he said above the banging and clanging. The racket became louder toward the rear of the kitchen where several prisoners were washing utensils in enormous sinks. Deputy Fritzsch was describing the kitchen equipment and appliances but I no longer heard him. The haunted look in the men's eyes was devastating. One had an open gash above his eye, another had a crudely bandaged hand. I was rooted to the spot while the annoying Herr Fritzsch kept jabbering.

"Come, I will show you the *Kasernen* and the *Krankenhaus*," my guide said. I replied that I would be most interested in the barracks and hospital while telling myself to keep a straight face. Do not fall apart in front of this Nazi. He continued to prattle on about the many other buildings: storage, showers, barbershop, general store, and the morgue.

Noticing the markings upon the prisoner's uniform, I asked him what they meant. "All the prisoners have the red triangle with the bold letter **P** in the middle for Pole but even that is subclassified depending upon the transgression. For example, for repeat offenders who are Polish a red line is added above that symbol. If they are part of the punitive group, a round patch with a black circle inside is sewn under their original triangle. *Verstehen?*"

"I think so. Only, why are some in the punitive group?"

"Oh, the reasons vary and are sometimes very random. Once a prisoner has that patch upon his clothing, they receive the most stringent of disciplinary measures. One of our guards disapproved of the way a prisoner looked at him so he got a new patch." He laughed and shook his head, "That particular guard takes offense at everything and still these Polish pigs do not learn." I really wanted to smack this man. "All identifications are on the shirt of the uniform," he went on, "as well as on their pant legs. If you would like, I could send you the complete chart explaining each badge. They have all been carefully thought out for each type of traitor in every country." I felt sure that would be very helpful, I replied.

As we continued on our walk, the scenery was becoming as far removed from the initial university-like surroundings as a cobra was to a kitten. There were no sidewalks here in the barrack area, only dark dank earth. The ground was solid today but I could imagine the sea of mud and slime during the rainy season. Noticing the careful placement of my feet, my guide informed me of the galoshes I would need later in the year. Either he could read my mind or my face betrayed my thoughts. Maintaining this pretense of nonchalant interest was more difficult than I had expected.

"Do you see the smoke in the distance, Fraulein?" I nodded as we walked closer to a belching chimney. I would see the black smoke billowing over the landscape for days on end. "That is the morgue where the dead are stored in a holding room until we place them in the ovens. Or I should say, until the prisoners place them. It's part of the duty roster, you see."

I could barely get the word out. "Ovens?"

"Where the bodies are burned, of course. Typhus is a very communicable disease, spreading very quickly. The only sure way to stop the transmittal of it is to completely burn the infected. It seems to work fairly well. Outbreaks are less frequent." I thought I would be sick and tried to push from my mind the picture forming of broken bodies being stuffed into a flaming oven. I swallowed quickly several times.

The barrack we entered was dark and it took a moment for my eyes to become adjusted to the gloom. I would have preferred the dark to what I saw. The floor was made of cement and bunk beds of rough planks were stacked three high. The mattresses were no more than filthy thick cloths and the entire building smelled like old people. At the end of the barrack was a tall, rectangular, heating unit that did not feel particularly effective.

"Conditions have improved since the camp was opened. We have only begun adding these bunks. In the early days, the prisoners did not have indoor toilet facilities then or mattresses. The showers and latrine were outdoors. Now indoor facilities are in each Kaserne and the beds are softer," he said in disgust. "I am against such coddling. These are prisoners, after all."

He showed me this improved area containing twenty-two toilets, urinals, and washbasins. As the only facility in the building, prisoners on both floors used it. Hundreds of men using twenty-two toilets, given only seconds to do so each day. And this was an improvement?

As we exited, he inquired if I was feeling all right. Of course I was not all right! Realizing he was waiting for me to answer, I needed an explanation for my silence. "Yes, thank you. I had not expected the...smell, that is all." He seemed to accept it and I tried to change the subject. "The brick looks lighter on the second floor of this building. Is this one of the original single stories the Kommandant spoke of?"

"Ah, you have a good eye. Berlin tried to send us the exact match but the old ones had weathered over the years." I had learned since I had been here that "Berlin" was often used as an analogy for The Nazi Regime and by extension Adolf Hitler. No matter where goods or materials had been requisitioned from, even if only a few kilometers away, they were always associated with Berlin as if God had personally sent it down. Camp personnel spoke very reverently of Berlin.

We walked still farther when I stopped to ask a question. "Between these two barracks. This wall with the black structure in the middle. What is this?"

Standing in front of a brick wall between two barracks stood a three-sided wooden structure covered in black cork. This was the Black Wall, he said, an execution point. The cork protected the bricks from bullet damage. He went on to point out the adjoining barracks.

"This building is Block 10, the medical building," he said, pointing to the left structure. "This one," he said, pointing to the right adjoining one, "is Block 11, our prison within a prison. Only the most hardened criminals or those who have transgressed in a serious manner are held here. Someone who has tried to escape, for example. It teaches them all obedience." He went on to describe the external elements of the building. At ground level, sat cement squares resembling shoe boxes minus their tops. These were called wells, which prevented prisoners an outside view from their cell. A small amount of light and air filtered into the cells through these. The upper windows were heavily barred. These were holding cells until the prisoner's trial; courtrooms were also located in Block 11. I could only imagine such a trial.

"Many of them arrive here previously convicted of crimes. Usually, local police units send along their files with notations reading "return not desired" or "do not transfer." Others have a red "X" on their file cover with the execution date specified. We sift through the files, pull a few, and proceed with the execution." His callous description of these acts of murder gave me chills.

As we walked to the other side of this Block, the morgue was in clear view. Long and wide, two slopes of grass grew from ground level to the roof on each side. A wide and tall chimney shot up through the roof, belching thick black smoke. Small flecks of dark ash were floating in the air and I quickly brushed one off my sleeve. "You will get used to that, Fraulein," he said. "That is the crematoria, the Krema. Would you like a tour inside?"

Good God, no, I thought. "Perhaps on another visit. My time is limited today, I'm afraid." I was amazed my voice sounded almost natural, far removed from what I felt.

As we retraced our steps, he turned my attention to the opposite walls of Block 11. There were no wells along these walls, only black metal angular boxes at ground level. Shaped like mailboxes, I knew they could not be that innocent and I waited for the deputy to explain. These were connected to standing cells in the basement as air vents, he said. Looking closer, the smaller holes could be seen. The cells, he said, were used as punishment, usually for twenty-four hours or so, and then the prisoner would be released to resume the rest of the workday. I still looked vaguely skeptical so he asked me if I would like to see one. Yes, please, I said, hoping, praying it would be vacant.

The building was freezing. I wondered if the courtrooms had heat. Probably not, I thought, the "trial" would last only long enough to pronounce sentence. Making our way to the basement, one side of the long room held doors of regular height but seemed much heavier than necessary for these helpless men. Each one had a round peephole in the middle.

Along the other side were several doors at knee level. I thought they were cubbyholes or some type of storage room. The deputy walked up to one and opened it, allowing me to peer through the metal bars of an interior door. It was a cold, dark cement hole (I cannot call it a room) no more than thirty-six inches square. A man could do nothing but crouch, elbows touching the side walls while his back and knees bumped the other two walls. They may be called standing cells, but no one could stand in these. Dear God.

"You say the men are usually in here for only twenty-four hours?" I asked.

"Usually. It depends, of course, on their crime. Sometimes the confinement lasts for days. One man got so hungry he actually ate his shoe. Can you imagine?" he said with a laugh. "Others drink their own urine. Animals!"

I'd had all I could take for one day. "Colonel Müller said we had only thirty minutes. I should return."

He looked at his watch. "Ach, *ja*. It is getting late. But I am so disappointed; you did not have time to see the medical buildings or the repair shops." I smiled, saying perhaps another time. The Colonel and the Kommandant were poring over maps of some sort when we returned. "You are late," grumbled Colonel Müller. I opened my mouth to apologize but the deputy began speaking first.

"It is my fault entirely, Herr Colonel. I was intent on showing her the entire camp and I lost track of the time. As it is, we did not cover everything."

As The Colonel rose from his chair rolling up the papers, I thanked the deputy for the very informative tour as the two of us left. As we exited the camp, I noticed a crudely made sign of three flat boards. It was white with a black skull and crossbones painted upon it, the word STOP printed in German and Polish. I hesitated for only a moment but the ever-watchful Colonel noticed my delay. "The high voltage, you see."

Our journey back was one of silence. I barely noticed how quiet we were since my mind was racing like a locomotive. I kept seeing the number 10,900 in my head. So many and still the world did not lift a finger. How could they, the other part of my brain said, if they did not know? That is why you are here. It suddenly occurred to me that not only had I failed to make contact with Prisoner 4859, I had also failed to find a hiding place for the key. Nevertheless, I had learned much about the camp today. I hoped Max would soon place a telephone call to me; I had much to tell him.

{ I }

When the elevator arrived upon our floor, I hurriedly made a mumbled excuse to The Colonel and ran for the Ladies. Quickly dropping the journals, I locked myself into a toilet stall, raised the lid, and vomited until I could only dry-heave and retch. Finally standing up, I blew my nose repeatedly trying to rid the smoke from my sinus, lowered the lid, and sat. The stress of continued politeness to the Germans while struggling with the fate of the prisoners caused me to shake. Wrapping both arms around my body, I began to rock back and forth, back and forth, my mind completely frozen. I kept repeating, "Oh God, oh God. How did it ever get to this? Why did You desert us?"

After an eternity, I heard the door creak open and Berta's voice call out, "Marta? Are you in here? Is everything all right?"

Taking a deep breath, I managed to croak out, "Here. I'm down here."

"Colonel Müller sent me. He called my office and asked if I would check on you. You have been gone almost an hour."

My sluggish mind finally arrived at an excuse. "Oh…yes, I am fine. It is just…uh…my monthly came early and, well, you know how painful it can be sometimes." There, I thought. No man in his right mind would inquire about a woman's monthly cycle.

"Oh, honey, I know. Come. Let me get you a hot water bottle or some aspirin."

I exited the stall and leaned over the sink, looking at myself in the mirror. God, I looked terrible. Splashing cool water on my face, I thought an aspirin might help the developing headache. I wondered aloud what I would tell The Colonel.

"Do not worry about your colonel, honey, I'll take care of him." Walking across the hall, she threw open the door and said, "Well, here she is. With rest, she will be fine tomorrow."

"Fraulein," he began, "are you sure you are well?"

"Nothing to worry about," said Berta, "just a little female troubles." The Colonel immediately looked embarrassed and mumbled something about "whatever you think best."

Locking the door of my sleeping cubicle and glad to be alone, I wondered if I could continue this. Perhaps I should tell The Colonel I wished to return to Bochnia. The AK would simply have to understand. I remembered what Max had said; I would see many terrible things and have to be strong. Luckily, I could retreat to my tiny cubicle if needed. As I thought this, I realized I had already made up my mind to stay.

Chapter Seven

February 1941

PRISONER 4859

*T*he following morning, I was inserting yet another form into my voracious metal machine, determined to complete these sheets with the least amount of trouble. "Now, listen up, you miserable Nazi beast," I threatened. "I do not want trouble today. If you so much as chew one corner of my paper, I swear I will yank out your lettering bars. Understand?" I doubted it would cooperate but I felt better.

First, I decided to decipher the massive book next to me. Opening the padded cover, the first page was clearly laid out before me; identity number, name, age, sex, height, weight, Kaserne where the prisoner was assigned, city of transfer, and a roomy line for comments. This usually entailed the person's crime, unusual features, previous occupation, or sexual proclivities. The last two columns had "date of death" and "reason for death." I forced myself to go back to the column marked "sex." It seemed important this fact be included; did that mean the Germans expected women? And if so, where would that leave the children? Shaking my head to rid myself of these thoughts, I skimmed through the book looking for prisoner 4859 and the assigned barrack. Here. I tapped my finger upon the name and number of the man I must search out. Kaserne number 13. Once I finished this paperwork, I could begin my search.

As I continued to browse through the pages, I noticed with shock the prisoners' ages. In the June, July, and August 1940 transports, boys of sixteen, seventeen, even as young as fourteen, had been interred beyond those humming fences. Fourteen! They were only babies! The more I typed, it was evident that many of the prisoners were highly regarded Poles: teachers, scientists, priests. Others had been machinists or accountants.

The death toll was enormous. Typhus caused the death of many Poles; or so the ledger indicated. I had been told several times that regular fumigation for lice, those nearly invisible causes of the disease, was performed in the camp. As a further precaution, all prisoners' body hair had been shaved off. How, then, could typhus be so prevalent among them? Additionally, an inordinate amount had died from various heart conditions, dysentery, and lung disease. There must be another reason for so many deaths. The Black Wall came instantly to mind.

Giving the Beast a much-needed rest, I counted the thousands of names. After adding and re-adding, subtracting those who had died, then deciding to add them back into the total, I felt I had come up with an accurate number. More than ten thousand men had died here within the year.

{ I }

It took another half day to finish the ledger before I could return it. Another guard, double gates, and I was let loose.

The lead guard was Josef Kramer, a large, heavy man with a huge head and mean eyes. He looked like a thug, someone who probably enjoyed using his ham-sized fists. I had asked Berta what she knew about him but she only warned me to stay away from him. Today he was prowling around the camp, his deep set beady eyes roaming over the compound when he spotted me. Be nice, I told myself, do not let him see how much he disgusts you.

"Was tun Sie hier?" he asked belligerently. "What are you doing here?"

Gritting my teeth, I smiled at him and held out my pass for him to see. "*Guten Tag,*" I began, wishing him a good day. "I work for Colonel

Müller. I have been sent to return this ledger to the Kommandant but I seem to be turned around."

Grabbing my pass, he perused it as if he was sure it had been forged. We stood there in silence for such an unnecessary length of time I was beginning to wonder if this gorilla of a man could read. *"Ja, sehr gut,"* he said finally. "Very good. Come. I will show you the way." His breath could knock over a moose, which surprised me, knowing how the Germans valued cleanliness.

While hatred simmered within me, I somehow smiled sweetly, allowing him to walk with me to the Administration Office hoping to engage him in conversation while staying downwind from his breath. The camp, he said, was somewhat self-sufficient. In addition to housing the prisoners, the camp also contained a tailor shop, leather shop, grocery store, laundry, sorting facilities, storage area, even a library. Everything was fully staffed by the prisoners who needed constant supervision and occasional discipline. He smiled when he said this and I shuddered. And the *Arbeit Macht Frei* message? I inquired. Was this true? Would a prisoner be set free if he worked hard enough?

He chortled at that. "Auschwitz is a Class I camp and that phrase appears on all such camps. I must admit, though, ours is the most grand. But the promise of freedom? That, I think, is up to interpretation. Kommandant Höss feels it refers to work as spiritually setting one free, not physically. Of course, the Polish pigs do not know that," and he laughed from his gut.

We finally reached my destination. Thankfully, this guard did not kiss my hand when he first approached me and I was not about to give him that chance now. I thanked him for his direction and scurried into the office door. I barely heard him say he hoped to see me again before I slammed the door behind me.

Once the massive tome was returned to its designated shelf I decided to search out my contact. Because I already knew where the Black Wall was, I opted to begin there to find Kaserne 13.

Reaching the wall took surprisingly little time so I took a moment to examine the corked structure. The brick wall behind the device was indeed pristine. I wish I could say the same for the corked enclosure. It was riddled with bullet holes and splatters so dark they looked almost black. As I stood there, I heard a voice in poorly pronounced German say,

"You should not be here, Fraulein." I turned around and found myself talking to a living, breathing skeleton. He was taller than I by a good foot but weighed much less.

Caught off guard, I apologized, saying I did not know the area was restricted. "Not restricted," I was told, "only dangerous."

I decided to throw caution out the window and spoke in Polish. His eyes went wide. Looking around furtively, he motioned me to follow him. Although I knew I could overpower this slight figure, I was still apprehensive. Foolish, I told myself. That overabundant imagination again.

His assigned quarters were just three buildings down on the right hand side. My shrunken escort touched my arm as we entered, causing me to jump slightly. He looked at me in amazement. "You are Polish?" I nodded. "What are you doing in this place?" It was a simple question but the answer was complicated. If I told him I worked for a Nazi colonel, would I be perceived as a traitor? Alternatively, was it safe for me to tell this man I worked for the underground? Max told me to trust no one and I believed that was good advice. He said when people are desperate, they would sell out anyone for their own survival. Physically this prisoner was no threat to me but if he imparted my personal information for extra food, I would not be able to help anyone. Least of all myself.

I compromised. "Well, it is a bit complicated. I'm actually searching for Kaserne 13 and I am afraid I am lost," giving the excuse I gave to Herr Kramer. I hoped he did not notice I had sidestepped his question.

He looked at me shrewdly and said, "This is number 13."

I was amazed. How could I have had such good luck? I hoped the man was not lying to me although I could think of no good reason for it.

"I am looking for Tomasz Serafinski. Do you know him?"

He hesitated a moment. He does not trust me either, I thought. Finally, he said, "He is on duty at the Medical Building. Would you like me to show you?"

"Thank you. I would be grateful for the company."

Peeking out the front door first, he opened it wide and we were off. I worried that he might get into trouble if caught walking with me. "We are allowed to walk the camp as long as we are working in some manner. Except for those too ill, of course. I was on my way to the laundry when we met. But Kramer does not need an excuse to beat us. He likes it."

"Tell me about that wall."

"The first shooting was November 22, last year, from midnight until 12:20 a.m. Himmler himself hand-selected forty Poles," he said derisively. Looking past me, his eyes were in the past, reliving the executions. Made very public, every prisoner was forced to stand witness. Those chosen were previously convicted of violence and assault upon German police officials. As such, they were held in Block 11 until forced to strip naked and face the Wall. After the obligatory shot to the back of the head, duty prisoners gathered the bodies and carted them to the crematoria. The switches on the coke-fired furnaces had been flipped the month prior and by now, men were well practiced in the science of corpse burning. All this in only twenty minutes.

"Tell me about the morgue and ovens," I requested.

"It would take too long. Perhaps if we meet again...?" He left the remark open-ended; unwise to plan for the future in this place.

The room I stood in was bright and medicinal white but far from sanitary. The back of a man in a white lab coat looked familiar. My guide said politely, "Excuse me, Mein Herr." When the man turned around, I squealed with delight. "*Wuj* Edmund!" and I ran into a great hug.

"Marta!" he was as shocked as I was. "Whatever are you doing here?" I had forgotten my guide until Uncle said, "Thank you, Pawal," and the stooped man slipped out the door.

I convinced him to explain his story first. "It was simple. I was married to a Pole so I either volunteered my services as an apothecary or would be sent here as a prisoner. Not much of a choice, really, and I thought perhaps I could do some good."

My aunt had been sent to Germany to live with Uncle's family. "I paid a small ransom to have papers forged for her but I knew it was the safest place. My family will treat her well." Antoni had not visited him in this place yet, he told me sadly, although each knew the other was here.

I knew I could trust Uncle so I divulged everything. "But, Uncle, I need to find my contact. His name is Tomasz Serafinski and the man who brought me—Pawal, you called him?—told me he was assigned here. Could I talk to him?"

Uncle became more serious and much quieter when he spoke. "We are all being watched, my dear, always. You must be so, so careful. The prisoners are not supposed to talk to us unless we engage them in conversation relating to the job. Wait—I know. Go down this hallway into office three. I will send him there to you, yes? Now, go…quietly."

Room 3 was proudly announced in old Prussian script over the door. I entered quickly and hid behind the door, feeling like a child about to be caught for stealing a cookie. It was only a matter of minutes before Tomasz entered.

"Talk quickly." He did not believe in wasting time, which I thought was an excellent idea.

Speaking as fast as I could, I told him who I was and why I was there. I pulled out the key from my pocket as proof. I told him about my meeting with his friend, Jan Slodarkiewicz, and our idea to get information back to him through my outside contact. (Max would have been proud of me; I did not use his name).

Now it was his turn. He asked how I found him and I mentioned Pawal. "Good. Then you have met a friend. We have an underground established within the camp and Pawal is part of it. He is a good man and if you ever need to reach me or send a message, go through him. Now, as far as the key…" I could tell he was thinking of a spot we could access. "Quickly, come with me." We walked out the door and down the two steps to look at the foundation. "Look, do you see this narrow crack? The key will fit tightly in there. We will set it at this angle if it's empty, this direction if full." I was relieved my two difficult tasks had been completed in a relatively short amount of time. "The next time you come into camp, I hope to have more time to talk. I will place my key here soon. Some information will not fit into any key and must be passed verbally." I let him go back to his duties while I hugged Uncle good-bye. He assured me he was being treated well—after all, he was not a prisoner—but I was still concerned for him. Before I left he said, "Marta, there is much you should know about this hospital. Next time, we will talk further."

As it so happened, Max called me two days later. "Oh, Max, I am so glad you called. I have so much to tell you."

"No names. Do not use my name on the phone, remember?"

"Yes, yes, I remember. Sorry," I said rather peevishly. I was bursting with news and he was worried about names. At least I remembered to speak in English. I launched into everything I could remember, speaking so quickly I was not sure if he caught it all as the connection was rather scratchy, and his English was sketchy. When I had finished, we set a rendezvous for Krakau instead of Bochnia. It would be better, he said, to change it up a bit. Just as I was finishing our conversation, The Colonel walked into my office.

"Oh, yes, Mother. I miss you as well. Please take care. I love you too." I hoped Max would get the hint. I hung up the receiver and turned in what I hoped was genuine surprise to see him in my office.

"English?" he said. "You are speaking English with your mother?"

I tried to look haughty. "Of course. Polish is banned, remember? I would not want my mother to be arrested while using a public phone"

"I was not aware she spoke English so well."

He was right; I had mentioned it to him once. "She is improving. We can learn quickly when we are forced to." I turned and went back to my paperwork hoping this conversation and my explanations were over. It was not.

He looked at me for a moment and then said, "Fraulein, I came in to let you know we will be receiving a visitor next week; the first of March, in fact. A very important visitor."

My interest was piqued. "Are you allowed to tell me who it is?"

He nodded and said simply, "Reichsführer Himmler."

Chapter Eight

March 1, 1941

THE VISIT

*H*e traveled in the grandest luxury and comfort, everyone ready to do his bidding, all eyes upon him as he passed throughout the Third Reich's territories. Still, he hated these tedious journeys. There was always something pending in Berlin that needed his attention and yet here he was listening to the constant click-click-click of the rail car. To be sure, his train was appointed with only the very best linens, tableware, velvet seats, and fringed shades. The chef was top notch, the bed extremely comfortable, and his personal masseur was always on board. The train contained a library, a dining car, an office, a card table of handcrafted wood, and leather club chairs. And why should he not travel in style? He was Himmler, after all, and nothing was too good for him.

Security had not been forgotten either. Just as on Hitler's train christened Amerika, Himmler's locomotive was reinforced with steel, bullet-proof windows, and carried a dozen bodyguards. He had plenty of room to stretch his legs along the many lengths of cars but it was still cage-like. Thankfully, this trip would end at the gates of Auschwitz.

There was a reason why Heinrich Himmler was one of Hitler's favorites: he could keep a secret. He also had the means whereby others would keep a secret as well. If they did not…well, his Luger came in handy for a variety of reasons. The secret of the camps was the greatest of all.

Thirty German criminals were initially brought to Auschwitz to act as functionaries within the prison system. Some were given trivial duties, others would act as privileged supervisors, the kapos, over the prisoners. The first "residents" of Auschwitz arrived on June 14, 1940—728 Polish political prisoners from Tarnow, Poland. Most were Intelligentsia who had not perished elsewhere. Another large shipment arrived during the first of Warsaw's transports in August but by now, the men were no longer Intelligentsia; that class had all but been wiped from the face of the earth. The Germans were now arresting Poles in area roundups, house checks, and sweeps of public buildings and streets.

The kapos were given much latitude when it came to keeping the inmates in line and could, at times, be more brutal than the uniformed guards. Concentration camps had been operational in Germany since 1933 but Auschwitz was to set the bar for all other future camps. Himmler could be proud of his efforts.

Recently, it had come to Himmler's attention that I.G. Farben Company had shown an interest in the area around "his" Auschwitz. The company was a giant German industrial conglomerate and the fourth-largest company in the world. Having ties internationally, Farben even conducted business with the Bayer Corporation in America. The reason for their interest in Auschwitz was simple; the natural resources located there. They had been experimenting for years in the manufacturing of synthetic rubber and coal, both essential to the Nazi war effort. The three main components needed were water, lime, and coal; Auschwitz had an abundance of each. Himmler had an audacious plan to encourage the Farben Company to build here. The land in question had been eradicated of five thousand Poles and the villages of Birkenau and Monowitz brought to the ground. This enabled camp expansion to encompass 425 acres and room for two hundred thousand prisoners. These people were like insects; the more you scratched the surface, the more of them appeared. Expansion was required.

He fairly shook with excitement when he calculated the millions and millions of RM this area would provide to the Third Reich. Himmler had accumulated the land at no cost and could therefore afford to sell it at a rock bottom cost. The low purchase price would be made up in the fees charged for prisoner labor. The SS, under whose jurisdiction the property belonged, would also sell Farben the raw materials they desired. The collection of prisoners' property meant another source of income. The entire project was a simple moneymaker that was exhilarating and pretentious.

Plans were being drawn for a vast ethnic German settlement with businesses, farms, and the inclusion of yet another Nazi Party Headquarters sprawling near the factories. Detailed plans for an additional home-away-from-home for himself was also part of the overall design. Everything from his sofa to wall hangings, occasional table to crystal drinking glasses; nothing had been forgotten. Construction for the town would also be supplied by the slave labor force while the camp would be completely transformed on the opposite side of the Sola River. Himmler was determined that Auschwitz not only meet his Fuhrer's standards but also expedite his own ambitions. Which brought him to his current musings; Hitler's obsession with England.

At their last meeting, Himmler was politely yet firmly presenting Hitler with reasons to avoid England. *Mein alter Freund*," began the Fuhrer, "my old friend, I know you have only the best intentions for our beloved country as well as for myself. But you must realize, I stand firm in my resolve to put England under our Nazi flag."

Unfortunately for his leader, thought Himmler, Prime Minister Chamberlain had resigned and in his place was a new prime minister, Winston Churchill. Himmler did not believe Churchill would be the useless pushover Chamberlain had been. No, he thought, assuredly Churchill was no pacifist. He had been the Lord of the Admiralty and would not run from a fight. He may even convince the Americans to join forces.

With these pressing thoughts, Himmler looked outside at the dark and depressing landscapes rushing by, and gathered his coat closer. March was a miserable time of year to be traveling here, he thought, no matter how important this visit was. He was arriving in Auschwitz to inform Höss of the expansion, to view the area, and to rate the current camp's effectiveness. It must run as smoothly as a well-oiled Franz Ketterer cuckoo clock.

{ I }

I was returning from lunch thinking of all the food laid out in the Kanteen. Fresh meats and vegetables, crème-filled delicacies and wines were all at the ready for the soldiers to eat their fill. All this, and those poor souls across the fences were subsisting on watered-down potato soup and one slice of bread. I could not even look at the food much less eat it. Berta asked me if I was feeling ill. I just shook my head and said I did not have much of an appetite today. Nothing ever seemed to bother her appetite or her playful mood; she was in the process of having a very good-looking guard lick her index finger, which she had slathered in whipped cream. I left her to her fun, giving the excuse of having work to do. I doubt they even heard me.

Walking past The Colonel's door, it suddenly opened and I was bade to enter. The profile of a man inspecting the toys made my blood run cold. Himmler. The man responsible for this camp, the man who had sworn, "All Poles will disappear from the world."

"Ach, Willie, you and your toys. So many new ones. Why not collect precious art or antique porcelain? After all, we have museums at our disposal."

The Colonel laughed, saying, "*Nein*, Heinrich, I much prefer my toys. My collection is so numerous I often alternate these with others from my home. Now, may I present to you Fraulein Marta, our secretary, and the one who keeps us on our toes."

Heinrich? Willie? What the hell was going on? Were these two men friends? Before I had time to speculate further, the second most powerful man in all of Germany turned to look at me. His photos did not capture him accurately, I thought. Resembling a turtle or perhaps a toad, the round spectacles enhanced this appearance for some reason. He took my hand and placed a forgettable kiss on the back of it. While his hand was lifeless, his eyes were clear and calculating. Although he smiled slightly, the smile never reached those eyes. "My pleasure, Fraulein. It is always good to see our women working for our Fuhrer's cause." I opened my mouth then shut it again, rather like a trout.

The image of Grandpapa's gun flashed into my mind and I was sorry I had not brought it from Bochnia. Then I smelled cigarette smoke and I noticed two men conversing in front of the fire and two others stationed by the doors, Lugers in their hand-tooled leather holsters. I would not have stood a chance.

They were apparently waiting for my response. "I had never expected to meet you, you see, and I am quite overwhelmed." They both seemed to buy that. After mundane small talk, I excused myself while again expressing my pleasure at the introduction and quickly snuck through the connecting door.

Leaning against the wall, I was sure they could hear the thumping of my heart. Himmler was right next door, I thought. I should let Max know and I raced to the phone. Perhaps an assassination attempt could be put into play. It was not until I had the receiver to my ear that I realized I lacked his phone number. At least, I thought, I can listen to their conversation. Perhaps they would speak of something important. It was not the finest plan but I took up position at the wall once more, pressed my ear against it, and waited. I jumped when Antoni strolled into my office. "Cousin, whatever are you up to?"

"Shhhh," I hissed, "I'm trying to listen."

He came closer with his head tilted to one side. "Yes, I can see that. The question is, why?"

It was no use; I would not learn anything with Antoni in the room. Sighing, I took my seat behind my desk. "Well, if you must know, Himmler is in there and I wanted to know what he was saying. There. Satisfied?"

"Indeed? I shall have to beg an introduction." He began to reach for the doorknob.

"Antoni, are you mad? You cannot barge in on Heinrich Himmler… can you?"

"I see no reason why I should not. I am a loyal officer and as such would like to meet him." Turning the knob, he walked into the room. With my ear once again pressed onto that yellow wall, I hoped he would be tossed out by his jackboots. Quite the contrary. Schnapps was handed around and the conversation now included Antoni. Damn!

It was not until Himmler's train pulled out of the vicinity two days later that I had a chance to speak with the Colonel Müller. Something extremely important must be afoot to have the Number Two Man make a personal visit and I hoped to learn the reason.

"So, Fraulein, it was surprising to meet Herr Himmler, *ja?* What did you think?"

How should I answer this? "Well, he looks different in person...ah... shorter." I left it at that but I could tell by The Colonel's smile that he was aware of the restraint I had shown in voicing my opinion.

"It would seem our camp has been so successful, there will be expansion. The town of Birkenau will be the site of a camp that will positively dwarf this one and factories will be constructed over the town of Monowitz. Kommandant Höss will remain in charge and this camp will continue as the administrative center. Over the course of the following year, we will be receiving more prisoners. I imagine your battle with the typewriter will increase somewhat." Although I tried to present encouraging looks to him, he would say no more.

Chapter Nine

March 7, 1941

TRAITOR

*H*e loved this room. Located at the rear of the home, this study was ostentatious and masculine with paneled walls, solid furniture, and heavy draperies now closed against Warsaw's cold morning air. Igo Sym stretched languorously in his soft, emerald-green, velvet easy chair, with his feet upon a damask footstool. Swallowing a large mouthful of imported coffee with heavy cream, he looked across the room at the movie poster sporting a younger rendering of himself. It was a 1925 advertisement from his first big movie, *Vampires of Warsaw*. He had lived the life of a matinee idol since then and at forty-five years old was still handsome and athletic, still attracting the ladies.

Sinking deeper into his chair, he reflected upon his life and career. An Austrian-born Pole, he considered his birth country home and as such had served as a lieutenant in the Austrian army during WWI. Afterward, he moved to Poland and served time in that country's infantry.

Often portraying soldiers and aristocrats in films, his star continued to rise until he was offered a movie contract and became a major European star, acting alongside Marlene Dietrich and Lillian Harvey. What a life!

Adoration and the best of everything. Deciding to try his hand on the Polish stage in the early 1930s, he was surprisingly a very good singer and dancer.

Taking a draw from the excellent cigar in his hand, he realized his political views were unexpected and radical; he was a staunch supporter of Nazism and Hitler. It had never detracted from his popularity, however; his fans loved him more than they hated Hitler. The fact that he was accorded privileges for his allegiance was secondary. He was a true believer.

Goebbels was elated to have someone with such widespread fame openly pro-Nazi and was determined to exploit that. Igo grinned. He knew his celebrity status was exploited but each side gained from the arrangement. He was now the Director of German Theaters in Warsaw and owned the Comedy Theater there. Allowed to stretch his talents further, he became the consultant of the "Only for Germans" cinema.

Much to his delight, the film he had been collaborating on, *Heimkehr* or Homecoming, debuted well. It was all Nazi propaganda, of course, which made it difficult to find Polish actors to take part. Difficult but not impossible. If money did not convince them, threats always did. Ahhh, he sighed, it had been a great undertaking and a cinematic success. His German associates were enormously pleased with his endeavors and continued to tout his participation in the glorious Third Reich. Tomorrow, March 8, he would be leaving for Vienna to continue his celebrity exposure enjoying the best restaurants, hotels, and perhaps a woman...or two. Yes, indeed; war had been good to him.

Eyes closed in a light slumber, this revelry was interrupted by the ringing of the doorbell. Glancing at the gilded mantle clock he thought, Good God! Only 7:10 a.m. Who could be rude enough to bother someone at this hour? Cursing himself for not employing a live-in housekeeper, he drew himself up to his considerable height and made his way to the door.

{ I }

Max received his instructions but was not happy about them. Perhaps another plan could be devised, he suggested. There is no other way, he was told. The underground must show the Germans that the movement was decidedly active, always vigilant.

That had been last night and now he and three others, traveling two by two, were strolling through the city as casually as possible without sweating profusely. Military haircut having long grown out, he looked like any other citizen, simply out for his morning ration redemption. Nothing more than that.

The first two men approached the door while he and his compatriot leaned against the stone balustrade, keeping watchful eyes while maintaining normality. The other two agents, the Rozmiłowski brothers, were dressed as mailmen, appearing cool and calm.

They were ringing the door now, answering the queries from a voice behind the door. "Mailman," Roman Rozmiłowski said. "Dispatch for Igo Sym." Max heard the clicking of the door locks. The occupant was asked to confirm his identity before Max heard a faint pop and saw blood run down the traitor's face.

The retreat from the flat was far from calm; the four men of the resistance ran like hell.

That same afternoon, the German loudspeaker trucks traveled through the city angrily announcing the brutal murder of the beloved actor, Igo Sym, and the capture of 118 hostages. Curfew from 8:00 a.m. to 5:00 p.m. would be strongly enforced, blared the speakers. The Germans gave Warsaw three days to relinquish those responsible or punishment would be dispensed to the hostages taken.

No one surrendered. On March 11, twenty-one hostages were executed while the rest, including several famous actors and directors, were sent to Auschwitz in retaliation.

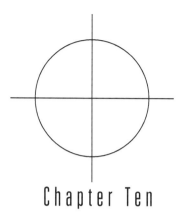

Chapter Ten

April 1941

GREED

*F*ilip awoke in his bed before the whore next to him stirred. They were in his rented flat outside Bochnia, close enough to surrounding towns to pursue his financial dreams. He yawned and smacked his lips loudly yet the disheveled trash next to him slept on. Ashtrays were filled with cigarette butts and empty bottles tossed everywhere, lending credence to the bacchanal he must have had. He looked again at his bedmate and did not remember her looking so, so...cheap last night. Skinny and young with matted bleached blonde hair, her excessive makeup was rubbing off onto his pillowcase. Well, what did you expect, he thought. Money for alcohol and not enough left to buy a decent girl. He would have to cut down on his liquor consumption—must have been unconscious to have given this one a second look. God, I hope she did not give me something, and he quickly raised the bed sheets to examine his shriveled member. Money was the answer to all his problems and he did not have enough. The partnership with the sergeant, formally private (hadn't Filip told him there would be promotions?), was profitable but by the time he paid rent, bought clothes, food, and liquor, enough never remained to get out of this dump and into something more suited to his status. He picked up an open bottle of vodka and swallowed a huge mouthful.

The woman next to him began to snore and drool slightly. He swatted her on her bare ass to wake her up. "Hey, I'm going to take a shower and I want you gone before I finish, understand?"

She turned to him with a toothless smile and smeared lipstick saying, "Sure, honey. I just need my money."

Christ! Hadn't he already paid her? He strode over to his chest of drawers, completely nude. Let her see what she'll be missing tonight, he thought. Looking at the bills folded in his wallet, he counted out two Marks. "How much?" he asked.

"If you promise to call me again, only three Marks."

He told her he would, of course, be calling her again but knew he would not. He did not even know her name and that whiny voice was already grating against his last nerve. He looked inside his wallet again, hoping he had counted wrong the first time. No, only two RM. Shit! He began pulling out drawers, and looking under the bed for enough change to make up the difference. The jelly jar in his poor excuse for a kitchen relinquished the final pfennig needed.

"Here you go, baby. Now get yourself dressed and leave." He thought about waiting to make sure she left without pinching anything but he had nothing left to pinch. Instead, he took another swig of vodka and jumped into the cramped shower to fine-tune a new idea for his financial success. He had one more bit of information to hand over to Sergeant Schafer. It was becoming tiresome finding those Jews and traitorous Poles. He needed an extra stake for the idea he had.

"Ten Marks!" yelled Sergeant Schafer. "That is outrageous." With his promotion came a sense of unwarranted self-importance. He called the shots, not this Pole. He would determine the amount any information was worth.

Filip shrugged. He needed the sergeant's support to continue this arrangement but he was not about to let the sergeant know this. "It may be outrageous, but that's the price. Perhaps I should go to your commanding officer and strike a deal."

The sergeant, on the other hand, also required Filip but was not clever enough to hide that realization. His face suddenly drained of all color and his eyes popped out even farther. Filip watched the man's fleshy lips quiver. "You cannot do that. I would be ruined."

"Oh, do not worry. I will not mention you. After all, have we not been friends as well as business partners? No, no, I shall merely propose doing business with your superior officer for less money than he is now paying. I would not dream of getting you into trouble. Why, you would probably be demoted to private again. Or perhaps not. What do your German officers do with liars and traitors within their ranks?"

They both knew what happened to liars and traitors; the word Auschwitz hung in the air between them.

"All right, all right. Here! Ten Marks. Not so much if I can get repaid from my major, *ja?*" said the show-off once again. "Only tell me, why do you need so much?"

"I have an idea to keep us in Jews for quite some time. Now, let me buy you a beer."

Filip did indeed have a plan and this one could not fail. In fact, if things went the way he anticipated, he would become a very rich man. Moreover, he would collect some self-satisfaction.

That very afternoon, Filip wandered into a boarding house and rented a room in the name of Edward Kazmaryk. The daughter of that household had refused an evening out with him. In fact, she had laughed in his face. Retribution time, thought Filip. After scattering food and used clothing in the space, he made his way to the Jewish sector of the town. There he sat on a curb, lit a cigarette, and waited.

At twilight, he began to see some movement on the streets. He had to look carefully to see them, so adept were they at moving within the shadows, but they were there all right. Although most of the Jews had left or been rounded up, Filip knew many had found some very ingenuous places in which to hide during the day. They were forced to find food and smell fresher air at night, the reason he sat on this filthy street. Dusting the dirt from his pants, he slowly and carefully made his way toward the movements, hugging the side of buildings and blending into the shadows like his prey. He was very non-threatening, obviously not a German soldier, and even the Gestapo dressed better. He was ready to begin this scenario.

Filip wandered down an alleyway to a group of men, offering them each a cigarette. They acted as if he was parting the seas; clearly, they had not tasted tobacco for some time. He began to talk about the sad events unraveling around all of them. Ease into a thing, that was Filip's way. One of the men mentioned his family and Filip began to reel him in. He knew of a place, Filip said, where the man and his family could be safe. He could bring them food and water regularly. In fact, it is already fully stocked. He expected compensation, of course, times being bad all around, and he would need to purchase more food, you see. But it could be done; not a single German had approached him. Filip could tell the man's brain was clicking away ferociously. He had seen enough calculating men to know the signs. How much would it cost him? the man asked. Got you, Filip thought. Well, that depends, he answered. Does your family eat much? The other men laughed and they were suddenly at ease. Can you afford, say, ten marks per day? The man was still thinking but he had not flinched at the amount. I should have asked for more, thought Filip.

"Done," said the man and they shook on it.

Half an hour later, the family was comfortably ensconced in the rented room and warned to stay quiet. The wife wept when she thanked him and he almost laughed aloud. A week's payment in advance was collected and Filip promised to return with fresh food in two days.

His next stop was to meet with Sergeant Schafer. Having settled upon a sum, twenty marks this time, the sergeant enthusiastically hurried to his major while Filip wandered off to the Kazmaryk house. He leaned against a streetlamp opposite the house, allowing the artificial light to embrace his face, and waited for his entertainment.

He was not disappointed. As if on cue, the Mercedes Benz staff car roared up to the home like a bat out of hell. The doors flew open and out heaved three large SS men and one obvious Gestapo officer, the requisite dogs leading the way. Amid much yelling of *"Raus, Raus"* from the Germans and denials of any wrongdoing from the family, the Poles poured from the house propelled along by a German kicking and dragging them. She saw him then just as he had hoped, across the street, legs crossed at the ankle, looking ever so smug. When he offered her a brief salute, Filip was pleased to see her eyes widen in understanding and watched as she was dragged away.

As they drove off, he realized the house had been left open. Well, well, thought Filip. We cannot have some unscrupulous person come along to conduct mischief to this beautiful home. With that, he pushed himself off from the lamppost and strode across the street whistling a German ditty. Whatever I cannot carry tonight I will simply lock the door and come back tomorrow for the rest.

What a perfect day, he thought; not only did I clear ninety Marks but I still have some of the sergeant's original ten Marks left. A small fortune in these times, not to mention whatever plunder he was about to find. He barely had to lift a finger. Revenge was better than sex. Well, at least a close second. At this rate, he should soon be rolling in it and began itemizing those who had slighted him over the years.

Chapter Eleven

April 6, 1941

EYEWITNESS ACCOUNTS

*W*e had finally reached Saturday and as such, the day was my own. If Uncle Edmund was not on duty, I could be directed to his whereabouts. Although the camp's operations stalled on weekends, the trains never stopped. As I passed by a particularly fat kapo, I asked about today's transport. From Pawiak Prison in Warsaw, I was told as he read his records, 1,021 men. Celebrities this time, he said. I looked around to see to whom he was referring. Actors! Several of our most famous Polish screen actors. Why? Other than repeating lines written for them in the movies, what could they have done wrong? Senseless, I thought, shaking my head and continuing on my way to the hospital ward.

As casually as possible, I pretended to drop something, while reaching inside the crevice of Block 10 with my fingers. Nothing. Perhaps Tomasz had not enough time to leave information for me. It was more important than ever to hear what the man had to tell me.

I was pleased to see my uncle when I opened the door. Kisses and hugs completed, he motioned me back into the cold. "I am so glad you came to see me today, my dear. I have a great deal to tell you. Since you were here last, I have been writing everything I can think of in a note-book. I want you to take the pages with you. It explains many things." He went on to tell me he had been copying details from the medical records for me. "The doctors here...they conduct medical experiments on the prisoners, all in the name of science. Hypothermia, warming...the list goes on." I asked him if he could quickly explain. "Do you know what mustard gas is? No? Armies have been using it since the last war as chemical warfare. It does not have an effect when it is first sprayed upon a man but within twenty-four hours, he develops blisters and lesions all over his body. Terribly painful and deforming. After applying the chemical upon a prisoner, the experiment is continued by saturating the wounds with various compounds to find a repellent.

"Then there are the hypothermia tests to determine how long a man can resist cold before dying—to prepare their own men for battle in the cold. Sometimes they strip a man naked and tie him to a stretcher, leave him outside in the snow, and tick off the hours or days until he freezes to death. If it is not cold enough outside, they use ice water and submerge him for hours at a time.

"Or," he continued, "the doctors test the increase of heat upon a man's skin. Again stripped, the prisoner is placed under heat lamps, and the heat is raised by increments. Marta, I have seen men's flesh bubble on their bodies and heard their screams. It's...it's...monstrous! Sometimes, they will retest the burned men in the extreme cold experiments, repeatedly put into the cold, into the heat, and back again. This place is no hospital! It is a test laboratory with an unlimited supply of subjects at their disposal." He was almost in tears. His mouth was very near my ear by now, whispering softly, hissing the 's' words and clicking the consonants, making his tale more unspeakable and indecent. "Thank God there are no women in this camp. I can only imagine what they would do to them. My papers have names and dates, the type of experiment and the outcome. One way or another almost all of the prisoners died." I stood there holding his hand.

"How?" was all that I could say. He merely shook his head and I remembered Mr. Klein telling me that they did this because they could. "Could I talk to Tomasz before I leave?"

"I can have him brought here on some pretext but not for long." Nodding my head in understanding, we made our way back into the building.

"We must talk quickly," Tomasz said and I marveled at this man who had volunteered to enter this hell. "Have you seen the ovens yet? No? You should. This camp has three double-muffle ovens. Do you know what that means? Simply put, each muffle is a compartment that can hold two bodies at a time. So this camp essentially has six heated ovens. The radiating source of fuel burns around each muffle, not directly in it. Understand?" I shook my head. "You will when you see one. Once stoked, they need little tending to stay at 1300 degrees Fahrenheit. They can burn three hundred bodies a day. Sometimes the bodies are burned in pits using wood or human fat as kindling. Ten thousand or more have been destroyed in pit fires. Next to the oven room is the morgue where they stack the dead like firewood.

"Have you seen Block 11?" Nodding, I explained about the standing cell I saw. "There is more. The other cells along that hallway are starvation cells. The Nazis literally throw one or more of us in there, slam the door, and then forget about us. No ventilation, no water, no food. There is a small peephole in the door to observe the prisoner without having to interact with him.

"The cells upstairs are for suspected criminals waiting for trial. Oh, you know of this already? Good. They are built to hold men but often one hundred will occupy the space. Everyone is always found guilty, of course, and it only remains a question of imprisonment or execution.

"Before we gather for roll call, we must make our beds. If the bed is not to a guard's liking, the man is punished. It takes hours to call each name and we stand there rain or shine. Should we misbehave, we are beaten until we can no longer stand. We are not allowed to help any prisoner or we will suffer the same consequence. Many of us drop dead at each roll call.

"Then we receive breakfast; ten ounces of bread, a small piece of salami or perhaps just some margarine, brown liquid that is supposed to be coffee. Another roll call, this time with a siren, and assignments are given out for that day. Thousands are taken to the fields working eleven or twelve hours each day. Lunch is thin soup of carrots and water. Occasionally we receive turnips or rutabagas.

"At the end of our day, another roll call, another four hours of standing. Then dinner; bread with rotten meat or cheese, sometimes margarine or jam, and water. Just when you think the day is done, the sirens scream again, calling for a penal roll call. This is a collective punishment for a crime, real or imagined, of one prisoner. All night long we stand. We stand in the snow, the rain, the cold, fainting from exhaustion. We have lost many men during these all-night calls. Some are shot, some are beaten to death, some simply fall down to die on their own terms.

"I am afraid we are becoming like animals. Those of us who reach the dead first begin to strip him of his clothes, shoes; anything that will ensure further survival. The greatest crime you can commit in here among the prisoners is to steal another man's food. Others have turned traitor among us to receive an additional slice of bread. The Germans actually foment this fighting among ourselves to reiterate their belief that we are subhuman."

"This is how we live each day, Miss, every single day. Here," he said as he reached into his drawstring, "it has taken me some time to acquire these. These will tell you how we are suffering. For all our sakes, do not lose this or let the Nazis find the pages. Get them out; get them out to anyone who can help."

He did not have much time left, I knew, so I quickly told him of Himmler and his plans for expansion. "We will be getting more prisoners before the new camp is completed. I got the impression it would be many, many more. What happens then?"

"Then?" he said sadly. "Then they will eliminate the excess to make room." With that, he got up and made his way out the door, smiling at me as he left. "Do not give up hope. As long as one of us is left to tell the world, we must never give up hope."

Gritting my teeth and nodding politely to the guards, I passed through the gate without incident and hurried back to my office. Once inside the room, I locked all three exits, cranked up the heating unit in my sleeping chamber, and finally climbed under the comforter. My uncle's notes had been neatly cut from a note pad and looked much easier to read. I began there.

I remembered Christmases and birthdays past when I would see his lovely script on gift cards and quickly shoved those memories aside, turning my attention instead to the pages at hand. Here he had enumerated other various forms of torture, all in the name of scientific experiments. Some had detailed descriptions while others were left to my imagination.

1. blood experiments.

2. if prisoners' treatment lasts more than four months, they are killed using phenol hexobarbitone or prussic acid. (I had no idea what these drugs were but I doubted it was a painless death.)

3. brainwashing—tried on the military prisoners using high doses of barbiturates and morphine.

4. cyanide salts injected into prisoners.

5. artificial injections of typhus into prisoners in attempt to establish cure.

6. starve prisoners and remove their organs after death to study results of starvation upon the human body.

With a feeling of dread, I turned to the rest of his notes. He had copied these from the original journal, I was sure, with information neatly arranged in rows and columns. Flipping the pages, I estimated there must be hundreds of names. The dates indicated these experiments began when the camp opened, over a year ago. Names with prisoner numbers, ages, heights, and weights were carefully noted. The description under Test were as my uncle had said: Hypothermia, Warming, Cooling. I was glad he had explained each one to me. Other experiments were more cryptic; LOST (I later learned this was the original abbreviation for mustard gas), H2O, and other initials that seemed to be in code for the doctors only.

I picked one and began to read the details of a submergence test. Every step of the experiment was neatly categorized from the body temperature when the prisoner finally died, to the number of times the man had been plunged. Another test ended with the patient dying by exsanguination; bleeding to death. Time and date along with amount of blood lost was carefully jotted down, even the amount of urine expressed from the bladders were in front of me. What did they hope to learn from all this?

Follow-up comments were appended as well. Some returned to their barrack only to die days later. Others had died before they had a chance to return. Some had the notation after their name of "permanently scarred."

I turned to the first page of Tomasz's missal. Each paragraph or page was in a different handwriting, some bold and strong, others shaky and faint. I started with the first page.

My name is Jerzy Bielcki, Polish political prisoner number 243. As punishment, the SS man wanted me to hang on the hook by my arms placed behind me and tied at the wrist. He said 'stand up on your toes.' Finally, he hooked me and then kicked the stool away. The terrible pain, my shoulders were breaking out from the joints, both arms were breaking from the joints. I had been moaning and he just said 'shut up, you dog, you deserve it, you have to suffer.' I hung there for hours.

One man in my barrack stole another's food. What do we do to get rid of such people? The other prisoners kill them at night. They put a blanket over his face and keep it there until he stops breathing. No one would ask questions. Many of us die each night, this was just one more.

I worked in the barber shop and was forced to cut the SS soldiers' hair or shave their beards. One day, Kommandant Höss sat in my chair. I had the razor in my hand and I thought about slitting his throat but I stopped just in time. What good would it have done? They would have destroyed my family still in Poland and killed many in the camp. Then someone else would have taken his place. It never ends.

My name is Albert. We all work so hard, get beaten for no reason. We sleep because we are exhausted and hope to have the strength to work again tomorrow. When we wake up, many are dead. The rest of us go through their pockets, take their shoes, blankets, anything they left behind. Once I searched a body's bunk and found an old dried piece of bread covered in lice. I shook them off and ate it.

None of us want to walk past Block 11. Sometimes we can hear the men screaming inside for food or water and we can do nothing to help. One of my friends was beaten while in a roll call line then taken there. I never saw him again.

I am prisoner number 563. I was on duty to clean the basement of Block 11. Some of the heavy metal doors were open on the starvation cells. There is no light inside, no air vents, just concrete. The door is paneled in wood and I saw fingernail marks down the length of the wood from men trying to claw their way out. Here too, are the 'dark cells.' The entire room is sealed and they are used to suffocate the men. Sometimes the soldiers light a candle in the room to use up the oxygen faster.

One of the old men fell during roll call this morning. The man next to him tried to help. In an instant, two SS men were beating them with clubs until I could not see their faces any longer, only blood. When the old man could not get up, one guard shot him in the head. The other man, the one who tried to help, was brought to his feet and told he must still work that day. I heard he died later in the fields.

We are always so hungry. We live with the pain in our bellies every day. Sometimes I can smell the food from the SS Kanteen but I cannot remember what it is like to eat real food. Sometimes I think I can feel my ribcage scratching against my backbone. If we scrounge for potato peels from trashcans, we are punished. We would all kill for more food.

It gets so cold here in winter. We are never given anything warmer to wear other than our shirt and pants, not even underwear. Because of the ice on the walkways, the Germans are afraid of slipping. Instead of using salt, we are forced to scatter the ashes of our friends along the paths so the Germans can walk upon them. Polish remains are cheaper than salt.

Karl Fritzsch is a monster. I remember Christmas last, the Nazis set up a Christmas tree with lights in the roll call square. Underneath it, Fritzsch had placed the bodies of those who had died by freezing to death during roll call. He called this "a present" to the living and forbade any Polish Christmas carols.

I am prisoner number 4685. I am a member of the orchestra here at camp. Every roll call we must play while the prisoners are counted, no matter what the weather is. After roll call, when our friends go out the gate to work, we play again. We are gathered to play in the evening when the men return. At official events, we play. We play when the trains arrive to make the men think this is not a camp of death. We must continue to play while our friends are beaten in line. If we stop, we are taken out and beaten too. I kept playing while my cousin was beaten to the tempo of our music. Many of us have committed suicide because we cannot stand to see all the suffering while we are expected to play cheery music.

We are punished for everything and for nothing. If we skirt work or perform in an unsatisfactory manner (which is up to the guards' judgment), wear non-regulation clothing, relieve ourselves at the improper time or take too long at it, or if we attempt suicide; punishment is in all things.

My brother and I are both here at Auschwitz. He was assigned to the morgue and ovens. He told me all about them but he was not supposed to talk. In the middle of the morgue is a drain for the blood to flow from the many bodies. When the dead are brought to this room, they are stripped and the uniforms and shoes are reused. Then anything of value is taken from them and sent back to Berlin.

When I have been assigned hospital duty, I have seen rats gnawing on the dead and even the sick. At night, I can hear them munching on those of us who are near death or the screams of others as they take a bite from their body. If you are bitten, you often become terribly ill.

We are worse than slave labor—we are expendable property. Equipment and machinery are treated better than us. At least the Germans maintain those items of property.

The psychological effects of Auschwitz are the worst. The guards deliberately do anything they can to strip of us our self-worth and human dignity, degrading us beyond belief. Even the most simple of tasks, that of attending to one's sanitary needs, cannot be done in private. The only method we have of rebellion is to stay alive as long as we can. Some of us cannot stand living like this any longer and commit suicide. When we hear a volley of shots fired, we know that someone made an attempt to jump the fence. They do this purposefully so the guards will shoot them and end their suffering. Some will grab and hold onto the wired fences, electrocuting themselves.

I pray each day. Is there a God? I was brought up to believe that God was in all things. If that is true, does that mean that God is in this suffering of ours? He watches, but does nothing? The priests here say we must not give up hope, we must believe God will stop this evil if we only believe in His love. If this is God's love, if this is the love I will receive in Heaven when I die, I choose hell.

I read until the sun went down.

The following day, April 17, the Chief of Political Department of the Gestapo Assigned to Auschwitz (a completely unpronounceable German commission),Maximilian Grabner, announced that urns containing the remains of Polish prisoners would no longer be shipped to the surviving families. All pretenses of normal deaths were eliminated. The cost of urns and difficulty in locating family members were the expected excuses for this action but the more likely reason was their need for camp secrecy. I was sure it would be only a matter of time before death notifications went out the window as well.

Grabner was particularly sadistic. His special domain was Block 11, inventing and enjoying punishments like the starvation cells. Although notification to the Kommandant was mandatory prior to each execution, it proved meaningless to any outcome; the fate of the prisoners was his decision. Tomasz and I were especially watchful of this man as squelching any resistance and escape in the camp was his primary duty.

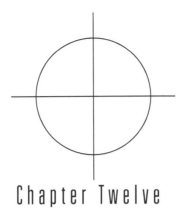

Chapter Twelve

June 1941

PROSTITUTION WITHIN THE REICH

"*W*here did you say we were heading, my friend?" said Filip. He strove to keep the question amiable although he was feeling quite disagreeable. He and Sergeant Schafer had been riding in the rented automobile for at least an hour and he was edgy. Granted the vehicle had been paid for by the sergeant and granted too, this evening had been promised to him as a surprise to celebrate their successful enterprise, but he could only take so much of the man, partner or not.

"Ah, mein Freund you are too impatient. Relax, I promise you will enjoy yourself."

The only way I would enjoy myself, thought Filip, is if I do not have to spend the next several hours in your company. Still, they had been good for each other monetarily. Recently, Filip began testing the waters of a black market enterprise. It was more difficult finding Jews to "position" for Gestapo raids and he had exhausted those Poles who had wronged him. Filip wondered when he had begun to think of his countrymen as "those" rather than "us." No matter; he owed them no allegiance. His moneymakers were the Germans now, almost his only family as well.

Beginning slowly, he sold his looted valuables to German soldiers seeking trophies for their loved ones. Eventually, soldiers began asking him to sell an item they had come upon for a good price. Of course, Filip was conversant in such idioms to know the item had been confiscated. It meant nothing to him as long as he could realize a finder's fee. So began a new phase of Wozniak & Schafer; buying, selling, and consignment agent of stolen property. Anything could be had for a price. This new subsidiary went hand in hand with murder or confinement of others, of course, but Filip had finally found a talent at which he excelled. Johann's ever-reaching connections had opened doors for them. It was symbiosis at its most appalling.

All this did not completely quell his desire to be elsewhere now, however. The sergeant laughed as he noticed Filip's fidgeting. "Fine, my friend, I will tell you. We are traveling to the most magnificent house of women," he said with some satisfaction and a smile upon his face.

Filip looked at him in surprise. A brothel? I do not need the services of a brothel, he sniffed, I can afford any woman I want.

Sergeant Schafer saw the skeptical look on Filip's face. "Ah, do not be so quick to judge. I was assured these women will do absolutely anything you require of them. Anything! They are placed in this remote location where only the most elite officers are permitted. My friend owes me for a very large favor (the sergeant neglected to tell his partner the favor was due to an inventive shortchanging of Filip's profits) and provided passes for the evening. The refreshments are very pricey, you understand, and top-notch but this evening is completely on me; my treat!"

Well, perhaps it would not be so bad after all, thought Filip. At least it will not cost me a pfennig. I might as well enjoy myself. He thought it only fair; he knew the favor provided to the sergeant's friend was some-how at his expense. He was not stupid, after all.

The exterior of the house was indeed elegant. Chimneys were smoking, window lights were twinkling, and they heard music upon opening the car doors. Johann instructed the driver to remain in the parking area and he would send refreshments to him. Filip wondered just how much this evening was going to cost his partner in crime. The Prussian lettering over the large front door was most descriptive; *Deutsches Soldaternhaus*,

German Soldier's House. It had other names too; DSH was the abbreviated version while the military regarded it as a *Militarbordellen* or *Wehrmachbordellen*. It was a German-operated bordello.

{ I }

It has been said that prostitution is the world's oldest profession. While most regarded this statement as unverified but probable fact, the Germans put their own particular spin to the ancient dealings of sexual gratification.

The German Staff realized its troops would indulge themselves in women and drink. Of the two, the women were their greater concern. The deliberate starvation of the overtaken populace resulted in emotional and physical tragedies to women, leading to prostitution and sexual favors in exchange for food or coin. Women and girls, along with the occasional men and boys, sold themselves to survive another day. Sexual acts were not limited to those who sold their bodies; civilians were often raped and mutilated, many perishing from their abuse. The Red Army considered such an act to a Pole a mere indulgence while the German officials understood "the needs" of their men, therefore rape was not considered a crime. The spread of disease from such unregulated actions was a worry, however.

Within the confines of the Wehrmacht offices, another unverified truth had made the rounds; French prostitutes had incapacitated more German soldiers than the French army in the 1940 occupation campaign. It was time to take control of the situation with the pragmatic, fastidious manner only the Nazi military could have initiated.

Initially, the Wehrmacht responded by conducting mandatory lectures on the dangers of unprotected sexual intercourse along with issuing pamphlets and condoms to the troops. Despite the shortage of rubber for nonmilitary use, free condoms were always available to their men. By October 1940, the Reich's chief sanitation officer issued memorandums to the General Staff; military-controlled brothels were essential for the soldiers' continued health and should be operated on a massive scale. Together with the civil authorities in place, complete and detailed manuals were circulated with official rules and regulations for all concerns established.

The organization of this solution varied by region. Some pre-existing brothels were simply taken over; others were newly established within hotels, bars, or private homes. They were classified into two types. Garrison brothels were created where large volumes of troops were either permanently maintained or processed through a transfer station. Field brothels traveled behind the lines to give relief to those men recently rotated from the front with a rest pass of a day or two. The officers had completely different facilities, especially within the garrison units. Those were slightly more refined with the officers expected to conduct themselves befitting their rank.

All units were under the administration of the Medical Division with regulations clearly laid out to each man. The soldier first reported to the *Sanitatssoldat*, medical soldier, to be declared clean and healthy. There he was given a pass certifying the same, indicating the date, time, and an official signature. Only the soldier's dog tag number was entered in a control book, allowing for some anonymity. This pass also indicated the name and location of the brothel where it could be redeemed and a separate line for the servicing woman to sign and place her identification number. After the issue of a condom and a small spray can of disinfectant, the soldier was free to enjoy the designated facility.

Documentation regulations were strictly upheld at each establishment. Field police, commonly called Chained Dogs among the soldiers, carefully reviewed each pass presented. All records remained at each house and additional prophylactic stations were required at each site. Prior to departure, the empty canister was returned to the appropriate official for his signature on the soldier's paperwork. This pass must be kept for three months by the guest and presented to any medical facility in case of a subsequent disease outbreak. In this manner, it was thought the spread of unnecessary disease could be stemmed.

As for the women, the method of their acquisition took many forms. Professional prostitutes were recruited from Germany and the occupied territories. Others fell into the political prisoner category and would be threatened with starvation or the barrel of a gun if they did not submit. These women were transferred from the all-female camp of Ravensbruck, located 90 km north of Berlin. Inmates here were from every country in occupied Europe but the largest nationality incarcerated were Polish.

A special corps formed of SS men completed the largest recruitment of women for these brothels. Throughout Poland, these men raided towns and cities, rounding up and kidnapping women at random as if they were cattle. Trucks carried girls as young as fourteen years of age to one of the Soldier's Houses. Frequently, they were beaten or had their performance abilities tested by their captors first.

Hundreds of these clubs were operational throughout occupied countries and the enormous amount of men facilitated there literally worked some of the girls to death. At the Wehrmacht brothel in Lublin, Poland, only four or five girls worked at servicing between one hundred twenty and one hundred fifty men per day. The demand upon the brothels was so high, the soldier's "time" was often called after ten minutes. A Gestapo report of a brothel located in Lodz, Poland, specified nearly four thousand men a month had been visitors. The sex-slave trade at the hands of the German military was the most heinous form of slave labor developed during the war. Although the men did not pay for any sexual act, alcohol and food could be purchased while they waited their turn, which was often longer than the time spent with the women. Inebriation was not condoned and an unruly man in such a state was booted from the premises, valid pass or not.

The women were subjected to weekly medical inspections and physicals. Occasionally, a man chose to pay for companionship rather than avail himself of the government-sanctioned brothels. If a soldier should develop an infection from such a private facility, he faced punishment. After all, clean females were provided to him at no personal cost. To avoid a blemish on his military record, the soldier often presented a signed brothel pass at a medical facility. It proved he was following orders; it was certainly not his fault the whore had the clap. The offending woman would be located and, surprisingly, Reich Marks were spent on her medical treatment rather than a bullet.

The women's existence rested in the hands of their jailers; clothing, food, and other necessities were provided to them and subsequently removed for noncooperation. Physical torture was also equally effective for those who did not obey. Many of the sexual encounters the women endured were violent. Perhaps the soldier preferred it that way or he had imbibed to the point of nonperformance, the woman presenting a handy punching bag for his wrath. They suffered further debasement after each sexual act by spreading their legs for the mandatory spray of disinfectant. Without hope for the future, thousands of women were nonetheless attempting to survive one more day in this enslavement.

{ II }

As Filip entered this particular gentlemen's club, he was quite taken with the interior. Considering himself a man of power and wealth, he had grown accustomed to the finer things in life this war had brought him. He had seen these Wehrmacht brothels before, of course, and had been amazed at the line of anxious soldiers winding down the street. Not the sort of place he could see himself frequenting, choosing the company of the private working girl instead. That had proven tiresome at times and expensive as well; an extra RM was occasionally needed to evict the woman from his bed.

But this place—this was more his style. He was surrounded by elegantly appointed furnishings, a small string quartet playing quietly in the corner, extremely fine alcohol served by tuxedo-clad bartenders, and intelligent conversation with impeccably groomed, albeit long in the tooth, women. Most of these, he later found out, merely acted as hostesses and supervisors to the women he would later bed. That was perfectly agreeable with Filip. He had often found that a woman who could intelligently converse with him was seldom the one he wanted to have spread her legs.

Of course, the requisite paperwork exchanged hands first, dates and signatures making the whole affair legal and safe. Finally, Filip was discretely approached by a concierge who informed him a room was waiting. Nothing overstated in this place, thought Filip.

The man led Filip up the thickly carpeted staircase, down a sconce-lit hallway decorated with artwork, finally arriving at a heavy oak door. Knocking softly upon the wood, the man opened the door for Filip to enter, biding him an enjoyable evening. At first, Filip had been slightly annoyed he could not choose the woman he wanted but as he stood in the center of the room and inhaled the perfumed air, he felt the familiar tingle of arousal and his irritation was forgotten.

The woman was sitting at a dressing table brushing her hair with her back turned toward him. As she stood, Filip noticed the long legs of a dancer. She came closer to him from the shadows and he got the first glimpse of her face. "I know you," he said to the woman, trying to place her name. "You are...are...my cousin Marta's friend. Arlene!" and he began to grin in sadistic delight. Arlene! That snippy, prissy girl who never gave him the time of day when they were younger. Now look at her. He noticed the look of fear upon her face and his member grew harder. "After all these years. Should I even ask how the world has been treating you, Arlene?" Slowly he walked around her, assessing her attributes. Her head flipped from side to side as she strove to maintain eye contact while he circled her. He flipped her skirt up and laughed aloud as she let out a whimper.

Finally looking her dead in her eyes, he said, "Tell me, do you remember who I am?" he asked. She nodded her head. "Yes? Then tell me. Say my name."

"Filip," she said softly.

"What? I am afraid I cannot hear you, *Liebschen*. Louder, little love," he shouted at her.

"Filip! You are Filip, Marta's cousin!"

He lifted her chin up so she could clearly see his face. "Very good. Who would have thought we should meet again in such circumstances?" and he reached out to roughly squeeze her breast. Nice, he thought, she must be well fed for her cooperation to the troops.

"Please, Filip, do not do this. I have some money, RM in fact. You can have it only please...do not do this."

He snickered cruelly in her face. "Money. Money! Do I look as if I need your money? Look at me! I am a wealthy and respected man now. Do you remember how you respected me when we were younger? You were always too good for me, never talked to me. Not too good for me now, are you?" he stressed cruelly.

Hoping for some sympathy from Filip, the frightened girl attempted an appeal. "Please, Filip, we were children together, played together. How can you think of going through with this?" One look at the response on his face told her; that is exactly why he would do this.

Reaching under her skirt he said, "Oh, Arlene—you and I will have some fun tonight. What should I do with you, hmmm?" and he shoved his fingers inside her as hard as he could, watching her flinch.

"Come, now. Let us see what you have under that outfit, shall we? Remove your skirt...slowly." She had no choice. This house looked very civilized and first-rate but she knew only too well what would happen if she refused. She still bore the scars on her back from the last refusal she gave. She tried to unbutton the back of the skirt but her hands were shaking. Impatient, Filip spun her around and ripped the thin fabric from waist to hand-stitched hem. "What is this?" he asked. Leaning down he read the words that had been roughly tattooed into her thigh. Although it was in German, the words were easy enough for him to read; Whore for Hitler's Troops. For the rest of her life, Filip thought, she would have to look at these words, remembering her debasement at the hands of... just how many men would the final tally be? This was just too good to be true. Turning her back around to face him, he looked her in the eyes while he caught the collar of her blouse in both of his hands and listened to the rending of the material. He grinned at her like a snake about to strike.

Pulling her breasts from the flimsy brassiere, he bit down on one until he drew blood. She suddenly saw all the nameless faces in her bed, remembered the days of starvation, the beatings she received, and decided if this pig was intent upon this path, she was going to let him know how disgusting she found him. "Do you know why no one respected you when we were children? I will tell you why! You were always a hateful boy who would lie and steal and no one ever wanted you around. You were a disgusting, conceited, smelly boy and an even more disgusting man. I will always be too good for you!"

She knew she was in trouble before he even raised his hand. He hit her in the face with a closed fist, and she fell backward onto the bed, struggling to remain alert. I am not going to let him rape me while I am unconscious, she thought, I want to remember this. I want to remember why I will make him pay for this one day.

Standing over her he slowly began releasing each button on his custom-made shirt, each one making a soft pop as it came through the finely stitched holes. Just as slowly, he unbuckled his belt and laid it alongside her. I may have use for this length of leather, he thought gleefully. Reminding himself to thank Johann later, he pounced on the trembling girl.

{ III }

The two men were enjoying the ride back to their respective domiciles, having been fully sated. Both were smoking cigars, another treat from the sergeant, and relaxing into the cushions. "My friend, I want to thank you for a most wonderful evening. This was truly something special," said Filip most sincerely.

"So, you did enjoy yourself. Did I not tell you the girls there were special?" replied Johann. "I am so pleased it met with your expectations."

Oh, yes, thought Filip; met and exceeded them. He would remember this night for quite some time. Imagine coming across Arlene in such a place. He laughed at his double entendre. He drove into her like a piston. Her ribs had been harder than he had imagined, so had her cheekbone, he thought, rubbing his bruised knuckles. She had never screamed, though. He would liked to have heard her scream. Perhaps she would have gotten into trouble with the household if she had done so. Still, that look of terror in her eyes was satisfying. The belt had come in handy too. He noticed the scars on her back and thought the house would not care if he inflicted a few more. He did so with a vengeance, thinking of her words of insolence, erasing the childhood memories with every strike. He smiled now, remembering her whimpers for mercy toward the end, almost as satisfying as screams. Yes, he and the good sergeant must plan another visit here. He leaned back into the headrest and smiled, watching the blue smoke of the cigar float around the interior of the vehicle.

Chapter Thirteen

June 1941

OPERATION BARBAROSSA

*M*y metallic tormenter and I came to an agreement in behavior and I was diligently typing without resorting to threats when The Colonel requested I come into his office. He reached out to brush carbon flakes from my cheek and we both jumped apart as if his touch had burned.

Clearing his throat and regaining his composure, he said, "I have been given to understand, Fraulein, that you have been spending much time in the camp. Specifically, the hospital wing. Is this correct?"

I was still feeling the traces of his touch upon my senses but I nodded and explained that my Uncle Edmund was positioned in the hospital. I further explained I was doing so on my own time and giving Uncle a hand while I was there. Would he prefer, I asked, that I not see my uncle?

He smiled at me for a moment before he answered, "Of course it is fine you should see your uncle. Only, be careful. The prisoners, for that matter the guards too, can be difficult to deal with. The reason I ask, however, is at the request of Kommandant Höss. He has heard from the doctors of your service in communicating with the prisoners as well as becoming quite competent in dosing medications. He would like to accept our offer of your translation services. Would it be agreeable?"

I told him I would be pleased to help. An even better excuse for me to be at camp, I thought. "Good. Also, he wanted to know if you spoke Russian." He looked at me inquiringly. Russian? Why Russian? Apologizing, I told him I could not. Reiterating my clumsy Yiddish abilities, he merely nodded his head and thanked me.

Shortly thereafter, on June 22, 1941, Germany shocked the world by invading the Soviet Union. Hitler was going to take on mammoth Russia. My God. Was he mad? Only two years since their nonaggression pact. I remembered the photograph of the smiling von Ribbentrop and Stalin, so secure with the treaty that had taken months to prepare. I thought of the screaming that must be echoing in Moscow now. I also understood the reason for The Colonel's question concerning my language skills.

{ I }

The Russian brigade was pushed farther and farther out of Poland. Germany had already captured Minsk, and Private Babikoff was not ashamed to admit he was relieved to retreat from the Nazi onslaught. He and his group vacated the east, retreating and fighting ever since. Before the Germans could reach Russia, they must pass through eastern Poland. That besieged territory became the site of an entirely new war campaign. What was left of the country stunk like a ripe whore, said the Russian private to a nearby compatriot. Decomposing and half-eaten bodies lay everywhere, starving people roamed the streets, makeshift hospital rooms were filled with the smell of necrotic flesh. The country should be burnt to the ground, thought Babikoff.

Stalin had called for a "scorched earth" policy, which suited the mood of the men just fine. Nothing was to be left behind for the Germans to use, stated the policy, everything of any possible value was to be confiscated or destroyed. Books were burned in the street, machines and tools lay smashed beyond recognition, men and horses were shot. The Russians rifled homes for anything resembling a weapon and destroyed it. Entire factories were set ablaze, even the few remaining electrical bulbs left in homes and buildings were shattered. Nothing was too trivial to destroy.

In one town, his captain had strung up the only remaining government employee outside a dilapidated post office. With legs and arms tied akimbo to protruding beams, he had slowly eviscerated the man in front of his family while they listened to his screams. Afterward, they had left his body to be eaten at the nearest pig farm.

The best part of their orders had been the women. Even they were left in a less desirable state for the Germans to use. The old and young alike had been left in misery. Some had been gang raped; others had received the attention of only one man. One woman wobbled along the sidewalk holding onto her chest where her right breast should have been, now only a gaping hole. Carving them up had been an effective way to let the Germans know the Red Army meant business.

One scene he had walked in upon had troubled him at first. A young mother was tied to a post while forced to watch one of his comrades rape her emaciated three-year-old daughter. When he finished, he sliced the child from groin to neck and tossed her aside like trash. Leering at the mother, he leaned in close to her when she suddenly spat at him. Spittle trickled down the Russian's cheek. At that display of disrespect, the private and the officer had both enjoyed the woman then used their bayonet on her as she pleaded for mercy. No one spits upon a Soviet soldier, he thought.

With a growing path of destruction in their wake, they were making their way systematically through each town and village, scorching each as they passed through. The Nazis would find nothing of use left by his brigade, by God. Not if he could help it. He knew other divisions were conducting the same decimation throughout Soviet owned Poland. Not only was the Polish land purged, but Polish men of any age were captured and inducted into the Soviet army. More than two hundred fifty thousand Poles had been forcibly drafted. It would take the Germans years of reconstruction for this portion of the country to be profitable in any way.

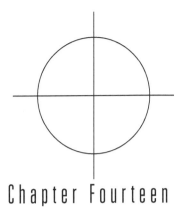

Chapter Fourteen

July 1941

FATHER KOLBE

*E*arly summer continued to be a warm, beautiful season that would normally lift one's spirits. This was impossible in our corner of Poland. The warmth only meant the decomposing bodies smelled of rot much sooner and the men in the furnaces could not keep up with the decay. Longer hours constructing Camp II meant more men literally worked to death. It was a repeating cycle. For every man who perished, two more arrived. Quarters became so cramped, prisoners took to sleeping on the floors. Perhaps the only advantage to the sultry air was not freezing to death, a temporary respite at best; winter would encompass us in darkness and ice soon enough. While the sun shone, however, I chose to visit my uncle.

Since receiving permission to spend further time in the camp, more of the guards seemed unconcerned with my presence, even greeting me at the gates. With their acceptance in mind, I devised what I thought was a wonderful idea to help the prisoners.

Using my most flattering approach to a loathsome kapo in the quartermaster's depot, I requested a blank journal from him as per

Kommandant's orders. He was a truly disgusting individual who would accidentally brush against my breasts or touch my fingertips when handing me anything, leering at me with his yellow teeth.

Having hollowed out the journal, I used it to smuggle in food to the prisoners. I carried an authentic journal along with the fake and, surprisingly, the idea worked. It was only a small measure of assistance though. How could I carry enough food for thousands of men?

Bringing it into camp with me today, I was well into the center of the compound when the sound of sirens and barking dogs broke through the air. The prickle on my neck began as I thought, this is it; I have been found out. Legs like jelly, I tried to retrace my steps. Before I could scurry away, Herr Fritsch approached me and ordered me inside.

Leading me to the prisoner formation, I was told my services were required for translation. "Repeat to them in Polish what I am about to say," he ordered.

Setting the books at my feet, praying a guard would not move them, I listened to his angry speech.

"Last night," I began translating softly then clearing my throat, I started again. "Last night, a prisoner escaped from Block 4. Herr Fritsch assures you he will be caught and dealt with accordingly." He motioned for me to go on and I continued our repartee of languages. "Because of this most heinous act, Herr Fritsch will be choosing ten of you from Block 4 to suffer punishment in his stead." I saw the news spread among the rows of prisoners like the ripples of a stone thrown into water. Some hung their heads, others sobbed.

Herr Fritsch sent a guard to walk among them and choose those to receive punishment. As the guard brought the selected men forward, Herr Fritsch again opened his mouth to speak. Before he could utter a word, I heard a frail voice call to him from within the crowd and watched as Father Maksmylian Kolbe was pulled out of line. A very kind and righteous man, he had been incarcerated for sheltering two thousand Jews at his friary. Occasionally, I had been present when he secretly held Mass within different barracks every Sunday. He faced corporal punishment if he had been caught but continued with the services each Sunday.

Surprisingly, Herr Fritsch did not shoot or beat the priest but permitted him to speak. With my help, Father Kolbe requested one chosen man, Franciszek Gajowinszek, be spared. He had a large family and the good priest offered to take his place. I saw a flash of anger in the German's eyes before he motioned to have the priest taken away with the other nine to Block 11. Prisoner number 10 was spared; Father Kolbe was not.

Their punishment had been the starvation cells. After two weeks without food or water and the last to survive, Father Kolbe was released and killed by phenol injection. I was told he had never complained, never asked for nourishment, only prayed with the other condemned and tried to keep up their courage. He was a saint of a man.

Chapter Fifteen

July 1941

JAZZ

I had decided to treat myself to a night of leisure, having recently returned from the Kanteen with a pastry and carrying a German military book. I was hoping the book would not only be interesting but would improve my wartime terminology as well. My life depended upon it.

As I walked down the hallway to my room, I heard the faint sound of music echoing down the hallway. It was different from the German tunes or the more popular war songs that so often played throughout the day. I could not hear the melody very clearly, but I definitely felt the beat. It was bright and sharp with drums and brass, carrying on as if in celebration. Idly, I wondered who else was spending a late night in the building. Probably a lonely staff member like myself.

As I neared The Colonel's door, I realized the music emanated from his office. I should have knocked but I was so curious, I quietly cracked open the door to peek inside. The very proper Colonel was sitting in his chair, poring over papers while moving his body side to side, slapping the desk to the beat, and bobbing his head up and down. Suddenly he began to whistle the next tune and I gasped; the whistling reminded me of Mama, something she had not done in quite some time. Naturally, he heard my short intake of breath and saw my pitiful plight; almost on my knees in the hallway, one eye peeking through the crack of the door, my dupa protruding in a most unladylike fashion. It seemed I was always in an unflattering position when he noticed me. I stood up and opened the door completely; crouching was hard on the back and he had already seen me.

When I was fully in the room, I noticed The Colonel had turned beet red. Having no intention of embarrassing any German officer, especially one in the SS, I held back my smile the best I could.

"Ah, Fraulein. You, ah, have, um, heard my music, *ja?*" I nodded to this question, hoping he would not berate me for spying on him.

"Do you like American swing?" he asked.

"I like Frank Sinatra. One of my cousins bought a Harry James record with Sinatra singing on it. We used to listen to it all the time before… well, just before. But I never heard that one," I said pointing to the now silent record. Then I became concerned; American music was banned now.

He must have seen my consternation because he said, "*Ja, ja,* I know. However, it is still very big in some Berlin clubs and I have always had a fondness for it. Besides, I am a colonel in the SS, after all," he said with a smile. "Also, Himmler has a weakness for the beat." With that, he replaced the needle's arm back on the rotating record and wonderful sounds came forth. A beat that had me tapping my foot as loud and brassy horns shouted out the melody, reminding me of the American movies I had enjoyed in another life.

"So, what do you think?" he asked me between songs.

I could not help smiling. "It's wonderful," I answered.

"This next one is my favorite. Benny Goodman, 'Sing, Sing, Sing,' he said. He pronounced it "Zing, Zing, Zing" but by now I was learning to interpret most of his oddly accented English. "Listen to the tom-toms." I was reminded of fun and laughter, something this country had not seen for a while.

"Do you dance? Or as the Americans call it, 'coot a roog'?" he asked.

I correctly assumed he meant "cut a rug" and I was appalled. Did he actually mean to dance with me or was he merely asking? "Only the polka, Herr Colonel, and my cousins tell me I tend to lead."

He laughed and said, "That does not surprise me. Come, I will show you." Before I had a chance to refuse, he had grabbed my waist and held my hand with his own. He performed a few steps then had me try along with him. Before I knew it, we were swinging and jiving all around the office, laughing and bumping into various pieces of furniture. I could not remember when I had such fun. Record after record, song after song, we danced to Glenn Miller, more Benny Goodman, and others I had never heard of. "Stompin' at the Savoy" was replaced by "Liza" (great drums on that one). When the piece "It Don't Mean a Thing" played, The Colonel began singing in that melodious Voice of his.

"It don't mean a thing if you ain't got that swing. Doo wop, doo wop, doo wop." He was pronouncing the words phonetically which made them easier to understand but not by much. I tried to sing along but it was harder than it looked to carry a tune while bouncing along the floor at a terrific rate. Plus, I knew none of the words, only chiming in on the "doo wops." He started to laugh so hard I thought he would drop me.

"No more," I gasped and laughed, "I can't breathe!"

"Here," he said, "let's try something slower."

He put on another melody, a bit bluesier, he explained. "Mood Indigo," he said, "one of the Duke's older compositions."

Slower than the previous melodies, he held me closer while showing me steps better suited to this beat. We were suddenly in sync as we glided across the floor and I felt my breasts against his tunic.

Another tune, "I'll Be Seeing You" echoed from the Victor Victrola's horn and he continued to sing in That Voice. Surprisingly, I understood him fairly well. Perhaps I was becoming accustomed to his oddly accented English.

"I'll be seeing you in all the old familiar places..."

It was suddenly difficult for me to hear the beat of the music over the pounding of my heart.

"...and when the night is new,
I'll be looking at the moon,
But I'll be seeing yooou..."

We had danced a few more steps before we realized the music had stopped and the scratching of the record was the only sound in the room. Finally, as the winding mechanism ran down, the beautiful old machine was silent.

Feeling his eyes upon me, I looked up into his. When his arm reached farther around my waist and his other slid behind my back, my heart was going wild. Flip-flops began in my stomach.

He leaned into me, crushing my breasts and planted a very light nibble upon my lips, nothing too insistent or frightening, but definitely noticeable. As he broke away, I was filled with a momentary sense of panic. He was my employer and a German officer; what would happen to me if I pushed him away?

He had not released me from his grasp, however, and I felt his lips travel along my jawbone to my ear lobes and finally to the hollow of my neck where they performed a seductive dance upon my throat. My hand gripped his shoulder tighter, giving in to my emotions. I was sure I would go straight to hell when my time came.

His lips were retracing their torrid path back to my mouth, strong fingers weaving themselves into my hair while his other arm engulfed me. His tongue made delicate circles upon my lips and I responded by tentatively kissing his roving tongue. Kissing again, softly at first then with intensity and passion until my head felt about to explode, I realized how long I had wanted this and I continued to respond in kind, inhaling his scent.

I heard a bell ringing suddenly and wondered if it was normal to hear such things in this circumstance. When he broke away from me, I opened my eyes as he smoothed down his tunic and reached for the telephone.

Only a phone call, I thought, and while he was so occupied, I quickly dashed from his office to the ladies WC. The mirror reflected my disarray as I ran my fingers comb-like through my hair and brought cold water to my still flushed face, trying to stop my hands from shaking. Hussy, I thought. First Antoni and now The Colonel. This man, though, could do much more harm to my family than Antoni ever could. What if he persisted? How would he react to my refusal? I thought of Arlene and Sister Lina and decided I would not broach the subject with him. It would be much more difficult to avoid The Colonel than Antoni. Had there ever been someone in such a mess, I thought. My reservation in hell had been confirmed.

{ I }

The next few days were an existence in heightened anxiety for me, jumping whenever someone approached unexpectedly. Each time I felt The Colonel about to begin a conversation concerning "that night," I would excuse myself, saying I was needed elsewhere. I tried my best to move silently about my office in avoidance of the two officers making it difficult to accomplish anything worthwhile. The situation was most distracting but I had only myself to blame.

Today I was so engrossed in paper work I must have let my guard down. Without warning, the connecting door between my office and The Colonel's swung open and he stood in the doorway. I rose to formally await whatever was coming next. "Herr Colonel," I said expectantly.

"*Setsen Sie, setsen Sie,*" he said. He waved his hand toward the two small seats in front of the table I proudly called a desk. As I sat in one, he sat in the other. Silence ensued.

He finally asked, "Fraulein, do you think of me as a friend?"

"Oh, ah...Yes, Herr Colonel."

"*Gut, Gut.* Then do you trust me?"

"Yeess," I answered slowly, wondering where this was heading.

"We should discuss the events of the other evening, I think." Without my answering, he went on. "I wish to apologize to you. I should not have approached you in that manner." I was truly confused. I had thought he would send me away or worse; blame me for the advances and send me to the camp. Yet he was apologizing to me.

Seeing the confusion on my face, he attempted to clarify. "I'm afraid I took advantage of you, placing you in a very awkward position. I realize you felt as though you had no choice but to submit to my rank. You were worried about punishment if you rebuffed me and I do not blame you for such thoughts. But I promise you, Fraulein, I would not have proceeded any further. And I do not blame you in any way."

I looked at him quizzically. I thought I knew to what he was referring but admittedly, I was naive in this area. Just how far was further? Perhaps I misunderstand his German. Would he have become violent? "Further? What kind of further?" I asked.

I had not expected the look of astonishment on his face. "Do you really not understand what could have happened?"

Putting my head down and blushing, I recalled Arlene's attack. "I...I think so, *mein Herr*. I have seen soldiers with women and heard the cries, but...is that what you mean?"

He suddenly looked very sad and reached for my hands, holding both in his, sending shivers along my spine. "*Mein Gott*! That is all you know of it. That is all you see every day, the abuse and killing. *Nein*, it does not have to be that way." He took a deep breath and looked me in the eyes, now even more embarrassed. "What I mean to say, I would never have... forced myself upon you in that, um, manner. Never! Did your mother not talk to you about the...uh...pleasures between men and women?"

"We've been so intent on staying out of harm's way...Besides, that talk is before the wedding night, I think. Is that what you mean?"

"*Ja ja*, that is exactly what I mean. What you see around us is not the way it could, rather should, be. People who care about each other do not behave in such a manner. I hope I did not frighten you too much?"

This last was a question I could tell he desperately wanted an answer to. I smiled at him. "No, Herr Colonel, you did not frighten me."

We were sitting with The Colonel's hands over mine when Antoni walked into the room and I pulled away guiltily. "Yes, Captain, what do you want?" Colonel Müller growled.

Antoni stared at me while answering The Colonel's question. "A message from Berlin, Herr Colonel," and he held out a teletype message, never taking his eyes from me.

"Thank you, Captain. That will be all."

Antoni gave the signature salute, The Colonel responded in kind, and my cousin retreated. Standing, would soon place a telephone call to me; I had much to tell him. The Colonel asked me, "So, we are still friends, *ja*?"

"*Ja, guten Freunden*," I replied with a smile. "Good friends."

He seemed pleased with my answer and walked back into his office, closing the door behind him.

I had come to the realization these past few weeks that I had strong feelings for the good Colonel and wondered if I could forget those kisses. Then I thought of Antoni and the way he had stared at me, totally devoid of emotion behind those chiseled features. I had the distinct feeling he was not at all happy and warned myself to continue my diligence with respect to my cousin.

Chapter Sixteen

SANCTUARY

*M*ax often arranged our meeting place in towns other than Bochnia. That was fine with me; Bochnia no longer felt like home. The presence of German soldiers increased my anxiety and I was assured of encountering several whenever I traveled home. Each time one glanced my way, I was certain of my impending arrest.

My house had suffered changes at the hands of the Germans as well. There are many items in life one can do without such as furniture and plates. Food, however, is not one of these and so we continued to sell our possessions to rid ourselves of the starvation that had claimed so many in my country. My large and displaced family members now resided with Mama, calling my childhood house their home. They were now all working long hours in the salt mines, slave labor but not yet encamped. We hoped that as long as they did as they were told, my relations would be allowed to remain in the home.

Today I was traveling by train to a remote village for our third meeting. During the trip, I kept repeating to myself key words, "Post, Goat, Expansion, Escapes" like a mantra, things I wanted to tell Max.

We met in a bombed-out church. Anything of value had been stripped or smashed. If the marble columns could have been carried away, I felt sure they would have. Damn Germans!

After genuflecting and praying quietly in half a pew, I heard a whisper from behind me. "Do not turn around. It is I, Max. Make your way to the confessional and go inside; the one in the corner. I will meet you." Obeying without question, quite unlike me, I might add, I walked to the fragile old confessional. Surprisingly, the door to the penitent's side was unlocked and I went in. As a Catholic, I was not unused to confessional procedures but I was startled when the grid in my cubical opened and the dim silhouette of a priest appeared.

"Do not be alarmed, my child. I am Father Klemens. Max will join us in a minute." True to his word, I heard the other cubical door gently open and close. Releasing the grid door on the other side, we three had a whispered conversation.

"Father Klemens knows me, do not worry," whispered Max. "Now, what news do you have?" I softly relayed the escape of the previous month and of the first attempt in June 1940, when one prisoner made his way out of the camp with the help of employed Polish civilians. The prisoner dressed like those employed and simply walked out the gate at the end of the day. Five of the captured civilians were sentenced to the camp and the entire prison population was punished, forced to stand in roll call position for twenty hours. I told him too of many civilians who smuggled food to the prisoners while they worked outside or took escapees into their homes, sending them on to partisan units. Also, I said, they often left bread and medicine outside the wire or smuggled prisoners' messages along to loved ones. Many prisoners are burying stolen photos and letters within the camp, hoping someday they will be found.

I explained the Post; a wooden cross-like structure. With a man's hands tied behind him, he was hung backward by the wrists so his feet did not touch the ground. After several hours, the prisoner frequently lost consciousness from the pain. More often than not, the tendons would rupture in his shoulder.

Then there was the Goat, a box that immobilized a man's feet and caused him to lean over with arms outstretched so the Germans could flog him. The limit was twenty-five lashes but often the guards conveniently lost count and started over.

Over thirty thousand registered prisoners had come through the gates, even more since those not registered were killed upon arrival and never counted. I told him I thought we would receive Russians soon and the camp was expanding to accommodate more prisoners and factories. If I spoke too softly, Father Klemens passed what I said to Max, as if we were on a telephone party-line; awkward but functional. I also had information in the key from my contact. At that, the rectangular screen lifted up just enough for me to pass it to the good priest and he to Max. Telling him it contained a microfilm of names and numbers of new prisoners, the priest returned it after Max relieved the key of its contents.

Thanked by both men, I exited from the confessional and made my way to the pew to say my penance. If anyone was watching, it would have looked suspicious not to stop and pray having just received absolution for my sins. My sins indeed. The Colonel and Antoni came to mind as I said one more Hail Mary for good measure.

Chapter Seventeen

July 1941

IDENTIFICATION

On July 22, the British signed a mutual assistance agreement with the Soviets. Germany and England seemed to be spreading themselves rather thin while the bloated Russian beast simply waited for everyone to come to her. Once again, I thought Hitler either mad or the recipient of extremely poor advice.

The battles along the Russian borders had a direct impact upon our area of the country. The screeching trains packed with Russian and Polish POWs were a common sight on our own private railway. Uncle explained the presence of so many new Polish soldiers by telling me of an old adage attributed to Arabian culture: "The enemy of my enemy is my friend." The Poles and Soviets were captured while fighting together against their common enemy and this was the end of the line, figuratively and literally, for the men arriving here.

By now, the numbering of prison uniforms was becoming cumbersome and difficult to maintain. When a prisoner died or was executed, the uniform was occasionally so worn-out it was of no further use. Additionally, a naked prisoner was impossible to identify. The Germans had a simple solution for this; rather than manually stamping numbers on every piece of clothing, simply number the man.

It was a most successful method in the eyes of the camp officials. The task was performed during registration and delousing in the main administrative building. Initially, a special metal stamp holding interchangeable numbers made of one-centimeter long needles was created for the purpose. With one blow, the entire serial number was punched upon the prisoner's left upper chest. Indelible ink was rubbed into the bleeding wound, the tiny holes catching and holding the black liquid.

Proving impractical, the camp abandoned the metal stamp for a single-needle device, a crude and painful tool. Originally, the numbers were placed on the outer side of the left forearm then later moved to the inner side. This method of identification began with the onslaught of the thousands of Soviets sent to camp, each number carefully notated in another series of ledgers. Transgressions and nationality symbols that had been so carefully designed were now limited to a meager few. Occasionally, a prisoner would receive a triangle or the letter P alongside their number but this was rare. Accessibility to the ledgers provided all the information anyone in the camp required. The entire process seemed so successful to the officers here, I often wondered why Auschwitz was the only camp employing such numbering techniques.

With the problem of prisoner identification solved, those in control of death within the Reich turned their attention to another situation. Senior SS officers informed Himmler of the trauma their death squads experienced by shooting unarmed civilians and children. They stressed the decline of morale within these selected troops and urged the general to investigate other methods of elimination. Himmler, having attended such an incident in 1941, agreed not only for the soldiers' mental state, but also for economic reasons; bullets were more important at the Eastern Front.

The sick in the camp were of no use to the Reich labor forces, yet ovens could not keep up with the dying. Gassing the sick prisoners in trucks and vans was expensive and clumsy. Embellishing upon the euthanasia idea, the officers and medical personnel developed an experimental solution.

An announcement was made during roll call of available transports to a sanatorium or to camps with lighter work details for the ill. Volunteers were encouraged and 573 Polish political prisoners from Block 15 did so. Added to this group at the last minute were two German criminals. The transport left in convoy fashion to Sonnenstein Castle in Germany on July 28, 1941. Since early 1940, three buildings of the castle were converted to one of the Reich's euthanasia killing centers. It was here all 575 prisoners were gassed in a bathroom by carbon monoxide released through showerheads. Effective but far from convenient. Other solutions must be sought.

Chapter Eighteen

August 1941

TRAGEDY

I took the opportunity to sort out my thinking as I lay in my room that night. It was a beautiful evening and the odor from the camp was not as prevalent. Or perhaps I was merely becoming used to it. A sobering thought, one I chose to put from my mind.

For years I had dreamed of Antoni returning my unrequited love. Now, when he treats me like a woman and no longer like his little cousin, I pushed him away in fear. Why? Wasn't this what I had always wanted? There had been more to that kiss than Antoni's teasing, no question. I was embarrassed to admit it but there had been more than a modicum of response from me too. My face felt hot remembering my shame and I punched my pillow.

My thoughts turned to the handsome Colonel. I melted just thinking of him. And That Voice—it was so...so...Oh, what is the word? Mellifluous! And honeyed. Smooth and sweet like honey. Oh, good God—stop this, I told myself. Sweet Jesus—what was wrong with me? In love with my cousin and now infatuated with a German! The ENEMY! Sick! I was a sick individual who would never see St. Peter to plead my case. No chance to redeem myself in God's eyes, straight to the fire with other sickies. Still, they both kissed so well. They smelled nice too. And That Voice! I remembered how he sang when we danced and I fell asleep, tossing and turning, hearing the mellow tone in my head…

{ I }

…I sat at my desk typing, as I did most mornings, listening to The Colonel sing in his office next door. It suddenly occurred to me I was not dressed properly for the office. I was wearing a long, black, beaded gown, cut so low my breasts threatened to pop out. What on earth had possessed me to put this on? As I sat there wondering where I should find a more appropriate dress, Antoni strode through the doorway. He was dressed in the most immaculate white tuxedo I had ever seen with his military medals fastened over his left breast pocket. It took him several steps to reach my workstation, as the room seemed to be stretching out before me.

The lights dimmed and I looked up to see the crystals on the chandelier were wiggling side to side and tinkling melodically.

"Another bombing," I said.

"Yes," agreed Antoni. "Perhaps the Americans have finally come to save you."

"They should get here soon, then, *ja?*"

By this time, he had reached my chair and brought me to my feet, which I happened to notice were shod in the most wonderful black velvet pumps with sparkling rhinestone clusters on each toe.

He lifted my face up to his and growled, "No one can save you from me. Not even the Americans. You do realize that, do you not?"

"Of course, Antoni. I understand. But I have to tell you I love their swing music."

He leaned down to my face and kissed me with such ferocity and passion that my knees buckled for a moment. His mouth was then kissing my neck, down to my chest and I gasped as he reached into my décolletage. "Oh, Antoni," I sighed, "this surely can't be a socially accepted practice. What if the Americans walk in?"

But he didn't stop and I was glad. Never had I felt so warm and yet my skin was tingling as if I had been immersed in an ice water experiment. He was cupping my rump, now, pushing me into him and my stomach flipped over.

Without warning, The Colonel stormed in, banging the connecting door against the wall, shattering the glass window within. His SS uniform had ashes clinging to it and the silver skull on his cap was mocking me, shrieking out, "Whore, whore, Fraulein is a whore!"

The Colonel slapped his hand over the bony head affixed to his hat to silence it.

"Hauptmann Schreiber, just what do you think you are doing here? You are supposed to be bombing the English, not kissing the staff!"

Antoni had released me and I was trying in vain to stay within the dress, which had shrunk two sizes.

"She is mine," said Antoni. "And I do not feel like bombing right now. In fact, never again!"

The Colonel quickly strode across what was now an extremely long room, wrapped his arm around my waist and kissed me, his tongue exploring my mouth. "I will show you who she belongs to," he said to Antoni.

"She is my cousin! I have rights by kinship!"

"And I outrank you!" The miserable shiny skull echoed this sentiment in a most annoying sing-song manner. "Outrank, outrank, the colonel outranks you!"

I saw the flash of steel in The Colonel's hand before Antoni did. He lunged at Antoni, stabbing him through, and I stared as the blood soaking into the once crisp white shirt tuxedo. How will he ever remove that stain? I thought ridiculously.

Taking me back in his arms, The Colonel and I danced around the now enormous ballroom to the music of "*Deutschland, Deutschland, Uber Alles.*"

Almost tripping over Antoni in midstride, I saw he was not as dead as I had thought. Grabbing my ankle, he was knocking on the side of the desk, calling out to me "Marta, Marta, can you hear me? Fraulein, can you hear me?"…

…"Fraulein, Fraulein, are you all right? Can you hear me?"

It was The Colonel. I was still in my cubical, lying in my cot. I must have cried out in my sleep. "Oh, yes. I hear you."

"I think, perhaps, you were having an *Albtraum, ja?*"

Oh yes, definitely a nightmare. *"Ja, Herr* Colonel. *Ein Albtraum.* But I am fine, really. I'm sorry to have disturbed you," I answered hoarsely. Why is he here already? Did I oversleep? I raised my head to look at the bedside clock. Only 7:00 a.m. "Is something wrong? Why are you here so early?" I started to get up and dress but my head was pounding, forcing me to sit back upon the bed.

"Nein, nein, I could not sleep. Take your time. We will take coffee together when you are ready, *ja?"*

"Oh, yes, that would be lovely," I answered. Oh, God, my head. I was shocked remembering brief scenes from last night's dream as they flitted in and out of my head.

Quickly dressing, I rushed into his office where he thoughtfully had a full service of coffee prepared with local pastries and fruit. He could be a most thoughtful man, I thought, and felt my face grow hot remembering my dream.

"Fraulein, are you well?"

"Oh, yes, *Danke*—just a headache."

"Restless sleep can have that effect. I hope I did not frighten you but you had called out quite loudly."

"Just the nightmare, I'm afraid. Luckily I do not remember too much of it," I lied, hoping to end this conversation.

"Not surprising. Having nightmares, I mean. Look around you—they are reality, I am afraid. I have a thought—you are quite caught up on duties, are you not? *Gut.* So then, perhaps you should go home for a few days, see your family."

It has been awhile, I thought. Perhaps I could contact Max while there. Still, I did not answer The Colonel right away. I wondered what he might be playing at—he had never offered this before.

"Today is already Thursday and I am quite capable of taking care of things here for two days," he dimpled at me. "Plus, tomorrow I must attend meetings regarding Camp II. Corporal Konig will drive you to Bochnia and before you leave, you will prepare a basket of food from the Kanteen to take home. So, all is settled, *ja?* Gut. I will see you on Monday, refreshed and ready for work. Now, we will have what I believe the British refer to as a 'shin vahg.' Is that correct? 'Shin vahg?'"

I thought he was trying to say 'chin wag,' English slang for a rather casual conversation between friends, but I was not altogether certain.

"I learned English in school, Herr Colonel, and was not taught many colloquial sayings." I hoped that would prevent me from correcting his English yet again—he seemed to take such pride in it.

"Ah, well, I believe that is the correct term for a chat. So, let us partake of this morning's *Frühstück* and talk."

I was so glad he did not attempt more English. Instead, we settled down to eat our lovely breakfast, and I found myself looking forward to going home. He really was a thoughtful man.

{ II }

Filip had established residency in a wonderful house within the better part of town. Happily, the exterior did not hold much appeal and he could think of no other reason why the Germans had passed it by while they ransacked the posh houses around him. It did not bother him in the least that it had been the residence of a family he had set up; it was now his. He thought briefly of that Kazmaryk girl. I bet she is not so arrogant now—if she is alive, he laughed to himself.

This house was perfect. The previous owners had very good taste. Furnished with quality furniture and precious knickknacks, it was warm and comfortable. A fully stocked larder and chopped firewood in the basement made life much easier all around. He even had a housekeeper/cook that came in daily "to do" for him and after enjoying her most excellent dinner tonight, Filip should have been in an equally excellent mood. His business venture was supplying him with more money than he could have imagined. Filip enjoyed all the trappings money could offer; tailor made clothing, custom shoes, the finest wines and spirits, the best table in any restaurant still open, even the most expensive and beautiful whores. And yet, he was not a happy man.

It was that family of his. That stubborn, meddling family who would always see him as a buffoon, the classic Falstaff, always compared to his dear cousin, Antoni. He had unexpectedly met Grandmother while shopping last week in one of the finer stores. The shops were now German owned with like customers or soldiers. A year ago, he would have been uncomfortable shopping side by side with them but he felt more relaxed around his former enemy every day.

He knew she could not afford the goods in those establishments, so what the hell was she doing there? He had made the mistake of greeting her—if he had simply walked on, she would never have seen him. Then he could present himself to the entire family as he had dreamed, showing them all what a great man he had become.

Instead, she looked him up and down in his fine clothes and berated him. Where did you get the money for those, she wanted to know. You must be up to no good to be able to afford those shoes. And why haven't you been to see your mother; she's been worrying about you. On and on she went, making him feel small and stupid. No one could ever see how brilliant he was, how destined he was for greatness.

And then, when he had offered her money out of the goodness of his heart, she refused his "ill gotten coin" and turned her back to him, shouting "God will see to your punishment." She should have been grateful, should have hugged and kissed him for relieving her suffering. But no; not Grandmother. Why, she acted as if he had offered her the biblical thirty pieces of silver, for Christ's sake.

Well, he would still show her—all of them. He would go to the butcher shop while family members were helping the old woman out, dressed in his finery, and bestow upon them a bundle of gifts. He began to run through his head a list of things he would bring. Wine, he thought, and fresh cheeses. No, not cheese, they had cheese in the shop. Flowers, then, and fresh fruit, even strawberries if he could find them. Oh, and fresh linens and some clothing. He had no idea what sizes to purchase but the women in his family were all handy with a needle and thread; they could make necessary adjustments to the garments. Yes, that is exactly what he would do. He would be so benevolent, so caring, they could not help but be impressed. Hah! Let's see cousin Antoni top that! He grabbed one of the cigars the previous owner had left behind and lit up, making plans for the prodigal son to return in glory.

Several days later, he was looking his best. Dapper, even. Freshly shaved with a liberal application of the best scent, a new suit, shoes shined, and his offerings gift-wrapped, he was already anticipating their esteem and admiration at so many gifts. He had even hired a driver for the day. And, best of all, Weegie was in town. Just as he was prepared to exit his room, the housekeeper knocked and stepped into the room.

"Excuse me, Mr. Filip, sir." God, he loved it when the people called him sir. "Excuse me, but Sergeant Schafer is here to see you."

"What? Now?" Damn! He did not remember a meeting with that irritatingly stupid man today. Well, he would go downstairs and get rid of him. He sighed and pulled himself together. "Thank you Mrs. Blonski, I will see him."

The man was waiting for him in the parlor. "Ah, my dear friend! Do not tell me I have forgotten an appointment with you today? I am so sorry. I was about to go out."

"*Nein, nein,* my friend. I just came by to inform you; the last traitorous family you put me onto was worth a king's ransom! They have implicated others and the major has given me a bonus. It would be impossible if not for your brilliant plan so I have come here to share it with you." And with that, he offered Filip twenty-five Reich Marks. Of course, the major had given the sergeant one hundred RM but Filip need not know. Give him enough to keep him happy, that was the sergeant's motto.

Filip was surprised. Imagine that, he thought, for once I really did lead the Germans to a true traitor. Would wonders never cease? Now the twenty-five Marks. Of course, Filip knew the sergeant's bonus was more generous than the man would admit but it would not do to rob him of this overtly magnanimous gesture. In all fairness, the sergeant had not been obligated to share his bonus. Filip thanked the sergeant very graciously.

"But you say you are going out? I had hoped we could dine together, have some wine, discuss your new ideas. I know, I shall accompany you on your errand and then we shall celebrate!"

Oh, no. Anything but that, thought Filip. He did not want this man along when he visited his family. It would not do for them to know he was on such familiar terms with a German, nor would it be prudent for the German in question to be reminded too often of Filip's nationality. He was becoming more ingrained into the German way of life, enjoying the sergeant's protection, small though it was, and did not wish that to change.

It was apparent Schafer was not to be gotten rid of so easily. Resigning himself to having a guest on this outing, he tried to look at the bright side. Perhaps the family would not be so thorny with a German in tow. He merely told Sergeant Schafer he occasionally looked after his relations, saving them from starvation and further hardships while this war business was sorted out.

"But what a kind man you are, Filip. Your family must be extremely grateful."

Let us hope so, thought Filip. If only there was some way he could shut up that cousin of his.

{ III }

Since we were forced to close by noon, we started much earlier in the shop now than before the war. People queued up outside before we opened, ready to use their ration coupons before the Germans decided to cut our allotments further or before we sold out of meat.

"I ran into Filip last week," said Buscha. "He was wearing some of the finest and most expensive clothing I had ever seen. I told him he must be up to no good if he can afford such things in these times."

"No doubt, Buscha. He always looked for the easiest effort in everything, even if it was illegal or immoral. That boy has always been a carbuncle on the ass of this family!"

"Marta," said Mama, "that is no way to talk!"

Buscha was laughing and coughing at the same time. "She's right, Birdie. He always has been a wrong one."

As we were talking, the object of our conversation walked in. I looked out the window and noticed a German was standing outside our door. We were not yet opened but Filip was still family and obviously felt he could come and go as he pleased. I looked again at the back of the soldier's head. Something looked familiar about him but I could not put my finger on it.

"Well, well," said Filip much too brightly. "My loving family. I have brought gifts to make your life easier in these very difficult times."

"You do not look as though you are struggling, cousin. Where did you get those clothes? And what is in this basket? Wine, fresh fruit; even clothing! What have you been up to, Filip? Knowing you, it cannot be good. Are you still trying to one-up Antoni?"

"Now, now, Marta. Filip means well," said Mama.

"Marta's right, Birdie. No one can afford this unless they are collaborators one way or another. Is that it, Filip? Are you a traitor to your people?" asked Buscha loudly.

This visit was not transpiring the way he had planned, thought Filip. That miserable Weegie—she is the cause of this going awry.

Just then, the loitering soldier walked through the door. "I heard yelling, Filip. Is all in order?"

I suddenly realized why he looked so familiar. He was That Private, the one who fought with Buscha over the sausage, the one who caused the death of my father and grandfather. "You! How dare you show your face in here! Get Out! Both of you!"

"You have no right to order us around, Weegie!" Filip's face turned red with anger.

Sergeant Schafer looked at this gathering with distaste. This was the family of Filip? These terrible shopkeepers who had no regard for the uniform of the Reich? They needed to be taught a lesson once and for all, although he thought it had been accomplished on May Day last. Apparently not.

"You let this little girl talk to you in that manner, Filip? These worthless Poles?" Filip responded in his broken German. I thought of The Colonel's recitation of his Pidgin English and smiled foolishly in spite of myself.

"Are you laughing at me, cousin?" yelled Filip.

"Laughing at you? When have you ever been funny, cousin? Absurd certainly, but never funny."

"I am an important man now, Weegie," he stressed. "One you should be careful of crossing. And let me tell you something, dear cousin," he hissed at me. "Antoni has nothing over me."

I walked up to Filip's face, "You know, you can put a suit on a worm but it's still a worm; it merely wears a suit." I turned to look at the Nazi. "Or a uniform."

Apparently, Sergeant Sausage was conversant in enough Polish to realize he had just been insulted. The thunderous look on the man's face was frightening but I refused to flinch. The hatred was obvious when he said, "Someone needs to put you in your place, Pole," he said in German.

"And you think you are the Nazi to do it?" I stood practically on tiptoes, bringing myself up to my full five-foot-nothing height.

"Marta, please, let's just calm down," said Mama. "Filip, I thank you for your gifts but perhaps you and your...ah...friend should leave."

Filip did not say another word, simply turned furiously on his heel and began to stride out the door. "Wait," I called to him. I grabbed the basked full of either stolen or black market items and thrust it into his arms. "You forgot this."

He slammed the door behind him and stomped off, he and his "pal." They deserved each other, I thought, and I hoped I would never see them again.

{ IV }

The two men were halfway down the street when Filip tossed the basket filled with his dreams of influence out the window of the rented town car. The story came out, as he knew it would, of Johann's involvement with "that family," his argument with "that old woman," the slaying of "the old goat." His telling differed from the truth, naturally. According to Johann, Filip's cousin had threatened the officer in charge. What other choice did the Germans have?

Knowing his family, especially that Weegie, it was a believable story. Filip would have expected troublemaking from her. What rotten luck. Of all the Germans invading his country, he was involved with the only one who had met up with Weegie's mouth. What were the odds? He could not lose face with Johann; this was too good an operation for them both. Since there was no shortage of carnage, murder and theft had become very good sources of income.

As if reading his thoughts, Johann suddenly said, "I should place a bet on something. Imagine. Becoming partners with you, never dreaming you are part of that family."

"I was a part of that family. I have not been so for quite some time. They do not think as I do—as we do," he said quickly. "All they do is pray for deliverance and starve while doing so. I believe in seizing any opportunity wherever it presents itself. No, my friend, I am no more a part of that group than you are." Christ, I hoped it worked, he thought. He had to keep this German on his side at all costs. He was too fond of the soft life he had finally found.

"Do not let it trouble you, my friend," said Johann, slapping Filip on the back in an affable manner. "You are a good and loyal partner. Is it well you are finally rid of them; you are unappreciated there." Johann's mind was working furiously, an exercise it did not often engage in. This development deserved some very careful consideration. Filip had made him rich; he did not fool himself into thinking otherwise. But that family of his…who would have guessed? They may become a problem to their arrangement, something he could not allow.

{ V }

"Good riddance!" I yelled after Filip.

"Oh, Marta, you shouldn't have done that. These times are so uncertain," said Mama.

"Rubbish," I answered. "This is Filip we are talking about. He has never been a threat to anyone except himself. And that German friend of his looks as if he repeated the same grade in school at least four times."

"I think they have much bigger ideas in mind than us," said Buscha. "Whatever he is up to, he is certainly excelling at it."

I had one more night in Bochnia before my scheduled return to Auschwitz and I wanted to spend as much time as possible with Buscha. Before we bicycled home, I promised to see her in the morning before Corporal Konig carried me back to Auschwitz.

{ VI }

Oh blast, she thought, I left my reading glasses downstairs; wouldn't be able to read the Bible without them. She was awake now anyway. Might as well go and search.

She had been nicely tucked into bed too. Her mother's quilt was wrapped around her and she had a weak cup of tea at her side. She must have used that teabag at least four times by now. She looked at her brooch sitting on her nightstand and thought of her husband, Roman. Oh, how they had enjoyed cups of evening tea together while they talked about the children and later the grandchildren.

Half absentmindedly, she attached the brooch on her nightgown and gave it a few short loving taps. With a sigh, she slipped out of bed, into her slippers and housecoat, and made her way down the narrow back steps to the shop. I hope some nasty German does not accuse me of being open late, she thought as she switched on the light. Against the rules, he would say! Hah. Who would be working in a butcher shop dressed in their nightclothes, I ask you! The shades were drawn, hiding her movements but there was nothing she could do about the light seeping into the outside world between the shade and windowsill. She hoped she would find those miserable spectacles quickly so she could return to her nice warm bed.

He was walking along the street, passing the closed-up shops after leaving the restaurant. The night was still young but enough shadows had fallen on the street to make walking among the rubble dangerous. Street lamps remained unlit but they clearly would have made his way safer had they been on. Too costly I suppose, he thought. Still, perhaps it was better this way; easier to hide in the shadows after curfew.

He turned the corner to see lights suddenly snap on in the store down the street, bright slivers of illumination edging their way into the gloom of the street. Well, well. What have we here? No one else in sight—perhaps he should pay the place a visit.

She was growing more and more irritated with herself. Lord, this getting old is such a nuisance. Where did I put those wretched things? She began digging through another drawer when she heard a knock at the door. Then another more insistent knock. She could not very well hide, she thought. After all, the lights were on. Having no choice other than to answer the insistent pounding, she shuffled over to the offending door and unlocked it.

Thrusting her head around the partially closed door, she began to say, "I am sorry, we are clos...." then she saw stars in front of her eyes. Her vision clouded and darkened as she slipped solidly to the floor. The last thing she remembered as she lost consciousness was the sweet smell of sawdust.

The man replaced his truncheon-like weapon into the back of his pants. That was easy, he thought. Slipping quietly inside, he made a beeline for the cash register. Pushing buttons, the metal machine opened its mouth to reveal drawers filled with Reich Marks and Polish zlotys. Hmmm, he thought, the zloty would be more difficult to spend. Apparently, not everyone complied with the order to exchange the Polish currency. Scooping everything out and placing it all in his pockets, he stood back and looked at the old woman. I suppose it should look like an accident, he thought, although one more dead Pole would probably not be noticed. Still, he did not want to take chances.

His eye fell upon the walk-in freezer. Perfect, he thought. She is nearly finished anyway. Freezing would be a plausible explanation. Picking her up was like lifting a child. Nothing but skin and bones, he thought.

Now that he had a plan, he was anxious to be done with this. Making his way quickly to the freezer, he opened the door and laid her as if she had struck her head on one of the lower shelves. As he stood up, his fingers grazed against something solid and oval-shaped under the housecoat. Tentatively lifting the edge of the garment, he was unprepared to see the lovely brooch fastened in such an odd place. Well, well, he thought, good fortune has certainly showered upon me this night.

Unpinning the piece, he placed it into another coat pocket. Remembering to strew around a few things from some of the shelves he closed the freezer door. Good. It will look as if she fell, hit her head, and froze to death. Perfect. Clicking off the lights and locking the entrance door after him, he made his way back into the night's cover.

{ VII }

The telephone was ringing insistently as the colonel opened the door to his office. Glancing at his watch he thought, only 0700. Who would be calling at this hour? He cursed as he tripped over the leg of a chair, banging his knee on the edge of the desk. He answered the phone with a sharp *"Ja, Hallo! Wer ist das?* Who is it?"

The connection was faint and scratchy but he heard her voice as she said, "Herr Colonel? This is Marta. Can you hear me clearly?"

The colonel sat in his chair and rubbed his knee while he answered, "Oh. *Ja,* Fraulein, only just." He thought he heard someone crying in the background and said more loudly, "Fraulein, what is wrong? Are you all right?"

He noticed the tension in her voice, tight and forcibly under control, "Oh, Herr Colonel, it's Buscha. She's gone. Dead. I do not…do not know what happened. Mama and I found her in the freezer. It looks as if she fell or something…Just a minute, Mama, I will be right there…

Oh, I just do not understand. It must have been the latch, that horrible latch! It should have been fixed years ago! The door was locked when we arrived this morning so I do not think it can be anything other than an accident but...I do not think I can come back today if it would not inconvenience you too much. I cannot understand it...she was going to bed. What would she be doing in the freezer? And I cannot find her brooch anywhere. She never lets that brooch out of her sight. And the money is gone from the till but if it wasn't an accident, why did she not use Grandpapa's gun? It makes no sense."

She was obviously distraught and the colonel was having a difficult time following her conversation, if one could call it that. She continued to talk about a brooch and the freezer, topics meaningless to him. He thought Buscha was the nickname she used for her grandmother.

"Fraulein, Fraulein, please...calm down. Do not worry about coming back today. Stay there as long as you need to. What can I do to help? This is your *Großmutter* we are discussing, *ja*? Would you like me to tell Antoni? She is his Grandmother as well, correct?"

She had forgotten about Antoni, she said, and he really ought to know. And she had to find her missing relatives, somehow, and inform them as well. Then she began rambling about the brooch and freezer again. He stepped into her conversation before she became too overwrought.

"Fraulein, is there something I can do for you, something else besides inform Antoni? Please you must not become distraught. There must be some assistance I can offer."

After a long and raspy sigh, she said, "There is one thing I would like very much if you can see your way to doing it. After my father and grandfather...died...a family friend buried them for me in the Church cemetery. He was not supposed to have done so...perhaps I should not have told you...I do not want to get him into trouble. He is very old. We are not really supposed to gather in groups even for funerals and burials; the men come by with wagons for our dead. I am afraid to do it on my own but I would very much like Buscha to be laid alongside my grandfather and father. Do you think that would be possible? Elias will not be in any trouble, will he?"

"*Nein, nein*, no trouble," he said wondering who the hell Elias was. It did not matter; if he was someone the family could rely upon, the man would not be in trouble as far as he was concerned. "I will contact the officer in charge there and arrange everything for you, *ja*? Marta? Can you hear me? Someone will be there within the hour. You will only need to show him where you want your grandmother buried, understand?"

He heard her faint affirmative reply before he told her once again to stay in Bochnia as long as she wanted and to call him immediately if there was anything else he could do. After hearing her promise, the conversation disconnected from her end. He sat there with the dead telephone in his hand, staring at the door to her office. I should have Corporal Konig take me directly to Bochnia, he thought. Hanging up the phone he thought better of the idea. It would not do to have a colonel in the SS appear at her doorstep. It could bring out the anger in her family. A long sigh escaped him and he shook his head. This war, he thought, this damnable war.

He sighed again and picked up the receiver once more. He had promised her his help and he must contact several people. His finger began dialing the operator to place the first call.

I stayed in Bochnia for two weeks. True to his word, The Colonel had arranged for a German mortician to arrive at the butcher shop in just over forty-five minutes. Rank definitely has its privileges. Surprisingly, the man had been very polite and deferential to our pain. Mama and I rode with him to the churchyard where we laid Buscha next to our other two beloved. The German offered to drive us back into town but we opted to walk home, both of us feeling the need to keep moving.

We had some decisions to make, Mama and I, about the shop and our livelihood. I should remain at home and simply tell The Colonel I wished to leave my position. Mama would not hear of it. My next suggestion to have her come with me was met with an immediate "No" as well.

Mama was hell-bent on staying in Bochnia. I was even more concerned about her safety after Buscha's death. In the end, Aunt Isabella, now also a widow, opted to live with Mama in Buscha's flat, run the store together, and give each other comfort. Although our shop was not as busy as it had once been, the German soldiers seemed to particularly favor our various wursts. Were it not for their business, I felt sure our shop would not remain open.

Before I left them, I found Elias and asked if he would mind living in the nearly empty storage room in exchange for the occasional sweeping and tidying up. Since he, not unlike the rest of Poland, was living hand to mouth, he readily agreed. I was glad to have him there—I could trust Elias with anything.

My last task was locating other family members to inform them of my beloved Buscha. I did not, however, seek out Filip. Perhaps I should not have been so heartless—after all, she was his grandmother as well as mine. I suppose if I searched my soul deep enough, I was hoping to make him as angry as I possibly could. It was not my most Christian attitude, I admit, but it was Filip, after all. I cushioned my guilt by notifying his parents.

Elias took me back to Auschwitz using our old rickety meat truck since we carried Buscha's prized dressing table. The Colonel was once again helpful in providing us with travel passes and a petrol ration.

While I had been searching for Buscha's brooch, I happened upon Grandpapa's pistol under the counter. It was one more piece to the puzzle; if someone had threatened her, why had she not used the gun? Since the till was emptied and the brooch gone, why had the pistol been left behind? It was valuable as well, especially if sold through the black market. Moreover, why was she in the freezer so late at night? My thoughts went round and round these details until my head ached. Slipping the tiny weapon into the table's secret drawer, it bounced along with everything else in the ancient vehicle.

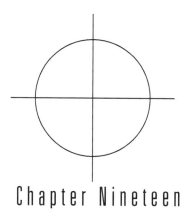

Chapter Nineteen

September 3, 1941

ZYKLON-B

*K*ommandant Höss' duties took him away from camp on September 3, leaving Karl Fritsch in charge. He was a man with ambition. His position as second-in-command at Auschwitz was a minor accomplishment compared to the heights he had set for himself. Today he would make a name for himself with Berlin.

Fritsch and Höss had engaged in several discussions regarding the clean and sure disposal of all undesirables. For some time, Fritz had been tossing about various ideas of extermination. After the gassing at Sonnenstein, using chemicals had been foremost in his thoughts specifically the large supply of pesticide in the camp. Easy to acquire, always plenty on hand—might need some slight modification—but all in all it seemed a very good idea indeed to try a quick experiment using this chemical; Zyklon-B. One added benefit—I.G. Farben held the patent for and produced the stabilizer for Zyklon-B. The resource would be even easier to acquire with the factory at Birkenau.

Today, Karl Fritsch chose 650 Russian prisoners from the infamous Block 11 along with 250 sick Poles from the hospital ward as his guinea pigs. They had limited time left anyway and this would probably be a more humane way to die. He did not particularly care either way. His goal was recognition. He ordered Block 11 to be locked down; no one enters or leaves without his express permission. Guards filled the floor vents in the basement with soil and tightly sealed all doors and windows. Rumblings were heard from some of the prisoners as they were forced into the tomb-like room. Their cries became more noticeable after the heavy doors were slammed and sealed, engulfing them in total darkness.

Several small holes had been drilled into the ceiling from the floor above, now occupied by Fritsch and several guards distributing large canisters among themselves. Tall and cylindrical, the cautionary script upon them was frightening; "Warning! Poison!" "To be opened by trained personnel only" "Zyklon! To be used against vermin!"

Even with their gas masks firmly attached, the guards did not feel completely safe with such great quantities of the chemical. Opening the containers with hammers and chisels, the contents were swiftly poured into the holes, and then the holes quickly sealed. Reaching the cell below, the blue pea-sized pellets released their gaseous acid. The smell of almonds alerted the prisoners to their fate and their screams were heard through the solid cement ceiling and walls. Fritsch could never understand it. Prison life in Auschwitz was intolerable; the SS had seen to that. Surely the prisoners knew they would all perish here eventually and yet, when death looked them in the face, they fought like animals to live in these wretched conditions.

Hours later, when the cries subsided, the door was unsealed. Through his gas mask, Fritsch saw a few men still clinging to their miserable lives. Resealing the door, another dose of Zyklon-B was poured into the chamber.

Twenty prisoners were handed gas masks, told to descend to the basement, and retrieve everyone inside. They were never to reveal what they would see under punishment of death. Once the door was again unsealed, the scene caused some to wretch inside their masks. The dying men had climbed atop each other to avoid the gas, bodies were piled at the door, fingernails torn out of bloody hands that had clawed and beaten against the exit. Their skin was blue tinged, their mouths wide. Severely stiffened limbs were intertwined with others, replicating a gruesome image of barbed wire. Hours were spent disentangling the bodies.

Tossing the bodies upon carts, the transportation to and from the crematorium continued well into the night. Herr Fritsch's quick experiment lasted nearly twenty hours.

Nonetheless, the deputy considered this trial a success. His one concern was the Krema. The ovens had taken too long to heat and could not efficiently handle the large load provided. Too much time had been lost and he knew the entire operation required expansion. It was another problem he would overcome.

{ I }

Kommandant Höss was livid although he did not let his deputy see his rage. He had known how determined Fritsch was to succeed in this Reich at anyone's cost, but how dare the man proceed with such an undertaking without his presence. He was forced to admit, in spite of his anger, his interest had been piqued by the use of Zyklon-B on the prisoners. He considered it his duty to improve upon the test.

Under the Kommandant's orders, SS engineers constructed an improvised gas chamber in the basement of Block 11. Refinements were made, eliminating the chemical's distinctive odor of almonds, and openings completely sealed. This chamber would be a temporary facility; a permanent gas chamber was already under construction in a building outside the compound.

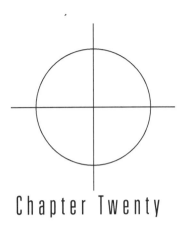

Chapter Twenty

October 1941

ENTER THE RUSSIANS

*I*n tandem with the arrival of so many Russians, so rose the structure of the second camp. Construction began in October under grueling conditions and for long hours. At times, I could hear whips cracking and German voices if the winds brought their sounds to me. I tried to pigeonhole it into the recesses of my mind along with the sounds of the train whistles, thinking how callous it was of me to block out someone else's plight.

The framework swelled in the distance like a child's building block set, the light yellow and red hues of the wood stretching farther each day. Sometimes the smell of freshly sawn wood wafted around my nose until it was chased back by the black smoke from the crematorium. The anticipated opening of Auschwitz II was scheduled for spring and I wondered what dignitaries would attend the momentous occasion, celebrating another secured complex where the erosion of human souls was encouraged.

I strove to learn all I could about the camp complex so I could relay the information to Max. Tomasz had been able to smuggle out several bits of information about the camp before I arrived. The Germans hired several men for specific jobs as electricians, plumbers, and the like from the local residents. Sympathetic to the plight of the prisoners, they would often smuggle in extra food and smuggle out the notes from Tomasz. He had been risking his life in such a manner ever since his capture in 1940. From what I had learned, thousands of AK members were risking their lives each day and yet there was no hint of salvation for my country.

Auschwitz-Birkenau was planned to contain nine separate segments, constructed over the next few years. Again, I managed to gain most of my information from Berta. She rattled off the segments and divisions between them as if she had a map in front of her. I tried desperately to remember everything she said but until I could see the camp, none of it would make very much sense.

From what Berta told me, Auschwitz II would contain 250 barracks, several kitchens, washrooms, bathhouses and storage buildings in each. Sector B2g would hold thirty buildings used as warehouses. Thirty! I could imagine why so many would be needed. All in all, the immediate plans called for 300 housing units, administrative buildings, kitchens, sanitary facilities, 13 km of drainage ditches, 16 km of barbed wire fencing, and more than 10 km of roads. The electrified subsections would be completely surrounded by another electrical fence and twenty-eight guard towers. With floodlights, patrolling guards, and dogs, it swallowed up 425 acres of once picturesque towns. The original camp would be dwarfed by the size of this newest cage and the place would be impenetrable.

The wooden barracks in Camp II were modeled after horse stables, each stable large enough to have housed fifty-two horses. The units were constructed with columns of brick bunks, three bunks high. Estimated human occupancy was two hundred thousand but, knowing how the Germans liked to squeeze prisoners together like sardines in a can, I thought this number optimistic.

After completion of the second camp, Auschwitz I would become the center of main offices, workshops, supply stores, barber shops, storage facilities, and the prisoner labor department. Those prisoners who were not assigned to the construction of the larger camp were usually appointed to work in these departments. Since Camp I already had many storage units, I wondered again at the thirty more that would be constructed in Camp II.

Chapter Twenty-One

November 1941

THE STORM

*B*oom! The crack of thunder woke me from a fitful sleep. The rain and sleet had been constant these past two weeks but tonight was torrential. The mud of the camp flowed between the Blocks like lava and I knew the remaining puddles would eventually become stagnant and develop that gooey rainbow-colored slime that floated on top. Four hour roll calls continued through the storm while the orchestra played on.

It was freezing in my room. Wrapping my arms around my thin flannel nightgown, I padded to the heater to stoke it. Damn, I thought. The coal basket was empty. Now what. The large fireplace in The Colonel's office came to mind. The man kept extremely unconventional hours, often popping in and out at odd times in the night but it was 1:00 a.m. and even he would not venture out on such a night.

Grabbing the down comforter from atop my bed, I tiptoed through the connecting door and built a raging fire. Much better, I thought. After moving the heavy sofa closer to the grate, I settled into the deep cushions and wrapped myself from head to toe with the comforter. The fire was mesmerizing to watch, the reflections of light bouncing off the marble floor, tongues of gold and embers in crimson licking the brick, and long shadows flickering against the paneled walls like a movie projector's light. Outside, I could hear the rain assault the glass panes, like a love-lorn suitor tossing gravel against his sweetheart's window. Enough, I told myself, time had long since passed for such foolish notions.

With the feeling restored to my limbs, I leaned into the corner of the sofa and closed my eyes. I had not slept well since my return from Bochnia. Nor could I rid myself of this solitary feeling within. Perhaps my lack of tears was a defense mechanism, preventing me from the pain of so much loss. Someday, when this war was over, then I would have time to cry.

Through my light slumber, I heard the click of the lock and felt the cold hallway air rush in as the door opened, revealing The Colonel who had half removed his wet topcoat before seeing me.

I stood immediately, professing the truth that I had never indulged in the luxury of his office before now, rambling on about the cold, lack of coal, and thunder. Until he stood staring at me without speaking, did I realize the glow of the fire through my old, worn nightdress left little to his imagination. I dove within the wrap of the comforter.

"I am sorry, *Herr* Colonel, I will go to my room," and I headed toward the door.

"And freeze? Sit, Fraulein, please." Removing his tunic, he placed it about my shoulders and I inhaled the scent of him in the fabric. "Here, drink this," he said, handing me a snifter of brandy. "It will warm you." Holding a snifter of his own, he sat on the sofa with me. My first mouthful caused watery eyes and a coughing fit. He moved slightly closer and pounded my back, something everyone thinks of performing when one is in my current predicament but actually does very little good. "*Ja*, it is strong. Take small sips and enjoy the bouquet."

Finally catching my breath, I did as instructed. The second sip was really quite good and I felt the heat reach my toes. Leaning my head against the back of the cushions, I sighed. "Thank you," I said, "for letting me remain."

"It would not do for one so lovely to become an icicle," he said as he loosened his tie. Turning my head toward him, I smiled and was greeted with his prominent dimples. The storm continued to pound the land, a bolt of lightning lit up the room, and I jumped at the thunder that followed. Laughing at my silly reaction, I inanely stated the obvious. "Quite a storm," to which he grinned.

As I stared into his cornflower blue eyes, my heart began pounding. Slowly, erotically, he leaned in and gently kissed my jaw bone, delicate nibbles like the touch of silk before he pulled away and looked into my eyes, questioning any hesitation I might have. In response, I slipped my hand around his neck and brought my lips to his. His fragrance enveloped me and his short curls of hair slid between my fingers. Holding me close, he nuzzled the hollow of my neck while his fingers wound themselves in my tresses. The heat grew between us as he withdrew his hand and sent it on a journey to my thighs, sliding up the hem of my gown and caressing my skin.

My body seemed detached from my mind and morals as I pressed closer against his chest, my heartbeat blocking out all sounds other than his warm deep breaths. Our tongues found each other, exploring, tasting, kissing. He was holding my cheek in his palm, suddenly whispering between pecks along my hairline, "I should leave." Abruptly, he pulled back and looked intently at me. "Shall I? *Bitte*, please, I need your honesty, with no fear of repercussions. Shall I stay? For if I do, I wish to stay the night and continue this."

I considered his statement but not for long. Wrapping my arm around his neck and leaning into his ear, I whispered, "Stay," and meant it.

Slumber was evading me but it was obvious from the ebb and flow of his breathing against my back, it had found The Colonel. How could he sleep when I was so racked with guilt?

Sliding carefully out from under the comforter, I slipped my arms into his discarded tunic and padded to my bedchamber. It was not only my abundant Catholic Guilt that had hold of me. The Colonel had been gentle and exciting, bringing me to emotional highs I never thought possible. But as he slipped into sleep, I could not help but think of my fellow Poles beyond the humming wires, contending with starvation, pain, and leaky roofs.

The sorrow on the faces of my father and grandfather in their final moments flashed across my mind as did Buscha, her halo of white hair as she waved to me, and the loss of her precious brooch, that last reminder of her. I had felt more alive and happy with The Colonel these past few hours than I had in several years. What right have I to feel joy with so much death around me? The tears rolled down my cheeks and would not subside as I sat on the edge of my bed.

"Marta, Marta, where are you?" I had awakened him with my silliness.

"Here," I mumbled. "I am in here."

He was at my side in an instant, holding me in his arms, asking. "*Mein Gott.* Did I hurt you? I am so sorry, *Liebchen*, so very sorry. I did not wish to harm you, little love." This show of concern only brought about more tears. With eyes running and nose dripping, I burbled and snorted my way through the reason for this sudden attack; I should not be happy, it was selfish of me and unfair to those in pain, those suffering around me on a daily basis. It was sinful of me to have been content in The Colonel's arms. When I noticed the mess I was making of his pristine tunic, I cried even louder.

Murmuring sweet encouragements and stroking my hair, we sat in this position for the remainder of the night while I cried myself dry.

At some point during the night, he left my side, for I awoke alone in my bed. Hearing his very angry voice through the walls, I crept to the connecting door to listen. I had never heard him in such a tirade. He was speaking on the phone in French to some unlucky person and although I did not understand a word of the conversation, it was obviously unfit for mixed company. Never hearing him raise his voice before, I wondered at the statement he made on the day we met; perhaps he was a brute after all.

Chapter Twenty-Two

December 7, 1941

JAPAN STRIKES

*I*t was barely dawn when the building came to life with feet pounding down the hall, doors slamming, voices raised, and phones ringing throughout the offices. What the hell is going on?

I tossed on the first dress I laid hands upon and ran into The Colonel's office. Empty. The lights were on in Antoni's office so perhaps I should try him. My inquisitiveness won out over caution so I entered his office just as he was hanging up the phone. The fire was burning brightly and warmly in the grate and I strolled in that direction.

"Antoni, do you have any idea what is happening? Everyone seems to be excited about something. I felt sure you would have the accurate story for me."

Putting his pen on the desk, he looked at me in that smoky, lazy way of his without commenting for a moment. "So, my little cousin, all these months of deliberate avoidance, now you require information and enter my office. I would call that rude." I really did not have an answer to that; he was right. Getting up from his desk and striding toward me, I noticed how elegant and handsome he looked in his immaculate uniform. He had been correct about that as well; the German uniform really did marvelous things for a man.

He placed one hand against the wall where I stood and leaned into me. Unless I skirted directly in front of the flames, I was essentially trapped. He always had a natural musky smell about him, even when we were younger, and now it was intoxicating. "Antoni, whatever are you playing at? All I want is information and if you are not willing to part with it, I shall find out from someone else." I edged to my left, trying to avoid my hem from catching the flames. Bringing his other arm against the mantel, he looked down into my eyes and said, "I do not think you should leave quite so soon. I would be more than happy to give you what you seek," by now he was murmuring in my ear, "and perhaps it will be what we both seek, *ja?*" His tongue was slowly gliding down the side of my neck until his mouth reached my throat. "It would seem," he said in between breathy kisses on my collar bone, "Emperor Hirohito has been causing trouble." His hand was sliding down the collar of my dress and began to slowly unbutton the top button. "His air force," the next button had been set free, "made a journey," he whispered as his kisses crept further into my cleavage, "all the way to Hawaii." I had no idea what he was talking about and did not care; I was beginning to breathe deeper and faster, losing track of time and place. "Early yesterday morning," and his fingers released two more closures, "they attacked Pearl Harbor."

Kisses on my flesh sent an electrical storm down my spine. His free hand had found its way under my skirt inching upward along my thigh. I cried out in shock and delight, throwing my head back and hitting it solidly against the carved marble mantle. The spell was broken. I was never so thankful for a bump on the head.

Opening my eyes, I looked at him in shock and embarrassment as I tried to straighten my dress. The pupils of his eyes were wide, baring the desire I saw within. Slipping the buttons back into their appropriate loops, all I could do was stammer an apology as I darted into the Ladies. I was becoming too familiar with these four walls; it seemed to be my constant refuge from uncomfortable situations.

It was not until radios were tuned to the news did I learn the full extent of Antoni's story. Japan had bombed America. Japan? Why? And what would this mean to the European war? The building continued to be in an upheaval for the next several days.

At midnight Polish time on December 8, the United States declared war on Japan and shortly thereafter, Britain did the same.

On December 11, Der Fuhrer addressed the world. Roosevelt deliberately brought this upon himself, Hitler declared. Promising no involvement in a foreign war, he had been secretly assisting the British. Because of Germany's alliance with Japan, Hitler was officially declaring war upon the United States of America. Several hours later, the United States returned the sentiment to Germany. Now it was truly a World War.

Part Four

NO END IN SIGHT
1942

Every day Hitler's firing parties are busy in a dozen lands. Monday he shoots Dutchmen, Tuesday Norwegians, Wednesday French and Belgians stand against the wall, Thursday it is the Czechs who must suffer, and now there are the Serbs and the Greeks to fill his repulsive bill of execution. But always, all of the days, there are the Poles.

Prime Minister Winston Churchill, 3 May 1941
BBC broadcast to Poland

Chapter One

January 1942

PERVERSITY ABOUNDS

"*Ja*, Herr Himmler, *alles in ordnung*. Everything is as ordered." Kommandant Höss sat in his warm office, holding the telephone receiver, glancing out the window at the murkiness and snow. Only one and a half hours of light each day in January, he thought. This detestable country! What he would not give to be home in Baden-Baden.

Conversations with Himmler, even by phone, made him nervous and he was beginning to sweat. Shuffling papers, he brought The Man up to date. "The Russians arrived on cue, ten thousand of them, and were immediately assigned to Camp II. Upon completion, it will house two hundred thousand prisoners. Since the Poles have essentially been eliminated, more room will be available in Camp I as well. We have begun converting the two farmhouses near the camp as per Eichmann's instructions. They should be fully functional by March, *mein Herr*."

And what of the chamber in Camp I, he was asked. "Still operational since fall. It is difficult to keep up with the demand in Krema I, however. Currently, we are able to hold approximately seven hundred in the gas chamber but the capacity of the three ovens is limited to three hundred forty bodies in a twenty-four-hour period. For expediency's sake, we bury many. Of course, after a four-month assignment, those prisoners detailed to the Krema are disposed of. It decreases the possibility of rumors spreading, you see.

"However, I am not sure if the Red and White Houses will suffice. Oh, my apologies. Because of the colors of each vacated farmhouse near Birkenau, those are the common terms applied to Krema II and Krema III. Of course, we still have the Black Wall. In November, another one hundred fifty-one Polish prisoners were executed there."

The penal colony—is that space still functional, asked Himmler. "*Ja,* it is currently full. Of course, it has been emptied of the Catholic priests originally housed there and now it contains common criminals. We sift through them as more arrive, eliminating many each day.

"I believe, however, the converted farmhouses will not be sufficient. The overall design is good; four hundred to eight hundred will fit into each chamber and each Krema contain fifteen ovens. Total capacity between all ovens should be two thousand bodies per twenty-four-hour period." Himmler paused for a moment, then simply told Höss to build two more. Twenty million RM had already been sunk into the project, what was another one or two more? "*Ja wohl, Herr* Himmler! We will begin immediately."

Himmler imparted further news; the first trainload of Jews would arrive at Auschwitz in February, not many, but they were to be gassed upon arrival. "All, *mein Herr*? Even those capable of work?" All, he was told. Later the selection process could begin. Women would arrive as planned in March. "Their temporary facilities will be completed by then in Camp I," assured Höss. "Birkenau will be totally operational by March as well, and I estimate Auschwitz-Monowitz to be ready in the fall." *Nein*; IG Farben wishes to have their facilities completed in July. See to it, Höss was ordered. July would also mean a second visit from Himmler, bringing a complete entourage to judge the efficiency of the camps.

After a mutual "Heil Hitler," Höss called in his deputy, informing him of the new time frames. "See to it," he told the man.

On schedule, the Jews came…and went. Amazing how they always believed the same tired reasons, thought the kapo. "You will be given showers," they were told. "What is your trade? Tailor? Wonderful, we need those," another guard would query. "Leave your belongings here and they will be returned to you in your barrack." "Clothing will be washed and returned; simply set them aside in the dressing room." Then the vultures would swoop in, those kapos and prisoners assigned to remove all personal belongings, and cart them to the sorting room. Everything was sifted through with care; valuables had been located in the soles of shoes, hems of shirts, linings of jackets, even between the leather of belts. Items of critical value were earmarked for Berlin, others were sorted into various bins. After the dead were withdrawn from the gas chamber, other prisoners would shave heads, pull gold teeth, and remove jewelry before placing the naked bodies in trolleys and wheeling them to the ovens. The January transport had the distinction of being the first to die in Krema II in the Birkenau camp. Never registered, never numbered, they remained nameless. The entire process was streamlined with assembly-line precision, a well-planned factory for killing.

First the Poles, then the Jews, now the women. On March 26, 1942, Camp I received 999 women from Ravenscroft camp and 999 Jews. On the following day, 127 Polish women political prisoners arrived by transport. A portion of the men's camp had been emptied and the women were assigned there.

A different form of degradation was inflicted upon the women. Upon arrival, their hair was shorn using old razorblades, their locks of hair bound and transported to Berlin. Wig manufacturing? I could think of no other reason for so much hair. Told to undress quickly, the clothes were torn from their bodies if they did not obey. Strapped to a table for a complete inspection of all body cavities, their pubic hair was shaved to further debase them.

Gas chambers were a talked-about and recognized secret. Even through concrete walls, one could hear the screams and pleas. A few fought back and gained a bullet for their troubles. Others looked numb and disbelieving. Some had survived in this hell over a year, hanging on by a thread, only to finally be gassed. It was not always the fast and painless method designed. Guards reveled in causing pain, cramming more than the allotted number into the chamber, causing less efficient chemical dosages. After the dissipation of the fumes, one or more would still be clinging to life, begging for mercy. A bullet would silence them. The sadistic behavior of the guards was unrelenting.

Only Russians were living in the incomplete Camp II where gas chambers and ovens had been the priority; those were fully operational while sanitary conditions were not. Officially called Auschwitz-Birkenau, among the staff, it was usually simply called Birkenau while the original camp was now referred to as *Stammlager,* the Main Camp. Of the ten thousand Russians first assigned to Birkenau's construction, only two hundred were yet alive.

Following the women, came the families. Arriving children were automatically exterminated as were children born in the camp. I made a point to visit Krema I as the doors were opened. Blood covered the walls and floor, many had been trampled to death in the ensuing panic, and children's heads popped open like someone had stepped on a pumpkin. They had been clawing, climbing, reaching for an exit that would never be, gasping for air while flesh turned blue and joints stiffened, and finally choking out their last breath. Their faces were frozen in masks of terror, mouths and eyes wide in silent reproach. It only took seconds to observe the scene, but one I can never forget.

December had been a busy month for deaths. Ninety-four Soviet POWs and twenty-three political prisoners died that month. A few days later, thirty-seven prisoners from Block 20 were murdered by phenol injections to the heart. This was becoming a pattern of sorts; an inordinate number of deaths in one month and then back to normal. I never heard of a satisfactory reason for this peculiar schedule. Killing was a corporate business and the Germans never tired of the enterprise.

Now we arrived at March, another busy month. On Sunday the fifteenth, twenty-eight prisoners died in the hospital of various illnesses but I knew better; other more sinister reasons were always the cause. On that same day before the morning roll call, drunken guards arbitrarily shot one hundred thirty-one prisoners. After lunch, another two hundred fifty subsequently died from past tortures; so I was told by Uncle in a brief note. In his particular shorthand writing, the note continued to inform me of more madness:

Prisoners' excrement used for industrial purposes
New epidemic control research and electro shock treatment
Tissue cut from hips of freshly executed prisoners, collected in
buckets, to breed bacteria
On commission from IG Farben- experimentation in tolerance of
new drugs

I could barely enter the camp or the hospital without covering my
nose. The odor of infection, filth, mildewed walls, urine, and fecal matter
seemed to be everywhere.

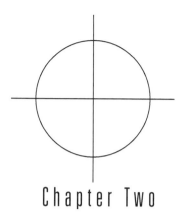

Chapter Two

April 1942

SABOTAGE

"*T*hey must be stopped!" Hermann Göring was appalled and furious. His gut jostled every time he raised his voice and his face was becoming quite red. "We cannot release troops from the front lines to keep these people in check. Wilhelm, you control the Wehrmacht—what is your solution?"

"As you say, Herr Göring. I do not think is wise to bring in troops to attend to this matter," said Keitel." What does Der Fuhrer say?"

"He does not know the extent of it," Göring said while wiping his face. "I want to present a task completed rather than more worries."

Josef Goebbels was rifling through various publications and announcements before sharing them with his colleagues. "Some of this is better than even my department can produce," he said, passing the papers around the table. "They have been issuing thousands of these. From what we know, they have an entire subdivision of men who study us; our various dialects, jargons, terms used in state administration, military opinions, structural changes, even how we communicate with the local communities. It boggles the mind." He picked out one official-looking notice and held it in front of him. "Do you see this? Very real looking, very professionally done. This was issued to our German citizens: 'Gas mask distribution will occur only two days a week due to insufficient supply.' It goes on to explain that masks were sent to troops and officials of the Reich! Complete bedlam ensued. Our citizens were rioting in the streets, believing they were left to die while government employees were receiving special consideration. Outrageous!"

"But surely, *mein Herr*," spoke Himmler, "They must have known it was a fake."

"Herr Himmler," said Goebbels with some frustration, "in this war, with our attention divided between so many, who is to know what is truth and what is not. The point is, this Polish underground has many such divisions destroying our people's trust in us. Look at this one. This was sent to over 209 of our German administrated factories ordering all workers to take a full day off—with wages—to celebrate the anniversary of the Nazi Party's inception. With pay! Can you imagine the uproar when the workers did as this flyer ordered then were told it was an error? Riot, upheaval! We finally had to pay them. Not only that, we lost thousands and thousands of man-hours in weapons manufacturing."

The men had a right to be concerned. Operation *Neimcy* (meaning Germany in Polish), also called Operation N, was a complex and effective action of sabotage, subversion, and black-propaganda activities. Carried out with extreme precision, Operation N was responsible for printing and distributing counterfeit newspapers, periodicals with radical articles, news of widespread anti-Nazi opposition within the German ranks, and numerous intelligent reports with one thought in mind; to confuse and undermine the morale of the Germans in a completely believable fashion.

"And what of Peenemunde? Have they learned of that?" inquired Himmler. Goebbels did not know for sure, better to inquire at the site directly, he was told.

In fact, the Poles had discovered the factory at Peenemunde and what Hitler referred to as his "secret weapon," the V1 flying torpedoes. This information was passed on to England using handmade crystal set radios, those frequencies undetectable by the enemy. Signals were decidedly weak and the operators often had to move within range but it represented hope.

The largest problem was English skepticism. How could any known fuel power a winged bomb? The underground was now in the process of procuring pieces of the torpedo to send across the British waters for proof. In the meantime, 43 percent of all strategic and tactical moves by the enemy provided to British Intelligence came from the Polish underground.

"These miserable Poles are now in collusion with the Soviets, attacking our transports of equipment and supplies to the Eastern Front, in addition to rail cars traveling to Germany with goods. Even border outposts are not safe from them. They have weapons now and have engaged our men in full scale battles! The physical damage they have wreaked upon us is immense. Here—I have some of the particulars." Himmler began shuffling papers until he found the one he sought. "These are the latest numbers; over six thousand damaged locomotives, seven hundred derailed transports, eighteen thousand railway wagons put out of commission, over five thousand army vehicles and fuel tanks destroyed. This does not include the damaged and burned locomotives, blown up railway bridges, or disruption to electricity. The Polish army and air force are fighting in North Africa, France, Britain…This cannot go on!"

It was estimated that an eighth of all German transports to the Eastern Front were either destroyed or severely delayed by AK actions. The generals were not aware, however, of sabotage conducted internally by the factory slave laborers. Polish workers made slight alterations on a massive scale to whatever weaponry the Germans produced. Built-in faults were added to aircraft engines, cannon muzzles, artillery missiles, air traffic radio stations, condensers, and electro-industrial lathes. Factory machinery would unexplainably freeze, incapacitating production. The sabotaged machinery and weaponry would not be detected until it malfunctioned in the field.

Polish troops had buried arms on the battlefields during the invasion, providing the Home Army with a large cache of weaponry once retrieved. Occasionally, arms were purchased on the black market, stolen outright from captured outposts and railcars, or smuggled from factories.

Amazingly, the tenacious AK manufactured their own arms in secret workshops, supplying the fighting forces with submachine guns, pistols, flamethrowers, explosive devices, road mines, hand grenades, and even converting Chevrolets into armored cars. Other devices to perpetuate sabotage included tire puncturing spikes, tool kits for unbolting rail girders, igniting charges, thermite bombs, clock bombs, smoke and signaling torches as well as chemical substances used to gas German cinema houses.

The control of the General Government was disrupted daily with acts of sabotage, espionage and military operations. Thousands of German troops had been recalled attempting to crush the Home Army with limited success.

"We have even offered arms to various communities in Eastern Poland for use against the Soviets; all very hush-hush, of course," said Keitel.

"And?"

William Keitel shook his head sadly. "The guns were turned upon the suppliers."

"They murdered Igo Sym, are you aware of that? He was of great assistance to us and not the only one killed in cold blood."

In response to the continued terror tactics of the Germans, the AK proudly established an Underground Court of Law for Crimes Against the Polish Nation. Holding formal trials, over five thousand prominent Nazi collaborators and Gestapo officers were compiled into a list of planned assassinations. The specialized unit assigned to this task had been very busy of late.

"And the Jews? Have those transports been attacked as well?"

"Only our military supplies and empty cars. The cars are destroyed before Jews are loaded and the captives spirited away. Poles and Jews have fled or are hidden by partisans while the explosions and fighting are ensuing."

"This is intolerable! Do you mean to say the Poles are continuing to hide the Jews? With a death sentence in effect? How is this possible?"

It was not only possible, but extremely organized and successful. Aware of their sentence if discovered, the Poles continued to provide sanctuary for Jews. In fact, it was the only occupied country to form an organization specifically for Jewish aid. Known as Zegota (code name for Council to Aid to Jews) the many members provided food, shelter, medicine, money, and false documentation for them. One Catholic Polish woman, Irena Sendler, was saving Jewish babies by using her appointment as a social worker assigned to inspect sanitary conditions in the ghettos. While there officially working to forestall typhus, she and her friends were really smuggling out babies and small children in her nurse's bag or packages.

Thousands of Jewish children were saved with the cooperation of Polish families and Roman Catholic convents. To those who could pass for Christians, priests would falsify baptismal certificates as proof of their Catholicism. The primary source of funds originated from the Government in Exile but members scrounged for anything of use when funds ran low.

Religious Sanctuary was not recognized by the Germans, and yet two-thirds of all nunneries were hiding and caring for Jews, mostly children, hundreds of those saved by Irena Sendler. Others lived under an assumed name with the full cooperation of their neighbors, vouching for them to inquisitive Gestapo. It was estimated that the work of ten Poles was required to save the life of one Jew.

Taking charge of the conversation, Keitel asked Himmler, "What of your *Einsatzgruppen* or *Sonderkommandos*? Both groups conduct furtive assignments, do they not? I think, perhaps, the elimination of these tiresome Poles should be the responsibility of the SS."

"Currently, they are both active in Russia doing what they do best." Although Himmler did not elaborate upon their activities, the men knew what the two groups were capable of. "The most equitable solution continues to be utilizing troops stationed in Poland and retrieving others from the Eastern Front if needed. Now with the Americans involved..." He left the sentence unfinished but understood.

"I warned Herr Fuhrer," said Göring. "My fear of the Americans becoming involved..." he shook his wattle-like double chin sadly, "I warned all of us..."

"So far, they are more concerned with Japan and the Asia-Pacific Theater of battle. However, if they should become more...troublesome, then any Polish resistance is secondary to that of defeating England and America. For the time being, I shall inform Der Fuhrer that we have a probable solution to the Polish difficulties...should he ask."

Chapter Three

May 1942

EXPANSION

*W*hen Auschwitz had opened in 1940, two hundred guards were stationed here. By June 1942, we had two thousand and more were arriving. The original kapos of German descent now consisted of any nationality willing to sell out their fellow prisoners for personal gain. Library privileges were no longer enough compensation for their exceptional actions. As incentives or rewards, the kapos were now granted the use of a woman prisoner for fifteen minutes.

The woman's block maintained two hundred of the nastiest female guards I had ever seen, more brutal than their male counterparts. Kommandant Höss described them as "mean and vulgar, prostitutes with multiple convictions and downright repulsive women." Forced to work just as hard as the men, the female prisoners' life expectancy was half as long as their male counterparts and their only hope was an assignment in tailor shops, kitchens, or office details.

Now that Auschwitz-Monowitz was opened, prisoners were transported not only for work detail in the factories, but to be housed there as well. The IG Farben Company began operations in synthetic rubber and liquid fuel in May using eleven thousand slave laborers. Smaller chemical plants and mines exploited another fifteen thousand with all producing a profit for the Reich coffers.

As near as I could tally, forty thousand prisoners were utilized somewhere within the 425 km area of the three camps but it was difficult to be completely accurate. Every few days, the doctors from Auschwitz II visited the work camps to select the weak and sick for elimination in the Little Red and White Houses.

Smaller areas, called satellite camps, were sprouting up outside the main perimeters. About a dozen were currently operational but plans called for another thirty-five, all staffed by prisoners at a daily rate paid to the SS. Some were designated Women Only but I could not learn the reason for this; only that they would be operated at a profit. The income must be monumental from this hellhole, I thought. No wonder people were brought in by the thousands, speaking every language imaginable.

According to Deputy Fritzsch, two thousand bodies could be burned each day with the multiple Kremas at their disposal. I hoped he was mistaken but I did not think he was; the past eight months had seen thirty thousand meet their demise in this fashion. Krema I was no longer in use, having been converted into a bomb shelter, but two larger versions were under construction in the third camp.

In addition to Kanada I in the main camp, Birkenau held Kanada II, another long paved area to conduct the selection process of incoming prisoners. Some were sent to the right end of Kanada, some to the left. Some would be encamped, others, almost three-fourths of each transport, would die immediately. All belongings were left in the gravel to be grabbed and taken to a Block to be sorted and stored in several facilities scattered between the camps. The question of thirty storage Blocks in the Birkenau blueprints was finally answered.

I visited one such separation Block and wished I had not. Everything was done with precision while several kapos looked on, speeding up the process, watching for thefts. The prisoners had no use for luxury items but shoes and clothing were another matter. Several soldiers wandered in and occasionally snatched up an item or two. The kapos did nothing, although the soldier could be severely punished for such actions. They could also do harm to the reporting kapos.

As goods were separated into similar lots, other prisoners carried them to storage bins. Following the men, I was agog at the amount of belongings separated within the building. Shoes, hundreds of them; eye glasses, too many to count; empty suitcases, each one carefully noted with the owner's name and address; locks of hair, further separated by color; metal and wooden leg braces, canes, and prosthetic legs, even pots and pans. Men might write about this someday, I thought, but no one will believe it.

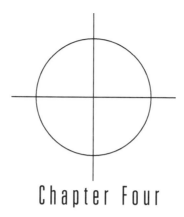

Chapter Four

June 1942

ESCAPES

$\mathcal{B}$erta came into the office in quite a state. "Did you hear?" she asked me. It was always better to answer in the negative with Berta; she was then more forthcoming with information. "An escape!" There had been many escapes from Auschwitz, some successful some not. I failed to understand her excitement until she explained.

That day, June 20, 1942, the most daring escape occurred in the camp. Four Polish political prisoners had disappeared without a trace. The four men had not only acquired German uniforms and weapons, they commandeered the Kommandant's staff car from the motor pool and calmly drove it out the front gate. (It took great control not to joyously laugh while Berta continued). Apparently, one of the prisoners spoke fluent German and, donned in an officer's uniform, commanded the guards to open the gate, as he was behind schedule. Marvelous!

Naturally, the entire camp was in total uproar and lock-down. I had never seen Kommandant Höss so furious. Not only were the prisoners gone, but his staff car as well. His screaming at the guards was wonderful to behold. Were they all idiots? Did they not recognize his personal automobile? Imbeciles!

More details were forthcoming from Tomasz. Prisoners had always worked in the shops in the camp, making it easy to abscond uniforms from the tailor's shop and guns from repair and weapons depots. At least that was his plausible theory. Punishment was naturally given to remaining prisoners but in this instance, many guards were punished as well. It did my heart good to see several transferred to demeaning details and black marks noted in their records. I only wished they had been put to the Post.

As long as I was at Auschwitz, the four escapees were never captured. It gave the camp hope, much more than the attempted escape ten days prior had.

The idea for that mass escape began in May of that year when four hundred Polish political prisoners were assigned to the Penal Block. Every few days, ten to twenty of these prisoners were randomly executed, a procedure that confirmed the death sentence hanging over all their heads. The possibility of one or more reaching freedom prompted a risky escape planned for June 10, 1942. The stop-work signal on the Birkenau drainage ditch was the cue to commence the plan. Mother Nature, however, had other ideas.

The pouring rain caused the Penal Block supervisor to call an early halt to the day's labor. Upon hearing the shrill whistle hours before the appointed time, prisoners were sent into confusion. Should they follow the plan and run now or wait until another date and time was set? Fifty men felt the time was at hand and made a run for it, many trampling over the kapos on duty.

Two men were caught immediately, thirteen were shot and carried through the gates while others were herded back into the camp. Two other escapees were caught five days later 25 km from the camp. Seven prisoners reached freedom.

Punishment for the living was swift. Twenty random prisoners were shot that day and 320 Poles from the Penal Block were gassed. Confident this example would deter escapes once and for all, the Germans were astounded when hundreds of prisoners continued escape attempts during the life of the camp.

Chapter Five

July 1942

DISCOVERY

*T*oday, I was alone in the offices, something I thoroughly enjoyed. I need not be on the alert for Antoni's advances nor did I have to be concerned with him deducing my affection for The Colonel. Last week, Antoni had sauntered in and seated himself in his customary position on the corner of my desk.

"So, my little cousin," he began while gently pushing an imaginary hair from my face, "you have been looking extremely lovely these past weeks." Leaning in, he grabbed a lock of my hair and inhaled. "Even your scent is different. Perhaps you are trying to gain the attention of someone, hmmm? A German, perhaps? What would your mother say?" His finger by now was tracing my arm up and down. Damn him, I thought. He still has the ability to give me chills.

"Perhaps you think it wiser for me to engage in an incestuous relationship with you?" I demanded.

"Ah, I can only dream of your heart softening in that regard," he grinned as he began nibbling on my ear.

"Antoni, please. I cannot work with you in my way. Can you not find some other Fraulein to pester?"

He chuckled as he rose and ambled toward our connecting door. "I noticed, cousin, you did not bother to deny my accusation." With another grin aimed in my direction, he proceeded into his office.

Damn, I thought. I must watch my step while bantering with him. He has a way of drawing out the truth from me every time.

Today, though, I was free from the mental stress of verbal fencing with my cousin. Alone and untaxed, I began rummaging in my desk for carbon paper. With so many copies demanded of every form, I constantly exhausted my supply and I did not look forward to the long trip downstairs to the quartermaster's office and maneuvering around that disgusting man today. I knew The Colonel hand wrote personal and classified letters, using carbon for his copies. It should be easy enough to find.

The drawer holding his completed letters contained the sole lock in his desk, nevertheless I felt uncomfortable searching through the other unlocked cubbies. Nonsense, I told myself, I only require one sheet of carbon paper; I am not interested in anything personal. I had almost given up when I opened the bottom drawer and found what I sought. I turned to leave when I noticed something odd about the drawer. Something I could not put my finger upon but niggled at my brain. Then I understood. The outer dimensions of the drawer were deeper than the interior. Much like Buscha's dressing table, it contained a secret space.

Did I really want to know its contents? It could be important information needed by the underground. Or I could be opening Pandora's box. With shaking hand, my fingers slowly searched for the spring latch I knew must be present. Go back just a little, that bump in the corner. There! Pressing firmly, I was rewarded with the pop of the false bottom. Empty! Well, perhaps it is a good thing, I thought, I did not want to know his secrets. And yet, my fingers sought the dark recesses of the space and brought forth a key. My key! No, mine was safe in the secret drawer. Then it had to be Tomasz's. Oh good Lord—we had been discovered! He knew!

Wait, I told myself, perhaps he does not know who is passing the key back and forth. If I just place it back, he need never know I found it. All his talk of affection and sweet lovemaking, how would he feel when he discovered I was a spy? It had been rumored that Kommandant Höss had taken a mistress from among the prisoners. When he had tired of her, she was eliminated in Krema II. Would I suffer the same fate?

I would have to tell Tomasz, of course, and my uncle; we could no longer continue this way. Should I remove anything inside? No, no; it would be too obvious it had been found.

I was frozen in this manner, behind his desk, extending the key before me like a beacon, when the door opened and Colonel Müller stood in the threshold. There would be no hiding now. Frantically, I began to rattle off excuses and apologies, blaming the carbon paper and attempting to place everything back from whence it came while wishing I had my pistol on me. He held up his hand to cease my inane jabbering. Closing the door behind him, he walked briskly to where I stood.

"It was only a matter of time, you know. I believe an explanation is in order," he said.

I could only open my mouth and stare at him. He had spoken in perfectly precise English.

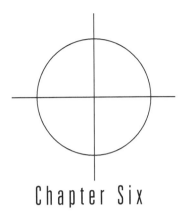

Chapter Six

BLACKMAIL

$\mathcal{F}$ilip lingered over his coffee—real coffee—in his bright and cheery dining room. Snow had fallen during the night but the fire in the grate kept out the fingers of the frost. The room was filled with beautiful and expensive items. Of course, most of his objects d'art were from another's home but it was convenient for him to forget that. They were his now and that's what mattered. He could afford to enjoy all the finer things this war had to offer him; this coffee for instance. Tins of expensive delicacies filled his pantry and silk sheets adorned his bed. The most satisfying of all was his ability to light fires in all his grates.

He had brought Mrs. Blonski with him to this new abode and she had proved to be an excellent cook, especially when he could provide such varieties of food with which to create meals. He entertained in style, often having German officers or government officials over to dine. Taking another long sip of the hot brown liquid, he added two teaspoons of sugar to his china cup. Normally, he never drank coffee with sugar but since he could afford it, why not indulge. Noises from below interrupted his quiet morning. The girls must be waking up, he thought and his mood immediately turned sour.

He had handpicked the women himself. No common street whores for his establishment. These women liked what they did and were worth every enormous fee they charged. Even the building had been carefully selected. It was once a hunting lodge for an obviously wealthy man who had all the latest comforts installed. It had taken skill and patience to acquire this place, not to mention a huge sum of money, but it was worth it. Situated in the wooded area outside of Krakau and constructed of hand sawed logs and river rock, it seemed to call his name.

He had, without much imagination, named his establishment The Lodge. It reminded him of the brothel where he had first enjoyed Arlene. Although not Wehrmacht controlled, the strictest rules applied; condoms and disinfectant always.

Membership fees were required to partake of the services but customers never complained once their pampering began. Only the best wines were provided along with caviar, the finest pastries, the loveliest ladies, even a four-course dinner in the dining room. All for an additional price, naturally. And that, Filip thought, is where the trouble began.

While he began this business entirely with his own funds, Johann felt their partnership should extend to this endeavor as it had in the others. As Filip expected, the man had neither money nor collateral to offer. He had frittered away his income on drink, women, and God-knew-what-else. Food, definitely, as the sergeant's waistline had grown considerably along with the contents of his wallet. His waistline remained engorged while his wallet did not.

It put Filip in a most difficult situation. If he refused, Johann would hand him over to the Gestapo for his prior transgressions. Once they knew he was Polish, it would be all over. No one would take a Pole's tale of innocence over the lies of a respected German soldier. He really had no choice but to offer Johann a cut of the profits, providing the loathsome man accept some responsibility for its operation. Looking back, perhaps it had not been his best decision, thought Filip as he paced his study. He had been carrying that bastard all these years and now Johann's blunder placed them in this current mess.

The women were complaining to Filip about the man as well. In Johann's mind, keeping the pantry stocked gave him access to the girls gratis. If the girls were not paid, then neither was Filip. I swear, vowed Filip, if he gave any of my girls the clap, I will shoot him in the balls myself!

To make matters worse, Johann had been pilfering supplies from the Officers' Kanteen as well as his Kommandant's private stock. Filip would never have known of the thievery, probably would not have cared, if Johann had not been caught. Idiot! Did Filip have to do the thinking for both of them? A Heer private was now squeezing them in return for silence. Hopefully, he was less intelligent than Johann, whose own was little more than a duck's. The private insisted on receiving a cut from their moneymaking venture or he would inform their Kommandant. The irony was not lost upon Filip; he was a victim of blackmail. Actually, when he considered Johann's original threats, it was double blackmail. Ignorant, stupid man! This was intolerable! It was like a scene from a bad American movie. He would laugh if it had not been his scene.

Perhaps Germany's engagement with Russia would prove to work in his favor. Nazi soldiers were shipped to the Eastern Front by the thousands leaving smaller portions in the Polish cities. The investigation into his activities could be minimal. God knew there were several he did not want them digging into. Even Johann was not privy to some of his more unsavory actions. Moreover, Filip had been noticing the remaining soldiers were much younger now, some not yet old enough to shave. Overall, he may get through this tight spot unscathed.

Time was growing short. He and Johann were to meet with the bastard in just over an hour. He had to finalize his plan to end this dilemma.

"What shall we do? How can we afford to give him our money? Everything must be purchased legitimately now. More expenditures, Filip. What are we going to do?" Johann's boiled eyes were near popping and looked rheumier than ever. Too much drink, thought Filip. He was panting as they walked to their assignation though the weather was cold and snowy. Too much food, thought Filip.

"Perhaps you should have thought of that before you put your hand into the Kommandant's wine cellar," replied Filip, slapping his gloved hands together to keep warm.

"*Ja, ja*. You are right. You are so right. But I was only trying to save us money, my friend. Only that," whined the man.

"You obviously did not," replied Filip tersely. Did he think me dimwitted? thought Filip. He knew for every bottle Johann pinched, he consumed another.

They were to meet the man in a crowded coffee shop although Filip had hoped to meet in some secluded alley or crumbled building but it was not to be. He had learned caution over the years; it was a pity Johann had not. Stupid, careless slob.

Acting more calm and unconcerned than he felt, Filip sat at a back table, ordering one coffee for himself from a skinny waitress. Let Johann order his own. He was past buying the man cups of coffee. Having unbuttoned his coat and taken off his hat, he was still sweating. Telling himself to relax or all would be lost, he spotted his tormentor walking through the door. Must not let him know how pissed I am, thought Filip, let him believe none of this really matters. He had become very adept at being friendly to people he hated.

The private strode up to their tiny table, and shook Filip's hand. Sitting down without an invitation to do so, the man was jovial and grinning, treating Filip as a friend and business associate rather than a blackmail victim.

Filip began the conversation. "My friend here informs me you have a proposition. I should like to hear it."

Grinning even wider, the man slapped Johann on his back, saying, "Sergeant Schafer is a good man—always has my back—and I appreciate him talking to you. So. I know what you two have been up to. I have seen the good sergeant with my own eyes in the Officers Pantry and I'm afraid he does not hold his tongue very well when he drinks." Filip kept his expression blank; so it was Johann's tongue, he thought. The sergeant began sputtering denials. Holding up a hand to quiet him, Filip allowed the private to continue. "You can see how this knowledge could get you in hot water. I propose we become business partners, friends even, and not a word of this will reach the Kommandant or anyone else. Of course, I shall want my fair share. Fifty percent should do."

Johann began sputtering again. "Fifty percent! Are you mad? We cannot give you that much. Tell him, Filip, tell him what..." Holding up his hand again to Johann, Filip began to talk.

"I'm afraid my friend here is right. That is much too steep. Even we do not net that much. You do not seem to understand the overhead we have. The girls must receive payment, the building needs repairs, and I pay the locals for protection. The biggest expense is the food and wine, which will increase now that you have forced us to buy from...

other sources. No, I am afraid we could become insolvent entirely and then what? Something along the lines of 10 percent, I think." Let the haggling begin, thought Filip. They ping-ponged back and forth with Johann occasionally throwing in a bluster or two. Finally, the amount of 25 percent was agreed upon and hands were shaken.

"I am fortunate to do business with two such reasonable men. And believe me, I will not betray you—you can trust me. Here, let me get your coffees. It is the least I can do." The waitress stood at the cash register and the private rose to stand in the queue.

As soon as he was out of earshot, Filip leaned into Johann while buttoning his coat. Under his breath he said, "Unsnap your holster."

"What? Why? What are you going to do?" said the sergeant worriedly, his watery eyes popping.

"Nothing," Filip hissed. "I just want you to be prepared. I do not trust him." Johann seemed to relax and look slightly proud; his military expertise was required. Filip heard a faint metallic pop from Johann's holster and nodded to the man.

The three men walked out of the shop in a much better frame of mind. In fact, when the suggestion of a drink came up, it was quickly accepted. Before long, the three of them were toasting to their continued good fortune and the drinks were flowing. Filip, however, professed a slight stomach ailment and continued to nurse one drink while his two partners made up for his temperance. Looking at his very expensive watch, he announced his departure. "I have the chance to acquire a very beautiful girl for The Lodge from another house. I have to promise the world to steal her away from her present spot but believe me, business will double when men see her. I have one more chance to present her with my final proposition." With that, he slowly rose from the table amid protestations from the other two men. "Oh, no," they said. "We should have a look at this piece of ass too, *ja*? After all, we are partners," they chortled loudly and sloppily. Agreeing, Filip and his two staggering partners made their way down a street with very few buildings still intact. Ignoring the slaps on the backs between the two Germans for the fine job their Luftwaffe had done, Filip stopped at a transomed door.

Trying to peer around a tattered blue shade, he said, "I do not think they are awake yet. Or perhaps it is their time off. I may have mistaken the day. If only I could see through that transom." He stood on his toes trying to do just that, but knew he was too short.

The private guffawed rudely and spoke in German to his fellow soldier, causing Johann to snicker. "Here, my pint-sized partner. Let me have a try." Pushing Filip to one side, he cupped his hands to the window in question and peered inside.

While the man was occupied in his task, Filip edged closer to Johann and quietly drew the gun from the sergeant's open holster. Creeping up to the private and holding the gun under the folds of his coat he said, "You know, I think I have had a change of heart." The man turned around and looked inquisitively at Filip. Leaning in closer to the private, he said, "I would rather burn The Lodge to the ground with the women inside than give you one pfennig of my business." Quickly touching the gun against the man's chest, he fired. The poor, stupid man had a look of complete surprise as he slumped to the ground.

Johann recovered from his shock in drunken surprise. "What did you do? Run. We have to run!"

"Silence," said Filip as he handed back the sergeant's gun to him. "I need you to keep your wits about you. I did what you should have done long ago. Now get down here and help me. We have to make it look like a robbery. Get his wallet and I will grab his gun." The sergeant did as he was told, following directions without hesitation. Filip stood behind him and asked, "Quickly, what else would you take from a soldier if you robbed him? His papers, perhaps? Or maybe his medals? Then grab those too."

"*Das ist alles*. I have everything," Johann said as he stood. "We should go now."

"Yes, I think that is a most excellent idea." As the sergeant turned to look at Filip, he heard a loud pop. The last thing he saw was the gun in Filip's hand as he joined the private on the street.

Quickly placing both guns into their respective owners' hands and possessions back into pockets, he thought it looked like an argument gone bad. Straightening up, Filip surveyed the blood seeping into the cobblestones and rubble. Thank goodness they had both been shot in the chest, he thought, harder to explain with a bullet in their back. It had all been over in a matter of seconds and as far as he could tell, no one had noticed. Killing the two men had been much easier than he thought but it had been his only way out. Finesse was never Filip's strong suit.

Turning on his heel, he walked quickly out of the street.

Chapter Seven

REVELATION

*T*hree hours ago, I feared for my life. Now I was settled comfortably in my Colonel's arms within his bed.

"Why did you not tell me?" I asked irritably for the third or fourth time.

"I could not. Plus, I admit, I was hoping you would fall in love with me as I am. Selfish, I admit."

Sitting upon my elbow and covering myself with the quilt, I responded, "Do you have any idea the turmoil and guilt I have been under? Involved with a Nazi? My God! My nerves were stretched to their limit." Then I had another thought. "You understood all my English phone calls!"

Dimpling at me, he admitted sheepishly he had. Flopping back into the feather bed with a groan, I stared at the ceiling trying to make sense of this afternoon's events.

Frozen in time with the key in my hand, The Colonel placed it back into its hiding spot, called for Corporal Konig, and led me gently out of the office. Shaking like a leaf, positive I would soon be the only prisoner chauffeured via staff car into captivity, I was speechless when the good corporal parked before a large home. The Colonel's home. My imagination took me from being held as a sex slave in his basement to a shooting against his back garden wall.

Instead, I was led into his study, poured a glass of brandy, and listened to him talk. The key was his, he said. And yes, he spoke perfect English. People often divulged information when they believe you do not understand them. And…he had been part of the Polish resistance for some time.

I sat before the fire in the cozy room, stunned, with so many questions I could not vocalize them. Thank God he stepped in with the full story.

He had been with the German military for many years, he began, but neither he nor his family were pro-Nazi; just the opposite. However, the lives of his parents, sister, and nieces were at stake. If he gave up his commission, suspicion would have attached to him and trouble would be issued to his family. (You have no idea the terror in my own country, he said). So, working against them from within was the answer. The fewer people who knew, the better. The key had been his idea as was my job offer.

"So…you know Max? He is your contact?"

"No," he said with an apologetic grin, "I am Max's contact. His directives are from me."

I could only shake my head. "And your personal letters? What were those?"

"Some are just that; letters home. Others are in code to various underground districts. Since the Poles sent an Enigma Machine to England along with the broken code, deciphering is much easier. Most of the information Britain acquires is a direct result of the code, did you know that? A most wonderful accomplishment by your people."

Rising, he walked to his great collection of toys. Picking up a little wooden carriage, he released a tiny panel in the underside. "This is where I keep microfilm before passing it along. My interest in toys is well known as is my dislike of others handling them. It proved a very safe hiding place especially since I often alternated those in the office. Several of them have hidden spaces. Very convenient to play upon my… eccentricity."

I suddenly remembered overhearing his angry conversation in French. "I was speaking to Max," he admitted. "Fortunately, he is not as conversant in the more...colorful verbiage of that language as I am. I wanted him to pull you out. After that first visit to the camp, I thought the conditions here were too upsetting for you. He assured me you could handle it. Then, after your torrential tears, well...It was the only time he disobeyed my order, although I am very glad he did," he finished with a grin.

Closing my eyes, I now brought the quilt up closer to my chin and asked yet again why he did not tell me the truth. Kissing the tip of my nose, he replied, "You are aware of the rules. I was trying to keep you and my family safe. By the way, I am not a Nazi."

"Well, of course I realize not really but..."

"I mean I am not a member of the Nazi party. Officers are not allowed to belong to any political party. We are here to protect the country, not a political party. Unfortunately, the Nazis are the country now and we have no choice but to follow their orders. Or be shot along with family members."

"I thought about shooting you, you know."

"Indeed?" His look was incredulous until I explained about Granspapa's weapon that I had begun to carry everywhere.

His shock turned to humor as he said, "Why am I not surprised? Only please, not in the camp, *ja*? If it should be discovered upon your person..." I nodded my understanding.

"Does your family know about your activities?"

"It is safer all around if they do not. Only Corporal Konig has been told. I know," he held up his hand to forestall my new irritation, "but he has been with me for many years and I could not have done this without his help. Besides, he was to keep you safe."

This explained his curious hours and days away from the office, even his suggested break from the routine so I could travel to Bochnia. Then I had a moment of panic. "And me? Do you mean to say he knew I was working for the underground? You told him? What about my cousin? Oh God, does the corporal know about...about...this?" and I waved my hand over his bed.

"The good corporal only suspects my feelings for you. As for Antoni... he is very much ingrained into the Third Reich, I am afraid, and he knows nothing. I could not take the chance of putting you in danger. I love you, you see." Noticing the look of surprise on my face, he smiled and said, "Did you not know?"

Smiling back I answered, "I could only hope. It was lonely being in love alone. With an officer in the SS, I might add, whom I thought to be my mortal enemy because he did not tell me the truth about himself!" I was not as angry as I pretended to be and he knew it.

"Do you know when I fell in love with you? No? When you first marched into the butcher shop to defend your grandmother. You stood up to me with such a stubborn look upon your face, as fierce as a tiger. I wanted to laugh and kiss you at the same time. That is why I offered you the job; I wanted you near. So tell me. Would you have truly shot me?"

I responded by leaning into his warm body, kissing him with abandon. It became a most interesting afternoon.

Chapter Eight

August 1942

DISBELIEF

*M*y interludes with The Colonel (somehow "Colonel" and "Fraulein" had become not only nicknames but terms of endearment between us) were carefully concealed. To be seen together outside camp might raise some awkward questions although I did enjoy dinner at his home occasionally. We tried to be as circumspect as possible but my main concern was Antoni. I hoped he was not suspicious but he became more direct and amorous in his advances giving me cause for wonder.

During my last phone call from Max, as vaguely as I could (remembering his "no name" rule) I managed to tell him I was privy to The Colonel's activities, making it much easier to converse.

He had two things to tell me, he said. The first regarded Jan Karski. He had finally made it to England and the United States armed with one of our keys filled with microfilm. With that and the testimonies from my end, he was sure of success. "They did not believe him, Marta."

"How could they not? Did they think he was lying?"

"No, that is the sad thing. The British ambassador was asked that very question. He said it was not that he did not believe him, but rather could not believe him, could not imagine human beings treating others in such unspeakable ways." I groaned, thinking we were out of options. "Wait, it gets worse. He had an audience with the president, the American president, who did not believe the information either. Jan was interrupted by the president who asked how the horses were treated in Poland. All these prisoners, tortured, dying, and he asks about horses! At least that is the rumor. I sincerely hope it is not true." Karski was still in America, trying to convince Polish and Jewish organizations there, begging for their assistance.

It would be an uphill battle to convince them. As long as I have been at this camp, I still have difficulties believing the atrocities I see here on a daily basis. How are English and American politicians to believe, immersed as they are in their everyday activities of a free society?

The second item on his agenda was more personal. "I'm leaving, Marta. Going to Zamosc County. Have you heard of the problems there? No? The Germans have planned to import sixty thousand of their ethnic countrymen to the region, necessitating the complete expulsion of 297 villages. The Poles are resisting, organizing self-defenses, fleeing into neighboring forests, bribing soldiers to release kidnapped children; complete mayhem for the past year. Some of my military colleagues and I will join in the fight." Afraid for his well-being, I tried to talk him out of the notion. He was doing so much good here, I told him, more than one man and a rifle could do there. It was all for naught. His mind was made up. I think he missed the action and I knew he hoped to make his way to England to fight from the skies. Pray for him, he told me, and he would try to contact me if he could. The possibility of that was slim to none, I knew, and I replaced the receiver feeling empty inside. He was a link to my childhood, our past life, and I already missed him.

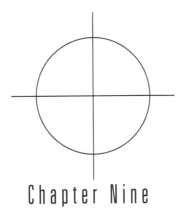

Chapter Nine

September 1942

THE GIRLS

*A*s I exited the camp, another of Eichmann's never ending death trains pulled in. Whistles were blowing, dogs were barking, and people were being dragged from the cars. It never stopped, I thought. No matter how hard we try, it never stops. Adolf Eichmann was much too efficient at his job.

I thought I overheard Polish spoken among the newcomers so I asked one of the kapos from where the train had departed. "Ispina," he said. I knew this little town. Sweet and friendly, the townspeople all knew one another and boasted one of the prettiest chocolate shops I had seen. I hoped it was still standing.

I slowly walked along the length of the train, trying to distance myself from Kanada, feeling useless and frustrated. People were dislodged from the cars in record speed, the separation process almost half done. As I passed the last car, I heard soft cries. Even though the lights barely reached this end of the tracks, I looked around for guards before I hoisted myself into the car. As my eyes got used to the gloom, I saw two little girls huddled together in the back corner.

Crouching down, I walked to them in what I hoped was a nonthreatening manner.

"Hello, there, little ones." I tried German first, still protecting my nationality from anyone who might be listening. When they did not respond, I repeated my greeting in Polish. At that, their eyes lit up and they began to cry a little louder. I placed my arms around them both, tiny wasted things that they were, and tried to comfort them. Their eyes were dark and wide with fear. It looked as though they had not bathed nor had a decent meal in weeks. My heart ached just looking at them. Seeing the large yellow stars on the their coats, I was reminded of that street scene photo of the young dying girl so long ago.

"Shhh, shhh. I have you. It's OK," I lied. "Where is your mother?" I asked. The oldest one pointed over my shoulder to a woman lying with other bodies at the far end of the car. She was in a most awkward position, arms and legs twisted and mangled like a pretzel. I knew without checking she was quite dead. I had seen enough bodies to be an authority on the subject.

By now, the littlest one was crying in earnest and I looked into her face, telling her I would make sure she would be safe. "But," I said, "it is very important that you do not cry for just a few minutes. Can you do that, both of you? We do not want any of the soldiers to know that we are here, OK?" I thought of my father and grandfather shot down in cold blood, of children's bodies dragged from the chambers, and I suddenly exploded inside with the desire to protect these two waifs. I could not allow two more innocents to be dumped or burned. There had been enough death for anyone's lifetime.

"My name is Marta. What are your names?"

The oldest girl said "I'm Magda Aleksy Walczak. I'm seven and this is my sister, Paulina Lucja Walczak. She is three. Our mother is dead, isn't she?" she asked matter-of-factly. I realized she too had seen enough of death to know its face.

I nodded my head and stroked her hair. "Yes, little one, I am so sorry. But I'm going to get you both out of here, OK? Come with me." At that, Paulina grabbed onto my hand with a strength I had not thought she was capable of in her half-starved state and she looked up into my eyes with complete trust. I put my finger to my lips and carefully peeked out the open door. Good, I thought, they are still caught up in the sorting drama.

I quickly tore off the golden stars from their coats and tossed them to the back of the car. Before we left the compartment, I searched through their bag for anything small I could carry. A photo was under a handful of clean clothes, the two girls and two adults I assumed to be their parents. Carefully slipping the clothes and photo down the front of my dress until it secured itself at my waistband, we turned to leave.

Jumping as quietly onto the ground as I could, I wrapped my arms around Magda and set her next to me. Doing the same with Paulina, I turned away from the crowd behind me. It was quite plain to see where the Star of David had been affixed; the imprint was the only clean spot on each coat. Gathering some dirt in my hands, I rubbed it on each void hoping I could obliterate the tell tale signs of their identity in Nazi eyes—enemies of the State.

"So, Magda Aleksy Walczak," I said in the most cheerful voice I could muster, "this is what we shall do. You walk in front of me, I will carry your sister, and we will make our way to safety." I adjusted the light bundle that was the three-year-old and held her slightly against my stomach as she latched on to me like a crustacean. I hoped Magda would be hidden if she walked calmly and quietly in front of me and Paulina's legs would not be seen if I kept most of her beneath my wrap. In this manner, we walked nearly ten steps before I heard a voice ordering me to stop. I turned only my head slightly and saw one of the many kapos. "What are you doing here?" he said in Yiddish.

I pretended not to understand him since no self-respecting German would know Yiddish, or at least not admit it to a mere kapo, but I worried the two children might answer him. Gripping them a little harder, I willed my warning to be understood. *"Meine papieren,"* I said in German, a phrase that all of us in occupied territories had quickly learned. Reaching inside my skirt pocket, I handed him my employment pass from The Colonel, hoping I could avoid turning completely around.

Apparently, he could read a little German or at least knew the signature of Herr Colonel Müller because he relaxed slightly. Then he saw Paulina's eyes from the folds of my wrap. His eyes narrowed and he came closer.

I stood a little taller and tried to assume an air of superiority over this traitorous excuse for a human being, speaking German as if he understood nothing of the language. Simply and slowly, gesticulating to the children, I said "My cousins. They were lost, understand...LOST!" I clenched my hand and made tiny walking movements with my two fingers. "Their mama, is my mama's sister, understand?...COUSINS." Please God, I prayed, let this work. My arms were aching and Paulina began to sob. I jiggled her and kissed her on the top of the head. I had no idea if he was accepting my story, as farfetched as it was beginning to sound even to me, or if he even fully understood it. By the grace of God, a voice rang out from the entrance of the camp that seemed to frighten him more than I ever could. He suddenly thrust my pass at me and motioned me to leave saying *"Schnell!"* as he ran toward the caller. Not wanting to give him the chance for a second thought, I grabbed both children and we moved swiftly down the dirt, edging farther and farther into the darkness, becoming one with the night.

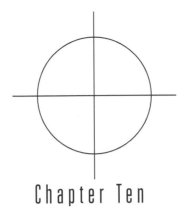

Chapter Ten

CORPORAL KONIG

Several hours later, I was standing in the dark waving good-bye to the staff car, my heart aching. I had only been with the girls a few hours but we had emotionally bonded. I spent several minutes convincing them of their safety away from me as I fed and washed them. When they saw Corporal Konig's German uniform they both clung to my legs. More promises and more minutes flew by before they entered the hiding place in the car.

I had done the right thing, I kept telling myself, they will be safe with Mama and Aunt Isabella. My fear of involving The Colonel led me to Corporal Konig who, thank God, agreed to my half-baked idea. It had been his idea to attach The Colonel's flags to the staff car, stocking the car with food, and preparing a comfortable hiding space under the rear seat. He was obviously much better at the cloak-and-dagger details than I.

It had been a long walk back to my office following my run-in with the kapo and the exhausted girls fell into a deep sleep straightaway while I called the corporal. I had no right to endanger him with my idea, I told him, and the decision was completely up to him. Once he agreed, we moved quickly, the three of us meeting him outside within a half hour.

Now I waited in my office for his return, hoping the flags of a colonel would prevent delays at the checkpoints. I should not have involved the corporal but my other choices were not viable. I could not purchase train tickets without current travel passes and walking by night with two half-starved girls was out of the question. The Colonel would have helped but I could not risk his involvement in hiding Jewish children. I had no other choice. I knew they would need identity papers but I had asked enough of Corporal Konig; papers could be dealt with later.

He returned safely three hours later. Everything was well, he said, although a German banging on the door at 3:00 a.m. initially frightened my mother and aunt, neither of whom had been overly surprised to receive such a package from me by the way, but promised to care for them nonetheless. Words could not express my gratitude to him but I sincerely tried.

Now I would have to get the girls out of the country. Somehow.

{ I }

Several days had passed and the colonel and I were spending a lazy Saturday afternoon in my room. I was curled upon his elbow which was partially behind his head. Gazing at the ceiling, he slowly said. "I recently had a chat with Corporal Konig." Damn! I could not believe the man would betray me. "Did you really think he would not tell me? With his loyalty?" He turned to look at me. "You did not trust me? I would have helped, you know." I knew that, of course, and I explained the dilemma I had found myself in, trying to protect him. "I can protect myself, Marta, but I appreciate your concern," he finished with a smile and a kiss. "So, we come to the question of the girls. How long do you think they can live with your mother before they are all in trouble? They have no papers, no rations cards, no travel pass to explain their sudden appearance..."

"Yes, well, I had not thought that far ahead," I admitted, "I hoped to pay for some false documentation and smuggle them out of the country."

"I see. And you have done this before? You know where false documents are printed? You have the necessary connections to send them to safety?" He knew I did not. The only thing I could offer was the notion of England and Olenka. I told him what little I knew about the town where my friend now resided and her mother's family name. "Inquiries will have to be made; subtle, quiet inquiries," said The Colonel. "Something you should leave up to me. In the meantime, I will arrange for papers to be delivered to your mother. Then we can work out their transport, *ja?*"

I showed him my appreciation in the best possible way.

Chapter Eleven

September 1942

COUSIN ANTONI

*H*immler had requested The Colonel come to Berlin for a personal discussion of the camps. Why The Colonel and not the Kommandant, I thought. Could you not request he come here instead? I asked him. He gave me a wry look and stated the obvious. Ask the second in command in all of Germany to travel here when he had already been summoned to Berlin? Tantamount to treason. Yes, I could see the reasoning in that. The Colonel was quite unconcerned which only fueled my imagination. Was he to be interrogated? What did Himmler know? He would be back soon, The Colonel said, and I promised to occupy my time with the business of the camp. Easy to do in these times.

Since the Americans had entered this war, the Germans were edgier than ever and Eichmann's trains rolled in more often, delivering prisoners several times a day, regularly filled with families and women. I remembered what my uncle had briefly mentioned, thanking God the camp contained no females. Considering the experiments conducted upon the men, it was not unreasonable to expect the Germans devising something grisly for the women. Then too, I thought it only a matter of time before they would be abused sexually by the soldiers if they had not already. I knew the female guards were not above servicing the soldiers but I did not know if it was for money or sport.

Sleep had been elusive through the night and it was nearly dawn before I finally dozed off when I heard the click of the door. Opening my eyes hoping to see The Colonel, I was shocked to see my cousin. Surprise turned into irritation as he sat upon my bed.

"So, my dear Weegie, it seems as if I shall be leaving your side."

Bringing the comforter up to my neck I asked. "Leaving? Where?"

"I have been offered a promotion of sorts which requires my reassignment to Berlin. Considering I made no application for this new position, I strongly suspect the intervention of someone else."

Could he mean me? "Antoni, even if I wanted to, I have no idea how to go about any such transfer. I swear I had nothing to do with it." He crept closer and stroked my cheek.

"Ah, *Liebchen*, I did not mean you. No, no. I believe your colonel's hand is in this. I wonder why he wishes to see me gone, hmm? I don't suppose you have any ideas?"

I have never mentioned my cousin's advances or teasing to The Colonel, and I told Antoni as much. Why would he want Antoni transferred?

"You have no idea? Really?" He snuck much closer to the head of the bed and to me. "My dear cousin. I know about the two of you, you see. Ahh! I have your attention." Slipping his hand under the bedclothes, he stroked my leg. "What would your mother say about consorting with the enemy?"

Drawing my leg away from his probing hand, I sat with my knees against my chest and my arms around them. "The Colonel is a good man, Antoni," I said, realizing I had just confirmed his statement. "Considering the turmoil in our lives, I doubt this would overly concern Mama."

"Perhaps not." He removed his tunic and tossed it on the window seat. "However, I am sure Kommandant Hoss would be extremely interested in your habit of feeding the animals. Strictly forbidden, you know."

Now I was slightly concerned. "Whatever are you talking about?"

Reaching under my bed, he brought forth my hollowed out ledger. "Antoni, you would tell Herr Höss? I do not believe it. Besides, these are not animals, these are your people, fellow Poles. You should be helping them as well, not letting them rot."

"Weegie, Poland is no longer a country, you must accept that. And our Poles in the camps…well, it's mostly Jews now, Polish or otherwise. Are you forgetting how my own mother forced me from this country long ago? I have no affinity for it any longer. So, yes, I would certainly turn you in."

"Whatever you have in mind, please reconsider. We are still blood, you and I."

Shaking his head side to side he replied, "Ah, Weegie, Weegie. Do you remember all those months ago when you asked me to free your mother? Yes? Then I am sure you will recall my warning at the time; you could only have that one favor. You were never to ask for another."

I simply stared at him. This was the man I had been so enamored of all my life and he was willing to hand me over to the Nazis with no concern for the family. If the Kommandant knew about me, my family would surely be harmed or killed.

Looking up at him, I realized he had thought of this act of retribution for my—our—family.

"What is it you want?"

As he began removing his boots and shirt, the answer was understood. "I believe you know exactly what I want. Deep down, I know you have always wanted it as well. I suppose it is too much to hope for some enthusiasm from you? *Nein*, I did not think so. Well, I will settle for compliance then, *ja*? As I recall, your fist can easily harm one's nose. And please, remove your scowl, Weegie. I promise, you will enjoy this."

I was not mistreated or taken by force like so many other women, I reminded myself, had not been dragged or beaten like Arlene. I was betrayed, surely, but was it rape? I did acquiesce, after all, and it had not been altogether disgusting. It was as much my fault as his. Still, I could not seem to scrub myself clean enough in the shower. I wondered if I would ever see Antoni again and if so, would I be expected to pay the piper once more?

As promised, Antoni left that day. The Colonel returned unscathed and I mentioned nothing of my victimization. Voicing the ordeal, releasing it from the recesses of my mind, would only breathe life into the sordid deed and perpetuate my guilt. Self-flagellation would not negate the coupling. I never mentioned my cousin's name thereafter. Neither did The Colonel.

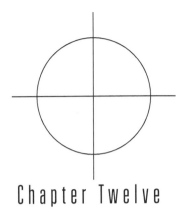

Chapter Twelve

August 25, 1942

BOCHNIA GHETTO

*M*y intercom system buzzed with The Colonel's voice requesting my presence in his office. Maintaining a businesslike persona while flashing him a broad smile, I seated myself in my usual club chair. When he did not smile back, I knew something was wrong. My brain was in the midst of clicking through one scenario after another before he spoke.

"Marta," he began, "there's been some trouble in Bochnia. In the Ghetto. Do you know of it?"

Of course. That was my first visit when Mama and Mrs. Feldman's daughter had been taken. What had begun as an unofficial settlement of Jews in 1939 was now a city within a city.

The Germans had expelled Jews from around the nation, resettling those in the Krakau district into Bochnia while moving the residents of those streets to other areas, allocating the needed space for the Ghetto. The first transport held about five hundred people with more arriving throughout the years. Not only was a hospital and a police force established there, but workshops employing almost two thousand people producing German uniforms, shoes, and other necessary goods for the war effort were operating within the walls.

"Jews from many others cities were brought to the Ghetto last week, one trainload from Wisnicz held fifteen hundred." The space allocated to the Ghetto was large but not that large.

The Colonel continued, "Yesterday and today soldiers began the rounding up of Jews from the Ghetto. Each policeman had a quota to fill or be shot. I have read here," he said tapping some papers, "the officers were obliged to include their friends and family members to meet their quota. At any rate, thousands were transported to the Belzec camp and many more were shot. I am guessing the overflow will be sent here. The entire community is in a state of confusion and panic. From what I have learned, your family is safe, as are the girls, but I think it prudent to step up our queries in England and get them far away from Germany."

He said he should have the details worked out in a week for the double escape. Initially, I had insisted on bringing them to England, resulting in several difficulties. The biggest obstacle was the permission for travel. The girls could not pass for German, provoking questions on public transportation. Plus, they did not speak German and their Polish, which was still outlawed, had a distinctive accent. If they spoke and were overheard we would be lost. Asking Corporal Konig to travel with us was not an option either. If we needed help from the AK at any time along the way, they would not do so with a German soldier tagging along, no matter how vehemently he was vouched for. I thought of beginning the first leg of the journey on our own which posed another problem; three females traveling alone would certainly be harassed even with passes which, since we did not have those valuable documents, brought us full circle in our dilemma.

Even then, it would be dangerous. Borders were heavily guarded and the Gestapo was abundant, longing for some escapee to capture and torture. Newly enlisted soldiers were waiting for an opportunity to bolster their image. And spies were everywhere, Poles and ethnic Germans alike. It would be a long and arduous journey, one fraught with complications the entire way. The various AK guides might resort to alternate routes if trouble arose along a preplanned course. Safe houses might have been raided and closed, necessitating last minute changes. Home Army contacts might not show at the appointed rendezvous point for a variety of reasons. Some had turned traitor, handing the escapees to the Gestapo for payment. The entire escape would be a miracle to pull off successfully especially with two such young girls. Even with the most detailed plans, many never made it to freedom.

The Colonel wanted to accompany me but that was ludicrous. Even in civilian clothing, his military bearing and haircut would arouse suspicion and give him away. Nothing could connect him with this endeavor not only for the safety of his family, but also for his AK connection. Even the girls' identification papers did not bear his signature. We came back to square one; the AK must be involved.

Chapter Thirteen

September 24, 1942

INTERFERENCE

I was en route to Bochnia courtesy of my friend, Corporal Konig, an ordinary journey on an ordinary day. We had done so on numerous occasions and this was no different. My jittery stomach and profuse sweating told me otherwise. We had finally gotten the go-ahead to release the "package," as The Colonel so vaguely put it. Vague terms seemed the norm at camp, every German sure they were being eavesdropped upon or watched. Dark and forbidding posters with warnings of "Spies Are Everywhere" and "Casual Conversation Could Be Overheard" were prominently displayed through the offices and, as I learned from The Colonel, throughout Germany. The intent was to prevent any information from meeting the ears of the enemy. Rather than allied spies, the Gestapo came to mind first, putting everyone further on edge.

We left after hours, again as usual, traveling our same route, avoiding suspicion at all costs. I had not even told my mother I would be arriving tonight, not wanting her to begin fussing and packing for the girls. Dropping me off at the front door of the butcher shop, the corporal and I confirmed the telephone call I would make when we could discuss my return trip. Since I had no idea of the route, we would have to improvise.

The family and girls were glad to see me, but upon arrival, Mama handed me a sealed note she seemed concerned about. "From Filip," she said gravely.

Filip? I thought we had seen the last of him. Reading the note, I realized we may never be free from my contemptible cousin. "I know," it began, which could mean a myriad of infractions. Directions to an old boarding house on the outskirts of town were included with instructions that I "should come alone" to discuss matters. How very Mata Hari-like of him, I thought, always so dramatic. The time stipulated was one hour from now. Damn!

"Mama, when did he drop this off?"

"Sometime last week. Monday, I think."

"Did he know I was coming here?"

"No one knew. Why?"

"Did he see the girls?" She did not answer immediately so I repeated the question.

"Yes. He went upstairs to use the facilities. I told him they were relations from my sister's side of the family but I do not think he believed me. Is everything all right?"

I only shook my head in reply not really knowing the answer to the query. That hateful bastard. When had blackmail suddenly become a family pursuit? I was short on time, not knowing when I would be contacted by the AK member. I had merely been told to be prepared and stand by.

Perhaps Filip did not know I had arrived in Bochnia, I thought rereading the instructions, his scrawl only stated to meet him an hour after I "received the note." I could leave with the girls and he would never know I had been here. No; he had only to revisit the shop to know of the escape. He would cause trouble, I was sure. Time-consuming, pernicious nonsense!

Telling Mama to get the girls ready and pack any food she could, I said I would return as soon as I was able.

"Marta, leave it alone. Please, do not see him."

Reassuring her with "It is only Filip, after all; I bested him when I was six and I can do it again," I followed the shadows out of town.

The place was worse than I remembered. Never an upscale establishment, half the building was now parted from the rest like a slice fallen off a cake. Not bothering to knock, I entered to find my dear cousin sitting in the only chair in the room, indeed the only stick of furniture in the apartment, smoking a cigar. One lone oil lamp, if it could be called that, was positioned in the room's center on the floor. Old and dusty, I could barely see the low level of oil through the glass base and the wick within sucking what it could of the cloudy oil. The brass burner was dented and the chimney, along with one of the brass tines to hold it in place, was missing. The glow from the short wick barely illuminated the decrepit state of the building.

"You've taken a step down in life, I see," I said rudely. "Still, I love what you've done to the place." My sarcasm was still spot-on.

"What? This?" He smirked at me while encompassing the building with the sweep of his arm. "Do not let the surroundings deceive you. This is not my residence, I assure you. I do have title to the building, however. Should be able to rent out the rooms soon. As you so charmingly pointed out, my decorator has not yet completed the job," he chuckled. Rising from the rickety chair and ambling toward me, he said, "Today, though, we are completely alone. No one to hear you for blocks." Backing me toward the flickering light, he reached out and stroked my cheek with the back of his hand. "Ahh, better. It will be easier to see your face in the light."

I struck away his hand saying, "You miserable cockroach. Give me an excuse to punch you again, Filip. Please."

Instead, faster than I thought he could move, he had made a fist and slugged me in the jaw so hard that I fell upon the floor, striking my head upon the wood. I saw stars for a moment but I kept thinking of the girls and the minutes ticking away. Raising myself upon my elbows, I tasted blood from a split lip and felt it roll down my jaw which was rapidly swelling.

"Cockroach! Cockroach! You have been a thorn in my side my whole life, Weegie." His shadow stretched and twisted against the wall from the meager light. "It's time I taught you some manners, showed you I am more of a man than Antoni will ever be." With that, he roughly parted my legs with his foot, dropped his pants, and fell to his knees between my own.

"Antoni!" I shrieked, "this is about Antoni?" I began laughing hysterically, tears rolling down my cheeks, and he looked at me as if I had suddenly gone insane. I howled even louder, doubling over on the floor, pointing at his member, now so shriveled it resembled a turtle retreating into a shell. "I have news for you, dear cousin; Antoni has already been here. First again! And believe me he had more to offer than you do," and I pointed to his crotch once more. Calming myself and wiping the tears of laughter from my face, I was back on my elbows, looking him straight in the eyes. "So you see, you puny son of a bitch, throughout your entire worthless life, you always came in second. You never beat our cousin at anything! Now get out of my way, I'm leaving," and I started to rise off the floor.

He roughly pushed me back down upon the filthy floorboards, his face contorted into a mask of hatred and his lips drawn back revealing his teeth. He never said a word, only reached into his pocket, bringing forth his closed hand. Thrusting it into my face, grinning even tighter, he slowly opened his fingers, one by one, until his palm produced Buscha's brooch!

I stared in horror as I understood. "You! You killed your own grandmother? What kind of a monster are you?" I grabbed at it with my left hand. He dropped the brooch and clenched my wrist while his other hand gripped my neck, squeezing the front of my throat with his short fat thumb. Scratching at his fingers and trying to pry them away from me, I felt myself grow dizzy and my struggles become weaker. Lowering my hand toward my hip, I felt the touch of cool metal and saw the shock in his face as he heard the blast. Filip's jaw gaped slightly awry and blood issued forth at a surprising rate. I had blindly fired Grandpapa's pistol through the pocket and fabric of my skirt and, judging from his face, the bullet had traveled into his right jaw.

The crimson fluid was everywhere, splattered across my face and down the front of my clothing. His hand released me and his fingers tried to curtail the blood while he gurgled and cursed me.

"I was actually aiming much lower. Be glad I missed," I said indicating his crotch. Rolling over and scrambling to retrieve the illusive brooch, I finally stood and ran for the door. Filip's half-naked body lunged the short distance between us, grabbed my ankle with his bloody hands, and brought me down like a wounded deer. Rolling over on my back, I kicked at his face with my free leg, again and again, and yet he hung on, cursing and screaming at me all the while.

In desperation, I reached for the oil lamp, my fingers inching ever closer, finally wrapping my index finger around one of the brass tines, burning myself in the process. By now, he was pulling me closer, his hands were wrapped around my thigh as I brought the lamp within my reach. Grasping it around the short neck, I brought the lamp down upon Filip's head. The light in the room intensified as he became a human candle, beating at the flames that were licking his face and shirt, rolling and screeching on the floor.

Rising up on my hands and feet, I half-ran, half-crawled out the door, not pausing to see if he was in pursuit. Bobbing and weaving between the town's buildings and ruins like an inebriated pugilist, I was relieved to finally see the back door of the butcher shop.

Mother and the girls were sitting in the gloom, waiting for my return. As I burst into the door, Mama lit a small lamp and stared at me. "My God, Marta! Is that your blood?" She followed me upstairs as I ran into the bathroom and surveyed the damage to my face. I was covered in blood and my jaw was turning blue. I began scrubbing myself clean as fast as my shaking hands would allow. Mama stepped in to complete the task and told my aunt to bring a coat: there was no time to wash the stains from my clothes, we could only cover them.

"Did I miss him?" I asked. "The man. Did he already come?"

"Yes, but he said he would return in an hour. Only ten minutes left now. We have to hurry. Let me get some ice for your face." Grabbing her arm before she could leave, I showed her what I carried in my pocket.

I watched as the horrible comprehension filled her face and she sputtered out quick staccato-like words. "What…you mean…how could he?…his grandmother?…His own grandmother?"

I nodded, told her to bring me a sewing kit, and meet me downstairs. Hugging and calming the girls, I tore part of the eldest's dress hem open. Taking scant seconds to hold the precious brooch to my heart and say a quick prayer, I opened it and removed the photo of my grandparents, placed it deep into my pocket, and pinned the brooch inside the gaping hole of the hem. Tearing Filip's note in half, I wrote my own letter to Olenka, telling her of the brooch and to use whatever money it could bring to care for the girls. Using the sewing items, I quickly stitched

Magda's hem closed around the treasured possession and sewed the letter to the inside of her coat while Mama was trying to cover my bruises with face powder.

"Magda, when you get to England, give this note to my friend, Olenka. Only her. Can you remember that? Good. She is one of my oldest friends. I have known her since I was younger than you. She is wonderful, and very smart. She will love both of you. I promise."

Just as I had finished, we heard a knock at the door. Praying it was not Gestapo or Filip, I slowly opened it to a man asking confirmation of my name. "Thank God you returned," I said. "I had a bit of trouble," and quickly told him I had been accosted, editing out a few choice segments. I was concerned he may cancel the escape if I told him of Filip's interference.

The man's plan had been to take the girls to a safe house but now he thought it better if we head straightaway to our first contact stop. I was insistent upon accompanying them, as were the girls.

We walked through the night, taking turns carrying the girls, resting only minutes at a time, hiding them as much as my face. We had found a stream to drink from and I attempted to remove Filip's blood from my clothing and stockings. My effort only smeared the blood in a diluted manner while soaking my clothes, making me extremely cold.

Our escort, Bazyli, said my eye was turning black and I could feel a blob of congealed blood on my swollen lip, plugging a new surge of blood like a cork. I had brought my mother's compact along and Magda considered it her solemn duty to apply the powder whenever my purple face made an appearance. An accident could explain my bruises but my clothes were another matter. Streaked with Filip's blood, I kept the old coat firmly buttoned.

We were off schedule now, he told me, and we may have to wait for the next contact. They always made two attempts so he hoped to make one or the other assignation. Huddled against the cold, we waited for hours and I took this time to tell the girls of Buscha and her brooch, of the love between her and Grandpapa, the many years of happiness I had with her. I was determined that along with her brooch, her memory should travel with the girls.

Bazyli held up his hand to quiet us and we heard the crackle of twigs in the woods and three short whistles. The newest guide emerged armed and suspicious until my contact confirmed our identities. Remembering warnings of traitors within the AK, I could not let this stranger take "my girls" without assessing his commitment.

I grilled him as though I belonged to the Gestapo. Where will you be taking the girls, how will I know if they made it to England, and on and on. The poor man was overwhelmed but answered everything he could. Too much knowledge could be dangerous, he said repeating the mantra with which I had become so familiar. I was sick of hearing it.

Both Bazyli and our new guide, Witus (at least I had wormed out his name) tried to impress upon me the need for urgency; they must continue this journey to meet their next link. Fine, I said. I am coming along. Bazyli who had taken to the girls, decided he could be of further help and insisted on accompanying us as well. As their arguments ensued, I calmly reminded them of their need for time, settling the situation. I gathered the girls' belongings and joined our small parade through the brush.

Chapter Fourteen

SEPARATION

*W*itus waited for me to catch up but I had the feeling if I lagged again, he would not be so accommodating. Paulina was firmly wrapped around my waist and Magda held Witus' hand. He glanced at me and asked what had happened to my face. Couching the terms so they were fit for young ears, I merely told him I had fought off an attacker. "You do not appear to have won," he replied.

"Yes, well, a .22 cal pistol made up for my size."

He looked at me in astonishment and with something else. Respect? Whatever it was, his attitude toward me was somewhat nicer.

We continued our trudge-like walk for hours, making our way through the debris of towns, wading through streams, stopping only now and then for the girls to rest. Once I asked Witus where we were headed. He looked at me and I stopped him before he could mutter the monotonous AK motto. "Never mind," I said.

Suddenly, he pulled us to the ground. We had been walking through desolate farmland, ducking behind old corn stalks until we now had the cover of a dense forest. In the distance, I could see crossed posts of wood connected to long lines of barbed wire. Border crossing or checkpoint? The nettles on the ground were poking Paulina and I tried to shush her whimpers by opening my coat and letting her lie on it.

"What is it? Germans?" Of course it was Germans, you twit, I told myself angrily. What else could it be?

"A checkpoint. They have upped the guards. Soldiers often roam the woods looking for escapees. We will have to go around them," he said and he pointed off to the left. Bazyli carried Magda and I had Paulina who by now was fast asleep and weighed twice as much as when she was awake. At least she stopped crying. "Step in my prints only, understand? Absolute quiet." Witus crouched silently forward, blazing the trail for our subsequent footsteps.

We were progressing slowly but safely, each of us stepping in Witus' matted down prints of nettles and leaves. The two AK members seemed well practiced in eluding such obstacles, but I wondered how the Nazis could not smell the fear emanating from me.

We had put some distance between the checkpoint and ourselves when Paulina awoke. I felt her first gentle movements and began to softly sooth her but I was not prepared for her to thrust herself suddenly away from me to point out a hopping rabbit. Losing my balance, I cried out as we both plopped to the ground, landing close to a tree and its various discarded twigs. Crack! The snapping of sticks seemed to echo and bounce off the great pines for miles.

"*Halt! Wer its das?* Who is it?" It was our worst scenario unfolding before us. Whistles blowing, the stomping of heavy boots searching us out, deep throaty barks of dogs, and Germans hollering instructions filled the forest.

"Hide," said Witus, "we will distract them." Hide where, I thought.

Grabbing both girls, I thrust them onto a limb of a thickly branched tree. "Climb!" I ordered. "Climb as high as you can. Stay behind the foliage. I will come back for you. Go!" I leaned in as far as I could to position them securely when I tore my dress on the bark. I thought the ripping sound would surely give me away. I ran in the opposite direction after watching the girls scramble up the branches until they were out of sight. By now, guns were firing from both sides. I could see Witus and Bazyli dashing to my right, shooting as they ran. I went to the left, hoping that among the three of us, we could lead them away from the girls. As I veered off farther, I saw Bazyli take a shot in his back and fly to the ground, arms splayed.

I kept running God-knew-where as I heard another shot. A final kill shot to Bazyli or at Witus? As I sped from tree to tree, my thoughts of survival ran willy-nilly through my mind. I could pass as German, perhaps as Witus' prisoner. My papers, though, clearly identified me as Polish. My Auschwitz pass, however, did not. It did have, on the other hand, The Colonel's official signature. It would be difficult to explain the disparity in surnames upon my documents without involving The Colonel. I had almost forgotten the blood on my wet clothing and the pistol in my pocket. Even more difficult to justify. I kept running.

I reached a small stream and I plowed through it, hoping to lose the dogs. After traveling upstream for several minutes, the black hole of a fallen tree trunk seemed to beckon me. Running through the muddy bank and up an incline, I lunged legs first as far back into the log as I could wiggle, preferring not to think of what other living things might be hiding within, and waited.

The heavy coat over my mouth proved helpful in covering the sounds of my intense panting. Straining my ears to hear over my heart beating, I was anxious to return to the girls. Stomping, and shouting in the distance convinced me to stay put for the moment. Were they coming closer or retreating? It was difficult to tell through the echoes.

I had no idea of the time but nightfall was upon us. Carefully poking out my head from the gaping hole of my tubular fortress, I tentatively peeked out at the world. Nothing. I had to get back to the girls. Witus could still be alive and waiting for me. If not, I knew the girls would still be sitting in that tree.

I must have walked in circles for hours. Dawn was fast approaching, giving me hope to find my way but losing my cover of darkness. As sunlight tapped upon my shoulder, so did the need for expediency.

A puddle of blood upon the forest needles told me I must be close. It had to be Bazyli's blood, I told myself, not the girls', only Bazyli's. Backtracking from there, I softly began calling the girls' names when the forest became more dense. Then I saw it. The piece of my dress caught in the slice of tree bark. Starting to climb, my calls became more desperate. I climbed higher and to the other side of the tall lush tree, in a panic by now. No, no! They have to be here, please.

I was sobbing uncontrollably, still softly calling their names, praying to hear their voices. The world was quiet. Even the Germans had gone back to their routine, no longer prowling the forest. Because they had the girls, I wondered, or given up their search?

I kept looking for any sign of an escape path but there was nothing to find. I still had six bullets left, I thought. I could…What? Capture a guard? Force him to tell me what I fear most? Go into their camp, gun blazing like a Hollywood Western? Foolish, I told myself. A foolish notion. As was this entire escape.

My only choice was to find a town with a working telephone and ring Corporal Konig. Obtaining his escort services to camp would present an entirely new set of challenges. Another foolish idea; insisting I come along on this folly. I did my best to backtrack our route to the last town and safe house we had found hoping it had not been evacuated..

My thoughts drifted to Filip as I walked and hid behind the tall forest trees. I was sure he still lived. He was too evil to die; even the devil would send him back. My cousin would live out of sheer spite.

And Antoni? What of him? Berlin was not far enough away to my liking. Would he expect to continue his extortion for his silence? I was sure to see him again, I worried, either during or after this war.

I ached to see the girls again. Would The Colonel be able to ascertain their whereabouts? The escape plan had been coordinated through various channels with no way of reaching Olenka directly. With the Germans' growing distrust of even their own, communication was more difficult than ever. I may have to face the fact that I might never learn what had become of my girls. It would be painful to accept.

When Max told me how difficult my tasks would be with the AK, I could never have imagined such sorrow. I reminded myself how I had requested an assignment other than the monotonous translation from Max. I almost laughed aloud at the irony. Three years, I thought, we have been suffering and dying for three years. We have very few healthy men or women left to continue the fight. How long can this persist? How many more unspeakable acts can human beings inflict upon each other?

Max had told me once, so long ago, fighting for our country does not necessarily mean shooting a gun or blowing up bridges. He was right. I renewed my resolve to inform the world of the travesties committed in my country. Poland had been under the thumb of dictators for many years and above all else, we wanted our freedom back. If we could survive this nightmare until the Allies had the upper hand, until they marched into our country, we may have hope. With luck, nations could learn from their mistakes, ineffective treaties, and betrayals that had brought us to this point in history. Hopefully, they would never be repeated.

Adolf Hitler, I felt, was a cruel and sadistic anomaly of human nature. Surely, I thought as I continued my tiring trek, the world could never produce another Hitler.

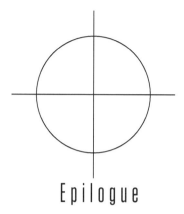

Epilogue

Present Day

SUSSEX, ENGLAND

"*O*h, darling," the woman exclaimed. "Come look at this." The newlyweds had been sightseeing and happened to stumble upon a shop the wife thought looked promising. It was a small brownstone standing a bit kilter on its foundation with the somewhat dubious words "Vintage Finds" in faded script letters posted over the doorway. The nursery rhyme verse, "There was a crooked man who caught a crooked mouse…and they all lived together in a little crooked house," came immediately to mind upon seeing the shop.

The beveled glass display window was stacked with goods of all kinds; some actually vintage, others looked like castoffs from attics and neighborhood jumbles. The couple had been browsing among the trinkets and old cheese pots when the woman had cried out with glee over a likely prospect. "Oh, no—how much will that set me back?" the man replied good naturedly. So far, he had seen nothing but dusty button-down children's boots and chipped pieces of old Spode china to catch his attention. He wondered what his lovely bride could possibly have found to elicit such excitement.

Overhearing this, the shopkeeper, as shopkeepers are wont to do, scurried over to the couple in the hopes of encouraging a sale. "Oh, you've found a luvly piece, there, ma'am," the eager owner said in a thick cockney accent. "Just the other day got that'n in."

The would-be customer looked down at the item she held in her hand. "Well, it's very pretty. But the price is a little dear. What is it, some type of porcelain?"

"Oh, no, ma'am. That there's Polish Pottery. There's a village in Poland, ya see, 'as the best clay in the world and each piece is still 'and made, though plates and bowls and such is more common. Since the 1500s I fink. See these flowers on it? The makers, usually wimen, in the old days used bits of p'tatoes cut into little such patt'rns and stamped it on the piece, then fired it up. And see 'ere? On the back is the name wrote of the maker's. But I never as did see such a one as this, with a tiny diamond set in the center of the big flower here and that's the truf."

"The silver work is lovely too," the customer said, "such sweet little filigree hearts all 'round."

"Oh, yes," the shopkeeper once again took up the recital, "yes, the, um, filleygray is surely sum'pin. Wonderful silverwork there. Known all over the world, it is. But there's som'pin really special about this 'n. I found this when I were cleaning it. Watch." And with a touch of his finger upon a hidden bit of silver between two of the hearts, the piece swung open. "See, it's a locket too. Must 'ave been made special, it was, 'cause I've never seen the like in forty years, and I've seen all kinds of pendants and lockets, I 'ave."

"Hmmm," the husband said aloud. He looked around at the various layers of dust and cobwebs and could certainly believe the store had been there for forty years if not longer. He was afraid he'd break out in a sneezing fit before too long. "There's an inscription of some sort inside. No photo, though, but a space for one. Do you know what it says?"

"Well, 'course it's in Polish in'it. Near as I've been able to figure from lookin' in one a' those Polish-to-English books, it says, 'to my loved one' or 'to the one I love,' som'pin like that. And there's a date too; '1 Maj'— that means May the first—'1880.' Long time ago. Must've been for a birfday maybe or som'pin special."

"I wish the photo was intact. I would love to have seen it. Maybe it was for an anniversary or an engagement present? It's in wonderful condition too." The more the young woman went on, the more her husband was sure he'd soon be digging in his wallet. "Do you know how it came to be in England? I mean, it survived two world wars and it's still gorgeous."

"Ahh, 'at's a mystery, 'at is," said the owner, tiring of this banter and eyeing another possible sale in the corner of the shop. "So, you'll be wantin' me to wrap it for you then, I'm sure. Be back in a jiff."

Out of earshot of the proprietor, the woman asked her groom with some concern in her voice, "Darling, do you think...well considering the wars...Do you think," she finished in a whisper, "there's blood on it. You know, some tragedy surrounding the piece?"

Her husband laughed lovingly at her. "What a funny little imagination you have, darling. I'm quite sure it's merely been gathering dust in an old lady's jewelry box." And with that he kissed her upon her forehead and began reaching for his wallet.

AFTERWARD

$\mathcal{T}$he Polish army, navy, and air force had the distinction of being the only national forces to fight on every battlefront of WWII including fighting Rommel in Africa with the British. Five thousand soldiers formed the Polish Carpathian Rifle Brigade, making such an impact during battle they were honored with inclusion to the unit known as "The Rats of Tobruk."

The loss of Polish military was 597,000 troops or 89.9 percent of the armed forces. Over six million civilians perished—22 percent of the total population—roughly half were Polish Catholics/Christians, half Polish Jews.

Poland lost 45 percent of her doctors, 57 percent of attorneys, 40 percent of professors, 30 percent of technicians, more than 18 percent of clergy, and most of her journalists in four years.

It's been estimated that at least one million Christian Poles were murdered at Auschwitz concentration camp, two million were deported to Germany for slave labor, and one million, seven hundred thousand sent to Siberia by the Russians.

By the time the Polish and Soviets resumed diplomatic relations in 1941, over 760,000 of those deportees to Siberia had perished.

Father Maksymilian Kolbe was beatified as a confessor by Pope Paul VI in 1971 and was canonized as a saint by Pope John Paul II on October 10, 1982. Franciszek Gajowniczek, the man Father Kolbe had saved in Auschwitz, was present at the ceremony. Franciszek Gajowniczek died in 1995 at the age of ninety-five.

To date, 6,135 poles have been awarded the title of Righteous Among the Nation by the State of Israel for saving the lives of Jews—more awards received than any other country during the war. Three million Poles are credited with saving the lives of approximately four hundred fifty thousand Jews. At least fifty thousand of these Poles were executed for their assistance.

In spite of the manpower and assistance given to Britain, Poland's representatives were refused permission to march in that country's 1945 victory parade; Great Britain was reluctant to offend the Soviet puppet regime in control of Poland after the war.

In 1992, after fifty years of official and public denials, the Russian government finally admitted to killing over 21,857 Polish military personnel and civilians in the Katyn Massacre after "discovering" long lost original execution orders signed by Stalin. Moscow refers to the travesty as crimes of war rather than intentional mass executions.

On April 10, 2010, Polish officials flying to commemoration ceremonies of the Katyn Massacre perished when their Soviet-supplied aircraft crashed in Western Russia. Ninety-six people, one-half of the Polish government including the president and his wife, were among the dead. After seventy years, the terrors of World War II continue to claim the Poles.

AUTHOR'S NOTES

*W*hile Marta, her friends, and family are fictional characters, I have drawn upon my own family history to provide details and background for those characters. My mother's family emigrated from Poland and my father's from Germany. My own grandparents owned and operated a Polish butcher shop. Additionally, my great-grandmother was trapped overnight in the shop's freezer and died of pneumonia shortly thereafter. As for my inspiration of Antoni and his dual mind-set, my parents told me of a high school friend of theirs, German by heritage but born in the United States, who decided to fly to Germany and fight for the Nazis when war broke out. He was killed in battle. The Polish wedding description came from Mother who did indeed fall asleep atop a pool table at a three-day celebration.

By contrast, events described, the destruction of Poland, its people and property, German officers, Auschwitz's camp buildings and tortures, activities of the Polish underground with Jan Karski, Witold Pilecki, and other brave members, even the murder of the traitor Igo Sym are a part of history and have been carefully and thoroughly researched.

My family's butcher shop, Orcholski Meats, circa 1925.

BIBLIOGRAPHY

History Place World war II in Europe Timeline, 26 March 2010 <http://www.historyplace.com/worldwari/timeline>.

Adolf Eichmann. 21 April 2010 <http://en.wikipedia.org/wiki/adolf_Eichman>.

Annexation of Austria. 22 May 2010 <http://ww2db.com/battle_spec.php?battle_id=86>.

Armenian Quote. 28 June 2010 <http://en.wikipdeia.org/siki/Armanian_quote>.

Armia Krajowa. 2 February 2010 <http://en.wikipdeia.org/wiki/Armia_Krajowa>.

Auschwitz Concentration Camp. 24 March 2010 <http://en.wikipedia.org/wiki/Auschwitz_concentration_camp>.

Auschwitz Concentration Camp—Definition. 17 January 2011 <http://www.wordiq.com/definition/Auschwitz_concentration_camp>.

Auschwitz Concentration Camp—The Historical Outline. 9 March 2011 <http://holocaustresearchproject.org/othercamps/auschwitzht.htmAusch-witz Concentration Camp: Pery Broad—SS Man. 22 January 2011 <http://www.holocaustresearchproject.org/othercamps/perybroad.html>.

Auschwitz Concentration Camp: The Basics. 18 February 2011 <http://www.holocaustresearchproject.org/othercamps/auschwitzbasics.html>.

Auschwitz Gas Chamber—Photos. 17 November 2010 <http://www.scrapbookpages.com/auschwitzscrapbook/tour/Auschwitz1/Auschwitz08.html>.

"Auschwitz Growth." Nizkor Project. 15 November 2010 <http://www.niz-kor.org/ftp.cgi/camps/ftp.ph?camps//auschwitz/auschwitz-growth.01>.

Auschwitz II—Birkenau. 17 November 2010 <http://www.scrap-bookpages.com/auschwitzscrapbook/history/articles/Birkenau01B.html>.

Auschwitz III—Monowitz Concentration Camp. 27 February 2011 <http://en.auschwitz.org.ph/h/index2.php?option=com_content&task=view&ik=5&pop=1&page=4&Itemid=5>.

Auschwitz III—Monowitz—History of the Camp. 17 October 2010 <http://www.scrapbookpages.com/poland/Auschwitz/monowitzHistory.html>.

Auschwitz Mechanisms for Mass Extermination: The Gas Chambers. 21 November 2010 <http://www.datasync.com/~david59/lengyel.html>.

"Auschwitz Scrapbook Tour." Auschwitz Main Camp. 17 November 2010 <http://www.scrapbookpages.com/auschwitzscrapbook/tour/auschwitz1/auschwitz12A.html>.

"Auschwitz Scrapbook Tour." Block 11 at Auschwitz 1. 17 November 2010 <http://www.scrapbookpages.com/auschwitzscrapbook/tour/auschwitz1/auschwitz06.html>.

"Auschwitz Scrapbook Tour." The Black Wall at Auschwitz 1. 17 November 2010 <http://www.scrapbookpages.com/auschwitzscrap-book/tour/auschwitz1/auschwitz05.html>.

Auschwitz: the Camp of Death. 17 November 2010 <http://www.holo-caust-trc.org/wmp17.htm>.

Auschwitz-Birkenau. 15 November <http://www.historylearningsity.co.uk/auschwitz-birkenau.htm>.

Auschwitz-Birkenau Concentration Camp Complex—data and sum-mary facts. 15 March 2010 <http://isurvived.org/AUSCHWITZ_TheCamp.html>.

Auschwitz-Birkenau: Memorial and Museum. 17 February 2011 <http://en.auschwitz.org.pl/h/index.php?option=com_content&task=view&id=18Itemid=3>.

Bach in Auschwitz and Birkenau. 15 November 2010 <http://www.cympm.com/orkest.html>.

"Barbarossa #5." World at War. Military Channel. MILI,1 May 2010.

"Barracks Buildings at Auschwitz 1." Auschwitz Scrapbook Tour. 17 November 2010 <http://www.scrapbookpages.com/auschwitzscrapbook/tour/auschwitz1/auschwitz09.html>.

Berghof (residence). 21 April 2010 <http://en.wikipedia.org/wiki/Berghof_(Hitler)>.

"Blowing Up History." Nazi Super Bombs. National Geographic Channel. NGEO, 19 September 2010

Bochnia Ghetto. 28 May 2006. 24 March 2010 <http://www.deathcampsorg/occupation/bochniapercent20ghetto.html>.

Bochnia Ghetto, The. 25 March 2010 <http://www.holocaustresearchproject.org/ghettos/bochnia.html>.

C. Mattogno, F. Deana. "The Crematoria Ovens of Auschwitz and Birkenau." 21 November 2010 <http://vho.org/GB/Books/dth/findcrema.html>.

"Cell of Father Maksymillian Kolbe." Virtual Tour of Auschwitz 1. 24 April 2010 <http://www.remember.org/auschwitz/aud.php?id=14>.

Chemistry of Auschwitz. 10 October 2010 <http://www.holocause-history.org/auschwitz/chemistry/>.

Chronology of World War II 1939. 1 July 2010 <http://ww2timeline.info.ww21939.html>.

Communist Crimes 1939-1941. 3 September 2010 <http://www.communistcrimes.org/en/Database/Poland//Historical-Overview/1939-1941>.

"Crematorium at Auschwitz I—Krema I—reconstructed ovens and brick chimney photos." Auschwitz Scrapbook Tour. 17 July 2010 <http://www.scrapbookpages.com/auschwitzscrapbook/tour/Auschwitz1/auschwitz08.html>.

Crematoriums/Body Disposal. 21 November 2010 <http://www.americanorphanpages.com/nazishowers.htm>.

"Cruise of the Secret Raiders." Secrets of World War II. Military Channel. MILI, 25 August 2010

Czortkow Uprising. 3 December 2010 <http://en.wikipedia.org/wiki/CzortkpercentC3percentB3w-Uprising>.

Discovery of Concentration Camps and the Holocaust—World War II Database. 17 April 2011 <http://ww3db.com/battle_spec.php?battle_id=136>.

"Distant War #2. World at War. Military Channel MILI, 2 June 2010.

Documents and Literature Third Reich. 12 October 2010 <http://65.160.172.250/doc2.html>.

Education in Poland during World War II. 3 August 2010 <http://en.wikipedia.org/wiki/Education_in_Poland_during_World_War_II>.

Education in Poland during World War II. 1 August 2010 <http://wapedia.mobi/en/Education_in_Poland_during_World_War_II>.

Einsatzgruppen of the Security Police and SD. 30 June 2010 <http://de.wikipedia.org/wiki/einsatzgruppen_der_Sicherheitspolizei_un_des_SD

Einsatzgruppen. 29 July 2010 <http://en.wikipedia.org/wiki/Einsatzgruppen>.

"Escape From Auschwitz." Secrets of the Dead. Public Broadcasting Station. KQED, 20 may 2010.

"Escapes, resistance and the Allies' knowledge of the camps." Auschwitz concentration camp. 18 February 2011 <http://en.wikipedia.org/wiki/Auschwitz_concentration_camp>.

"Euthanasia Program." Holocaust Encyclopedia. 5 September 2010 <http://www.ushmm.org/sic/en/article.php?moduleid=10005200>.

"Fast Attach Boats." Weapons of World War II. Military Channel. MILI, 4 August 2010.

"FDR." Decisions That Shook the World. Military Channel. MILI, 31 August 2010.

File: The Bochnia massacre German-occupied Poland 1939. 1 April 2011 <http://en.wikipedia.org/wiki/File:The_Bochnia_massacre_German_occupied_Poland_1939.jpg>.

Five Underground Churches from Around the World. 22 April 2010 <http://blog.hotelclub.com/underground-churches/>.

French and British Betrayal of Poland in 1939. 10 July 2010 <http://www.worldfuturefund.org/wffmaster/reading/history/polandbetrayal.htm>.

"Fun Facts About Josef Stalin." Yahoo Answers. 15 June 2010 <http://uk.answers.yahoo.com/questions/index?qid=20090303084053AAje9qW>.

General Government. 26 March 2010 <http://www.search.com/reference/General_government>.

"Genocide #20." World at War. Military Channel. MILI, 29 June 2010

German Camp Brothels in World War II. 30 October 2010 <http://en.wikipedia.org/wiki/German_camp_brothels_in_World_War_II>.

German-Polish non-Agression Pact. 22 June 2010 <http://en.wikipedia. org/wiki/GermanpercentE2percent80percent93Polish_Non-Agression_Pact>.

Gertjejanssen, Windy Jo. PhD, University of Minnesota. Victims Heroes, Survivors: Sexual Violence on the Eastern Front During World War II. 2004. 30 October 2010 <http://www.victimsheroessurvivors.info/ eastern_front_gender-viloence_>.

Gianfranco Moscati Collection-wartime rationing. 30 June 2010 <http:// www.iwm.org.uk/service/show/nav.22753>.

"Gliders." Weapons of World War II. Military Channel. MILI, 25 August 2010.

Halbmayr, Brigitte. Sexualized Violence and Forced Prostitution in National Socialism. 22 March 2011 <http://www.theverylongview. com/WATH/essays/sexual.htm>.

"Treasured Polish recipes for Americans." Hawks, Mrs. Stanley. Forward. Polaine Club, 1948. 7-15.

Heer Brothels. 30 October 2010 <http://www.ww2incolor.com/forum/ showthread/php?10828-Heer-Brothels>.

Heinrich Himmler. 20 April 2010 <http://en.wikipedia.org/wiki/ Heinrich_Himmler>.

Hermann Goring. 22 April 2010 <http://en.wikipedia.org/wiki/ Hermann_CpercentC3percentB6ring>.

Jewish history in Poland during the years 1939-1945. 25 March 2010 <http://members.core.com/~mikerose/waryears.htm>.

"History after World War II." Zamosc. 5 February 2011 <http:// en.wikipedia.org/wiki/ZamopercentC5percent9BpercentC4 percent87>.

History Place: World War II in Europe. 27 march 2010 <http://www. historyguide.org/europe/lecture11.html>.

"Hitler and world War Two." 16 August 2009. The history guide Lecture 11. 16 July 2010 <http://www.historyguide.org/europe/lecture11. html>.

Hitlerjugend. 21 march 2010 <http://www.shoaheducation.com/HJ.html>.

"Hitler's Biggest Gamble #3." Clash of Wings. Military Channel. MILI, 5 August 2010.

"Hitler's Stealth Fighters." National Geographic Channel. NGEO, 19 September 2010.

"Holocaust Encyclopedia." United States holocaust memorial Museum interactive site. 2 December 2010 <http://www.ushmm.org/wlc/en/media_nm.php?ModuleId=10005070&MediaId=2372>.

"Holocaust Encyclopedia." Tattoos and Numbers: the system of Identifying Prisoners at Auschwitz. 6 February 2011 <http://www.ushmm.org/wlc/en/article.php?ModuleId=10007056>

Home Army and V-1 and V-2. 4 February 2011 <http://en.wikipedia.org/Home_Army_and_V1_and_V2>.

"Home Run From Colditz. WWII In Color. Military Channel. MILI, 3 December 2010.

Identification in Nazi Camps. 19 May 2010 <http://en.wikipedialorg/wiki/Identification_in_nazi_camps>.

IG Farben. 17 October 2010 <http://en.wikipedia.org.wiki/IG_Farben>.

IG Farben Building. 21 September 2010 <http://en.wikipedia.org.wiki/IG_Farben_Building>.

Igo Sym. 24 January 2011 <http://en.wikipedia.org/wiki/Igo_Sym>.

"Interactive map of Auschwitz." BBC History World Wars. 3 November 2010 <http://www.bbc.co.uk/history/interactive/animations/auschwitz_map/index_embed.shtml>.

Introduction To Nazi Euthanasia. 5 August 2010 <http://holocaustresearchproject.org/euthan/index.html>.

Invasion of Poland. 15 May 2010 <http://en.wikipedia.org/wiki/Invasion_of_Poland>.

Jan Karski—How One Man Tried to Stop the Holocaust. 1 February 2010 <http://www.holocaustforgotten.com/karski.html>.

Jan Wlodarkiewicz. 26 October 2010 <http://en.wikipdeia.org/wiki/Jan_WpercentC5percent82odarkiewicz>.

Joseph Goebbels. 20 April 2010 <http://en.wikipedia.org/wiki/Joseph_Goebbels>.

Karl Fritzsch. 17 November 2010 <http://en.wikipedia.org/wiki/Karl_Fritzsch>.

Katyn Massacre. 1 February 2010 <http://en.wikipedia.org/wiki/Katyn_massacre>.

Katyn. Dir. Andrzei Wajda. 2007

"Killing Hitler." Public Broadcasting Station. KQEDL, 14 May 2010.

Knight-Jadczyk, Laura. Born From the Ashes and Blood. 24 March 2010 <http://www.cassiopaea.org.cass/coming2.htm>.

Poland in WWIi. Born From the Ashes and Blood. 24 march 2010 <http://www.cassiopaea.org.cass/coming2.htm>.

Koscian and the Euthanasia in Poland. 4 August 2010 <http://www.deathcamps.org/euthanasia/t4poland.html>.

Layers of History and Grief in Katyn. 14 march 2011 <http://thelede.blogs.nytimes.com/2010/01/10/layers-of-history-and-grief-in-katyn/>.

"Maginot Line." France Falls. Military Channel. MILI, 30 January 2011.

Molotov-Ribbentrop Pact and its Secret Protocol. 16 June 2010 <http://en.wikipedia.org/wiki/MolotovpercentE2percent80percent 92Ribbentrop_Pact>.

"Munich Conference." World War II Europe: the Road to War. 14 April 2010 <http://militaryhistory.about.com/od/worldwarii/a/wwiierucauses_2.htm>.

"Nazi Plundering of Europe." Secrets of World War II. Military Channel. MILI, 4 August 2010.

Nazi Crimes Against Ethnic Poles. 6 April 2010 <http://en.wikipdeia.org/wiki/nazi_crimes_against_ethnic_Poles>.

"Nazi Euthanasia." History Place: World War II in Europe. 26 March 2010 <http://www.historyplace.com/worldwar2/timeline/euthanasia.html>.

"Nazi Secret Weapons." National Geographic Channel. NGEO, 19 September 2010.

"Nemesis #21." World at War. Military Channel. MILI, 29 June 2010.

Neville Chamberlain. 22 May 2010 <http://en.wikipedia.org/wiki/Neville_Champerlain>.

"Nizkor Project." Shofar FTP Archive File: first execution at Auschwitz. 19 February 2011 <http://www.nizkor.org/ftp.cgi/camps/ftp.py?camps//auschwitz/first-execution-shooting>.

Occupation of Eastern Europe. 11 August 2006. 8 April 2010 <http://www.deathcamps.org/occupation/occupationintro.html>.

Occupation of Poland (1939-1945) (1/4). 1 August 2010 <http://wapedia.mobi/en/Treatment_of_Polish_citizens_by_occupiers>.

Operation MOST III. 4 February 2011 <http://en.wikipedia.org/wiki/Operation_Most_III>.

Operation N. 4 February 2011 <http://en.wikipedia.org/wiki/Action_N>.

"Owinska." Owinska Mental Home and Poznan Fort VII. 5 August 2010 <http://www.deathcamps.org/euthanasia/owinski.html>.

Poland—Hitler's first Target for Annihilation during the Holocaust. 28 June 2010 <http://www.holocaustforgotten.com/poland.htm>.

Poland. 30 June 2010 <http://www.poland.pl/archives.ww2/article,,id, 271230.htm>.

"Poland-Great Britain Agreement of Mutual Assistance." American journal of International law, Vol.35, No.3 (Jul., 1941), pp. 173. 10 June 2010 <http://www.jstor.org/pss/2213497>.

Polish Armed Forces memorial-National Memorial Arboretum. 25 October 2010 <http://www.derekcrose.com/post.aspx?ik=95>.

Polish contribution to World War II. 4 February 2011 <http://en.wikipedia. org/wiki/Polish_contribution_to_World_War_II>

Polish Culture During World War II. 10 June 2010 <http://en.wikipedia. org/wiki/Polish_culture_during_World_War_II>

Polish Facts and Figures in World War II. 2 august 2010 <http://bole-kchrobry.tripod.com/polishinformationcenter19391945/id9.html>.

Polish Fighter Pilots of World War II. 28 June 2010 <http://www.world-wariihistory.info/Polish/fighter-pilots.html>.

Polish Pres. Lays Blame at WWII Anniversary. 24 March 2010 <http:// www.thenewamerican.com/index.php/world-mainmenu-26/ europe-mainmenu-35/1798>.

Polish Resistance Movement in World War II. 28 June 2010 <http://en. wikipedia.org/wiki/Polish_resistance_movement_in_ world_War_II>.

Polish Resistance Movement in World War II (1/3). 25 October 2010 <http:// wapedia.mobi/en/Polish_resistance_movement_in_World_War_II>.

Polish Underground State. 28 June 2010 <http://en.wikipedia.org/wiki/ Polish_Underground_State>.

Rakowice-Czany Airfield—Aviation Museums on Waymarketing. com. 1 April 2011 <http://www.waymarketing.com/waymarkd/ WM30YV_rakowice_Czyany_Airfield>.

Ravensbruck Concentration Camp. 30 October 2010 <http://en.wikipedia. org/wiki/ravensbrpercentC3percentBCck_concentration_camp>.

Recipes of Wartime Europe. 30 June 2010 <http://timewitnesses.org/ english/food/index.html>.

"Remember #26." World at War. Military Channel. MILI, 18 July 2010.

Rescue of Jews by Poles During the Holocaust. 17 February 2011 <http://en.wikipedia.org/wiki/Rescue_of_Jews_by_Poles_during_the_holocaust>.

Rhineland 1936. 22 May 2010 <http://www.historylearningsite.co.uk/Rhineland_1936.htm>.

Rudolf Hoss. 19 May 2020 <http://enwikipedia.org/wiki/Rudolf_HpercentC3percentB6ss>.

Rudolf Hoss—(1900—1947). 10 October 2010 <http://www.jewishvirtuallibrary.org/jsource/biography/Hoess.html>.

Rudolf Hoss—Commandant of Auschwitz. 10 October 2010 <http://www.bbc.co.uk/history/worldwars/genocide/hoss_commandant?auschwitz_01.shtml>.

Salt Mine in Bochnia. 22 April 2010 <http://www.bochnia.starostwo.gov.pl/en/tourist-attractions/the-salt-mine-in-bochnia.html>.

Second Polish Republic (1918—1939). 30 June 2010 <http://en.wikipedia.org/wiki/List_of_polish_heads_of_state_(1918percentE-2percent80percent93present)>.

Second World War. 15 May 2010 <http://www.pasprzyk.demn.co.uk/www/history/WW2.html>.

"Secrets of the Battle of the Bulge." Secrets of World War II. Military Channel. MILI, 1 September 2010.

Sexual Enslavement by Nazi Germany in World War II. 3 October 2010 <http://en.academic.ru/dic.nsf/enwiki/1487375>.

Smith, Bradley. Codoh founder. Capacity and Role of the Auschwitz Crematoria. 27 February 2011 <http://codoh.com/butz/di/dau/nmufa.html>.

Smuggling Children out of the Ghetto: Irena Sendler, Poland. 29 April 2011 <http://www1.yadvashem.org/righteous_new/poland/sendler.html>.

Sonderaktion Krakau. 10 June 2010 <http://en.wikipedia.org/wiki/Sonderaktion_Krakau>.

Soviet Invasion of Poland. 1 August 2010 <http://en.wikipedia.org/wiki/Soviet_Invasion_of_Poland>.

"Stalingrad #9." World at War. Military Channel. MILI, 18 July 2010.

Standing Cell. 17 November 2010 <http://en.wikipedia.org/wiki/Standing_cell>.

Stefan Rowecki. 25 March 2010 <http://enwikipedia.org/wiki/Stefan_ Rowecki>.

Stolarski, Rafal E. The Production of Arms and Explosive Materials by the Polish Home Army in the Years 1939-1945. 22 March 2011 <http;//www.polishresistance-ak.org>.

Surprising Beginnings: Episode 1. Auschwitz: Inside the Nazi State. 15 November 2010 <http://www.pbs.org/auschwitz/about/transcripts. html>.

"The Fall." Third Reich. History Channel, 16 December 2010.

The Place Formerly Known As Salzberg. 1 April 2011 <http://www. visit-salzberg.net/travel/salzberginformation.htm>.

The Seven Gas Chambers at Auschwitz. 6 February 2011 <http://www. deathcamps.org/gas_chambers/gas_chambers_auschwitz.html>.

"Typhus Myth." Body Disposal at Auschwitz: The End of Holocaust— Denial. 20 November 2010 <http://www.holocaust-history.org/ auschwitz/body-disposal/>.

"Undressing room—Krema II gas chamber." Auschwitz Scrapbook Tour. 27 February 2011 <http://www.scrapbookpages.com/auschwitzscrap book/tour/Birkenau/TuinsII01A.html>.

Volksliste. 24 January 2011 <http://en.wikipedia.org/wiki/Volksliste>.

"Blowing Up History: Nazi Super Bombs." Ed. Michael (Director) Wadding. National Geographic Channel. NGEO, 19 September 2010.

War Crimes of the Wehrmacht. 24 March 2010 <http://en.wikipedia. org/wiki/War_crimes_of_the_Wehrmacht>.

Western Betrayal. 10 July 2010 <http://en.wikipedia.org/wiki/Western_ betrayal>.

Wiki: War Crimes of the Wehrmacht (1/2). 1 August 2010 <http:// wapedia.mobi/en/War_crimes_of_the_Wehrmacht>.

Wilhelm Keitel. 20 April 2010 <http://en.wikipedia.org/wiki/Wilhelm_ Keitel>.

Witold Pilecki. 26 October 2010 <http://en.wikipedia.org/wiki/Witold_ Pilecki>.

Women in Auschwitz. 17 February 2011 <http://www.wsg-hist.uni-linz.ac. at/auschwitz/html/Frauen.heml>.

"World at War—weaponry." Military Channel. MILI, 20 July 2010.

World War II Crimes in Poland (1.5). 1 August 2010 <http://wapedia. mobi/en/World_War_II_crimes_in_Poland>.

World War II Timeline. 10 July 2010 <http://everything2.com/title/Wor ld+War+II+Timelinepercent253A+1939>.

14423948R00239

Made in the USA
Charleston, SC
10 September 2012